WOMAN *of a*
THOUSAND SECRETS

Also by Barbara Wood

Daughter of the Sun

Private Entrance

Star of Babylon

The Blessing Stone

Sacred Ground

Perfect Harmony

The Prophetess

Virgins of Paradise

The Dreaming

Green City in the Sun

Soul Flame

Vital Signs

Domina

The Watch Gods

Childsong

Night Trains

Yesterday's Child

Curse This House

Hounds and Jackals

The Magdalene Scrolls

WOMAN *of a*
THOUSAND SECRETS

BARBARA WOOD

ST. MARTIN'S GRIFFIN ✦ NEW YORK

WOMAN OF A THOUSAND SECRETS. Copyright © 2008 by Barbara Wood. All rights reserved. Printed in the United States of America. For information, address St. Martin's Press, 175 Fifth Avenue, New York, N.Y. 10010.

www.stmartins.com

Library of Congress Cataloging-in-Publication Data

Wood, Barbara, 1947–
    Woman of a thousand secrets / Barbara Wood.—1st ed.
        p. cm.
    ISBN-13: 978-0-312-36369-7
    ISBN-10: 0-312-36369-9
    1. Orphans—Fiction. 2. Quests (Expeditions)—Fiction. 3. Prehistoric peoples—Fiction. 4. Central America—Fiction. I. Title.

PS3573.O5877 W66 2008
813'.54—dc22

2008021149

First Edition: September 2008

10 9 8 7 6 5 4 3 2 1

This book is dedicated, with love,
to my husband, George.

Acknowledgments

Deepest thanks to three amazing people: my editor, Jennifer Enderlin, who has an uncanny knack for saying just the right words; my dear friend and assistant, Sharon Stewart, who helps me more than she knows; and Harvey Klinger, the greatest literary agent in the world.

WOMAN *of a*
THOUSAND SECRETS

Revenge was in Macu's heart as he searched for the girl who had humiliated his brother.

Pretending to be interested in her as a prospective bride, he asked about Tonina in the village and was told that she could be found on the beach of the western lagoon, where the pearl divers were hauling in their oyster catch for the day.

Macu's brother, who was at that moment on the other side of the island with their canoe, had begged Macu not to go. It was bad enough a girl had bested him in a swimming contest, but Macu exacting revenge would only make matters worse. "She *is* a better swimmer," Awak had said. "You cannot beat her, Brother." But twenty-two-year-old Macu of nearby Half Moon Island was proud and vain and despised girls who thought they were better than men.

Pearl Island was a small, verdant dot on the green sea off the western tip of a landmass that would one day be called Cuba, and it had only two accessible harbors: the western lagoon and a cove on the northern tip, where Macu and his friends had paddled their canoe between rocky shoals and made landfall on a tiny beach. From there, a trail led through dense trees and brush to a lively, bustling village where children played, women stirred cooking pots, and men toiled in tobacco-drying sheds.

As Macu marched through the settlement and down to the beach, he was followed by an excited entourage. He ignored the chatter as he curled his hands into fists, vowing to exact revenge. He strode with a firm step across the hot white sand so that egrets and pelicans flew up out of his way, and men looked up, startled, from their work repairing canoes and fishing nets. Naked children digging for clams in the calm, warm surf of the peaceful lagoon watched in curiosity as the stranger marched past.

Macu was dark brown, stocky and muscular, his nearly naked body scarred and tattooed with myriad symbols and decorations. His black hair hung long, indicating his unmarried state, and besides a loincloth made of woven palm fibers he wore numerous necklaces and protective amulets. That he was an outsider was evident by the clan tattoo on his forehead. The group that followed him beneath the warm tropical sun, traipsing over the wide swath of sand between the lime green lagoon and the lush inland jungle, was made up of the young men who had accompanied him from Half Moon Island and a few villagers who had abandoned their labors as they sensed an afternoon's diversion.

A man was showing interest in poor, plain Tonina!

The pearl divers were clustered at the end of the beach where a rocky cliff rose against the sea. Ranging in age from twelve to twenty-three, the girls laughed and joked, their dark brown bodies glistening with seawater, as they unloaded nets of oysters from their canoes, piling the shells onto the cool sand beneath shady coconut palms. Although Macu had never met or seen the girl he had come to challenge, he was able to spot her at once. "She isn't beautiful," his brother had said. "In fact, she's homely." He had gone on to describe her, and now Macu's eyes went straight to the grass-skirted girl called Tonina.

His brother was right. Although Tonina's hair was worn long and loose and decorated with many shells, and although her face and arms were painted with myriad white symbols and designs, she was not at all fetching. No wonder she was still unmarried. Everything about Tonina was wrong. Her coloring was too light, her hips too narrow, her waist too slender, and, by the gods, Awak had spoken the truth: The girl was *tall*. If Macu had not seen the swelling breasts, golden-skinned and still wet from her dive, he might have suspected she was a man.

Macu raised a hand in friendly greeting and called, "Hello!"

The girls turned and, taking stock of the attractive young man, immediately adopted flirtatious attitudes.

Tonina paid no attention at first—young men never looked at *her*—until she realized in shock that the charming smile was directed at her.

She wondered why, having no idea that he was the brother of a young man she had bested at swimming days ago.

As Macu took the measure of this tall, plain girl, he thought of his cunning plan to get back at her for what she had done to Awak. A plan that involved the ghost of an ancient sea monster.

All the nearby islands knew the legend of the beast that slept in a forbidden area of Pearl Island's lagoon, near the opening in the barrier reef, where calm water met the choppy sea. It was said that the skeleton of an enormous sea monster occupied the ocean floor there, and that the monster's ghost haunted the waters.

No one swam there, ever.

Because Macu had not grown up here, fear of the sea monster's spirit had not been cultivated in him. But he knew that Tonina had lived her life hearing about the ghost and would be terrified to swim near it. Beneath the warm afternoon sun, as trade winds whispered through the swaying palm trees and gulls circled overhead, Macu played his role to perfection.

"Are you the one called Tonina?" he asked.

Tonina smiled shyly, unused to male attention. Boys did not like girls taller than themselves, but as Macu was of equal height, she decided he must not mind.

As the pearl divers stood in a group around the two, their curiosity piqued, Macu introduced himself to Tonina and boasted about his skill and prowess at spearfishing, as was the custom when beginning a courtship. He exaggerated his accomplishments as he carefully laid his trap. The islands' courting ritual involved each prospective partner proving himself or herself.

Secretly pleased with his cleverness, Macu fixed his smiling eyes on Tonina as he said, "Are you brave enough to swim with me to the haunted place and bring back one of the monster's bones?"

G uama! There is a boy here from Half Moon Island. He is interested in Tonina!"

Tonina's grandmother, in the tobacco shed rolling leaves into cigars, looked up. "What? A boy? Are you sure?"

"They are at the lagoon. And he is challenging her to a contest!"

Guama blinked. A boy was interested in her granddaughter? Tonina was twenty-one years old and still unmarried. Every spring, when boys and men from other islands came to Pearl Island to select a bride, Tonina was always overlooked. So why was this boy from Half Moon Island suddenly showing such interest? Had the impossible finally happened?

Guama prayed so. The girl must get married, otherwise what sort of life would she have? With no children to raise, no man to cook for, what use was a woman? Tonina was a fine pearl diver, one of the best, but pearl divers did not live long.

As she followed the boy down to the beach, old Guama remembered the swimming contest a few days prior, when Tonina had bested all the boys, even though Guama was always telling her she must let the boys win. Unfortunately, Tonina was cursed with an ingrained honesty that wouldn't allow her to cheat.

"What sort of contest?" Guama asked now, suddenly suspicious.

"To swim out to the bones of the sea monster."

"*Guay!*" the old woman cried, voicing her dismay with a word that, in the language of the islanders, conveyed pain, surprise, or distress. She broke into a sprint, running as fast as her ancient legs could go.

To Macu's shock, Tonina accepted his challenge.

The onlookers gasped. Contests of depth and endurance were daily occurrences—deep water and fierce waves and rip currents did not daunt the islanders—but swimming into haunted waters was something else. Macu had been confident Tonina would refuse the contest, giving him the victory.

But what Macu did not know was that Tonina was not afraid of sea monsters or their ghosts. Nothing in the ocean frightened her. Now he did not know what to do. With all eyes on him, Macu had to reach a swift decision. He could not back down on his own dare, and so he had to go through with a contest in which he had not expected to compete.

His anger flared anew, but he kept it masked as he smiled and said, "Very well!"

Tonina wore the grass skirt all island females wore once they began menstruating. She removed it now, leaving her in a simple cotton modesty apron hanging from a string around her waist. As she followed Macu into the surf, the crowd watched anxiously. No one had ever visited the bones of the monster. Would Macu and Tonina make it back alive?

G uama arrived too late. She could only stand helplessly on the beach and watch the two plunge into the water and swim toward the reef.

Guama's white hair was combed back into an intricate knot and tied with palm-fiber string, but a few long wisps had escaped the knot and whipped about her face in the tropical breeze. Brushing the hair from her face, she kept her eyes on the swimmers, terrified that this was the final sign. The sign that she had been dreading for six days—ever since the dolphins arrived. And so she wondered now, not for the first time, if Tonina's unmarried status was a message from the gods. That she was never meant to stay on Pearl Island.

Was that why the gods had been so cruel to Tonina, Guama wondered. Was that why they had created her to be displeasing to a man's eye? Although the girl laughed easily and possessed a warm, trusting spirit, there was her unfortunate golden coloring, long limbs, slender hips. Guama had tried over the years to conform her adopted granddaughter to the island's beauty ideal, rubbing tobacco juice into her skin to darken it, fattening her on cassava root to make her plump. But the tan washed off and the fat melted from her lithe form. At each yearly wife-selecting *barbicu*, men from the other islands always overlooked Tonina so that she still wore the cowry shell belt of maidenhood. A badge of honor for younger girls—the cowry belt symbolized the girl's virgin state, not to be removed until the wedding night—there came a time when the purity belt became a badge of shame, as it was for Tonina, telling all the world that at the age of twenty-one she was still a virgin, that no man wanted her.

Guama glanced up at the cliff rising above the lagoon and saw her husband at his post, reading the wind and sky and sea for signs of a *huracán*. An aged, potbellied man in a palm-fiber loincloth, his wrinkled nut-brown body painted with the symbols of his sacred calling, he was the most important man on the island, more important even than the chief.

Since there was never any way of knowing when a *huracán* was coming, there was no way to prepare, to hide, and so such storms were known for wiping entire tribes out of existence. But Pearl Island had been blessed with a man who descended from a long line of storm-readers, who possessed the ability to sense a *huracán* far beyond the horizon, to know how strong it would be, to know when it would make landfall.

Guama saw that her husband's attention was not upon the horizon, but upon the young people below. And when she saw how intently he stared at Tonina, Guama knew it was because of the dolphins.

Ever since the pair had been seen cavorting beyond the reef, Guama and Huracan had been watching for signs and omens to understand the wish of the gods. Did they want Tonina back? Had she been sent here only temporarily? *And are they now,* Guama wondered in sudden fear, *about to take Tonina from us as she swims into the taboo water?*

The lagoon was deep and warm, with gentle currents, the water clear to the sandy bottom where spiny urchins and starfish dwelled. Tonina and Macu swam wordlessly side by side, the shore dropping behind and the great coral reef drawing near. The wave action grew stronger, and kelp beds now appeared. Spurred by anger, Macu pulled ahead, his mind working on ways to humiliate this girl who thought she was better than a man. He dived under the kelp to appear a moment later on the other side.

Tonina stopped swimming and began to tread water as she watched him. She was recalling the many times Guama had advised her to let a boy win a competition. This time I shall do it, Tonina decided. She liked Macu's smile, and felt a new flutter in her heart at the sudden attention from an attractive stranger. Perhaps, if she let him win, he would come back to Pearl Island and court her until they wed.

And then she would be like everyone else, and accepted at last.

Finally she dived, disappearing from view. But instead of swimming under the kelp bed toward the haunted water, she swam to a sunlit area of the coral reef that was alive with life.

Here she swam with joy, joining the colorful schools of fish that darted this way and that. She floated over coral fans and sponge beds, smiling at a bright golden fish that glided by. Tonina was suddenly happy. The way Macu had looked at her, chosen her! An outcast all her life, shy about her plain looks, Tonina finally felt the joy of receiving a boy's attention.

Rolling onto her back in the placid water, she looked up at the surface where sunlight swirled and glittered. She would spend another moment here, then swim back to the other side of the kelp and surface before Macu, allowing him to be the winner of the contest.

Macu had sucked lungfuls of air before executing a sharp downward dive. Now a world of wonder filled his eyes, as living coral danced and swayed in dappled sunlight and colorful fish flashed by. When he saw the massive skeleton ahead, faintly illuminated by sunlight filtering through the water, his bowels tightened. The monster really existed. And it was enormous! He cautiously swam closer. The spine of the giant creature lay on the sandy bottom and its ribs curved upward in queer shapes. Strangely, the bones were brown.

His fear turning to curiosity, Macu swam down and placed his hands on a rib. It was made of wood!

His eyes widened. This was no sea creature but a fantastically large canoe. But not a dugout, as the islanders' canoes were. This vessel had been made from separate wooden planks pieced together, as he had seen in some war canoes. However, this was not of any island manufacture he was familiar with. Who had made it? When had it crashed on this reef?

Something shimmered in the sand. It looked like a jellyfish, yet it was strangely shaped and appeared to be scored with bright green and blue scars. Plucking it up, Macu found the object was as hard as rock, yet transparent.

His lungs tightened. It was time to surface. A current eddied around him, caught his body, and turned it in an arc so that he floated sideways to the boat. When he saw the fearsome head looming over him at the end of a long, arching neck, with open jaws displaying jagged teeth, Macu realized in fright that it was a sea monster after all.

In sudden terror he frantically swam away, still clutching the object he had pulled from the sandy bottom, and in his panic swam blindly into the kelp bed. Flailing his arms and legs, his lungs fighting for air, his chest shooting with pain, he became trapped in the dense tangle of seaweed.

From the beach, Guama watched, tense and anxious. How foolhardy of the boy to challenge Tonina to swim into taboo waters. And how naïve of Tonina to accept. Guama knew that her granddaughter feared nothing in the sea, and while it was true Tonina was under the special protection of dolphin spirits, surely there were limits.

When she saw Tonina resurface at the edge of the kelp bed, Guama sighed with relief. But Macu had yet to surface. Time stretched, and then suddenly Tonina dived back under the kelp bed.

She found Macu entangled and unconscious, floating with vacant, staring eyes, his hair streaming out and drifting gently on the current. Tonina dragged him to the surface, tearing him loose from the clinging leaves and tendrils, and swam back to shore, pulling him along.

Guama was there to meet them, being experienced with drownings. As soon as others pulled Macu onto the sand, she dropped to her knees and placed her hands on his chest. He was not breathing but his heart was still beating. She rolled him onto his side and thumped his back. Then she pried his mouth open, tugged his jaw down, and thumped his back again. She called out the names of various gods, invoking their mercy and their power, while the group stood in anxious silence.

The third thump made him cough. The fourth sent water spewing from his mouth, and he sputtered and hacked and fought for breath.

As Macu's friends lifted him to his feet, the others stepped back to make way for them to pass. It was a silent group that watched Macu stumble and stagger, aided by comrades, down the beach. And then the young islanders turned to stare at Tonina, who was herself heaving for breath, dripping with seawater.

Slowly, they backed away from her. She had swum in taboo waters. The sea monster had tried to claim Macu, but Tonina had defied the monster.

Guama watched in sadness as the islanders moved away from Tonina, tracing protective signs in the air, and the old woman knew this was the omen she had been watching for, to tell her that it was indeed time for the girl, this precious child who had brought joy to a childless couple, to leave Pearl Island.

The others returned to the village while Tonina, as she had so many times over the years, disappeared into the jungle to be alone. The beach was growing cold with the setting sun, and Guama started to leave when her toe nudged something hard in the sand. She looked down and saw a dead jellyfish lying there, curled into a ball. She frowned. No, not a jellyfish. She picked it up and brushed it off.

The object was still wet, which meant it must have come with Macu and the kelp. She had no idea what it was—hard, and yet not stone or clay, and transparent, with rich colors woven throughout so that it resembled a globule of petrified water with plant life imprisoned within. The shape, however, was familiar, for the object sat in her hand the way a drinking gourd did.

Guama did not know that the wondrous transparent material was called glass, or that it had been hand-blown in a cold-climate land on the other side of the world, called Germany. She could not guess that the goblet had passed from owner to owner until it became the cherished possession of a red-bearded explorer who carried the drinking glass with him in his dragon-prowed ship to a new home called Vinland.

Guama knew none of this, only that she had seen the strange vessel clutched in Macu's hand when Tonina brought him ashore. And as everything happened for a reason—this Guama believed most deeply— she suspected that this curious object must somehow be tied to Tonina's destiny. And so she would keep the goblet, to give to her granddaughter.

But as she struck off toward the village, Guama sighed wistfully, because she was reminding herself for the hundredth time that the girl wasn't really her granddaughter. She was no one's granddaughter.

Tonina wasn't even human.

❧ 2 ❧

This was Tonina's favorite place to be alone, a rocky cove of mangroves from where she could hear the whispering surf, the gentle *shush* of distant waves. Few ever visited this remote inlet that had no beach, and so it had become, over the years, Tonina's private refuge.

It was here, twenty-one years ago, that she had begun her life on Pearl Island.

Guama's husband, Huracan, high atop his lookout cliff, had spotted a pair of dolphins that seemed to be playing with something. A small brown thing bobbed between them as they flew up out of the water and then back down, crying and squeaking as if trying to get the storm-reader's attention. He had hurried down to the water's murky edge and watched as the dolphins guided the object closer to land and then, as if satisfied that the current would do the rest, leaped high out of the water, in perfect synchrony, splashed back in, and swam out to sea.

As the object floated near and then was caught in gnarly mangrove roots, Huracan thought he heard an animal crying in pain. Wading out, he saw that the bobbing thing was a waterproof basket with a lid, and from within a creature wailed in distress. Caution made him leery, but curiosity drew him closer until he recognized the cry of a human infant.

Carefully lifting the lid of the basket, he peered in and saw a baby with a scrunched, red face swaddled in embroidered cloth, bawling lustily. He had hurried into the village with his precious discovery, taking her straightaway to Guama, who would know what to do. Six babies she had brought into the world, and all six she had outlived. When the final remaining daughter died, Guama had wanted to sleep and never wake up. And then the tiny mewling creature had been placed in her arms and she had come to life.

They named the baby Tonina, which in their language meant "dolphin," and because she was not dark brown like the islanders but the color of golden sand, Huracan and Guama privately believed she was the offspring of a sea god. They also believed that the gods, in their compassion, had sent the baby to be a comfort to the pious couple in their old age.

As the child grew, however, her strange physical appearance had made people wonder, and soon she became an outsider. Children had teased her cruelly, saying that she had been put on the sea because her family didn't want an ugly baby.

Mystery had always been part of her life. What, for example, was the meaning of the strange amulet that had been on a string around her neck when Huracan found her? Who had placed it there, to what people did it connect her? Long ago Guama had woven a little jacket of palm fibers, enclosing the amulet completely and sealing it, which meant that no one but Huracan and herself had seen it; not even Tonina had laid eyes upon it, although she had been told that the magic stone was a vibrant pink, and translucent when held to the sun, with magical symbols engraved upon it. Guama had told Tonina that she could uncover it when she felt the time was right. Tonina had been tempted many times to look inside, but had stopped. The talisman of "rare material and strange engravings" would only alienate her further, she realized, and make her even more of an outsider.

Then there was the curious cloth swaddling her infant body— precious cotton, a rarity on the islands. Another connection to unknown people.

She thought of Macu. Tonina had not so much fallen in love with him as with what he stood for: the *belonging* she had always dreamed of. Marrying Macu would give her a place in a tribe, it would connect her to other people, and she would no longer be alone.

As she rose to her feet, her hand brushed the fiber thong that hung from her waist, strung with cowry shells, denoting her virginal state. The belt had been tied around her waist when she had begun menstruating, and it was to remain there until her wedding night, when it was the husband's happy privilege to remove it.

Lifting the string of cowries into the last light of day, Tonina sadly wondered if the belt was ever going to be removed.

On the other side of the island, a silent and sullen group sat around a campfire, the flames illuminating the flat, dark brown faces of young men who tried to ignore the night's darkness.

A mystical event had taken place, involving sea monsters and near death, and each tried in his simple way to make sense of it. Macu had drowned. Tonina had pulled him to shore. And the old woman had smacked him back to life. Had the ghost of the sea monster tried to steal Macu's soul? The young men were speechless in the face of such mystery.

Macu himself, however, was not embroiled in the mystical complexities of near death and revival. He had come to Pearl Island to teach the girl a lesson and had ended up being humiliated.

His thoughts were black all evening, as they had cooked and eaten their fish. With each bitter mouthful, the malignant thoughts in Macu's mind flew to one conclusion: The girl must be punished.

≈ 3 ≈

G uama lifted the little ark from the rafter where it had been stored for twenty-one years and tenderly set it on the floor of the hut.

It was time to say good-bye.

The problem was, how to make Tonina leave Pearl Island?

Guama knew she could order her to leave, but it would be an event of such sadness that it would be like a death. And what misery for the girl herself, paddling away from her beloved home, being cast out without fully understanding why, even though Guama would explain it was the will of the dolphin spirits.

Guama decided that she needed to invent a reason for Tonina to go, one that would ease the pain of leaving.

She looked down at the little basket that had sailed the seas, the folded cloth in it, and an idea came to her. A deception . . .

The old woman shivered with fear. She knew that Pearl Island was not the limit of the world, nor even the center of it. To the north, east, and south, hundreds of islands dotted the sea. Many of her people had sailed to them. On those islands, people lived much as her own did with little difference in custom, language, or religion. To the west, however . . .

She shivered again and said a silent prayer to Lokono, the Spirit of All.

To the west lay something called Mainland because people said that it was not an island but a land that went on forever, with no ending. Some said there was a whole other world on that hidden side, where people lived in trees, or walked upside down, or gave birth through their mouths.

While it was the sea gods who had brought Tonina to her, and while the superstitious and religious part of Guama believed the girl came from the gods, in her practical woman's mind she knew Tonina had been born of a human mother. The amulet and swaddling cloth were proof of that. But why that mother had placed her baby in the care of the sea gods was a secret Guama could not fathom. Had the child been a sacrifice? And what, therefore, when Tonina went back, would happen to her?

Would they sacrifice her a second time?

Guama closed her eyes and silently prayed: Great Lokono, guide me.

"Guama," came a soft voice, and the old woman's heart leaped, thinking the god had answered. But when she opened her eyes, she saw Tonina standing in the doorway.

"There you are! You know better than to be out at night, child," she said. No one ventured out after dark, when spirits and ghosts roamed the land.

Tonina's features were freshly painted, as all islanders' were, with symbols and attractive designs, but it could not hide her homeliness. Yes, Guama thought in resignation, the gods had indeed created Tonina this way on purpose, so that she would not catch a man's eye. This way, she was alone, and free to return to the sea.

It was time to tell the lie. "Your grandfather is ill. Gravely ill, Tonina, although he hides it from the others."

Tonina looked around the spacious hut and saw, by torchlight, her grandfather slumbering in his *hamac*. Tonina's eyes went round with fear. "Is he dying?"

Guama lowered her voice. "Not now, not today. He will enjoy good health until the day comes when he will not open his eyes again."

"Can you not cure him?" Guama was famous for her knowledge of healing herbs and charms.

"We do not have the medicine on our island. But I have heard of a plant . . . a red flower with petals like this," and she formed a blossom with her hands, joining her wrists, fingers spread and curved, pointing to the floor.

"The flower does not grow upward, facing the sun," Guama said, "but downward, facing the earth, like the red heliconia that grow on our island."

"Perhaps the flower grows in a tree?" Tonina offered.

Touched by Tonina's eagerness to help, Guama's throat tightened. Outside the hut, village life went on as usual—families gathered around fires, children running and playing near the light—while a fat moon sailed across the heavens. "It is said that the petals contain powerful spirits that will heal any illness, cure any trouble."

"Where can this flower be found?" Tonina asked.

"Mainland."

Tonina fell silent. Mainland was something heard of only in myth and frightening stories. "How shall we obtain it?" she asked, imagining the chief selecting teams of strong oarsmen and sending them forth in the island's sturdiest canoes.

Guama took Tonina's hands and said, "You have seen the dolphins playing in the water beyond the reef?"

Tonina smiled. She had swum out to the pair, to speak to them and swim with them.

"They are not here by chance, Tonina. They bring a message: that you sail to Mainland, find the magic healing flower, and bring it back."

Tonina stared at her in shock. "Me, Grandmother? Are you sure?"

"The message is clear."

Guama fixed tired old eyes on the girl who stood a head taller, called "ugly" by others but whom Guama thought beautiful. "After you return, you will be loved for what you did. Saving Huracan's life means saving the people of the island," she said softly. "This quest will be spoken of for years to come. Your name will be praised around every cook fire. This will be known as the Year Tonina Saved Pearl Island."

This will be known as the Year Tonina Returned to the Sea.

She reached up to touch the face of the girl she loved more than her own life, this child who had brought such joy into the days of a broken-hearted mother, and said, "And then men will call you beautiful."

Tonina tried not to show fear. Mainland! It terrified her to think of leaving Pearl Island, of traveling across the wide sea and setting foot in that unknown land. But Grandfather needed her.

"I will go," she said.

Although Guama had known Tonina would accept the challenge, her heart dropped. She would forever remember this night as the worst in her life. "As you know, the big storms rest between the winter solstice and the summer solstice. You must come back by then, Tonina. When we celebrate the spring equinox we shall begin to watch for your return before the big storms start again."

As the winter solstice lay just one month away, Tonina felt sudden urgency. Squeezing the aged hands, she said with passion, "I promise I will return with the healing flower. I shall pray to my dolphin spirits for help."

B rother!" Awak cried as he ran into the camp in the tiny cove, waking his friends. "Something has happened!"

They rubbed their eyes and listened as he told them of a magical red flower and Tonina's mission to find it. "They are gathering now at the lagoon; the great canoe is soon to depart."

Macu saw his chance at once. He would show everyone who was superior. *He* was going to be the one to return with the magic flower. And his humiliation at the lagoon would be forgotten.

As they would forget Tonina, who was not going to return at all.

G uama and Huracan kept their deception a secret, reasoning that, should their lie anger the gods, the punishment would be upon their heads alone.

All the tribe was gathered in the dawn light to witness an event that would be spoken of for generations to come. The twenty men who had been selected to paddle the great canoe were excited about the adventure. This was not a mere island they were sailing to, but Mainland!

When Huracan had pulled the basket from the shallows twenty-one years prior, he had studied the winds and the tides, and had determined that the little ark had been set upon the sea from the southern coast of Mainland, perhaps from a land called Quatemalan. He had decided that must be where Tonina came from, and so that was where she would find her people. Therefore that was where, he said, the flower grew.

As they stood on the crowded beach in the early light, while women placed supplies in the large dugout canoe, Guama looked at the girl who had been delivered to them one miraculous day on the sea. From that moment, Guama thought, Tonina had never been far from water, never out of view of the ocean around them. The sea was in her veins. How would she survive on a land that never ended?

The same frightening questions had occurred to Tonina. To go to a place where the sea could not be seen? She would not think of it, only the sacred task for which she had been chosen.

As Huracan supervised the placement of food and water into the boat, he studied his granddaughter. Standing among the islanders, she looked less like one of this tribe and more like a stranger, as if the transformation had already begun.

It was because of the clothes.

As he tried to think of ways to keep Tonina safe once she was on Mainland, Huracan recalled a Taino trader who regularly visited Pearl Island to exchange cotton for pearls. The man had spoken of the strange customs on Mainland. "They wear a lot of clothes," he had said, "especially the women. Modest creatures. Bare breasts are taboo."

This worried Huracan, as Tonina's lack of attire would point her out as a foreigner, and who knew what those savages did to foreigners? Huracan had explained the problem to Guama, who had seen the solution in the palm-fiber *hamacs* the villagers slept in. Using sharp clamshells, she had cut and stitched two *hamacs* into a loose blouse that hung halfway down a *hamac* skirt. Behind Tonina's back, the other women giggled, saying she looked like a giant fish trapped in a net.

As Huracan watched the men load the canoe with sun-dried salt fish, jerked turtle meat, and hard cassava cakes, he recalled other tales the trader had told. "They are not like us, those savages on Mainland. The men mutilate their genitals and call it a sign of bravery. They pierce their privates with thorns and fibers so that over the years their members grow pebbly and distorted."

He pushed such unthinkable notions aside as he made sure the oarsmen were prepared for defense. The men of Pearl Island were not warriors and therefore their weapons were simple wooden spears and stone knives. Huracan saw that they added clubs and a few bows and arrows.

Finally it was time for departure. Guama chanted prayers to Lokono as she painted protective symbols on Tonina's face and arms. Then she gave her the vessel made of hard transparency.

As she pressed Tonina's fingers against the cold glass, Guama sensed the goblet's strange power. Guama could not begin to guess that on this important day of Tonina's departure from Pearl Island, the country of the goblet's origin was referring to this seasonal cycle as the Year of Our Lord 1323. She did not know that, in that country on the other side of the eastern sea, pale-skinned men encased their bodies in chain mail and armor, the women in tight bodices and heavy gowns. Guama did not know of kings and armies that waged war with crossbows and war horses, that only one God was worshiped, and that two hundred years hence, those same pale-skinned people would come to Pearl Island and, in the name of their one God, change the islanders' way of life forever.

All Guama could say on this important day beside the sunlit lagoon was, "This vessel came from the sea monster. It contains great power. Keep it with you, beloved granddaughter, and it will see that you come back to us safely." Guama's voice broke as she spoke the lie, and she felt a sharp pain in her breast as she saw the loneliness of her life in the days to come.

As Huracan pressed a small bag of pearls into Tonina's hand, he looked deep into her eyes and said, "You will see wondrous things on Mainland, Granddaughter. Towering hills called mountains, and streams that fall from them, called waterfalls. When you return," he said in a tight voice, "you will tell us of all the wonderful things you have seen."

"I shall, Grandfather," Tonina said, excited, frightened, and wondering why Macu was not there to see her off. She embraced the sweet old couple whose white heads barely came to her shoulders.

Before stepping into the canoe, Tonina bent and scooped up sand and put it in her little medicine pouch that also contained a small blue periwinkle and a dolphin's tooth, powerful talismans that would connect her to this place.

"This I promise to you, dear Grandfather: I will find the flower and I will return so that you will live many more years to protect the people of this island from storms. I swear this vow upon the spirit of my dolphin totem."

She looked at those standing around her and saw the looks of admiration on their faces. At long last, Tonina had a taste of belonging. When she brought back the healing flower, she would be accepted at last.

As she embraced the others, saying good-bye, Huracan drew the chief oarsman, Yúo, aside and said quietly, "I must now take you into a special confidence, Nephew. When you reach Mainland, set up camp on the beach the first night. While Tonina sleeps, you and your crew quickly carry the boat into the surf and set off at once for home."

For a moment, Yúo looked surprised, and then, looking into his uncle's eyes, he suddenly understood. "Will she find her people?" he asked softly, wondering what strange fate lay ahead for the girl.

Huracan shook his head. "I do not know. I have done my duty. She is in the hands of the gods now. Tonina's time among us is at an end."

As the canoe with its twenty oarsmen sailed through the break in the reef and out onto open sea, with Tonina kneeling in the prow, her face into the wind, Huracan turned his own face toward the east and caught his breath sharply.

He had been so distracted by Tonina's departure that he had not been about his daily duties as a storm-watcher. But he sensed now that a storm was gathering. A big storm. A terrible storm.

He looked back at the small, frail canoe with its fragile cargo and realized in horror that he had no way of calling it back, no way of warning Tonina and the men.

A hurricane was coming.

BOOK

ONE

~ 5 ~

Pearl Island slipped behind the horizon until the long dugout canoe, with twenty rowers, one captain, and one passenger, was alone on the high seas. No longer did seagulls follow them, no longer could the crashing surf be heard. The endless silence of the open ocean surrounded them, broken only by the rhythmic splash of oars into water. Kneeling in the prow, her face set toward the frightening west, Tonina squinted in the sunlight that glared off the surface of the choppy water.

The sun beat down upon the backs of the rowers, while salt spray shot up to cool their faces. Oarsmen born and bred, Yúo and his men never knew such pleasure as when they raced a craft over the open sea. However, as Yúo struck the drumbeat for the oarsmen, he was filled with regret. Only he knew that the quest was a sham, that they were to abandon his uncle's adopted granddaughter on Mainland.

The great canoe, carved and painted with magic symbols and blessed by the Spirit of All, Lokono, had entered a body of water that had no name but which in a future time would be called the Yucatán Channel. Here, the winds came from the north, and because the wind was against the stream, the sea grew rough. But Yúo and his men were skilled and strong, and rowed swiftly through the choppy waves. Their vessel, hewn from a mighty tree and hollowed out with axes and fire, was sturdy and seaworthy and capable of traveling great distances. But rain squalls were a constant hazard in these waters, dark clouds producing short-lived blasts of high wind that demanded the rowers' full attention, and so Yúo kept a keen watch on the sea from horizon to horizon.

And suddenly he saw—

His eyes widened. Another watercraft. *"Guay!"* he called out in alarm.

The twenty rowers looked anxiously to the south. Was it a war canoe from Mainland? Tales about the ferocious Mayan warriors who prowled these waters came into mind as each man rowed with all his strength, eyes wide and focused on the approaching vessel.

And then they realized in puzzlement that it had come from the direction of Pearl Island.

When Tonina saw the captain of the smaller canoe, standing in the prow and waving, her heart leaped. Macu!

The two islands of Pearl and Half Moon had been friends for so many years, trading goods and brides, that Macu knew the men in Tonina's boat would not be expecting an attack. With his brother Awak and their friends lying low in the belly of their own vessel, leaving four rowers visible, Macu waved in a friendly fashion as they raced toward the other canoe. He gauged the wind and the current, and his vessel's speed against that of the larger one. Just before they collided, he would give the signal for his men to jump up and send arrows and spears flying.

Macu smiled. A perfect plan. Tonina's twenty oarsmen would be dead before they even knew they were under attack. And Macu would deliver the lethal blow to the girl himself. After that, they would help themselves to the provisions in the other canoe, sink it, and head for Mainland where the magic flower awaited.

Recognizing the young man in the rapidly approaching canoe, Yúo waved back. Tonina's heart raced. Why was Macu here? Was he going to escort her to Mainland?

When the smaller canoe was nearly upon them, Yúo gave the order for his men to raise oars. Macu grinned, and gave the secret signal for his hidden men to ready themselves.

"We come to wish you good luck!" Macu shouted as his boat drew near.

"Thank you," Yúo called back, white teeth flashing in his dark brown face. "May the gods bless us all on this journey."

Both teams of oarsmen ceased rowing so that the day was silent, filled only with the sound of waves slapping the sides of the long narrow boats. As Macu's canoe maneuvered alongside, close enough for a man to jump from one dugout to the other, he turned to give his crouched men the order to attack. But as he opened his mouth, he felt something sharp strike his thigh.

He looked down in surprise. A burning arrow was lodged in his flesh.

In the next instant, a hail of fire arrows rained down upon the smaller canoe. Macu's men jumped up, retaliating with their own arrows and spears.

Tonina watched in bewilderment as chaos erupted.

She did not know that her grandmother had held a private conversation with Yúo before they set sail. "I do not trust the boy named Macu. When Tonina saved his life, and his friends carried him from the beach, I saw him look back and give her the evil eye."

"We shall be prepared," Yúo had assured her. He knew what to do. With Tonina riding in the prow of the canoe, her attention focused upon western landfall, she would be unaware that at the back of her long vessel Yúo's men were crouched in readiness to defend themselves with fire arrows. The arrows were coated with flammable sap and, ignited with embers placed on board for making camp on Mainland, they would be hard to douse once lodged in the other canoe.

As Macu's canoe had neared, Yúo had studied the boy's stance, the nervous faces of his oarsmen, noting that there were only four rowers in a canoe outfitted for twelve. And then he had seen the crouched men. And so Yúo had been able to strike first.

As small fires now broke out on Macu's canoe, with men frantically scooping water from the sea to douse them, others leaped onto Tonina's canoe with knives and axes. Suddenly men were fighting hand to hand, yelling, stabbing, punching. The canoe rocked dangerously. Tonina grabbed the sides and felt a shout tear from her throat.

Smoke billowed from the smaller canoe as the ocean current tugged it away with the men stranded upon it, desperately fighting to extinguish the fires.

Tonina saw Macu through the smoke, his face twisted in fury as he brought a club down upon Yúo's head, cracking the skull. Huracan's nephew dropped and Macu stepped over him, raising his club, to bash it down on another Pearl Islander's head.

Tonina watched in frozen horror as the hand-to-hand combat escalated, grew frenzied and brutal, the air filling with cries of pain. Bodies now floated in the rough water, crimson blood streaming in every direction.

Tonina's canoe continued to rock dangerously beneath the feet of so many fighting men. And then the unthinkable happened: The canoe tipped once more from one side to the other, and then it capsized completely, tumbling combatants and Tonina into the water.

While she seized hold of her upturned dugout, the men frantically swam back to the smaller canoe, where the fires had been put out, scrambling up and over the sides, pulling up wounded comrades, and enemies, too, as men from both islands, forgetting the brief conflict, lifted one another into the canoe.

As the Half Moon Island dugout was pulled away on the strong current, and cries for help filled the air, Tonina stayed beside her own capsized boat, desperately treading water, trying to see whom she could save. She was a strong swimmer and at home in the water, but she had never swum so encumbered before. Although the travel pack she wore on her back was buoyant, the fibers of her *hamac* clothes swelled and became so heavy she could hardly move her legs. As she held on to the upturned hull with one hand, she used her free hand to untie the knot at her waist, allowing the heavy skirt to sink.

She swam first to a Pearl Island man and brought him back to their capsized canoe. But as she placed his hand on the hull, she realized he was dead. His hand slipped and he floated away, facedown in the water.

She swam to another and saw that although he was alive, he had lost an arm in the fight. As she struggled to help him back to the upturned hull, she heard panicked shouts, and turned to see the smaller canoe start to sink. It was filled with too many men. They screamed and scrambled over one another as the canoe disappeared beneath the choppy water. Tonina waved her arms, calling to them. Her canoe was larger and sturdier. If they could manage to turn it upright—

Then she saw the sharks.

Fresh screams erupted from the men struggling to get out of the sinking canoe to swim to Tonina's. Cries of terror and pain rose to the sky as dorsal fins circled among the panicked men. The day took on a horrific aspect, filled with frantic splashing, men's shrieks, scarlet water.

When Tonina saw Macu bobbing in the water, faceup and unconscious, she seized him and pulled him to her. With great effort, she was able to haul herself out of the water onto the keel, and pull Macu with her. She sat trembling and afraid on the rocking hull, her arms holding tight to Macu.

The canoe was caught in a crosscurrent, carrying Tonina and Macu away from the sharks and death. She watched in disbelief as the scene of carnage gradually fell out of sight, the survivors unable to reach the sturdy, capsized dugout. Of thirty-one islanders, only Tonina and Macu rode the drifting hull.

Tonina's arms ached as she held on to the unconscious Macu. She didn't understand what had happened. Why had he and his friends attacked her canoe? Why was she now, once again, holding his life in her arms? Pressing her face against his cold, wet hair, she sobbed. She did not know how much longer she could hold him out of the water. Her strength was fading. Her muscles screamed with pain. She watched for sharks.

And then one appeared. It was a small one, young, and drawing swiftly closer. With one smooth gliding motion, it widened its jaws and severed Macu's leg below the knee. The water turned crimson. Tonina cried out. Struggling to keep her own limbs out of the water, she fought with all her strength to pull Macu higher onto the hull.

She saw the fin turn, come back. Tonina tightened her hold around Macu's chest, but instead of gliding by, the creature slammed into the boat, jolting Tonina's arms loose, and suddenly Macu was in the water. She watched in horror as his head went under, and the shark, seizing the unconscious boy, swam away, trailing a bloody wake.

Tonina stared in dumb shock. Alone on the vast sea beneath a cloudless blue sky, with no land in sight—not even the bodies of the other men—Tonina felt her muscles go limp, and then darkness closed over her.

~ 6 ~

Tonina dreamed she rode on the back of a great gray beast.

It was the sea monster from the lagoon, she realized, mysteriously alive, flesh and skin padding his gigantic bones. He had come to carry her away, and she rode him now, holding on to a dorsal fin as they glided together over the sea.

But when she awoke, she found herself on a deserted beach, and wondered if perhaps it had not been a dream at all but her guardians the dolphins, once again bringing her to safety.

She lay still, listening to the surf, the wind in the palm trees, and looked up at deep blue sky. The sand beneath her was warm and dry. But her legs felt strange. Pushing up on her elbows, she shook sand and seaweed from her face and looked down at herself.

Her legs were bare. And then she remembered that she had abandoned the *hamac* skirt in the ocean. It felt odd to have her legs exposed while wearing a cover-up on top when she was used to going barebreasted with her legs covered. The whole effect felt upside down, and she wondered if she had landed in an upside-down world.

She scanned the beach to the right and left and found no other survivors from the brief sea battle that had ended in tragedy. There was also no sign of her dugout canoe or the store of provisions it had held. But her waterproof travel pack was still strapped to her shoulders, and she thanked the gods for that.

Rising shakily to her feet, she turned in a circle to take in the unfamiliar landscape. No lagoon separated this beach from the sea, so that mighty breakers crashed on shore. Behind her, a thick green forest rose like a wall. She realized in dismay that she was not where she was supposed to be.

Grandfather had described the place where the healing flower grew as having great craggy coastal cliffs and dangerous rocky coves. This was a wide, white beach with palm trees. Was she even on Mainland?

Unshouldering her travel pack, she opened it and inspected the contents lovingly packed by Guama—salt fish, dried coconut and berries, medicines—all dry and intact.

Thoughts of home brought back memories of Uncle Yúo and his terrible death, Macu's treachery and Tonina's desperate fight to save him. She started to sob, and then collected herself. No time for sadness or self-pity. Noting the position of the sun, she determined that south lay to her right. If she followed the curving coastline she should reach the coast where she hoped the red flower grew.

Among her provisions was a small coconut bowl filled with the white paint islanders used to cover their faces and arms with protective symbols. She took a moment to take this precaution now, knowing that her face must have been washed clean in the sea, leaving her vulnerable to evil spirits and bad luck. She carefully traced lines and circles, dots and zigzags on her forehead, cheeks, nose, and chin until her face was protected once again.

Then she shouldered her travel pack and, whispering a prayer for the men lost at sea—and a prayer of thanks to Lokono and her guardian dolphins—she struck off down the beach.

She had not gone far before a mangrove forest blocked the way, huge trees with broad trunks rising like giants refusing to let her pass. But Tonina pressed on, climbing over the tangled roots that arched out of the water, slogging through swamp and muck until her legs grew heavy. Clouds of mosquitoes buzzed about her and she stayed alert for poisonous snakes.

Finally she had to lean against a tree to catch her breath and survey the dense wetland forest that had no end. It was no use. She must turn inland and find firm ground before resuming a southward trek. But fear stabbed her. Going inland meant turning her back on the comforting sea.

Nonetheless, she went, and by late afternoon she was out of the marshes and could no longer hear the cries of shorebirds, or see such familiar friends as sea turtles laying their eggs in the mud. She was deep within dense, dry forest with no sight of another shore. Her heart pounded. Pearl Island was so small that a person could cross it in less than a day. A short trek over low hills, several streams, and thick forest at its heart brought the comforting sea back in sight again.

But not here.

This *must* be Mainland, Tonina thought as she paused frequently to sniff the air and note the position of the sun. Unless this was a very large island. But if it *was* Mainland, then it was not much different from Pearl Island, for here the trees were familiar, bearing fruits and nuts that had sustained her people for generations. The flowers were familiar, too, and the small creatures that darted across her path. From tales around the campfire, Tonina had thought Mainland would be such a fantastic place that she would recognize none of its weird features.

She was about to turn southward and head for the coast when she picked up the scent of smoke.

A campfire? Taking heart at the possibility that someone might direct her to the flower, she cautiously followed the smoke and arrived at a clearing occupied by men sitting around a fire, quietly talking and smoking pipes. Tonina's eyes widened. They looked no different from the men of Pearl Island. Except for the brown and black stripes decorating their bodies, they could be members of her own tribe.

Then she saw the cages.

Constructed of poles and twine, they resembled lobster traps, except that these were much larger and held, to her shock, captured eagles.

Tonina gasped softly. Eagle hunting was taboo on Pearl Island. But she had heard of men who did not respect the gods and who thought themselves greater than the spirits of nature. These would not be friendly, she decided, and so she would retrace her steps and continue on her way.

But something stopped her. In the farthest cage, another sort of captive was being held—a young man, wearing only a white loincloth, bound wrist and ankle and looking terrified.

Tonina crept closer through the dense brush, and when she reached his cage, the young man turned, as if sensing her there, and Tonina was startled to find a pair of yellow irises fixed on her. She sucked in her breath and traced a protective sign in the air. She had never seen golden eyes before.

Her heart thumped. She wanted to turn and run, but the look of pleading on his face rooted her to the spot. And then she saw the wound on the boy's forehead, the blood trickling down one side of his face.

Keeping an eye on the men at the campfire, Tonina quietly approached the cage and inspected the closure. It was simply a matter of cutting the twine. She removed the knife from her travel pack and severed the ties. Then she crept in and cut the bonds on the boy's feet and hands.

Without a word he scrambled out of the cage and darted into the trees. When he stopped to look back, tense and coiled to spring away, he seemed for a moment to Tonina like a wild creature. She put her finger to her lips, and then pointed to the eagle hunters. "Make no sound," she whispered.

Yellow irises looked at her in confusion.

She pointed to the ground where dried twigs were strewn, remnants of the cages' manufacture. "Be careful where you step. We must not make noise."

He frowned down at the ground, and then his eyes fixed on her bare legs.

Looking down at herself, Tonina remembered what Grandfather had told her about people on Mainland not liking to look at women's bare skin. She scanned the encampment, where food was heaped along with waterskins and weapons, and she saw, on the other side of the clearing, several white cotton mantles draped over large fern fronds, spread out as if to dry.

Placing her finger to her lips again, she motioned for the youth to follow, and together they crept silently around the perimeter, and when they neared the large ferns, Tonina reached for the nearest mantle. She had seen cotton traded for pearls in her village, and so she planned to leave three perfect round pearls in the place of the mantle.

But when she plucked the cloth from the fern, a sudden cacophony erupted in the air.

Too late, Tonina saw the string attached to the mantle, leading to another looped up into the overhead branches of a tree. One tug and down came a rain of rocks, shells, and coconuts, clattering to the ground in a great noise.

The hunters were instantly on their feet, reaching for weapons.

"*Guay!*" Tonina exclaimed under her breath, and turned to flee into the forest with the yellow-eyed youth close on her heels.

They plunged through the trees and brush, jumped over fallen logs and around thorny bushes; they flew across the dry, twiggy ground, glancing back to see the hunters pursuing. Tonina said, "Quick! We must climb!" and they clambered up a tree thick with leaves, high enough in the branches to be hidden and yet still see their pursuers below. Holding their breath and not moving, Tonina and the youth watched the brown-and-black-striped men run past and disappear into the forest. The two waited until stillness lay around them, broken only by birdsong and the rustling of small creatures in the underbrush, and then they cautiously slipped back to the ground.

Tonina massaged her aching limbs and came to a swift decision. The hunters had run south, their camp lay eastward, and going north would only take Tonina farther from her destination. That left west. She had no choice. For the moment, staying alive was more important than finding the flower.

She looked at the boy. His head had stopped bleeding, but dried blood caked one side of his face. When she reached up to touch the injury, he flinched. "Are you all right?" she whispered.

He stared at her lips, and when she repeated the question, he nodded.

"We must find water and clean your wound. Do you know this place?"

He looked around, golden irises taking in dense trees, many without leaves, the vegetation yellowed and sere. It was autumn and the lowland forest was retreating into dormancy. He shook his head.

Realizing that she still clutched the stolen mantle, Tonina shook it out and tied it around her waist so that it formed a sarong to mid-calf. "This way," she said, and they struck off through trees growing dark with the dying day.

As they made their way through dry country, encountering thistles, thorns, and burrs, traipsing across a forest floor thick with dead leaves, they searched for water and shelter for the night, watchful of the hunters. Tonina grew curious about her strange companion.

His face was oval instead of round like those of her tribe, and he was almost taller than she—the first person she had ever met to be so. His long black hair hung in different lengths and was tangled, as if it had never been groomed. She guessed he was about her own age, but there was nothing about him to identify his tribe or clan. Except for a loin-cloth, he wore nothing on his person, and his skin was unmarked. Tonina had never met someone who wasn't covered in tattoos and piercings. He looked strangely naked and vulnerable, like a newborn baby.

They pushed on through the dying day until they came to a small clearing and found themselves standing before a structure that made them both stare in wonder.

Towering over them, carved out of rock and covered in vines and creepers, was a giant monkey. He squatted on a stone platform that had long since been claimed by moss and lichen, the gray bricks broken by tree roots. Stone monkey paws were clasped over his potbelly, and nesting in them were birds of different kinds.

"*Guay!*" Tonina whispered in alarm, tracing a protective sign in the air. "What is it?"

Her mute companion shook his head in awe.

Tonina saw that the monkey's mouth was open, as if it yawned in a silent scream, and it looked large enough for two people to hide in. Although Tonina thought the builders of this shrine must have been giants, it was apparent they had not come here in years, so it must be safe. They scaled the giant statue, helping each other up until they clambered into the gaping mouth and were able to look down from a good vantage point, should the eagle hunters come prowling about.

Within the safety of the man-made cave, Tonina sat cross-legged on the stone floor and slipped the travel pack from her aching shoulders. Reaching inside, she pulled out a small pouch that contained one of Guama's healing salves. "I wish we had water to wash your wound," she said as she dug her finger into the green paste and tenderly applied it to the injury. "Why were those men holding you captive?"

When the boy did not respond, she said, "Do you understand what I am saying?" Grandfather had said that the people on Mainland spoke different languages. "Can you even hear me?" she mused aloud, wiping her fingers on her sarong and replacing the pouch in the travel pack.

The youth's thin black brows furrowed, and then his face cleared in comprehension. When he nodded, Tonina said, "If you understood my question, then you speak my language. I wonder how that is. You do not look like an island boy. What is your name?"

He stared at her lips.

"Your name," she repeated. Then she tapped her chest and said, "I am Tonina. Who are you?"

His lips moved as he struggled to form a word. But no sound came out.

Tonina sat back. Perhaps the wound on his forehead had injured his ability to speak. And then another thought occurred to her. "Do you *know* your name?"

Golden irises fixed on her as he seemed to retreat into thought. When he shook his head, Tonina decided the head wound had injured his memory. "Can you remember *anything*?"

As the boy shook his head once more, Tonina noted again his lack of protective tattoos and body piercings, the absence of feathers, necklaces, amulets. She said, "Without a name, you have no protection against evil spirits."

She withdrew into solemn thought. Deciding upon a name was no light matter. Her own people devoted days to selecting a child's name because it not only provided protection against evil, but was destiny as well. Thinking of the cage he had been kept in, and the great birds of prey occupying the other cages, Tonina decided that, until he remembered his real name, he should be called Brave Eagle.

When she told him so, he smiled in such a beautiful way that it took her aback. Suddenly she wanted to give him more. Recalling the string of periwinkle shells Guama had tucked into the travel pack for good luck, Tonina lifted the necklace out and draped it over his head, settling the charms on his pale chest. "These are sacred to Lokono, Spirit of All," she said, adding, "now you are twice as safe," and was rewarded with another beautiful smile.

"I am searching for a flower," Tonina went on as she produced nuts and dried berries from the pack, offering them to Brave Eagle, wishing she had water. "Perhaps you know it?" She formed cupped petals with her fingers, the way Grandmother had, and added, "It is as red as blood, and possesses a magical healing spirit. Have you seen it?"

Brave Eagle munched on berries as he stared at her hands. He thought hard about it, then shook his head.

They silently consumed their modest rations while watching the forest deepen into darkness, as the night came alive with nocturnal sounds. "We should sleep," Tonina finally said to Brave Eagle, whose luminous eyes mesmerized her. There was an air of mystery about this attractive mute boy. Vulnerability, too. The tender wound on his forehead, and the welts on his wrists where he had been bound, moved her heart and made her want to take him into her arms.

While Tonina studied him, he did the same with her, moving his golden eyes from her head to her toes and up again, not in the disrespectful way some men had of looking at a woman, but in almost innocent curiosity. When he settled his eyes on the many necklaces resting on her breast, he picked up the amulet encased in palm fibers.

"I have never seen what's inside," Tonina said. "Grandmother said I would know when the time had come for me to open it. So far, the time has never seemed right."

He gently let the talisman fall to her breast and met her eyes in the deepening darkness. The stone chamber was small, and the night was growing chill. When Brave Eagle stretched out on his side, folding his arm beneath his head for a pillow, Tonina removed her sarong and, lying down to face Brave Eagle, spread the mantle over them both. "Why can't you speak?" she murmured, touching a fingertip to his silent lips. "You can hear, and you can understand me. Yet you cannot speak." She yawned and drifted off to sleep while Brave Eagle stayed awake, keeping his eyes on her.

As the night grew colder, he drew the girl to him, slipping an arm under her and gently pulling her slumbering body against his. He held her until he, too, fell asleep, and thus they slept together, protected within the sacred shrine of the monkey god so covered in vines and creepers that they could not be seen.

7

Unearthly shrieks shattered the dawn silence.

Tonina sat up and, clamping her hands over her ears, turned frightened eyes to the opening of the shrine. The unholy howling was deafening. It was the sound of people being slaughtered!

A dark shape flew past, and then the shrine trembled, as if struck by something heavy. "We are under attack!" Tonina cried, and she held on to Brave Eagle as the assault continued.

But when pale daylight streamed inside, Tonina saw that their attackers were not human at all, but enormous red monkeys, and that the shrine was not under attack. The howler monkeys had simply greeted the day as they always did, with great noise and excitement, and when the chorus died, the howlers grew quiet and settled down to the day's business of survival in the lowland forest.

Tonina laughed nervously. And then she remembered that she was now a whole day on Mainland and had yet to find the flower. "We must go," she said, shouldering her travel pack and whispering a prayer of thanks to the monkey god for harboring them.

Her body ached. She had never slept on a hard surface before. She glanced at Brave Eagle, recalling how she had wakened during the night, confused and frightened, and then found herself in the boy's comforting and warm embrace. Her cheeks burned at the memory. Tonina was unused to the feel of another body against hers because her people slept separately in *hamacs*. She wondered if she had broken a premarital taboo.

Brave Eagle pointed to his mouth and made dry, smacking sounds.

Tonina nodded. She was thirsty, too. "There must be water nearby."

But as they descended by way of sturdy vines, they heard men's voices. Tonina recognized them as the eagle hunters. And they were approaching from the southeast.

The two young people stayed on the move, always ahead of the hunters, creating a zigzag trail, turning around, retracing their steps, then breaking off to follow another tack until they no longer heard their pursuers. Toward late afternoon they came upon a small clearing where they saw women lowering gourds into a well sunk into the natural limestone.

Gesturing to Brave Eagle to stay hidden, Tonina approached the women with a smile and a friendly greeting. They smiled back, and then, eyeing her curious attire—a man's cloak for a short skirt, the loosely woven blouse—they giggled. Now Tonina saw proper women's dress: an ankle-length skirt and a long tunic top with short sleeves.

Indicating that she was thirsty, and producing a handsome abalone shell from her travel pack, Tonina was able to purchase a gourd of freshwater. "Where am I?" she asked. "What is this place called?"

One of the women smiled and said, "Yucatán."

"Yucatán?"

The woman nodded.

"Are we near Quatemalan?"

The woman worked her lips over toothless gums and shook her head. Holding out her arms, she said, "Yucatán."

Tonina thanked her and, returning to Brave Eagle, said, "At least we know where we *are*. Now we need to find out where we want to be."

~ 8 ~

Pushing her way through trees and dense brush, using her knife to cut thick growth, Tonina suddenly came to a halt. The leaf-littered forest floor had come to an end, and a new sort of ground began. "What is this?" Tonina whispered as she bent over the strange surface, inspecting it.

Brave Eagle squatted and, reaching out a tentative hand, touched the curious surface with his fingertips. He looked up and shook his head.

It appeared to be stone. But very white stone, and unnaturally smooth and flat. Tonina's eyes took in the dimensions of the new forest floor: Its width was the measure of ten men standing shoulder to shoulder, and the length of it—

She peered ahead and could not see the end of the straight stone way. On either side, trees and shrubs flourished, as if giving way to the march of this peculiar stone. Tonina started to put a foot on the white surface, then withdrew. What if this path was reserved for the gods and therefore taboo? "We'll go around," she said to Brave Eagle, and they delivered themselves into the forest, skirting the road for its entire length, which proved to be nearly a day's march.

With each footstep west, Tonina's anxiety grew. Twice they had tried to turn back or to go southward, only to hear the hunters still in pursuit, spread out like a fisherman's net. Tonina wondered why they were so determined to get the boy back.

They ate Guama's salt fish as they walked, and shared the precious gourd of water. When they came to the first stone building, Tonina surmised that it was a dwelling of some sort, or a shrine to local gods, but she had never seen a building made of stone before. She looked in and found it empty.

After a short walk, they came upon more stone structures; some intact, others crumbling and overgrown with vines, but all deserted. Blackened fire pits were evidence of habitation at one time, but long ago.

Even so, there might still be people nearby, and the prospect lifted Tonina's spirits. She had inspected the few flowers they had encountered along the way, but as this was autumn, little bloomed. She vowed that if this day, when it was done, had not produced results, she would head north, as far as she could go to be sure she was out of the range of the hunters, and then turn east to the coast and from there follow the beach to Quatemalan.

The forest began to thin and the vein of flat white stone that ran through it came to an end. Tonina and Brave Eagle found themselves standing before a structure for which they had no explanation—a vast field, clearly man-made, embraced within two steep, sloping walls. As they walked its length, wondering who had constructed such a fantastic place, they arrived at a platform built of human skulls.

Tonina cried out and spoke a quick protective prayer to Lokono before she realized the skulls were carved from stone, row upon row of them.

And then Brave Eagle saw the pyramid.

He broke into a run and sprinted across the open space where no trees grew, just weeds and wild grass, and when he arrived at the base of the stone steps that rose to the sky, Brave Eagle was overcome by the need to climb to the top. With Tonina calling out to him, he scrambled up the steps, and when he reached the top he opened his arms wide, flung back his head, and released a high, keening cry.

Tonina followed him up to the summit and was astonished by what she saw—forest as far as the horizon. And not a glint of the sea. Now she knew for certain she was on Mainland. She was also suddenly gripped with panic at the sight of the dizzying open expanse. Dropping to her knees, she started for the steps, but Brave Eagle lifted her to her feet and, holding her in his arms, calmed her.

Now she marveled at this fantastic construction that rose brick by brick toward the sun, and wondered about the giants who had built it. But weeds grew on its slopes, tufts of grass broke through the stone, and at the top where a curious stone building stood, stunted trees had taken root. Like the shrine of the monkey god, overgrown and neglected, whoever had built this structure had not returned to keep it clean, to keep nature from claiming it.

Tonina felt Brave Eagle stiffen at her side. His eyes were fixed on the forest below. "What is it?" she asked.

He pointed, and although Tonina could not see what he saw, she knew it was the hunters. To her horror, Brave Eagle pointed in three directions. The hunters had spread out and were approaching from the north, east, and south. "We must hide!" she said, and they hurriedly climbed down the pyramid, finding the descent more difficult than the ascent, as the slope was steep and the steps shallow. They went backward, on hands and knees, frequently looking out at the open space to see if the hunters had broken through the trees.

When they reached the base, they searched for a hiding place. "There!" Tonina whispered, pointing to a low stone structure that appeared to be half underground. They explored the crumbled walls covered in weeds and moss and found a partially collapsed doorway. It was a tight squeeze, but they were able to insinuate their slender bodies through and into a dark, narrow passage. Creeping cautiously forward, Tonina and Brave Eagle stretched their eyes against the darkness, feeling themselves descend deeper into the earth as the passage sloped downward, and presently they saw a thin shaft of light ahead, like a beacon.

They came upon a stone chamber that had no other entrance or exit, but a curious opening in the ceiling that pierced layers of rock and opened to the sky. The narrow shaft was no wider than a man's fist, and admitted fresh air as well as light.

And sounds. The hunters were nearby, their familiar grumblings funneling through the vent into the buried chamber. Tonina and Brave Eagle looked at each other in the dank, mysterious room, praying that the men did not notice the partially collapsed doorway. They waited, listening, until the voices faded, and the two released shaky sighs of relief.

But they could not yet leave, and so they took stock of their new refuge. Tonina stared in amazement. She had never seen wall paintings before. It took her a moment to comprehend what her eyes beheld.

"Men," she said softly, reaching out to touch the painted figures. "These are men."

The mural was old and covered with a creeping mold, the paint fading and chipped. Tonina was filled with a sense that this mural would not last for many more years and that what was recorded here would some-day be forgotten.

The three walls seemed to tell the story of a tall, white-skinned man with hair growing from his chin. On the first wall, he appeared to be a king sitting on a throne while watching a battle. On the second, the king was seen throwing himself onto fire and then descending into the Underworld where the souls of the dead greeted him. But on the last wall he was alive again and his people were bowing to him. Finally he was standing on snakes forming a raft, and he was sailing over the sea toward the rising sun.

In this last painting Tonina spotted a familiar object. She stared at it, then reached into her travel pack and brought out the glass goblet. It was like the one the king held in the painting, so that Tonina wondered if one of those giant serpents was the sea monster whose bones lay on the floor of Pearl Island's lagoon.

"We will stay here for the night," she said, suspecting that this chamber had once been a holy sanctuary and that, like in the monkey god shrine, she and Brave Eagle would be protected here.

Tonina was suddenly tired and hungry and homesick. Thinking of Uncle Yúo's death, and sharply missing Guama and Huracan, wishing she were back in the village, Tonina wept into her hands. Brave Eagle embraced her and she cried on his shoulder. They were both strangers in a strange land, they knew only each other, and had quickly come to depend on each other. And now he was comforting her.

As her tears subsided and she drifted again into slumber in Brave Eagle's arms, Tonina thought: I shall take him back to Pearl Island. . . .

~ 9 ~

Brave Eagle dreamed of mist-shrouded mountains and pine forests blanketed in snow. He dreamed of speed and wind and freedom. He saw, in the dream, the man-made mountain with its stone steps rising to the sky and he felt again, when he had reached the pyramid's summit, that he was *home*. This area is called the Lowlands, he thought in his dream. I do not belong here. The eagle hunters carried me far from my people.

I am Eagle Clan. We are the caretakers of—

He awoke suddenly, blinking up at the stone ceiling, wondering in the darkness where he was. As he wondered, the dream faded. Though he tried to hold on to it, as he climbed to full consciousness, the dream vanished. And with it, the answers to who he was and where he came from.

He lifted himself up to gaze down at the girl sleeping at his side, and a wave of tenderness washed over him. Tonina had shown him kindness. She had severed his bonds and set him free, had shared her food and water, had put medicine on his wound, had kept him warm and safe—all at great risk to herself. Although he still did not know who he himself was, he knew who *she* was. His savior. And for that, his gratitude would know no bounds. There was nothing, Brave Eagle decided in that moment, that he would not do for Tonina.

Dawn came and they crept from their hiding place to see that the hunters had established four small camps at the edge of the forest, aligned with each of the cardinal points so that they formed a perimeter around the pyramid's compound. Once again, Tonina wondered why her mute companion was so valuable to them.

The pair made a stealthy circumnavigation of the pyramid and saw that, of the four camps, the western one was momentarily unoccupied. "I must go east toward the coast, but those men over there will see us," Tonina said quietly. "This way we can get through, and perhaps if we go far enough west, we can find a safe place to turn south."

10

Trekking westward through woodland, they finished the water in the gourd, and consumed the last of their dried berries and coconut. Three times they doubled back, retracing their steps, creating false trails for the hunters to track. And when night came, they found refuge in the embrace of an ancient fig tree long past fruit-bearing, its mighty branches forming a V wide enough for the two to sleep in, above the ground and in safety.

Then came another day of walking westward, of increased hunger and thirst. When they came upon a cluster of avocado trees, they scaled the thick trunks in search of food, but the avocados were small and bitter, months away from being ripe and edible.

The sun was nearing the western horizon when Tonina and Brave Eagle, thirsty, tired, and ravenous, pushed through dense scrub forest and suddenly heard shouts and cries ahead. They knew it was not the hunters, for it had been nearly a day since they had sensed their presence behind them. These were new voices, new men.

The two froze, trying to see through the trees. And then a queer creaking sound was followed by a horrific crash.

Picking their way closer, they came to the edge of the forest and saw a vast clearing before them. There was no more woodland, just fields dotted with tree stumps and thatched huts, and around the periphery, men laboring to cut down more trees. They wielded stone axes and knives. Some scaled the mighty trees to tie ropes to the top; others held the distal ends of the ropes to pull the trees down.

Tonina's eyes widened. Hundreds of men and boys were at work, more men than she had ever seen in her life, laboring industriously as they filled the air with their yells and shouts, and trees toppled and crashed to the earth. Other men were moving through the fields, bent over their digging sticks and dropping seeds into the soil. Other fields already supported mature crops, and men walked among these, too, weeding, pruning, harvesting.

So much food, Tonina thought as she and Brave Eagle found a well-worn path and followed it. Enough food to feed her own tribe for years. What were the men going to do with so much squash and corn?

The answer came soon, as she and Brave Eagle entered more densely populated fields, where huts now clustered together and children played among tame dogs and turkeys. The newcomers saw women bent over cook fires, stirring pots or basting meat on spits. Women also sat at looms or spun cotton while nursing babies.

Fields grew smaller and huts became more numerous. And there were more people—Tonina had not thought there were this many people in the whole world.

And then the fields were gone and the huts were separated by mere garden plots where a few stalks of corn struggled for space, and turkeys scratched in the dirt. The smoke from so many campfires filled the air and nearly blotted out the late afternoon sun.

Finally they came upon a sight that made Tonina stare in wide-eyed wonder.

When Brave Eagle gave her a questioning look, she said, "I think," trying to remember what Grandfather had said about Mainland, "I think that," and she pointed to the high stone wall, the tops of buildings on the other side, the towers and guards, the pennants snapping in the breeze, "I think that is something called . . . a *city*."

11

One Eye the island trader was scanning the crowd for female companionship for the coming night when he spotted the strange pair on the far side of the marketplace.

Newcomers, he decided, noting the expressions of wonder on their young faces. And not the usual sort of first-time visitors to Mayapan. Travelers generally arrived bent beneath heavy burdens, or with families in tow. These were a pair of tall ones, a head above the crowd, the boy pale-skinned and lanky, and the girl— What *was* she wearing? It looked like a man's mantle tied around her waist, and on top some sort of crude mesh that resembled a fishing net. She carried a modest travel pack on her shoulders.

One Eye's curiosity was piqued when he noticed the way the girl kept touching the small bag that hung from her belt. Something valuable inside? Looked heavy. Cacao beans, perhaps. Or jade pieces.

One Eye smiled as he reached for his knife. His luck had been bad lately, but it appeared to have suddenly turned for the better.

Tonina stared in amazement.

Although other islanders came to Pearl Island to trade, she had never seen a marketplace. The great gathering of noisy commerce took place in the precincts outside the city, in the clearing between forest and high stone walls. Tonina's eyes widened at the profusion of people sitting on blankets with wares or food spread around them; crouching beneath thatch umbrellas and calling out to passersby; standing in front of crude huts that had only one wall, with goods hanging on strings from the ceiling poles. Tonina and Brave Eagle made their way among market stalls offering raw cotton, rare tropical woods, cacao beans, leather, featherwork cloaks, chilies, and caged macaws, each merchant hawking his merchandise in a language the two newcomers did not understand.

Night had fallen and torches were lit, filling the air with smoke and dancing shadows. Tonina watched as customers exchanged cacao beans for blankets, gourds, feathers, onions, and avocados; haggling, arguing, or nodding in agreement while beans were meticulously counted and scrutinized. She had never witnessed such behavior before. And the people themselves! They ranged from poor beggars dressed only in dirty loincloths to men and women arrayed in colorful capes and dresses, their hair adorned with plumes and beads, their feet clad in fine sandals. On Pearl Island, everyone dressed the same. With the exception of the chief, it would not have occurred to any of Tonina's people to array himself differently.

The din of the throng made Tonina's head swim. And the aromas from so many delicious offerings caused her stomach to rumble. With her mouth watering, she said to Brave Eagle, "I am hungry."

He nodded, eyeing a savory display of fried fish speckled with herbs.

Then Tonina spotted the flower sellers' stalls and was there in a dash, looking for an opening among the throng to push through, her eyes frantically scanning the colorful and fragrant offerings. There was a red flower! And another. And another. She picked up each, studied it by torchlight, then replaced it to pick up another until one of the merchants barked at her to make a choice or move on. When Brave Eagle reached her with a questioning look, Tonina said in disappointment, "It is not here."

W atching the young pair as they left the flower stalls, One Eye discreetly followed them through the crowd until opportunity arrived. He bumped into the girl, muttered an apology in Mayan, and disappeared.

Out of the sight of others, he opened the pouch he had cut from her belt and his single eye bugged out. Pearls! Round and flawless. What were those two doing with such a fortune? It didn't matter. One Eye almost danced with glee. Now he could leave this miserable country and retire to an island where he would build a fine house and marry a fat woman who would give him ten children. He would dine every day on meat and lobster. He would wear cotton and feathers and call himself king. He would—

"*Guay!*"

Startled, One Eye turned. The girl had discovered the theft and was wailing in alarm. "*Guay!*" she cried again, while the throng milled around her without interest.

One Eye froze to the spot. The girl was chattering in dismay to her companion, and the words that flowed were distinctly from an island dialect. One Eye's jaw dropped. Now he saw the white facial paint, and the long hair decorated with shells. She was an island girl!

Cursing his luck and the gods—sparse though his scruples might be, One Eye could never steal from a kinswoman—he did some rapid thinking and finally hurried after the pair to say, "Is this yours?" He spoke in Taino instead of Mayan, and the girl exclaimed with delight.

"I saw the thief lift the purse and I gave chase," One Eye said as he reluctantly handed the small bag back.

As the girl thanked him profusely, One Eye realized in relief that she was indeed one of his own, for she prattled in his native tongue with perfection, as one born to the islands, though with the accent and idioms of a western tribe.

"May the blessings of the gods be upon you and yours," One Eye said, suddenly coming up with an idea. There were other ways to relieve the girl of her pearls and still leave his conscience in peace. "Will you and your friend join me at my fire?"

As Tonina and Brave Eagle followed him through the crowd, Tonina looked down at One Eye the trader, who wore a plain loincloth and an orange cloak knotted at the neck, and who walked with a curious rolling gait. "Are you a midget?" she asked. Tonina had heard of such people, but had never seen one.

"I'm a dwarf," he said indignantly. "There's a difference, you know."

When they reached his camp near the main city gate—a patch of ground claimed by blankets spread out between two noisy families—One Eye said, "Got to grab every bit of space you can," and crossed his legs to sit down. Tonina and Brave Eagle sat shoulder to shoulder, there was so little room between the two loud families who ate and argued and screamed with laughter. As the trader stirred the embers in his fire, he studied the feminine boy and boyish girl. Lovers? No. Virgins, he would bet on it. How did they know each other and why had they come to Mayapan?

"Are you here for the games?" he asked.

"Games?"

He waved a stubby arm. "All these people. It's the games. Mayapan isn't always this crowded."

When the girl gave him a blank look, he asked, "Where are you from?" wondering how it was possible for someone not to be aware of the Thirteen Games.

"Pearl Island," she said, her attention singularly focused on the corncobs roasting in the embers.

"Never heard of it. I am from Borinquen, which means 'land of great lords.'"

He looked at her expectantly, but Tonina shook her head. One Eye shrugged. It didn't matter. An island possessed many names: the one the inhabitants gave to it, the name other islanders called it, how the island was called by the ancestors, and how future people would refer to it—in One Eye's case, his descendants would one day say they lived on the island of Puerto Rico.

He narrowed his good eye and scrutinized her. It was a known fact that one could tell the origin of a man's people by the color of his skin. The Mayans, coming from the south, were red. In the west and north, where the Nahuatl-speakers flourished, people were copper-toned. And those from the east, on the islands, were a handsome, rich brown, like himself. But this girl defied the rule, her skin the gold of wild honey. Where did *her* people originate? He said, "You don't look like an island girl. Where I come from, the women are short and plump and dark."

As Tonina told him her story, he listened with keen interest. It was not unusual for a tribe to sacrifice a child to the sea gods; to place it in a waterproof ark, however, with blankets and spirit-protection, was. She had been abandoned by her people for a reason, yet the intent seemed not that she should perish.

Tucking the information away for possible use at a later date, he offered a waterskin, and the two drank so deeply that he thought of asking a pearl in payment. And when he offered to share his corn, they looked at the cobs as if they were made of jade.

"You had better put that purse away," he said, giving the corn a turn in the heat.

Tonina agreed and, opening her sharkskin travel pack, tucked the small pouch within. When a glint in the torchlight caught One Eye's attention, he leaned over and said, "What's that?"

Tonina showed him the glass goblet, and the trader's eye went big and round. He had never seen anything like it and decided he would have that *and* the pearls.

They accepted hot tortillas with eagerness. Although the boy so far made no sound, the girl said between bites, "All these people . . . Where do they find water?"

"This is a dry land. No streams, rivers, or ponds. They get their water from something called a cenote—a deep well sunk into the limestone."

Tonina nodded, recalling the women she had met fetching water at a well.

"The one here at Mayapan is far underground. A ladder of a hundred rungs descends into the earth, and men labor day upon day, going down, coming up with baskets of water."

"So many strange things in this strange land," Tonina murmured.

One Eye gave her a skeptical look. Something strange to this girl was probably commonplace to anyone else.

"White stone," she said. "Growing through the trees in long straight lines, smooth and wide. Lying flat on the forest floor."

The dwarf blinked. "You mean the roads?"

"Roads?"

"Called White Roads because of the color. The Maya make them. Religious pathways for walking from shrine to shrine."

She frowned. "But where do they find rock so smooth and flat?"

"They don't find it, they *make* it. They cook rocks until they turn to dust, then they stir in water and spread it about. It's called cement. It's what holds their buildings together. Piled-up bricks with cement mortar in between. How do you think that pyramid stays up?" He jerked a greasy thumb toward the high wall that encircled the inner city.

Tonina squinted in the torchlight and saw, shrouded in smoke and backdropped by stars, an imposing structure rising beyond the wall. "We saw a mountain just like that," she said. "We climbed to the top and could see the forest all the way to the end of the earth. Nearby there was a platform made of stone skulls. And an enormous field embraced within two sloping walls."

One Eye nodded. "That is the City of Water Wizards. What the Maya call Chichén Itzá. It was once a thriving city but now it's deserted. They still use it as a religious ceremonial center, though. They hold festivals there on holy days. Fanatical calendar-keepers, the Maya. Every day needs a festival. And it isn't a mountain, it's called a pyramid. On top is a temple to Kukulcan, one of their gods."

He handed them each an ear of corn, which they accepted with gusto. Before sinking her teeth into the cob, Tonina plucked a few hot kernels and threw them into the fire as an offering to the gods.

"What happened to your eye?" she asked.

"Which one?"

She reddened in embarrassment.

"Lost it in a fight with a jaguar," he said, tapping the leather patch that covered his left eye. "But the tragedy has turned into a blessing. Dwarfs are considered lucky. People like to have us about. But a dwarf with only one eye must surely have the favor of the gods." Further sign of the gods' favor, he could have added, was his graying, thinning hair. Forty years upon this earth and not dead yet.

While they ate, Tonina's eyes roved the busy marketplace where more camps were being established, and industry continued beneath torch-light. When she saw a man plastering what looked like a coconut with a white, milky substance, and asked about it, One Eye said, "That's rubber. He's making a ball."

"Rubber?"

"The sap of a local tree. The Maya use it for a hundred things. They adore their rubber goods."

"It stinks."

"But it bounces well," he said, eyeing the ball that was bound for a game. "Hard, though. One blow to the head with that ball can kill you. So what brings you to the city?" One Eye asked, wondering how to relieve the girl of her pearls and transparent drinking vessel as honorably as possible.

"We are here by accident. I am supposed to be in Quatemalan, not in Yucatán."

He stopped stirring the embers. "Eh? What did you say? Yucatán?"

"Is this city not in Yucatán, or did we travel out of that land?"

He frowned. "Where did you get the idea you were in *Yucatán*?"

"We met a woman at a well, and when I asked what this place was called, she said Yucatán."

The dwarf howled with laughter. "*Yucatán* in their dialect means 'I don't understand'!"

Tonina stared at him. And then she realized that, if she was going to survive in this land and accomplish her goal, she must learn the language. She asked One Eye if he would teach her.

He brightened and quickly agreed. He would trade lessons for pearls.

"The Maya are a wonderful race," One Eye said as he sank his teeth into a roasted corncob and talked with his mouth full. "You will never meet a friendlier, more hospitable people. And so respectful! When husband and wife sleep at night, side by side, they do so head to toe so that should one desire to smoke, it won't bother the other. But those in there." He jerked his thumb toward the walls. "The nobility. Can't say the same of them. Self-involved. Look at themselves in mirrors all day."

"Mirrors?"

"It's something you look into and you see yourself."

"*Guay!*" Tonina held up a hand. "How can someone see his own face?"

"It's called a reflection. Have you never looked into water?"

She thought back to her childhood, when the girls knelt on the grassy bank of the island's placid lagoon and gazed upon the surface. They had thought the faces looking up at them were water sprites. Tonina pondered this now. Was it possible she had seen her own face?

One Eye looked Brave Eagle up and down. Weird skin coloring, sickly pale, and his features were delicate. One Eye thought the boy curiously feminine. He had heard of creatures called hermaphrodites and wondered if a peek inside the lad's loincloth might divulge a surprise or two. No tattoos or body decorations, just a periwinkle necklace. "What's the matter with your friend? Doesn't he speak?"

"He hurt his head. I think it knocked his memories out."

As he watched his two guests, One Eye thought: A pair of innocents. Unwise to the ways of city life. Especially the girl. Once her pearls were gone, she would have to resort to selling her body. The boy, too. Typical of young folk fresh from the farm.

"How far are we from the sea?" Tonina asked.

One Eye jerked a thumb over his shoulder. "That way, north, three days is the great Bay of Campeche. We are sitting on what is called a peninsula. A big spit of land protruding from the mainland. That way many days," he said, pointing west, "is another ocean."

Her eyes stretched wide. "*Another* ocean? How can that be?"

"Up there," he flung a stubby arm in the direction of northwest, "is a stretch of land that goes on for eternity, so they say."

Tonina was silent. She could not picture so much land, and so far from the sea.

But then, she would never have imagined so many people, yet here they were, amassed against the city walls. Although the camps were noisy and full of life, with people eating and laughing, playing flutes and drums, Tonina saw a lot of hunger among them, and remarked so.

"There isn't enough food," the dwarf said. "There isn't enough land to grow more food. And more people are coming to the city every day."

"The poor children," she murmured, eyeing the family squatting next to them. "They look starved."

"They're all right," One Eye said with a shrug. "The parents make a tobacco paste and rub it on the children's gums. Staves off hunger."

Tonina nodded. Although hunger was rare among her own people, it was known that the spirit that resided in tobacco leaves suppressed the appetite.

A sudden commotion in the marketplace caught their attention.

Trumpets blared and guards with spears pushed through, making way for a small procession. When word spread who was coming, people jumped up from campfires and ran to see.

One Eye and his companions had a good view, as the procession was aiming for the main gate, and presently they saw a swaggering, thickly built man, resplendently dressed, every inch of his skin painted bright red. He wore such a tall headdress that he looked as if he might topple over. Tonina had never seen anything like it. Petals were strewn in his path, mothers held up babies for him to bless, and people fought to touch his shadow, jostling one another while guards with whips kept them back. The man had an arrogant air and did not look at the worshipful mob but kept his eyes over their heads.

"That is Balám," One Eye said, seeing Tonina's look of wide-eyed wonder.

"Is he the king of this place?"

One Eye snorted. "Someone more important than that."

"A holy man?"

"More important yet."

She gave him a startled look. "Who is more important than a king or a holy man?"

One Eye sucked a tooth and said, "A ballplayer."

She gave him a blank look. "What is a ballplayer?"

The girl truly came from a backward island! Even the crudest village had its playing field and team. "It is a game played with a rubber ball, and that man is Prince Balám, the captain of his team. He is of royal blood. His uncle is the king of Uxmal. The rulers of these cities exchange family members in order to ensure the peace, you see, and so likewise the king of Mayapan's son lives in Uxmal."

But Tonina wasn't listening. Her attention was fixed upon the second man emerging from the mob, also regally dressed, with magnificent feathers rising from an impossible headdress. "Is he a prince, too?" she asked in awe.

"Kaan? No. He's a commoner."

"But a ballplayer?"

"And a better one than Prince Balám, so in a way he is a better man, despite his bad blood."

"Bad blood?"

"He belongs to an inferior race called Chichimecs, which means 'wild people.' Scattered tribes of unruly, uncivilized wanderers. Normally he would work as a slave or servant and be despised for his inferiority, but because of his skills as a player, he is a hero of the people. When a man scores points, people forget his blood."

"Chichimec," she murmured, unable to take her eyes off him. Taller than Prince Balám, Kaan the commoner walked with a long, proud stride.

"Not many of his race in these parts," One Eye said. "They roam the high valleys in the far northwest. Ignorant, inept warriors. Call themselves by different names—Mexica, Mixtec, Zapotec—as if their names for themselves meant anything. Barbarians is all they are. Like others of his pitiful kind, Kaan's parents came to Mayapan hoping for a better life among the Maya. His mother still works in the palace kitchens. His father perished while felling trees. But Kaan has a Mayan wife, he owns a villa in the city, and as you can see, dresses and acts Mayan. He denies his Chichimec blood, which any smart man would do."

How strange to deny one's blood, thought Tonina, who yearned to know who her people were, the ones who had set her on the sea in an ark.

"Unfortunately," One Eye added, "he can't help his looks. A man can dress in all manner of finery and speak Mayan, even marry a Mayan woman, but his face will always be his face."

"What's wrong with his face?" Tonina thought Kaan was handsome and said so.

One Eye stared at her. Handsome! Kaan the hawk-nosed Chichimec was not handsome. Now, One Eye the crafty Taino trader, *there* was a handsome fellow. One Eye had seen himself in a mirror and so he knew. Despite the stunted arms and legs attached to a thick torso, and his over-large head that tended to wobble, and despite the lack of an eye, the dwarf knew he was devilishly attractive to women. Didn't his many sexual conquests attest to that?

"Notice how different Kaan is from Prince Balám and the nobles walking with them," One Eye said. "The Maya have high cheekbones, slanting eyes, and a natural reddish tint to their skin. They flatten their babies' heads by pressing the soft skull between two boards until it stays that way. They force babies' eyes to cross. And they make a cut in the skin here," he said, tapping the bridge of his nose, "and insert an appliance that gives them that beak I am sure you have noticed. The Mayan beauty ideal is receding chins and protuberant front teeth, such as you see on Prince Balám. But Kaan is nothing like that. Nice round head, like mine, and that big nose is all his. Anyone can see he is not Mayan.

"Nonetheless, he is our greatest ball-game hero. His name tells you everything, for in the tongue of the Maya, *chak* means 'great,' and *kaan* means 'snake.' He was so named for his agility and speed on the ball court, and because he never loses, in the same way that a snake never dies."

Tonina watched the crowd in curiosity, their frenzy to get close to the two men, their fever-pitch excitement over their presence. When she asked One Eye why the people were acting thus, he said, "Everyone loves to worship a hero. Were there no such men on your island?"

She had to think. There were some who were revered and respected, such as Huracan and the chief. Perhaps an excellent swimmer. Or a boy who had tangled with a barracuda and won. But no one ever received such passionate adulation as these two men did.

As the procession drew near, she noticed how differently each hero treated the cheering crowd. Kaan the commoner smiled at the people and bestowed his hand upon children's heads, patient and playful with his young adorers. But Prince Balám did not even acknowledge the mob, striding past with his huge artificial nose held high. One Eye said, "They're like brothers. Not blood brothers, but such close friends that they might as well have shared a womb."

Tonina studied the smiling, friendly Kaan, and the aloof Prince Balám. "They are so unalike," she murmured.

In more ways than the girl knew, One Eye thought. Prince Balám was wed to a fat, juicy woman suited to the prince's appetites. But Kaan was married to Lady Jade Sky, who, from what One Eye had heard, was a quiet, shy, and rather "dry" woman. More bones than meat.

Kaan paused in the crowd to bestow his smile upon his admirers, and when his dark eyes fell upon Tonina, who stood a head taller than those around her, he seemed startled, and he came to a momentary standstill.

Tonina met his gaze, also briefly taken aback, without knowing why. Their eyes locked, and as the moment stretched, One Eye looked from one to the other and wondered if something was at work here, the magic of the gods perhaps, or destiny; something more than was apparent to the casual observer, or even to the girl and Kaan themselves.

Kaan seemed to remember himself, resumed walking, and the procession finally moved through the wall, with the gates closing behind them, people returning to their camps, talking excitedly.

Tonina remained standing, peering through the smoke-filled night toward the closed wooden gates, deaf to the noise of the marketplace, blind to any other sight than the gates—and, in her mind, the face of Kaan the hero ballplayer.

She finally sat down, while One Eye contemplated the curious, brief interlude between Kaan and Tonina, wondering if this might be something profitable down the line. "So how did your friend hurt his head?" the trader asked as he picked his teeth with a twig.

As Tonina recounted how she and Brave Eagle met, and told of the eagle hunters who had chased them, One Eye studied the youth. There was something strange about him. With those yellow eyes so luminous and penetrating, an air of enchantment hung about the boy like a morning mist. The trader's mind shifted to thoughts of profit. The boy was worth something if what the girl said about the eagle hunters was true, that they had tracked him for such a long distance. Perhaps he *was* a hermaphrodite. Certain freaks and human oddities commanded a good price.

"What do these hunters look like?" he asked. "I mean, we should keep a lookout so we can hide you from them."

Tonina described the brown-and-black-striped men, and the one with a crooked arm whom she assumed to be their leader, and One Eye tucked the information away for a future time.

"How long are you staying in Mayapan?"

"We are not staying," Tonina said, her thoughts still on the hero Kaan, unable to put his face from her mind, and not knowing why. "We will buy provisions and then we go to Quatemalan. I am searching for a rare flower, and that is where I am told it grows."

"What sort of flower?"

When she described it, One Eye said, "Quatemalan, in the language of that region, means 'land of many trees.' Therefore it is possible the flower you seek is a tree blossom, hanging from a branch, as you say."

His thoughts raced. He needed to get these two inside the city and keep them there until the hunters showed up. He had been trying for days to get inside the walls, but the city was so crowded that entry was selective. The guards demanded costly bribes, and One Eye was, for the moment, impoverished. But the pearls would guarantee entry. . . .

"This special flower you search for," he said. "There is a garden in the royal palace that is rumored to hold every kind of plant in the world." One Eye held a brief, mental conversation with his conscience, saying that stealing was one thing but a little creative truth was quite another. He did not know for certain that the red flower was in the palace garden, but on the other hand, he did not know for certain that it was not.

Tonina was instantly animated. Was it possible she could have the flower tomorrow, and in a few days find a canoe and be heading back to Pearl Island? "But how can we get into the palace?" She had seen people try to pass through the great wooden gates beneath the massive stone archway, only to be turned away by the guards.

One Eye gave this some thought. Once the bribe was paid, he himself should have no trouble, as royals and nobles always liked having a dwarf about. But the girl? "We need to get you properly dressed," he said, wrinkling his nose at her ridiculous attire. "And then you will need—"

"Brave Eagle, too," she interjected. "I do not go anywhere without him."

One Eye had no intention of letting such a catch out of his sight. He looked at the boy and decided that Brave Eagle could get into the palace with his looks alone. His lack of tattoos made him an oddity, and if he were a hermaphrodite, all the better. The girl, however, was a problem. Could she dance? Sing? Play a flute? Tonina said no to each. And then an idea came to him: "You will be a fortune-teller."

"But I cannot tell fortunes!"

"It doesn't matter. You simply tell people what they wish to hear."

"Will they believe me?"

"They will if you use that." He pointed to the strange transparent cup that jutted out of her travel pack. "Everyone will believe that such an unusual vessel has special powers."

Tonina was about to protest further when she was suddenly overcome by fatigue. It had all caught up with her—leaving Pearl Island, the battle on the canoes, Macu killed by a shark, finding herself on a deserted beach, rescuing Brave Eagle, and their perilous trek to this amazing place.

"Take my space," One Eye said as he cleared his few belongings. "You can both sleep here."

Gratefully, Tonina and Brave Eagle curled up together, as naturally as if they had been sleeping thus all their lives. She recited silent prayers to Lokono and her dolphin spirits, and as sleep stole over her, as she mentally thanked the friendly dwarf for helping them, Tonina felt a new thought nudge the edge of her consciousness. Too mind-weary to grasp it, she sensed only that it had something to do with One Eye claiming to be a trader, and yet he had no goods, no porters. Her last thought before she slipped into troubled dreams was that he wasn't a trader at all but something else, perhaps even something sinister, and that, at first light, she and Brave Eagle should get as far from the dwarf as possible.

~ 12 ~

It had been so long since anything had shocked One Eye that he had thought himself immune—until Tonina stripped naked in the marketplace.

Before they could enter the city, the trader had told her, she must procure decent female clothing: a skirt that reached the ankles and an over-blouse that came past the hips, with sleeves partially covering the arms. "Mayan women are modest," he had said.

And then, before his startled eyes, she had accepted the clothing he had purchased with one of her pearls, set the garments down, and, in the bright morning sunlight, had removed her sarong and *hamac*-blouse. She was not entirely nude because she wore a modesty apron beneath the sarong, but it was enough to shock those nearby, and to cause One Eye to stifle a squeal and throw his spare cloak over her.

Tonina laughed. Used to swimming nearly nude and hauling her oyster catch onto the beach in view of others before putting her grass skirt back on, she realized this modesty was a custom to which she must quickly adapt.

As One Eye secured his two travel packs over his shoulders, he found troubling thoughts invading his mind. The sight of Tonina's body had aroused him, not an unusual condition since he spent much of his time thinking about women and sex. But in this case it was her lack of modesty—it reminded him of how island people lived, making him realize it was years since he had been home.

I have lived among the Maya too long, he thought, overcome with nostalgia. But if his secret plan turned out successful, he could retire to the islands and to a way of life for which he now suddenly yearned.

The plan was a good one. Unfortunately, one element of uncertainty could spoil it: his young companions. Their only interest seemed to be in finding a red flower and leaving. One Eye was going to have to find a way to delay that hasty departure until he made contact with the eagle hunters. He must also find a way to make it easier for the girl to let go of the youth. She might wail in distress as she had over the loss of her pearls, and that was something One Eye's conscience would not abide. So in addition to seeking a place to house the two for a while, he needed to come up with an emotional distraction for Tonina. Get her interested in someone else while he stole Brave Eagle from her.

After a night of fitful sleep—because of his young guests, One Eye had forgone the pleasure of a bedmate—they had breakfasted on hot tortillas filled with beans and chilies, shared the dwarf's water (for which he charged them a pearl), and now they were ready to attempt entry into the city. One Eye welcomed the diversion. From the moment they awoke, with city guards dousing the torches and blowing trumpets on the walls, Tonina had been insatiable in her thirst for the Mayan language. "What do you call this?" she had asked before One Eye had opened his one good eye. "How do you say that?" When she heard the nearby families bickering, she had asked One Eye to translate.

It was annoying. But at least she had a sharp memory. He never had to say anything twice. She was also surprisingly tenacious. As soon as the flower stalls were open, Tonina had run to them, looking for that red flower, coming back disappointed and saying, "How soon can we enter the city?" And now that they were ready, the girl in proper modest attire with a few Mayan words and phrases in her vocabulary, she took Brave Eagle by the hand and walked ahead of One Eye, as if *she* were leading *him*!

As they pushed through the morning crowd, One Eye studied Brave Eagle more clearly in the fresh sunlight, and could not believe how smooth and unblemished his skin was. Not the smallest tattoo. Not the most modest of piercings. People were going to make fun of the boy. Everyone snickered at an untattooed man. It meant he feared pain.

And yet the boy did not seem afraid of anything. He looked about himself with the curiosity of a small child, as if everything he saw was new to him and intrigued him. In fact, One Eye thought, the boy's own body seemed new, for in the morning light the dwarf saw that there was not the slightest scar or mark on that smooth skin. No man on earth made it to early adulthood without the marks of childhood mishaps.

Thinking back to what Tonina had told him of the boy's story—held in a cage meant for eagles, pursued relentlessly by hunters determined to get him back, the amnesia and lack of speech—a thought occurred to One Eye that so shocked him, he cried, *"Guay!"*

Tonina turned, and the dwarf quickly recovered, saying, "I stepped on something sharp." The girl resumed walking while One Eye examined this new thought.

Brave Eagle . . . was it possible? Could he be a *shape-shifter*?

Unaware that a shocking new idea had just occurred to their short-statured host, Tonina held fast to Brave Eagle's hand. She saw how people ogled him. He himself did not seem to mind as he moved through the crowd, golden eyes wide with wonder, occasionally frowning as he seemed to struggle to grasp an elusive memory. The wound on his forehead was healing, she saw, but his mind was not.

Tonina was grappling with an elusive memory herself. The night before, as she had drifted off to sleep, she had worried about something. It had had to do with the dwarf. She could not recall it, so she put the problem from her mind. A palace garden lay beyond these tall wooden gates, along with the possibility of the red flower growing there.

The surly guards at the stone archway inspected each visitor, pawed through travel packs, spat on the ground, and turned people away for no apparent reason. But One Eye was able to negotiate a bribe—two of Tonina's pearls and, from his own pack, three precious cacao beans—and then he said to his companions, "We must get to the main plaza, quickly."

The city turned out to be as crowded as the marketplace, although with a vague semblance of order. As One Eye led the way in his peculiar rolling gait, he explained that the majority of the city's populace resided in densely packed quarters identified by profession—the Wood-Carvers' Quarter, the Stonemasons' Quarter, and so forth—their humble stone-and-wood houses crammed into meandering lanes and alleys, with gardens in between, and low stone walls marking off property lines.

Smoke from thousands of cook fires filled the morning air. The night silence had given way to a din created by children shouting, dogs barking, women calling to neighbors, and the peculiar pat-pat sound of a multitude of hands slapping cornmeal into breakfast tortillas.

"That's how they beautify their children," One Eye said when Tonina came to a sudden standstill in front of a white stone house where two women were cooking breakfast in the courtyard. On a blanket between them lay a small baby, its head pressed between two boards. The planks formed a V, with the narrow end at the crown. "When that contraption comes off, the child will grow to look like everyone else—pointy-headed and cross-eyed."

Except for Kaan, Tonina thought, surprised that the ballplayer should suddenly come to mind. *His* head had not been pressed between boards.

Finally they came to the end of the path as it emerged from between two towering stone walls, and when the trio stepped into the main plaza, where there was open space and more breathing room, Tonina looked across the paved expanse and received another shock.

Across the plaza, a pyramid rose to the clear blue sky in majestic splendor. It was a smaller version of the one at the place One Eye had called Chichén Itzá. But unlike that neglected, weed-ridden monument, Mayapan's pyramid was coated with stucco so smooth and red that the walls gleamed like blood in the sun. It rose dizzyingly in levels and steps, and at its top stood a temple, smoke rising from sacred censers, long feathered pennants floating on the breeze.

Smaller pyramid-temples stood on two sides of the plaza, their sloping walls painted bright red and decorated with colorful designs and friezes, flags snapping from spires. On the fourth side stood the palace, a blinding red edifice with steps, levels, and colonnades. It seemed to Tonina that the Maya were obsessed with steps and stairways. Except for small dwellings, no building appeared to be entered at ground level.

Like the marketplace, the plaza teemed with people. But these were more splendidly dressed than those beyond the walls, for here the nobility and the rich conducted their business, men and women more radiantly dressed than Tonina could have dreamed, in cotton dresses and cloaks of vibrant colors, loincloths weighted with jade and gold, basket-work headdresses fitted with feathers and beads. Wrists, ankles, ears, and lips were laden with jewelry.

And then Tonina noticed something odd. Nearly every person she saw, whether noble or city guard or fruit peddler, wore a strip of cloth tied about his or her upper arm. And the cloth was either green or blue. When she asked the meaning of it, One Eye said, "It's for the games. The people are showing their support of a team. Green is the Mayapan team, and blue is the team from Tulum. Everyone has a favorite."

"*You* are not wearing a ribbon."

"I support both teams," he said with a grin.

As Brave Eagle followed closely behind Tonina across the paved plaza, his yellow eyes were drawn to the topmost places—the temple crowning the pyramid, the spires reaching to the clouds. Noticing this, One Eye thought: He is searching for an eagle's aerie. And the dwarf's suspicion of the boy's true nature grew.

As the main steps of the palace were crowded with public visitors who had business with the government, One Eye led his two new friends around to the side where a narrow alley, paved and clean, led to another stairway carved into the towering wall. Here they encountered people bearing travel packs like themselves, variously dressed, some in costumes, all having come in the hope of receiving the king's generous bounty.

"We are in luck," One Eye said as they fell in with a troupe of musicians carrying rattles, conch-shell trumpets, and tortoise-shell drums. "The annual games draw many visitors to the city, which means the king will be entertaining more guests than usual tonight. They will want variety."

He turned to Brave Eagle. "I will play a flute. All you have to do is move to the melody. Can you do that?"

Brave Eagle nodded. One Eye was confident the boy's natural grace and unusual looks would be entertainment enough, even if he could not dance. He also had confidence in himself to please the audience. But the girl and her fortune-telling . . . She was cursed with innate honesty and was probably a terrible liar. "Remember," he said once again to Tonina, "if you feel the need to tell the truth, make it a *pleasant* truth."

When he saw the uncertainty in her eyes, he added, "Listen, girl. It is not you doing the prophesying. It is the water. Do you understand? As you might have discovered by now, water is a precious commodity in this land where there are no streams, rivers, or lakes. The Maya believe that water, like blood, possesses profound powers. Fill the goblet with water, have someone drink, and then 'read' his or her fortune in it."

At the great arched doorway, guards once again interrogated visitors, demanded bribes, and pushed their weight around. One Eye paid two cacao beans, explaining that he had come with rare and exciting entertainment for His Exalted Goodness. When the guards made lewd comments to Tonina, thinking she was a prostitute, One Eye intervened, explaining that she was a respected fortune-teller. And he thought: This is a first. He had never had to *protect* a woman's virtue before.

It was necessary for them to be escorted along an inner corridor because the palace was a confusing maze of stairways, courtyards, chambers, galleries, and tunnels, and when they neared the heart of the massive complex, they heard music and voices. The escort brought them into a large chamber where entertainers were awaiting their turn to perform.

As was his habit, One Eye made a quick appraisal of the crowd of tumblers, jugglers, magicians, dancers, and jesters, and when he spotted a pair of contortionists limbering up, he sent a suggestive wink to the female partner, who wore a curious costume: a short doeskin wrap around her hips and a band of soft doeskin covering her breasts. When she blushed and smiled back, One Eye rubbed his fat little hands together. He had spent years perfecting the wink, which involved his entire face, and it never failed. He wondered if the male partner was husband or brother. He had never shared a bed with so agile a female and speculated on the possible delights.

"What do we do now?" Tonina whispered to One Eye.

"Through that doorway," he said quietly, pointing to a brightly colored tapestry hanging from a lintel, "is the Grand Hall. The king and his courtiers are having a feast in there, and these people are the entertainment. We await our turn."

"How do we get to the garden from here?"

"The garden? Oh! The garden! Well—" He scratched an ear. "We have to provide entertainment first, and then we see what our reward is."

"Do you know where the garden is?"

"On a terrace," he said vaguely, pointing upward. He didn't know if there *was* a garden, but if one existed, he imagined it would be above them.

The steward of the waiting room, a pompous man with jade plugs in his ears, nose, and lips, looked over the newcomers with a haughty air and said, "I cannot guarantee your packs will be here after your performance."

Grasping the man's meaning, One Eye shot back: "It is worth one cacao bean, which is reasonable. But if I find that these packs have been disturbed in any way, I will expose my evil eye to you."

As more entertainers were sent into the Grand Hall, the trio maneuvered closer to the doorway where they could peek around the hanging. Standing behind One Eye, Tonina was able to see nobles seated on cushions made of jaguar pelts while a coterie of dwarves, hunchbacks, scribes, servants, fan bearers, and entertainers catered to their every need. They all had the Mayan sloping forehead and crossed eyes, and all were burdened with massive headdresses constructed of wicker, feathers, shells, cotton, and jade.

The expansive hall was decorated with ceramic censers, stucco heads, jade masks, terra-cotta figurines, and great carved limestone lintels. The walls were painted with brightly colored murals, and the air was filled with smoke from pipes and cigars. The ruler of Mayapan, whom One Eye had called His Exalted Goodness, was a large fat man wearing only a loincloth, his corpulent body painted bright red, his headdress simply a topknot of long quetzal feathers. He sat at the head of the hall, on a dais so that he was higher than his guests. One Eye jabbed Tonina in the thigh with his elbow and warned, "Do not look at him! No one looks upon the king."

"What is he doing?" she whispered back, bending slightly so that the dwarf could hear. The king was staring at a large round object being held up before him by a servant.

"That's a mirror. His Exalted Goodness watches himself at all times."

Tonina blinked. The king was sitting on a stool that was propped on the backs of two men crouching on all fours. Seeing her look, One Eye

murmured, "Captives in a recent battle. The Maya don't kill their enemies. They prefer humiliation as a punishment."

Servants were continually refilling cups from decorative jugs. The
drink, One Eye explained, was called *pulque,* an intoxicating mixture of
maguey cactus and the root of a bush called "evil wood." And because the
guests poured a small libation to the gods each time they drank, slaves
were also needed to constantly mop the floor.

Seductive aromas wafted from an endless parade of platters heaped
with roasted birds and rabbits, steaming sweet potatoes and corn, glistening papaya and guava, pumpkin and honeycombs. Tonina could not
identify some of the offerings, which One Eye called tomatoes, wiping his
salivating mouth as he spoke.

And then something caught his eye that gave him what he considered
a brilliant idea: Kaan the ballplayer was among the guests. Could *he* be
the diversion that would draw Tonina's interest away from Brave Eagle?

A team of acrobats finished their performance and ran from the hall,
and when the off-key voice of a solitary singer drifted on the air, One Eye
whispered, *"Guay,"* for he knew what was coming.

A bellow of protest cut the song short. It had come from the king. Immediately guards came running with large earthen pots. The hapless
singer fell to the ground and covered his head as the pots were decanted
over him, covering his body in urine.

The guards then picked up the hapless man and dragged him from
the hall.

One Eye said, "If an entertainer does not please the audience, there is
punishment." He licked his lips with a dry tongue. Sometimes the punishment was whips. "Make sure you please them, Tonina."

He said this for more reasons than to avoid humiliation. In order for
his secret plan to succeed—to sell the youth to the eagle hunters—One
Eye needed to secure accommodations for a few days, to keep the boy
with him, and here in the palace would be best. If they entertained the
king and his courtiers to great satisfaction, they might be kept for en-
cores.

It was to this end that, from behind the tapestry, One Eye searched the
Grand Hall for a possible contact. When he espied a man who, judging

by the elaborate staff he carried, was the chief steward, responsible for the smooth running of the king's household, he smiled.

Gambling was a universal passion. One Eye had never met a man who didn't lay odds on one thing or another, even if it was only the weather. Men of means, as surely the chief steward was, gambled on goods in the market, creating games of buying and selling merchandise or food in bulk.

Before coming to Mayapan, as he was on the road from Uxmal, One Eye had chanced upon a camped caravan and had been welcomed to share food and drink. Despite his short stature, One Eye could hold twice the alcohol as a normal man and soon had the caravan master's tongue loosened. His cargo was amber from Chiapán, the man had boasted, where it had become so abundant that its worth had plummeted. The financial backers of the amber trade were hoping for higher profits in the lowland cities.

A dwarf on his own traveled faster than one hundred heavily burdened men, and so he had arrived at Mayapan days in advance of the caravan. One Eye was certain the chief steward would pay handsomely to know that there was about to be a glut of Chiapán amber on the market. If the chief steward had any to sell, he should do it now and command a high price.

All One Eye was going to ask in return for this valuable information was lodging within the palace for as long as he needed, for himself and his two companions.

This was One Eye's trade—in goods so small they needed no packs or porters, only his brain. The Taino dwarf was a professional spy.

A snake charmer pleased the audience, and was directed to an outer chamber where limitless food and *pulque* awaited, and so finally it was their turn. The steward of the waiting room drew aside the tapestry and One Eye shambled out, followed by Tonina and Brave Eagle.

The Grand Hall buzzed with interest. Not so much over the girl, but the dwarf, who was always welcome, because he had only one eye and that meant he was greatly favored by the gods. What particularly had everyone's attention was the pale youth who had not a mark on his body.

Tonina stood nervously with her eyes cast down as One Eye introduced his "troupe" in a loud voice. As he spoke, holding the courtiers' attention, his sharp eye scanned the gathered guests, making mental note, sorting, filing away. He had visited royal palaces in other Mayan towns, and the villas of the rich, the nobility. But this was his first time in the Grand Hall of Mayapan and he planned to make good use of the opportunity.

While One Eye waxed eloquent for the court, Tonina made a surreptitious sweep of the hall from beneath her eyelashes, seeing now the full grandeur of the gathered royalty and nobility, taking in their radiance, the abundance of food. And then she saw the two ballplayers who had strode through the marketplace the night before.

Prince Balám did not interest her. He looked like all the rest, with his red-painted skin, sloping head, and augmented nose. But seated next to him in what was obviously a place of honor was the commoner Kaan, resplendent in scarlet loincloth and sky blue cloak, his head adorned with feathers. She noted again his features that were so different from those around him: the clearly defined jaw, high forehead, and large straight nose.

Next to him sat a woman Tonina assumed was his wife, whom One Eye had mentioned the night before, a Mayan lady named Jade Sky. Like the other ladies in the Grand Hall, her small form was laden with more clothing than Tonina thought necessary: a brightly patterned dress overlaid with a shawl fringed with beads and shells, a girdle belt likewise fringed, and more necklaces and bracelets than Tonina thought the woman could carry. Her sleek black hair was gathered up in a brightly colored scarf, the long tresses spilling down like the branches of a weeping willow, to frame a face that Tonina knew by now was the ideal of Mayan beauty: a beaked nose and slightly receding chin, fleshy lips barely covering prominent front teeth. Lady Jade Sky's forehead sloped back into an elongated skull, causing her slightly crossed eyes to slant.

Tonina's gaze went back to Kaan, whom she still thought handsome. His skull was not misshapen, the large nose was his own, and his physique was trimmer than that of his plump companions.

And then a jolt went through her. Although she had thought she didn't mind about the humiliation, because she had been taunted and mocked all her life, for her looks, for being an outsider, she realized now that when her turn came to perform, she suddenly did not want to be humiliated.

Not in front of *him*.

Because One Eye had perfected the skill of doing one thing while thinking about another, he was able to flatter the king and courtiers, filling their ears with flowery compliments, and at the same time note that Tonina was staring at Kaan, her eyes fixed on him as they had been the evening before in the marketplace. Unaware of the scrutiny, the hero ballplayer was drinking and laughing with his companions. But the girl— What was it about Kaan that captivated her so?

One Eye was pleased. Judging by how hypnotized she was by Kaan, she might not even care at all if Brave Eagle vanished.

Tonina's eyes went back to Jade Sky, Kaan's wife of three years and as yet childless, according to One Eye. Tonina noticed now that Jade Sky would rest her hand on her abdomen once in a while and smile in a satisfied, secretive way. But as soon as Kaan turned to say something to her, she quickly withdrew her hand and assumed a bland expression. Tonina had seen such behavior before, and guessed at the reason behind it.

One Eye stepped aside, held up his flute, and now it was Brave Eagle's turn. The courtiers had seen dancers before, so they returned to their conversations, chatting and laughing and helping themselves to more roasted pheasant, more *pulque*. One Eye's flute could barely be heard above the din—a simple eight-note melody that Brave Eagle soon adapted himself to as he held out his arms and moved in graceful steps.

As the smooth-skinned youth, willowy and silent, glided over the polished floor, pirouetting, rising on toes, forming a circle with his limber arms, the Grand Hall grew silent until only the flute could be heard. All eyes were fastened on Brave Eagle, mesmerized by his slow, soaring movements until he seemed not to be a boy anymore but a fascinating creature out of myth.

When Brave Eagle sank gracefully to the floor, draping his willowy arms over his head, and the melody stopped, the Grand Hall remained silent. Not a whisper, not a cough was heard. One Eye lowered his flute and looked around. The guests sat as if hypnotized. And then the whispering began, nods of appreciation, remarks of wonder, and he realized that someone might snatch Brave Eagle for themselves.

"Heavenly ladies and gentlemen," One Eye quickly called out, "Most

Exalted Goodness and Lady Starlight Beauty, I now present to you the foremost seer in all the land." Impatiently gesturing for Brave Eagle to step back and out of the audience's focus, One Eye waved Tonina to come forward and stand before the king's dais.

Like dancers, fortune-tellers were ubiquitous in Mayapan, and so audience attention once again drifted and Tonina was in danger of losing their interest altogether until she produced the glass goblet that she had been carrying at her side, lifting it up to the light and turning it so that facets flashed back. As one by one the courtiers stared at the goblet, One Eye declared it to be an instrument of the gods themselves.

The king fixed a curious eye upon the object, then gestured to one of the servants, who took the glass from Tonina and handed it up to a better-dressed servant, who passed the goblet to a yet more impressive-looking servant, who handed it to a noble who gave it to the king.

Everyone watched in anticipation as His Exalted Goodness inspected the strange object, holding it up, turning it, tapping it, finally licking it with a jade-studded tongue. Then he returned it to the noble, who passed it along until the goblet was in Tonina's hands again.

She spoke through One Eye, who translated. When she called for water, a slave filled the goblet. Tonina swirled the water, looked into it, and then said in a loud voice, "The water has chosen. . . ." She turned in a slow circle, and One Eye was pleased to see eagerness among the courtiers, each hoping the girl would choose him or her.

As everyone watched in delighted anticipation, Prince Balám felt his wife stiffen at his side. He knew she wanted to be the chosen one. Lady Six Dove had a passion for fortune-tellers.

But when the tall girl pointed to Kaan's wife, Balám heard a whispered oath from his wife, and he knew there would be no peace at his home tonight. Lady Six Dove hated Jade Sky, and now Balám would not hear the end of it—the fortune-teller had chosen the wife of a commoner over the wife of a prince. Balám shook his head. The girl with the island tattoos did not know it, but she had just made a terrible mistake.

Tonina approached Lady Jade Sky and saw now the details of Kaan's wife: the thick cosmetic on her face and arms, the jade plug piercing her nasal septum, the gold plug in her lower lip, the heavy earrings. Tonina also saw, beneath the powder and paint and facial tattoos, a shy young woman not much older than herself.

"Me?" Jade Sky said in surprise. Everyone laughed and urged her to participate.

"Take a sip, my lady," One Eye said in Mayan.

Jade Sky delicately sipped through prominent teeth while the Grand Hall watched in silence, and Kaan kept his dark eyes on the new fortune-teller. When the goblet was returned to her, Tonina again swirled the water, pretending to read its message, and, with her heart thumping, decided to take a chance on what she had observed earlier—the lady's secretive, satisfied behavior. If she was wrong, what would her punishment be?

Taking a breath for courage, Tonina said, with One Eye translating: "You are going to have a son."

Lady Jade Sky gave her a skeptical look. Fortune-tellers always predicted sons. "What year will he be born?" she asked in amused challenge.

Tonina met her eyes directly and said, "His life has already begun."

"*Aii,*" Jade Sky declared softly. "It is true! She speaks the truth!"

The hall erupted in exclamations as the lady turned to her husband with a radiant smile to tell him that it was so, she was pregnant, and that she had planned to tell him that evening, while One Eye leaned close to Tonina and murmured, "Well done, girl. We will be richly rewarded for this."

Tonina beamed. She was going to ask to be taken to the royal garden.

"Will my son be healthy?" Jade Sky asked. "Will he grow to manhood?"

One Eye did some rapid thinking. "Forgive us, dear lady," he said. "But the glass makes but one prediction per day. Its power is exhausted now."

"What does the fortune-teller wish for a reward?" Kaan asked.

One Eye translated, and Tonina replied, "To stay here in the palace, my lord, and be allowed to visit the royal garden."

The dwarf was tempted to lie and tell them she had said something else. He did not want her to find the flower so soon. But he could not run the risk that someone here understood Taino, and to tell a lie in the presence of His Exalted Goodness was bad luck. So he told Kaan the truth, and Lady Jade Sky waved a dismissive hand, saying, "The girl will come and live with *us.*"

As One Eye turned with a smile to Tonina and said, "They are grant-ing your wish!" he did not see—no one saw—the vengeful look that sud-denly filled Lady Six Dove's eyes.

"May I go to the garden now?" Tonina asked.

One Eye cleared his throat. "Um, the lady wishes you to visit her home first. You will be given lodging there, and while you stay there, you will be free to visit the gardens." He shifted his eye from side to side, to see if anyone had caught the untruth. But everyone remained silent.

"Please tell the lady that I will be happy to visit her home, but tell her that you and Brave Eagle must be allowed to come with me."

One Eye was happy to pass along the request, for lodgings in the resi-dence of so famous a person as Kaan could be profitable.

As they were escorted to the outer chamber, where dancers and tum-blers and the snake magician were filling their bellies, One Eye's thoughts followed yet another new track. He was impressed with how cleverly Tonina had worked her "fortune" for Jade Sky, that she had simply stud-ied the woman's body language and had leaped to a correct conclusion. This island girl is almost as good as me, he thought as he seized a roasted rabbit from a platter and sank his teeth into it. She and I would make a great team.

As Brave Eagle and Tonina helped themselves to the generous offer-ings, One Eye examined ways of keeping Tonina with him after he sold the youth to the eagle hunters. He would have to make sure she never found the royal garden, never found the red flower, because then she would hurry home. Did she say she wanted to go to Quatemalan? Easily done. Especially since the girl had no idea where Quatemalan was.

Y ou have made me the happiest man in the world," Kaan declared as he knelt before his wife. "I do not know what I did to deserve such blessings."

Jade Sky, seated on a stool in the morning sunlight, smiled and stroked his hair. "I wanted to surprise you."

"You did surprise me!" He laughed, then he rested his head on her abdomen and, closing his tear-filled eyes, imagined the baby slumbering in the warm, salty sea within. His son . . . his *Mayan* son.

Kaan the commoner, called great by the people, hero ballplayer and devoted husband, embraced but one ambition in this world: to see his son play in the sacred ball court.

"We will keep the island girl with us," Jade Sky said decidedly. "She will read our fortunes every day. We will guide our lives according to the prophecies spoken by the transparent cup. And when our son is born, and grows to manhood, the girl will read his fortune every day, and guide him."

"We will keep her . . . ," Kaan murmured into the soft fabric of Jade Sky's dress. "The island girl . . ."

He frowned. Twice now, for reasons he did not understand, he had stared at the girl named Tonina. He supposed it was because of her uniqueness. Kaan had seen many women from the islands. They tended to be short, plump, and dark brown, but this one was tall with skin the color of honey. And yet her face was painted in white symbols in island fashion, and she spoke only Taino, with the dwarf translating.

Startled by his thoughts—why was he thinking about the girl?—Kaan rose and looked tenderly down at his wife.

He wanted to take her to bed and make love to her. But he could not. The Twelfth Game was tomorrow. He must keep himself pure and spend the next hours in prayer and fasting. If he committed the slightest transgression, it might cost his team the game. And he must also think of Jade Sky's delicate condition. She had barely survived the miscarriage.

Kaan looked at the things strewn about his wife's private bedchamber, the trappings of her obsessive hobby, which she had taken up after miscarrying their first child: feathers of all varieties, large and stiff ones from birds' wings and tails, smaller flexible plumes, and fluffy breast feathers, all the colors of the rainbow. Strips of leather and cotton, awls for making holes, and maguey thorns with fibers still attached.

Jade Sky made exquisite feather bracelets, giving them as gifts to friends. Kaan marveled at her talent. She could look at a pile of mixed feathers and see the pattern in them, the beauty and harmony. The hobby, Kaan knew, took the place of a baby.

"Where is the girl?" Jade Sky said anxiously. "She should have been here by now."

"I will go and see," he said, kissing her on the cheek.

As Kaan passed through the spacious villa where servants were sweeping floors and airing out the rooms, he glanced out the window at the private garden and saw, in shock, an old woman making her way through shrubs and flowers.

He rushed outside, crying, "What are you doing here?" and startling the intruder.

"Forgive me," she said. "I heard that your wife is pregnant. Is it true?"

Kaan was so stunned by the old woman's presence and her question— she was the last person he had expected to see at his home—that he was speechless.

Tonina and her companions had spent the night in the servants' quarters in the palace, and were now being escorted to the residence of Lady Jade Sky. The lady had inherited the property from her wealthy parents, One Eye explained. When she married Kaan, the rumors went, Jade Sky the aristocrat had brought wealth, status, and bloodline to the marriage. Kaan the ballplayer had brought only a winning streak.

A row of majestic villas fronted a paved plaza, their walls high and covered in smooth white stucco, with narrow windows admitting light and air, and guards stationed at each doorway, looking both fierce and bored. This was the wealthy quarter, where the nobles and prosperous merchants protected their families and their luxurious way of life. The trio was led to a tall wooden gate painted bright red for good luck. Two men with spears guarded the entrance to Lady Jade Sky's villa, and they pulled the double-doored gate open to admit the visitors.

A spacious garden opened before the newcomers, and a fountain sprayed droplets into the morning air. Tonina's eyes widened. How could water be made to shoot upward? One Eye was saying something about underground pipes and masterful engineering, but Tonina wasn't listening. At the end of the path that led through luxuriant plants and flowers stood Kaan.

He was dressed in a colorful loincloth laden with jade, and a bright orange and yellow mantle tied at the neck. His long hair was drawn back from his face and tied in what Tonina had learned was called a jaguar-tail, caught up nearly on the crown of the head so that the black tresses streamed down his back like a cat's tail. On Pearl Island, boys and men cut their hair short into a "bowl" cut and only women wore their hair long.

Kaan was speaking sharply to an old woman, who bowed humbly and hurried away. Tonina realized she had seen her before. Where? Then she remembered. In the marketplace two nights prior, when the two hero ballplayers had strode through the crowd, the old woman had been following at a distance.

When Tonina quietly remarked on this as they waited on the path, One Eye whispered, "That is Kaan's mother."

"His mother! But she is dressed like a servant. And see how he is sending her away."

"He's ashamed of her. She works in the palace kitchens. When Kaan began to rise to fame, and then married a Mayan noblewoman, he severed ties with his mother."

Tonina was horrified. "Why?"

"He doesn't like being reminded of his barbaric bloodline. And he doesn't want his admirers to be reminded of it either. He strives to be as Mayan as he can."

Tonina recalled what One Eye had told her two nights prior, about Kaan's parents leaving their homeland far in the northwest because of an endless famine, coming to this distant Mayan city in hopes of a better life. And this was how he treated his mother! "I feel sorry for him," Tonina said.

"Don't ever let Kaan hear you say that," One Eye cautioned.

In that moment, as if he had heard, Kaan turned and stared at the strangers in the garden. His dark, enigmatic eyes scanned Brave Eagle and One Eye, and then Tonina, his scrutiny resting there.

Again, that locked stare, One Eye noticed. What did it mean? The two were looking at each other for the first time, really. The prior occasions had been in the flickering torchlight of a crowded marketplace, and in the smoke-filled Grand Hall. Now Kaan and Tonina faced each other in the freshly washed light of a new morning, and One Eye thought: The girl is fascinated by him and doesn't know why.

It was obvious that Tonina did not see what others saw, that she shared physical traits with Kaan: the same clearly defined jaw so different from the soft Mayan chin, the high forehead, and the fact that both clearly had more bone in the nose—no need to insert the enhancing appliance the small-nosed Mayans used. But Tonina would not recognize her own features, One Eye realized, would not even be able to describe herself if asked, because she had never looked into a mirror. Therefore she could not guess that she and Kaan might be of the same race.

But did Kaan? Although Chichimecs from the far northwest visited Mayapan, and many even lived there, their differences to the native population were enough that seeing two together—Kaan and Tonina, if One Eye's guess was right—was noticeable. Was Kaan wondering the same thing One Eye wondered: How did a Chichimec girl end up being an islander?

They were led through a house made airy with open colonnades and windows set high in the thick walls. Tonina had an impression of corridors and doorways and rooms, and could not imagine two people occupying such a commodious space. "Wait here," the servant said.

One Eye looked around, his single eye drinking in all that it saw—the potted plants and statuary, the rugs and tapestries—his sharp mind analyzing, memorizing. He planned to put his time as a guest in this house to good use. So many servants, so much information to gather on the great hero Kaan. The dwarf could not believe his luck. He would stuff his head with facts and stories about Kaan and his wife, as many secrets as he could glean from the household staff, and then find buyers for them.

Footsteps sounded in the corridor, the door hanging moved aside, and the great ballplayer himself came in.

This close up, Tonina saw the scars and old wounds covering his body. Nobles weren't supposed to be scarred like that, not from injury. What had caused them? He was a ballplayer. She still did not know what that was.

Through One Eye, Kaan said to Tonina, "My wife is not strong. Do not say anything that will upset her."

Kaan's chest rose and fell in a shaky sigh, as if deeply felt emotions were trapped there. Or held tightly, Tonina thought. Kaan had a way of speaking that was both powerful and constrained. He was not a man who shouted. He did not need to. His powerful voice, though softly spoken, conveyed meaning. "You say my child is a son."

"He is," she said, her own chest tight because now she was lying. She had no idea if the baby was a boy or a girl, but something told her that Kaan wanted a son.

He seemed to relax a little. He held his dark eyes on Tonina for a moment longer, and she thought she saw something going on behind that enigmatic gaze, as if the great Kaan were wrestling with a mystery, and then the hero ballplayer turned and strode away.

Finally they were escorted into Lady Jade Sky's private quarters, where she was sewing small red feathers to a strip of linen. Tonina was speechless in the midst of such splendor—the white stucco walls hung with colorful tapestries, green plants growing out of large pots, reed mats covering a polished floor. No cooking hearth, no crockery, no rafters from which all earthly possessions hung, no fishing nets piled in the corner, no *hamacs* for three people. A room just for one woman to make feather bracelets!

Jade Sky looked first at Brave Eagle, pausing as if to address him, then said to One Eye, "Tell the girl that we will have readings each morning, mid-morning, noon, afternoon, sundown, and evening."

When One Eye translated, Tonina panicked. That would leave her no time to search for the red flower. "Remind her of what you said last night," she said to One Eye. "That the cup of prophecy works only once a day, for its powers must be allowed to regenerate." Lady Jade Sky would be having Tonina cast fortunes all day long with no respite. Tonina was now five days from home, and her anxiousness was growing.

They watched as Lady Jade Sky next engaged in a brief, puzzling task. Using a brush dipped in red ink, she drew a glyph on a small piece of paper. "What is she doing?" Tonina asked.

"She is writing the name of a goddess. She will then put the paper in fire, and as it burns, the smoke will take the message to the spirit world, letting the goddess know that her attention is requested."

Having never seen paper or writing before, Tonina watched in fascination as the lady dropped the scrap of paper into a bowl of red embers, whispering a prayer as it caught flame and was consumed. Then Jade Sky traced a sign in the air, touching each of the cardinal points to form a cross. She addressed One Eye. "I wish to know when my son will be born. Precisely what day?"

One Eye translated for Tonina, who said, "It should be a simple thing to calculate."

But One Eye explained that the complex Mayan obsession with time and dates, and their complicated calendar system, was nothing Tonina was familiar with. The island people knew only two calendars: solar and lunar, from planting to planting, full moon to full moon. But the Maya had more than just these, One Eye explained: the Venus cycle calendar, the solar and monthly calendar, plus a sacred calendar of 280 days, and two calendars of years. It took a vast priesthood of astronomers and mathematicians to keep track of all the days, months, and years, to know which god governed which particular day, which years were auspicious, which months were ill-lucked. It took decades of devoted study to be able to read and decipher the complex map of the calendar-within-calendars, and thus the priests were kept busy offering their services to the public.

"Mayan women," One Eye murmured to Tonina, "will drink a brew that induces labor in order to have the infant enter the world on a lucky day."

"What are you two whispering about?"

"I am explaining the Maya way of computing time, my lady. The fortune-teller is unfamiliar with your calendars."

The Maya made a special drink from cacao beans mixed with vanilla obtained from the black orchid pod, and a dollop of honey stirred in. They called it *kawkaw* and drank it all day long. Lady Jade Sky sipped some now as she anxiously waited for Tonina to read the swirling water.

Like most of her people, Jade Sky was fearful of the world around her, which was why her race was so obsessed with calendars, astronomy, and mathematics. They needed to understand the cosmos in order to assuage their fears. They needed to live in an *orderly* world, and so they mapped the heavens and could predict the motion of the stars and planets with fanatical accuracy. When a predicted eclipse took place, they rejoiced, because they had known about it ahead of time and therefore reassured themselves that there was indeed an order to things. It was also why they were passionate about divination and fortune-telling. If the future were known, they slept better at night.

While Tonina swirled the water, she spoke to One Eye in Taino, but in a way that Lady Jade Sky would not suspect a conversation was going on. As if chanting a prayer, Tonina said, "What can you tell me about this woman's history with children? Why has she had none until now?"

"The rumor is, last year she miscarried in her second month."

Now Tonina understood the lady's withholding of the news from Kaan until she was past the date of the miscarriage. From beneath her lashes, Tonina scrutinized the small form. Jade Sky was not as elaborately attired this morning as she had been in the Grand Hall. As she wore a simple cotton shift, Tonina was better able to assess her physical condition. No belly showed yet, but her breasts strained against the fabric of the dress. She had not yet changed to a larger garment, which meant she was probably in her third month.

When she had passed this information to One Eye, he tried to calculate ahead in time, stressing his brain over the various Mayan calendars, recalling the gods that ruled each of the twenty days that made up the eighteen Mayan months, recalling also that each day was assigned a number. He determined that the child must be due sometime in the month of Lamat, but which were the lucky days? He chewed his lip. Nine or thirteen. These people were in love with those two numbers. Cursing the Maya for their stars and days and months and years, he said to Tonina, "Say anything and I shall pretend to translate."

Tonina said in Taino, "Please choose a good day," and One Eye said to Lady Jade Sky, "The girl says your son will be born on 13 Lamat."

"*Aii!*" Jade Sky cried in delight, and One Eye released a sigh of relief. Then he said, "That is all for now, my lady. The cup of prophecy needs to rest for a day and a night." He was anxious to get started making the acquaintance of the household staff, the females especially. And then a foray into the marketplace beyond the city walls, to look for the eagle hunters.

As they started to leave, Jade Sky said, "Wait," and rose from her stool. Approaching Brave Eagle, she looked deep into his eyes and said softly, "You are a beautiful and gifted dancer."

He smiled.

She saw the wound on his forehead. "What happened?"

"He cannot speak, my lady," One Eye said.

"Can he hear?"

One Eye was about to reply when, to his shock, Brave Eagle nodded. Tonina looked at him. "You understand Mayan *and* Taino?"

When Brave Eagle nodded again, One Eye whispered, "Great Lokono." The boy *must* be a shape-shifter, to adapt so quickly to changing surroundings! One Eye mentally tripled the reward he was going to ask of the hunters.

"Poor boy," Jade Sky murmured, reaching up to touch the injury on his forehead. She studied the small scab for a moment, then turned to scrutinize the featherwork supplies spread around the room. Tapping her receding chin in deep thought, she picked up a basket, sorted through its contents, and brought out a beautiful shimmering blue feather.

"Take this," she said with a smile. "Place it against your head and say a prayer to your gods. In time, your wound will heal and so will your voice."

With a smile of gratitude, Brave Eagle accepted the gift and tucked it into the waistband of his loincloth.

"Please leave me now, for I am fatigued," the lady said, and servants immediately rushed in, as if they had been listening at the door.

"Now we can find the royal garden," Tonina said eagerly, looking up and down the corridor, determining which way to go.

"Not today," One Eye said. "We have only just arrived. If the lady should suddenly wish our company . . ."

But Tonina said, "No, I will go to the palace now."

"You cannot get in, silly girl. We must obtain special permission, and that takes time, bribes."

"Then I will seek flower vendors within the city. There are sure to be some."

"But you cannot go out alone!"

"I will have Brave Eagle with me," she said as she turned in the direction of the main entry hall.

Grunting in exasperation, One Eye hurried after the pair. He had potential profit riding on them. He could not let them out of his sight.

Although the flower vendors within the city walls offered more variety and fresher stock than those in the marketplace, none could produce the blossom Tonina described, nor did any know where she could find it. But she was not discouraged. Standing at the base of the Kukulcan pyramid, she squinted across the sunlit plaza at the shimmering red building that rose in many stories and levels and stairways. But Tonina saw nothing that resembled a garden. And then Brave Eagle suddenly made a strange sound and pointed upward. One Eye wrinkled his eye and said, "I don't see anything."

But Tonina did. "On the fourth level," she said excitedly. "Above that row of columns. There is greenery. That must be the garden!"

When she started toward the palace, as if she were going to walk right in and straight up the many stairways, One Eye seized her wrist and said, "You cannot go in! The guards will throw you in a cage and you will never get out. I will ask the great Kaan to help us," One Eye added, knowing that tomorrow was the day of the Twelfth Game and that the palace would be closed and locked tight with everyone attending the contest.

By the time they returned to the villa, the day was dying and lamps of coconut oil and fish oil were being lit in Mayapan's thousands of homes. Windows covered with lattice shutters or cloth curtains or oiled-paper shades glowed in golden rectangles of light.

After a supper of spiced beans and squash, shared with the servants in the kitchen courtyard, Tonina, Brave Eagle, and One Eye were shown to the crowded dormitory where the household staff slept. During the meal, the dwarf had perused the available females and, catching the attention of one he found pleasing, had sent her his famous wink. She would be his for the night. But first he had business in the marketplace.

As it had been several days since she was shipwrecked, days since she had been in water, Tonina did not feel clean. Was there somewhere she could swim and bathe? From the servants she learned that water was such a precious commodity, having to be drawn from the cenote and hauled to each house, that she must satisfy herself with a sweat bath, scraping the moisture from her skin and then rubbing herself with scented leaves.

Afterward she shared a sleeping mat with Brave Eagle. When she felt him trembling at her side, she took him into her arms and stroked his hair. "What's wrong?" she whispered.

He could not understand it himself. Strange images had invaded his thoughts, frightening cravings, and the growing sense that he was urgently needed elsewhere.

"Do not worry," she whispered as she held him. "Tomorrow you and I will find the palace garden. We will find the flower and we will make our way back to the sea."

One Eye waited until the night was filled with the sounds of snoring and furtive sexual couplings. As he knotted his mantle around his neck, he looked in on his young friends and saw that they slept in an embrace. Since Tonina still wore the cowry belt of purity, he knew they had not yet been intimate. He shook his head. How could people sleep together and not have sex?

One Eye hurried through the slumbering city like a shadow, bribed the guards at the main gate, and slipped out into the marketplace, where bodies snoozed on mats or under crude shelters, and hundreds of camp-fires died down into acrid smoke. Groups were still awake here and there, sharing tobacco and *pulque*.

It was at the edge of the great human gathering that he saw the strangers, numbering six, their bodies painted in brown and black stripes. The leader had a distinctive disfiguring mark: His right arm was crooked, as if it had been broken and not set properly—just as Tonina had described it.

W hy should Jade Sky have the girl? *I* want the fortune-teller."
Prince Balám was sitting on a woven rug, playing with his daughter, Ziyal. Although he must soon begin the ritualistic preparations for tomorrow's game, he could not part from the little girl who was his sun, moon, stars, and life. "If you remember, my love," he said to his wife, who was into her fourth mug of *kawkaw*, "it was not the girl but the *cup* that chose Jade Sky."

Six Dove made an impatient sound and signaled to a servant to bring more of the frothy chocolate. Every day she listened to rumors in the marketplace to see which hero was the more popular—her husband or Kaan. Mostly, they were in equal favor. But sometimes Kaan was the pub-lic's favorite, and it stuck like a thorn in Six Dove's throat. "It is late, Hus-band. The child needs to go to bed."

Balám sighed. He would never understand why his wife wasn't as worshipful of their beautiful daughter as he was. Maybe it was just dif-ferent between mothers and daughters. Maybe if his son had lived, Balám would see the same devotion between Six Dove and the boy as he shared with little Ziyal.

He lifted the child into his arms, a chubby girl who was denied noth-ing, and as he carried her to her private bedchamber, he clasped her tightly to him as he had the day when she was born, when she was placed, bloody and crying, in his arms. In that moment Prince Balám had been rocked by emotions both fierce and tender, and from that day he had cherished his daughter more than the beating of his own heart.

She giggled as he danced about the room with her in his arms. "Faster, *Taati*," she said.

Balám could weep with ecstasy each time she called him that. His own father had been a rigid, distant man who wanted his son to call him "my lord." Not even *taat*, Mayan for "father." But Ziyal used the diminutive *taati*, and no music on earth sounded sweeter to Balám's ears.

When he returned to their bedchamber, having laid his daughter down and kissed her dozens of times and led her in her nightly prayers, Six Dove picked up the thread of conversation as if there had been no interruption. "I want the fortune-teller to live with us." She was still bristling from the fortune-teller's announcement in the Grand Hall. Not only was Jade Sky pregnant, but with a son.

Balám agreed. Why shouldn't the island girl live with them? After all, *he* was a prince. His wife was wealthier and more important than Jade Sky and therefore should have anything she desired. Balám adored Six Dove precisely because she was so overbearing, physically and in her personality. She reminded him of his mother, the great Lady White Heron, the formidable force of nature who ruled Uxmal (although no one would dare tell that to the *king* of Uxmal). Six Dove was fat, greedy, and voracious. And Balám loved her.

He knew she would be relentless in this pursuit. Once Six Dove set her mind on something, she was like a dog with a bone. All of Mayapan was aware of Six Dove's fiercely competitive nature, that she must always outdo Jade Sky, whom she detested, even though Jade Sky herself did not seem interested and did not compete. And now the puny creature was pregnant! Six Dove would not be outdone. She, too, would produce a son, and *he* would be a prince. "Dearest," she said now, setting aside her sixth mug of *kawkaw* as she reached for her spouse.

"I must not," Balám said reluctantly. "It is the night before a big game."

But Six Dove thought: This is the *best* time. It was when her husband was at his most potent. Tonight he would give her a son.

Though Balám tried to dissuade her, he could not resist her big brown nipples.

As Six Dove spread her fleshy thighs and drew her husband to her, she thought in satisfaction: I shall have my son *and* the fortune-teller.

❧ 14 ❧

As dawn broke over the city, and Lady Jade Sky's villa came alive with noisy industry, One Eye's first thought was to go to the market-place and meet with the eagle hunters. When he had found them the night before, he had decided they looked too hungry and mean for de-cent business negotiating, and so he had retreated, determined to return today. Tonina's waking thought was to visit the royal garden. And Brave Eagle, who had slumbered fitfully in troubled dreams, awoke with a sud-den urgency to find his people.

But their plans were quashed when the chief steward entered the ser-vants' quarters and informed them that Lady Jade Sky was calling for a reading of the prophecy cup, after which they were to accompany her to the ball game.

While Tonina and Brave Eagle were dismayed over this, One Eye was ecstatic. To attend a royal ball game! He had only watched games in small towns and villages, where teams of little consequence played for in-significant prizes. But this was *the* tournament of the year, when all the best teams participated in thirteen matches. Today it was Mayapan against Tulum, and it was rumored that the stakes were high.

After a breakfast of beans and tortillas in the kitchen, Tonina took an-other steam bath, cleaned her teeth with a mixture of ash, honey, and mint, and changed into fresh clothes. She and Brave Eagle were then taken to the mistress of the house.

Jade Sky, a deeply religious woman, started each day by reading from the Book of Creation to her slaves and servants. This was the *Popol Vuh*, sa-cred text of the Maya. "In the beginning," she read in a reverent voice, "all was suspended, all was silent and motionless, and the sky was empty. There was only the placid water and the calm tranquil sea. Then came the Word. Tepeu and Gucumatz appeared in the darkness and they talked together. As they talked, they united their thoughts until they became words."

The household workers were then dismissed—not silently as was their habit, but with enthusiastic chatter, for even the lowliest had placed a wager on today's game—and Tonina was taken once again to the lady's private suite, where Jade Sky sipped from the glass goblet and looked hopefully at the island girl. "Will my husband's team win today?" she asked, and One Eye translated.

Tonina did not want to venture to guess the outcome of a game. She also did not want to lie. So she said, "I cannot read the fortune of those who have not sipped from the water, my lady. The spirit in the cup can only speak for *you*."

Lady Jade Sky gave this some thought, then said, "Very well, will I be the wife of a winner today?"

Very clever, thought One Eye, who noticed how the lady wrung her hands. Jade Sky was clearly worried. He said to Tonina, "I am going to say yes to the lady. If we are wrong, and Kaan does not win today, I will tell her I misunderstood her, that my Mayan is not that good. Pray that it saves our skins. Now say something as though you are reading the water."

"I want to go to the palace garden," Tonina said.

Giving her a look—Tonina was annoyingly single-minded—One Eye turned a smile to Jade Sky and said, "My lady, the cup of prophecy says that you will be beyond a doubt the wife of a winner."

"*Today,*" Jade Sky said pointedly, letting him know that she was aware of how fortune-tellers were notorious for being purposely ambiguous.

"Today," One Eye grudgingly conceded. But then he brightened when he remembered that he was to attend the great game. And afterward, a secret meeting with the eagle hunters.

One Eye had new plans. Although he had originally decided not to come back to Jade Sky's villa once he gave Brave Eagle to the hunters, the Taino dwarf had decided that, instead of taking the reward and heading for the coast to buy a small boat and sail to an unoccupied island, he was going to continue his profession as a trader between Mayan cities—with Tonina as his partner.

He could not get over her remarkable and convincing performance at fortune-telling. What a pair they would make, what profits they would reap! He was confident that he could convince her to join him. No woman had ever resisted his charms. And while Tonina wasn't as plump or experienced as he preferred, and was a bit tall—especially next to a dwarf—she was a fast learner and he could teach her many tricks. Perhaps they would eventually retire to a private island. . . .

Lady Jade Sky finally left for the ball court. She was accompanied by six attendants, two of whom were skilled midwives who watched for the slightest sign of trouble with the pregnancy. Behind them came guards from the villa, as splendidly outfitted as palace guards, and finally Tonina and her two friends. Along the way, as the small procession moved through the central plaza, past the mighty Pyramid of Kukulcan, and down a busy avenue, people cheered and shouted—here was the wife of the great Kaan!—and threw flowers in her path. Jade Sky did not acknowledge them but walked serenely with her mind on the spiritual plane. The annual Thirteen Games tournament had its roots in religion many generations prior, and although most of the ritual significance was lost and people simply wanted the spectacle, the players' families were required to maintain proper religious decorum.

When they arrived at the ball court, a playing field swarming with spectators, Tonina realized that the curious man-made field she and Brave Eagle had explored at Chichén Itzá had once been a place for holding the curious ball games. But while Mayapan's ball court and surrounding environs were packed with humanity—food vendors, acrobats and jugglers, men frantically placing and taking wagers—the one at Chichén Itzá had appeared to have been unused for generations.

When Tonina saw curious activity in the throng—clumps of men furiously passing strange objects back and forth—she asked One Eye who they were.

"They are called *koxol*," he said. "That is Mayan for 'mosquito.' They are professional bettors who can read and write and are schooled in numbers. They carry strips of bark paper upon which they write the gambler's name and how much he is betting. The one placing the wager then pricks his thumb with a thorn and stamps it to the paper."

"Why are they called mosquitoes?" Tonina asked, marveling at how quickly they wrote on the paper and sent it back for a thumbprint, and then scribbled more, passing the pieces of paper over the heads of men at lightning speed.

"It's a very old nickname. I assume it has to do with them being very quick, hard to catch, and hard to run from. And they will always suck the blood out of you!" One Eye laughed, then shrugged. "Or maybe it is because of those tall, pointy hats they wear. Make them look like mosquitoes."

"Why do people go to those men?"

"How else are you to make wagers above two cacao beans?" The girl's ignorance on important financial matters was appalling.

"What are those things they are handing out?" she asked, referring to the small scraps of paper the *koxol* were exchanging with their customers.

"Gambling pledges," One Eye said. "Let's say you wish to wager five pearls on tomorrow's game. You show the *koxol* your pearls, he writes on a piece of paper the commodity you are wagering, the amount, and your name, which you then stamp with your blood. In return, he gives you a note stipulating what you will gain if you win. For example, you might wager pearls against cacao beans. After the game, if your team loses, the *koxol* gives you the note you stamped with your thumb and you turn over the pearls to him. Or, if your team wins, you give him the note he gave you, and he pays you the cacao beans that were promised."

It seemed to Tonina a lot of work to earn a little extra wealth, and a big risk. She had no intention of wagering her pearls on anything.

Trumpets blared, and people began to gather at the playing field. Nobles and royal members took their places along the tops of the sloping walls that embraced the field, so that they looked down upon the game from a height. They sat on mats, blankets, or stools, while behind them, lesser nobility and the rich stood. Then came the general population, who struggled and fought for a glimpse of the action below. The ends of the enormous ball court were open. At one end sat His Exalted Goodness with his family and courtiers, while the other was reserved for the families of the favored players. Plump wives with many children, all beautifully dressed, occupied stools and mats. Lady Jade Sky took a seat of honor next to a larger woman who Tonina learned was Lady Six Dove, the wife of Prince Balám. Her sloping head, crossed eyes, and protuberant front teeth gave her a vague resemblance to Jade Sky. But the similarities ended there. Six Dove was enormously fat, and required two stools beneath her impressive buttocks.

Tonina and Brave Eagle took a place behind Lady Jade Sky while, thoughtfully, the lady gave One Eye a stool to stand on so that he could see over the heads of those seated in front. Together the three looked down the length of the empty field in anticipation. From this distance, Tonina felt free to stare at the king, and she saw that even here he gazed into a mirror held before him by a kneeling noble.

And then she wondered where Kaan was. She had wakened during the night to see him being escorted from the villa by a whispering procession of heavily cloaked men.

Trumpets blared and the crowd roared. From a hidden doorway elaborately costumed musicians emerged, blowing conch shell trumpets, playing flutes and whistles, banging on drums, and shaking gourd rattles. Behind them marched stately priests bearing smoking censers as they incanted prayers blessing the ball court, the equipment, even the rubber ball. Finally, the two teams strode into the sunlight and the roar of the crowd was deafening. They walked in counter circles—scarred, muscular men whose pride was evident on their faces and in their posture as they raised their arms to the ecstatic observers and let shouts of adoration wash over them. Each was a group of six; one team wore green plumes on their heads, the other, blue. All twelve were dressed in a curious costume that Tonina could not comprehend.

"That contraption around their waists," One Eye murmured to her, almost at ear level since he stood on a stool, "is called the yoke. It's made of cotton padding set in a wooden frame. The men also wear knee pads and elbow pads. It's for protection but they still get hurt, sometimes even killed."

As the players paraded the length of the field, Tonina heard how the roar of the crowd increased when Kaan walked by. It baffled her, this love the people held for their ball-game heroes. One Eye had told her that although

Kaan was of inferior blood, they did not look down upon him for it. In fact, they seemed to worship him for having risen above his lowly race to gain fame. Balám, on the other hand, was a prince of noble blood and Tonina saw that the people loved him for *that*!

The two teams came to a standstill before the row of priests and joined together in a strange, collective mumbling.

"What are they doing?" Tonina asked, seeking out Kaan and finding him. His torso gleamed in the sun, as if it had been oiled. Without his mantle in the way, she could see the tight musculature of his back and arms.

"Confessing their sins," One Eye whispered. "In case they are killed in the game. The Maya live in constant fear of dying with sins on their souls. They believe that when a person is killed or sacrificed, his soul does not die but only goes dormant, awaiting rebirth. They call it the resurrection of the soul. Without confession, the soul is doomed to the Nine Levels of Hell, never to be reborn."

After a lengthy blessing by the priests, the players arranged themselves on the field, the two teams facing one another.

One Eye explained, "The first team to get nine points is the winner. Points are scored when opposing ballplayers miss a shot at the vertical hoops—you see them there, sticking out at the center of the side walls? A team also scores if the opponents are unable to return the ball before it bounces a second time, or they allow the ball to bounce outside the boundaries of the court. Not only do points accumulate but scores could go down, too, often making for a very long game. That is why those scribes you see are recording the action, and their tallies will be compared at the end."

It made no sense to Tonina, but she did not care. Caught up in the energy and excitement of the thousands of onlookers, she felt a strange new thrill rush through her. And when the ball was thrown in, and the teams jumped into play, she felt a scream tear from her own throat.

The action was fast and violent, and Tonina had difficulty following it. She often lost sight of the ball and was startled when the spectators cheered. But she soon saw that the sloping walls that formed the sides of the court were used to bounce the ball off to keep it in play. The men also kept the ball in play by hitting it with their upper arms, torsos, and thighs. They ran up and down the field, sending the ball into the air with great speed, agility, and quickness. Players collided, jumped to their feet, and continued to run. It was a breakneck pace, breathless even for the onlooker.

"In spite of the protective padding," One Eye said, "players are often severely hurt. But the dangers are insignificant compared to the glory which is attained by the greatest players. Most honored of all is the player who sends the ball through one of those stone hoops. Kaan has done that. And that is why he is a hero. It is also why he is so rich. Winners receive great prizes. They also wager on their own teams, and become even richer."

One Eye snorted as a Tulum player missed a block and was booed by the crowd. "They don't always get rich. They gamble away their homes, their fields, their corn granaries. They sell their children in order to bet and even stake themselves and become slaves if their family cannot cover the bet. That fellow there, who missed the ball, I would wager he has just now lost an orchard or two."

The sun rose high and the day grew warm. The game did not stop. If a player fell, he was replaced. Vendors shouted their offerings as they moved among the spectators. Cups of *kawkaw* were consumed and thrown to the ground. Tortillas stuffed with beans, corn, and chilies were devoured as eyes remained on the play below. And servants discreetly placed ceramic pots underneath their noble masters to allow them to answer nature's call.

The players grew sweaty and filthy, and even bloody, but did not slow down. Back and forth the ball went until Prince Balám slid to the ground and, deflecting the ball in a surprise move, shot it into the air and into the face of an oncoming opponent. The ball knocked the player off his feet. He flew up and landed on his back with a sickening thud. The crowd cried out, and then fell silent as a trumpet blared and robed officials ran onto the field. Tension solidified the air as everyone watched the men examine the fallen player, bending over him in anxious concern, touching his arms and legs, placing their ears upon his chest, until finally one rose and, holding his arms aloft, shouted, "Blessings of the gods, Yaxik of Tulum is dead!"

Pandemonium erupted and Tonina feared there would be a riot, but then she saw that the mood was one of joy, and that even people wearing the blue ribbon of Tulum cheered at the death of their beloved player.

Seeing the perplexed look on her face, One Eye said, "They are happy for him. Even his widow is happy, for he has gone straight to the Thirteenth Heaven where he will live with the gods for eternity."

Tonina chanced a quick look at Jade Sky, who, though her face was powdered with yellow cosmetic, had gone visibly pale. She also trembled, and Tonina wondered if it was out of fear for her own husband. Would she rejoice if Kaan were to die in this game?

And then Tonina realized in shock that she herself was fearful for Kaan's life, and wondered why she should care—why, in fact, she should suddenly be filled with worry and anxiousness over his safety.

The game resumed and as play continued with the same energy and determination, Tonina began to see a pattern in the chaos. The intricacies of the play mesmerized her, how connected the team members were to one another, as if by invisible threads, as if they could read one another's minds. She watched Kaan jump out to meet the ball, while the chunky Mayan, Balám, danced around him, blocked a Tulum player, and together they raced the ball to the other goal in victory. Yet Tonina had detected no communication between Kaan and Balám.

At that moment the ball whizzed through the air and came within a whisper of Kaan's head, but Balám swiftly intercepted it with a high jump and deflection with his thigh. Tonina gasped. One slack instant on Balám's part and Kaan would be dead. What was it like, she wondered, to place one's life in the hands of another, as these ballplayers did? Diving for pearls was a solitary occupation; Tonina had always worked alone, relying on no one but herself.

When the game was over, with Kaan scoring the final goal, and the people were swarming onto the field to lift their favorites onto their shoulders, Kaan marched to the end of the field to ceremoniously lay the ball at Jade Sky's feet. He was grimy and sweaty and bleeding, but his manner was one of respect and adoration as he placed the trophy before his wife. When Tonina saw the look in his eyes, she was surprised to feel a stab of envy.

As the crowd came running, and city guards formed a circle around Kaan and his wife and friends, Tonina withdrew from the mob, saying to Brave Eagle and One Eye, "Now we can go to the palace garden."

"Yes," One Eye said, now eager to accomplish an errand himself. "And I will take Brave Eagle to the marketplace. He needs a cloak. And a haircut. People have been staring."

Tonina turned to Brave Eagle and said, "Do you wish to go with him, or come with me?"

Brave Eagle answered by touching her arm.

The dwarf suppressed a scowl. He had come to regard Brave Eagle as a personal investment, and so he could not risk letting the boy out of his sight. "I will come with you then, for I am most curious to see what a royal garden looks like." And he smiled, mentally cursing Tonina's stubbornness.

The short-statured trader did not understand her insistence upon going *now*. Surely tomorrow would be soon enough. Why not attend the feast and enjoy herself?

What One Eye did not know, as he grumbled and fell into step behind her, was that Tonina herself could not define the root of her sudden urgency to get to the royal garden and, afterward, away from Mayapan. It had to do with more than saving her grandfather and her people. The desperation to stay away from the villa of Lady Jade Sky had been born out of frightening new feelings as yet vague and without form, but which filled Tonina with misgivings and ill-ease.

They had to do with Kaan. It was *him* she suddenly needed to stay away from.

A celebration was in progress at the villa, but Tonina and her friends arrived before anyone had noticed their absence. They had been unable to gain access to the palace garden, and so Tonina needed to think of a new strategy.

As the wife of a winning player, Lady Jade Sky was distributing gifts to her friends—feather bracelets that she had crafted herself. While the ladies remarked with delight as they held up their wrists to admire the clever and attractive adornments, Lady Jade Sky voiced her desire to have her fortune told, despite the fact that Tonina had done a reading that morning.

It was the opportunity Tonina was looking for, to gain entrance to the palace garden, and so she said that, although the prophecy cup normally did only one reading a day, because of the great victory on the ball court, she could do a second reading.

Once again, she hated to lie. As she swirled the water and looked into it, she tried to think of something to say that would be the truth, yet sound like a prophecy. And then something came to her: "A stranger will visit this house very soon. He will ask for you, lady."

One Eye gave her a briefly startled look and then translated.

"A stranger?" said Jade Sky.

"A hunchback."

The ladies cried out with delight. Hunchbacks were the luckiest men in the world. Hunchbacks were so rare that any such man who survived to adulthood was considered blessed by the gods.

Tonina wondered: Where did that come from? It wasn't a lie. Yet how do I know about the hunchback?

Lady Jade Sky said, "Is there anything else?"

Tonina looked deeply into the swirling water and said, "Darkness . . ."

Jade Sky clapped her small hands. "Then he will come at night!"

Tonina thought: No, it is another kind of darkness.

"What is your reward, honorable fortune-teller?"

"I wish to visit the palace garden."

Jade Sky exchanged an amused look with her friends. "Such an odd request."

"I am searching for a rare flower. It is for my grandfather, who has a sickness. And I want to help my friend remember his memories."

Jade Sky looked with sympathy at Brave Eagle and said, "The palace garden is a place of healing botanicals. Ask for the caretaker, whom we call the *h'meen*." In further generosity, Jade Sky gave Tonina a note of free passage, written on paper, and a house guard to accompany them.

One Eye suggested once more that he take Brave Eagle into the marketplace for a new cloak and a haircut, saying, "We cannot present him to so lofty a personage as the *h'meen* looking like this." Were the eagle hunters still even in Mayapan? All this wasted time!

But once again Tonina asked Brave Eagle what he wished to do, and again he chose to go with her. As they retired to the servants' quarters for the night, Tonina made a whispered promise to her young companion: "Tomorrow we will find the red flower, and then we will leave this place."

~ 15 ~

Wait!" One Eye called after Tonina, who strode ahead in such haste that the dwarf had to run along the palace corridor to keep up.

Having finally gained admittance to the royal residence, Tonina was eager to be up on the fourth level where, according to the servant who escorted them, "every flower, tree, and shrub in the world" grew. She had not a moment to waste. The magic flower was soon to be in her grasp, and then she would be on her way back to the coast, to find a canoe and sail home.

One Eye was not so eager to find the flower—not until he had completed his transaction with the hunters, who he prayed were still camped beyond the city walls.

His hope to find a diversion for the girl, so that she would not become hysterical over being separated from Brave Eagle, was answered yesterday, at the end of the game when Kaan had knelt at Jade Sky's feet in a touching gesture of tribute. The Taino dwarf might only have one eye, but it would take a man blind in both eyes, he thought, to have missed the brief but telling glance that was exchanged between Kaan and Tonina.

That women were universally fickle was a truth One Eye had learned in his years of traveling the width and breadth of this land. Tonina was no exception. Already her attention was straying. Whatever she felt for Brave Eagle (which the dwarf mistakenly took to be sexual attraction, unable to imagine that a woman could feel sisterly toward a man who was not her brother), her loyalty was shifting toward the more powerful Kaan. Was there a reciprocal attraction budding in the scarred chest of Kaan? What was it that, on more than one occasion, had drawn them to share a glance? Did they recognize their resemblance to each other in this land of shorter, plumper people with the sloping heads and crossed eyes? Perhaps not consciously, One Eye thought, but on an instinctive level. Blood recognizes blood.

With the germ of the attraction already planted, One Eye knew it would be a simple matter to get Tonina's devotion shifted from Brave Eagle to Kaan. A word in her ear that the hero ballplayer found her interesting was all it would take. No woman could resist a man who was interested in her. It was the world's oldest aphrodisiac. In this case, it did not even have to result in physical consummation. One Eye doubted, in fact, that Kaan would commit adultery. He was known for his moral conscience. All that was needed was the bee in Tonina's ear. Let her *imagine* that romance was possible, and she would not even remember Brave Eagle's name. And then One Eye would be left with a clear conscience when he sold the youth to the eagle hunters.

Brave Eagle, as he hurried at Tonina's side down the palace corridor, exhibited an optimistic eagerness. More dreams had plagued his sleep, to vanish upon wakening and leave him only with an increasing feeling that his people desperately needed him. Was there an herb, a root in the royal garden that would restore his memory? Then he, too, would be on his way home. When One Eye called out again, Brave Eagle swooped down and, lifting the little man into the air, settled him on his broad shoulders and they continued on their way.

More stairs, more corridors—with the dwarf ducking his head under lintels and beams—and finally they stepped through a doorway and out into open space.

The royal garden was enormous, spreading away from the inner wall to the edge of the terrace. The three paused—it was like being in a forest that floated in the air, and a low hedge was all that stood between them and the teeming plaza below. It terrified Tonina and One Eye, who froze beneath the vast blue sky.

But Brave Eagle loved it, running to the precarious edge with his head back, his arms held out as if waiting for a thermal to lift him up and carry him away.

Tonina finally found courage to move among the rows of shrubs, flowers, bushes, and vines, wondering what the names of these plants were. She did not wish to remain dependent upon One Eye to translate for her. Before falling asleep the night before, Tonina had mentally recited the Mayan words she had learned that day—"team," "ball," "dead," "victory," "hunchback," and a score of others—committing her new and expanding vocabulary to memory.

She paused beneath a trellised arbor from which autumn-ripe berries hung, and looked out over the city, at the thousands of rooftops, gardens and narrow lanes, the temple-pyramids, and pictured the forest and White Road that led to the sea. Her chest tightened. The ocean called to her.

Bringing herself back from the painful and fruitless search for a glimpse of blue water, Tonina saw nearby, through the smoky haze, the high wall that surrounded Lady Jade Sky's villa. And Kaan materialized in her mind, as real as life, his muscled and scarred body towering before her in vivid detail.

As she had left for the palace earlier, she had seen Kaan slipping into the steam bath attached to the back of the house. He was in there now, she knew, praying and meditating in preparation for the final game tomorrow.

Tonina had never been so curious about another human being. She could not stop turning him around and around in her mind. Kaan was so strong, powerful, and confident. He was proud, too, and a man of honor—or so everyone said. But how could a man be so honorable on the playing field, yet be so disrespectful to his mother?

Tonina pulled herself back to the garden. She would never know the answer because she was leaving Mayapan. To that end, she had brought her travel pack with her to the royal garden, shouldering everything she owned in the world. If she found the red flower today, she was going to make straight for the coast and then home. If she did not find it here, then it was on to Quatemalan to search for it there. Either way, after she left this garden, it would not be to return to Lady Jade Sky's villa where Kaan, handsome and strong, was at that moment in communion with his gods. . . .

Another victory, Kaan pondered solemnly as he inhaled the hot moist air of the steam bath. Why did he not feel jubilant? Yesterday's win over the Tulum team had heaped more honors and praise upon his head, yet he felt inexplicably morose.

It was because of the future. For the first time in his life, he was examining the unknown path that lay ahead. How many victories were left to him? How many more years of playing the game? He was twenty-seven. Most players retired after thirty. Their bodies could not take the punishment; their reflexes slowed; and spectators always loved to embrace a newcomer.

The newcomers, he thought with a ragged sigh. Young, wild, arrogant. Kaan had been such a one, once. As soon as they hit the playing field they singled out the hero players and went after them, more intent upon bringing down the hero than winning the game. The people loved it. There was one player like that on the Chacmultún team, and Kaan would have to face him tomorrow. . . .

Was tomorrow the day Kaan would be so injured that he could no longer play? Would he die? Yesterday, Yaxik of Tulum . . . the ball hitting him in the face, killing him. *Is that me tomorrow?*

Kaan's throat tightened. He ran his hands over his sweating face and swallowed down his fear. But it was not fear of death that gripped him now, in the dark privacy of the sweat bath where he crouched naked and alone. He had played a good game yesterday, or so it appeared to the spectators. But Kaan knew the truth: His reflexes had been a fraction sluggish, his attention not one hundred percent on the ball. Why?

It was the distractions. First, his mother appearing in the garden, and then again among the spectators. It had momentarily thrown him off. Why was she there when she had promised she would never come? And then the island girl, sitting with Jade Sky. There had been a moment in the game when Kaan had realized he was playing as much for her as for his wife. Why? Never had his mind been so full of questions, so troubled. Was it because he was about to be a father? Or were other forces at work?

Splashing more water on the hot stones, he filled his lungs with the invigorating mist. And then he shivered again with fear.

Despite the moist air, Kaan's mouth was dry. Not a day went by in which he did not worry that someone might uncover his dark secret. Kaan knew how the world saw him—filled with confidence and unshakable faith in himself. What no one knew—not his wife, not Balám, not even his mother—was that the great Kaan, most famous ballplayer on the peninsula, was terrified of failure.

"Do not ever be a failure," his mother had said when he was a boy, and it had become his personal credo. To lose was to be perceived as weak and, by extension, inferior—and it would prove that, despite extreme efforts to appear Mayan, the great Kaan was after all just a lowly Chichimec.

He struggled daily to overcome his bloodline, to be better than his birthright, to prove that he was the equal of his Mayan teammates. And because it was a constant struggle simply to be their equal, he had declined the honored position of team captain. What if he accepted and failed? To fall from such a height! The mob was fickle. A hero one day could be reviled the next.

Every time he walked out onto the field he wondered if that was the day he would fail in front of the people. Which was why he must forever keep his wits about him, his mind sharp and focused, without the distractions that were plaguing him of late. Especially the fortune-teller with her news of Jade Sky's pregnancy.

Why had the gods brought the island girl into his life *now*, when the ball game was the most important thing in the world? She would not leave his mind, but troubled him like an annoying moth, to distract him, weaken him, and expose him to risk of failure and death.

As he poured more water on the hot stones, intoning prayers to Mother Moon, patron goddess of ballplayers, Kaan wondered if there was a way to get rid of the island girl.

The servant announced the arrival of the *h'meen*, and Tonina, Brave Eagle, and One Eye stared at the remarkable person who emerged from inside the palace and into the sunlight of the terrace. The tiny creature—a small, white-haired woman with curious facial features—looked older than time. "Blessings of the gods upon you and yours," she called softly.

Barely taller than One Eye, the ancient shaman approached in a long white dress embroidered with symbols that indicated she was a healer and a wise woman, for that was what *h'meen* meant in Mayan. "I greet the friends of Lady Jade Sky. How may I be of service to you?"

Speaking through One Eye, Tonina explained about the red flower and demonstrated its appearance with her hands.

"Yes, we have that blossom!" the *h'meen* said, and she led a suddenly hopeful Tonina to a bush of clumping red flowers. But when Tonina saw the familiar lobster-claw shape, she realized it was the heliconia that grew on her own island.

"The flower I seek looks more like . . ." She looked around the garden and, finding flowering red zinnias, said, "Like that, but upside down."

Bright round eyes embraced in folds of wrinkles seemed to withdraw into thought. "A moment please," the *h'meen* said, and she vanished within the doorway, returning with a wrapped object in her arms and a fat little dog frisking about her feet.

"This is Poki. He is my life companion. My dear one." She bent to pat the pudgy, hairless little animal and received a grateful lick in return.

Then she opened the cloth wrappings to expose something Tonina had never seen before, but which did not surprise One Eye at all. It was called a book, he said, and explained its purpose to Tonina.

The *h'meen,* who had told them to address her as H'meen, for that had become her name, waited patiently as Tonina was illuminated on the concept of paper, writing, and record-keeping. When One Eye was finished, H'meen opened out the pages folded accordion-fashion, and Tonina saw the drawings painted upon them.

They were lists of trees, grasses, shrubs, roots, leaves, and flowers, each with a written commentary as to properties, medicinal powers, and where it could be found. Tonina looked anxiously at the glyphs, hoping to recognize the flower. But the symbols did not resemble flowers or trees, they merely *represented* them, H'meen explained. One by one, the folded paper squares were turned, but no flower such as Tonina had described appeared.

"I am sorry," H'meen said humbly. "Everything that grows within this garden is recorded in this book. And I do not recognize the blossom of which you speak. I pray the gods lead you to it."

Tonina released a disappointed sigh, then said, "Can you help my friend? He suffered a blow to the head and now he can neither speak nor remember."

The diminutive woman with a high forehead and narrow, pointed chin gazed thoughtfully at the tall youth. She shook her head. "Memories come from the gods. They must have taken them back. As for speech, this comes from the soul, not from medicine. Again, I am sorry."

Tonina's shoulders slumped. She and Brave Eagle now faced a long journey to the Quatemalan coast. "Thank you for your help, good mother," she said, addressing her with the honorific of the islands.

H'meen looked at her, and then said, "Oh, I am sorry! I forgot." She laughed. "I always forget. I am not a mother, I am not old enough to be a mother."

When Tonina gave her a puzzled look, H'meen said, "I am only four-teen years old!"

Kaan poured water on the hot stones and inhaled the steam, his thoughts continuing along their troubled path.

He thought of the supposedly friendly wager Balám had proposed before yesterday's game. "If I score the final victory, the fortune-teller comes to live with us."

Kaan had laughed and said, "The final victory will be mine, brother," but he had had no intention of honoring the wager should Balám win. Kaan was going to hold on to the fortune-teller for the same reason Balám wanted the girl: to please his wife.

Jade Sky . . .

There was a time when the game was all that mattered to Kaan, when he had no other interests, when it was his life, his future. And then he had met and married Jade Sky. He had expected to have the family started by the end of the first year, giving him responsibilities beyond the ball game, and a future outside the playing field. But Jade Sky had difficulty conceiving, and then had suffered a miscarriage. The midwives had warned that because of Jade Sky's frailty, she might never conceive. And Kaan had wondered where his life would go once he was too old to play.

But now Jade Sky was pregnant—with a son!

Scooping a handful of bay leaves from a basket, he rubbed them over his bare arms and torso, filling the steam with pungent aromas. He was supposed to be praying. But his thoughts were on earthly matters.

Last night, as they had lain in each other's arms, with Jade Sky whispering her hopes and dreams to him, Kaan had been overcome by intense feelings of protectiveness. At the celebration that evening, Jade Sky had become too excited after the fortune-teller's prophecy of the hunchback visiting the house. Jade Sky needed to be quiet, to rest. There was too much excitement going on for her delicate condition. Kaan also did not trust Balám's wife. He had seen how Six Dove had looked at Jade Sky in the Grand Hall when the fortune-teller broke the news of the pregnancy. And then there had been Balám's wager before the game. Kaan knew that Six Dove would stop at nothing to steal the fortune-teller for herself.

Kaan recalled a private villa near the coast, which the owner, recently widowed, was eager to sell. The villa had its own vegetable gardens and fruit orchards. He would stock the yard with turkeys and dogs. It was a peaceful atmosphere with plenty of fresh air. Jade Sky would enjoy a serene pregnancy as there were no nearby neighbors, and no need to have contact with the city. He would tell no one, not even Balám, the location of this new place. And there they would live until their son was five years old.

Most especially, there would be no risk of Balám finding a way to steal Tonina the fortune-teller from them. At the same time, it solved the dilemma of how to get Tonina out of his own life and thoughts, for Kaan would visit the villa only sporadically.

As the steam began to abate and the small stone hut cooled, Kaan closed his eyes and breathed in the fragrance of the laurel leaves. He did not like the island girl living in their home, although he could not say why. She was quiet and stayed to herself. But he had found himself dreading an accidental encounter in a corridor. The way she had looked at him at the end of yesterday's game when he had laid the ball at Jade Sky's feet . . . He had glanced up and the girl was staring at him, a spellbound look on her face. It had captured him for a brief instant before he was able to collect himself.

Was she a sorceress as well as a fortune-teller? Had she powers to cast spells as well as to read the future? It did not matter. All that concerned him was that Jade Sky wanted the girl with her. And so, immediately following tomorrow's game, he would move his entire household to the secret villa on the coast, including the fortune-teller.

I am fourteen years old," H'meen was saying. "And I will die soon."
As Poki the fat little dog stuck his nose into the myriad pots and planters in the garden, H'meen told her story. She had been taken in as apprentice to the former *h'meen,* and in order to sharpen and quicken her mind, since the prior herbalist had sustained an injury and was soon to die, the child had been fed a plant that did indeed quicken her mind, giving her the learning and retaining capacity of an adult. An unfortunate side effect was that it had rapidly aged her body as well.

Tonina was speechless in the face of such tragedy. But then she said, "The flower which I seek is one that contains great magic. I was told it cures all ailments. Perhaps it can help you as well."

"Where does it grow?"

"In Quatemalan."

H'meen sighed. "That is very far away, and I have never stepped beyond the city walls." She smiled, showing young white teeth that sharply contrasted with her aged face. And as she spoke, telling a little of her sheltered life in the palace, Tonina realized that she was grasping some of what the girl was saying before One Eye translated it.

As they made to leave, the girl-woman said, *"Ka x'ik teech utsil."* Which meant "Good luck to you."

And Tonina, without thinking, said, *"Béey xan teech."* Which was Mayan for "The same to you."

One Eye was thrilled. Tonina was a quick learner. What a pair they would make! He would teach her all his tricks, the confidence games, and together they would grow rich.

Outside, in the plaza, Tonina said to One Eye, "We are not returning to the villa. We are leaving the city now. Thank you for all you have done for us." She reached into her travel pack and produced two pearls.

As she handed them to him, One Eye panicked. "Let us stay for the Thirteenth Game, at least."

"I do not wish to tell any more fortunes. I will tell no more lies. Thank you for all your help. But we must find the road to the southern coast."

To her surprise, Brave Eagle started shaking his head and gesturing frantically. "What is the matter?" she asked.

"I think he wants to return to the villa," One Eye said.

"Why?"

Brave Eagle struggled in frustration to form words, to produce voice.

"Do you think the hunters are out there?" Tonina asked, pointing in the direction of the walls and the marketplace beyond.

He nodded.

One Eye seized upon this and said, "The boy might be right. We have only been in the city for three days. If they followed you here they would not give up so quickly. We are safe at the villa. Eventually, they will give up, but until then we dare not venture out."

"But I did not want to return to the villa," Tonina said unhappily. Reaching the southern coast was a journey of many days. After that, she had to search for the flower. Time was precious. But as she looked more closely at Brave Eagle, she saw something else in his eyes. "What is it?" she asked quietly. "Why do you want to go back?"

He could not explain it. The trouble did not lie in his inability to speak, but in his chaotic thoughts. Even if he had voice, he would not have the words. Since the day Tonina had freed him from his cage, vibrant and lifelike dreams had visited his sleep, leaving him only with the sense that he was on an important errand. The house of Lady Jade Sky seemed to be part of it, but in ways he could not fathom.

"Brave Eagle, I do not know if they will let you stay there without me. And I must go."

He implored her with his golden eyes, his hands on her arms, squeezing them, to impart his desperate need.

"Very well," Tonina said at last. "If you feel safe there, we will return. But only for a few days. And then I must go."

One Eye hid his relief as he said, "I have business in the marketplace. I will return to the villa tonight."

Tonina touched his arm and said, "Take care, for although you are a dwarf and respected, there are dangerous men out there." And then she turned reluctantly in the direction of Lady Jade Sky's villa, where, at that moment, Kaan was informing his wife that she and the entire household, including the fortune-teller, were to relocate to a villa on the coast, where they would live in seclusion until their son came of age.

16

As Prince Balám sang a lullaby to his daughter, he felt like laughing, he was in such a good mood.

For a day and a night he had tried to think of ways to get the fortune-teller away from Jade Sky. Finally it had come to him. Bribe the girl. Offer her anything she wanted if she left Jade Sky and came to live under his roof. Just the chance to live in the household of a prince should be incentive enough, but the girl would most likely demand something else— jade, cacao beans, cotton dresses. And there was nothing Kaan's wife could do to stop it because Jade Sky would not be able to top Balám's offer. After tomorrow's victorious game, he was going to be the richest man in Mayapan, if not in the whole world. And there would be nothing he would not be able to buy for his beloved Six Dove—least of all a simple girl from the islands.

Little Ziyal grew sleepy and her father was about to launch into another song when a servant came into the bedroom to inform his lordship that he had a visitor.

"Tell him to come tomorrow," Balám snapped. Time spent with his daughter was never to be interrupted.

But when the servant told him the visitor's name, Balám froze.

And suddenly his good mood was gone.

As One Eye left the city, he ran the scenario through his mind: He would tell the hunters he knew where the boy was and then announce his price for the information. They in turn would tell him to lead them to the boy. One Eye would then say he wanted payment up front, and they would counter with "half now, half on delivery," which he would accept. He would take them to Jade Sky's villa, point to where the boy was sleeping, take his payment, and leave. But first he would lure Tonina away and the two of them would be on the northern road before anyone knew what was happening.

"My friends," he called out as he neared the hunters' camp. Because of tomorrow's game, the marketplace beyond the city wall was more crowded than ever, rowdy with laughter and arguments, children kicking balls; a festive atmosphere. But there they sat, six dour men, their brown-and-black-striped bodies hunched over—the only ones here not thinking of tomorrow's match. "Have you a morsel to share with a hungry traveler?" As a dwarf and his good luck were always welcome, they offered him a place at their fire and gave him tortillas and corn.

He threw some crumbs into the fire for the gods, and then proceeded to eat with gusto, and as he did, sized them up with his good eye. Edgy fellows, he thought, not at all happy to be so far from home. Not relaxed as one was supposed to be at a supper fire, but alert, nervous, and constantly surveying the marketplace crowd. "So," he asked casually, "what brings you to Mayapan?"

They were not very talkative.

"If you are here to buy or to trade," he said, licking his stubby fingers, "perhaps I can help. I know many of the merchants here and can see that they do not cheat you. Just mention the name One Eye and they will tell you I am the most honest man in the land."

The leader, who wore three precious eagle feathers in his hair, grunted and said they were looking for a runaway slave. "We think he came here in the company of a girl."

One Eye shrugged. "Many boys and girls in Mayapan. But perhaps I have seen them. Can you give me a description?"

When they did, One Eye said, "A tall island girl in the company of a pale-skinned youth who wore not the smallest tattoo? I saw such a pair in this very marketplace, camped over there by the main gate."

When two hunters started to rise, spears in their hands, he added quickly, "Oh, they are not there anymore."

"Tell us where they are."

"Well, I have to think." He looked from one to the other of the faces glowing in the campfire light. Not pleasant men; too deadly, he suspected, and wondered how far he dared go in his bargaining.

But the chief hunter sighed and said, "How much do you want for this information?" and One Eye grinned. He pretended to think, then said, "Twenty cacao beans."

The payment was handed over.

One Eye looked at the precious beans in his chubby palm and, thinking of the rest of the payment he would demand and how it would enable him to retire to a life of women and ease, he lifted his smiling face to the hunters and, pointing over his shoulder, said, "Eastward, to Tulum on the coast. They left yesterday."

N o one knew where the roots of the mysterious ritual lay, or its original significance. Some said that the cloaked priests coming in the middle of the night to escort the players to the field was a reenactment of soldiers long past taking prisoners to their chief. Others said it was merely a secure way of getting popular players from their homes to the field without being accosted by admirers. Whatever the reasons for the rite, Kaan followed strict protocol as he prepared himself, binding his wrists and ankles with leather strips while he prayed to Mother Moon. When the chief steward of his house came in and, bowing low, said, "My lord, you have a visitor," Kaan looked startled. "So soon?" The priests never came this early.

"It is Prince Balám, my lord."

Balám! "Show him in."

When Balám entered, Kaan was shocked by the haggard look on his face. "What is it, brother?" Kaan asked in deep concern.

Balám was perspiring heavily, despite the cool night, and his color was the gray of dead ash. "Have you something to drink?"

Kaan ordered *kawkaw* but Balám asked for something stronger. *Pulque* was brought and, to Kaan's shock, Balám gulped it down in one upturn of the cup. On the night before the most important game of the year!

Balám wiped his mouth with the back of his hand, faced his old friend squarely, and said, "Brother, I am in serious trouble."

O   ne Eye muttered to himself as he waddled along the torchlit av-
enue, the only soul afoot at this late hour. His stunted shadow formed strange shapes on walls as he hurried to Lady Jade Sky's villa. "One Eye, you fool! You idiot! Have you lost your brains? You were one word away from being a rich man—all you had to say was, 'Come, I will show you where the youth is,' and *what fell from your mouth?* Tulum!"

He did not know why he had lied to the eagle hunters. His own words had surprised him. And as he had returned to the city gates and looked back, he had seen the hunters already breaking camp. They would be on the eastward road before midnight, and well away from Mayapan by dawn. Why had he committed what could only be called the stupidest mistake of his life?

Tonina. On the palace steps. She had put her hand on his shoulder and, instead of asking for luck as everyone else did, had told him to be careful. No one had ever thought of *his* welfare before. One Eye decided that that small act of kindness must have set deeper thoughts and emotions into play because, as he had been about to divulge Brave Eagle's whereabouts, a curious thought had sprung into his mind: that he did not want to encourage Tonina's interest in Kaan after all.

He sighed now as he hurried down the narrow lane between dark and silent houses, telling himself that he was getting old and soft. But not all was lost. Before visiting the camp of the eagle hunters, he had gone to one of the many *koxol* gathered near the gate, frantically taking wagers from bettors on tomorrow's game. Though he had had but the few cacao beans from the eagle hunters, One Eye had been able to place a large bet all the same. Because he wore an embroidered loincloth and his mantle was of finely spun cotton, proof of his prosperity, and because he was after all a dwarf, he had been able to place bets with the *koxol* with only his thumbprint on a piece of paper, wagering a fortune that he did not in fact have.

As he consoled himself with the knowledge that the Mayapan team would win and that tomorrow evening he would be a man of means again, he saw, in the lane ahead, a dark shape knocking at the wooden gate of Lady Jade Sky's villa.

One Eye knew of the pregame ritual of priests coming for the players. But it was too early, and this was only one man. When he saw that the man was Prince Balám, One Eye fell back into the shadows and watched as Balám was admitted, the gate closing behind him. Then One Eye knocked, was allowed in, and he slipped through the garden with a practiced light step from years of spying. Instead of going to the servants' quarters, he tiptoed through the sleeping house, down corridors he had memorized, until he heard voices and saw light up ahead. Prince Balám was in Kaan's private bedchamber, and they were talking.

Creeping close and making certain that no servants were about, the dwarf positioned himself at the tapestry hanging in the doorway so that he was able to see as well as hear.

Balám had thrown off his cloak and One Eye saw that he wore upon his belt the jade emblem of Uxmal, which identified him as a prince of the royal line of that city and a direct descendant of Hun Uitzil Chac Tutul Xiu, founder of the great city of Uxmal. Everyone knew that Balám had been delivered to the royal court of Mayapan in a traditional exchange of princes to ensure peace between the two kingdoms. The sons and daughters of other royalty in lesser towns also resided in the Mayapan palace, just as Mayapan's princes and princesses had been sent to be raised in the houses of other rulers. The time-honored practice kept political stability in the region.

But why, One Eye wondered, was the prince wearing his official emblem tonight when it was usually reserved for state occasions?

Balám cried, "Disaster has befallen me, brother! I am a dead man." And One Eye, thinking of profits, listened keenly, committing every word and gesture to memory.

"Calm yourself," Kaan said. "Is it Six Dove? Your daughter—?"

"It is all of us!" Balám wrung his hands and said in a lower voice, "I am heavily into debt, brother."

Kaan was not surprised. All men gambled; it was a passion shared by Chichimecs as well as Maya, and even islanders. For Balám, however, the pastime of wagering ran so deep in his blood that it sometimes consumed him. And now Kaan learned the shocking truth of just how dangerously far his gambling had gone.

Most men who used the services of the *koxol* had to show the items they were wagering, such as jade jewelry, or proof of ownership of what was being wagered. But Balám was a prince and so the *koxol* took him at his word. Unfortunately, this enabled him to extend himself beyond his means.

"Do you remember, Kaan, last year, when Six Dove and I took Ziyal to visit my parents in Uxmal? We came home to discover that thieves had broken in and stolen some of our most valuable possessions?"

Kaan waited while Balám took a drink and then wiped his mouth with the back of his hand.

"Those possessions were gone before we even left," he said miserably. "I used them to pay gambling debts. Six Dove doesn't know that I had lost her favorite jade earrings on a dog fight. That was why I took her to Uxmal, so that she wouldn't notice things missing."

Kaan became alarmed. He had thought Balám had his gambling under control. He had hidden it well, from his wife, his teammates, his best friend. "I have lied to you, my brother. To everyone. To my own mother! She gave me a gold cup encrusted with the purest jade and I lost it on a bet."

Balám's tone turned earnest. "It has not all been bad luck. I have won, too. That is what is so confounding! I have brought home fabulous riches, which I hid away as a surprise for Six Dove, only to have to give them up a day later. Brother, I cannot seem to stay lucky enough to get ahead. The more I sink into debt, the more I gamble to get out of debt. I was balancing it well for a while, but now . . ."

"How bad is it?" Kaan asked.

Balám swallowed with difficulty. "I owe everything . . . my lands, my wealth . . . and more."

"Mother Moon," Kaan whispered.

Tears rose in Balám's eyes. "Six Dove is insatiable. I love her. I cannot refuse her anything."

Kaan thought how unalike their wives were; Jade Sky like a small sparrow, Six Dove like a massive gobbler turkey.

"She wanted an avocado orchard. So I wagered with a man from Yaxchilan. It was a roll of knucklebones. I lost. We played again. I kept losing. He had a piece of paper drawn up and I made my mark on it. So I went to another man to cover the debt. It got out of hand. . . . When those I wagered with demanded payment, I could only cover it by borrowing or gambling with other men."

Kaan wanted to say, "Take all that I have," and had this happened just days earlier, he would have said those very words. But now Jade Sky was pregnant. Kaan had to think of his son. "What about your family in Uxmal?" he asked. According to Mayan custom, a man's relatives were expected to come to his aid in times of need.

"It would impoverish them," Balám said miserably.

"So great is the debt?" Kaan said in astonishment.

He waited, sensing that this was not the reason Balám had come to see him at this sacred hour when both should be preparing for tomorrow's game. The debts could have waited. Something else, however, could not.

Finally Balám said, "I had a visitor just now. He represents a consortium of rich men intent upon becoming richer. He held all my markers. Every piece of paper I signed, from all over the city, wagers with different men, he had them."

"How—?"

"This consortium is very rich. Richer, it is said, than all the local kings combined. They bought all my markers, Kaan. They paid off all my debts."

Kaan frowned. "Why would they do this?"

Balám looked at him with haunted eyes. "Don't you know?"

Kaan shook his head.

"They . . ." Balám licked his lips. His eyes shifted around the room. He swallowed for courage and then said in a strangled whisper, "They want me to make sure we lose tomorrow's game."

Silence fell. Sounds drifted through the open window—a man and a woman arguing several houses down, an owl calling from a rooftop, footsteps staggering drunkenly down the lane. Still eavesdropping, One Eye could hear his heart pounding in his ears.

"I don't understand," Kaan finally said, although deep inside he did.

"If I throw tomorrow's game, they will erase all my debts."

"They are betting on us to *lose*?"

"It is that simple. They have wagered heavily on Chacmultún to win."

"But why don't they just bet on *us* to win?"

"A victory can never be guaranteed, brother, but a defeat can."

Kaan suddenly felt sick. "Balám, do not ask this of me. Winning or losing is in the hands of the gods. It is already fixed in the divine plan."

"But you and I both know we can change that. Nothing is so fixed that a man cannot alter it."

"But changing the outcome of a game is sacrilege!"

"Do you think I do not know this?" Balám cried. "But if I do not do this, the consortium will call in my markers. As I have no way of paying my debts, they will take my wife and daughter and sell them into slavery. I will be stripped of my lands and my wealth. I will be thrown off the team and never allowed to play again. My friends will reject me. My family in Uxmal—my parents, my uncle the king—will spurn me and expect me to do the honorable thing by hanging myself!"

Kaan's throat ran dry. "Balám, we pledged with our blood to live by a code of honor. We spoke an oath before Mother Moon never to lie, steal, or cheat. Without honor, we are nothing."

"And if we do not lose the game, *I* will be nothing!"

Kaan paced. He rubbed the back of his neck. He stopped and turned. "I can sell my orchards. I have a newly purchased villa near the coast."

But Balám was shaking his head. "If His Exalted Goodness *and* my uncle the king of Uxmal combined all their wealth, it would not be enough. I have only one recourse." Balám held out his hands. "To lose the game."

When Kaan looked at him in horror, Balám quickly said, "The gods will see into your heart. They will understand that you are helping your brother. They will see that your actions are those of self-sacrifice. You will not be punished, rather you will be blessed."

The prince began to sob. "Forgive me for having brought this disaster to your doorstep. I desperately need your help. I remember a time when I went to your aid, and you did not even ask for it."

Kaan closed his eyes, tears forming at the memory. Living in the palace kitchen with his mother, young Kaan alone and without friends because he was a Chichimec in a Mayan city. A gang of boys cornering him in an alley. A young prince coming to his rescue, befriending him, and eventually securing young Kaan's admittance into the famous ballplayer academy.

"If you do this tomorrow, my brother," Balám said, "all my debts will be cleared. I will be a new man. I will never gamble again. On my daughter's life, I swear this."

Kaan said in a tight voice, "You have promised so many times before."

"I have never come so close to losing my family before! This was the shock I needed, brother. For Ziyal's sake, I must become a new man. I will swear off gambling entirely."

Balám carried Ziyal's first tooth in a pouch around his neck, and he showed it now to Kaan. "Upon this powerful talisman I swear my oath. I cradled her in my arms when she cried while teething this first tooth. And when she came running to me to proudly show off how painlessly she had pulled the loose tooth out, to make room for her permanent teeth, I threw a party in her honor. This tooth reminds me of her smile, and of my eternal devotion to her. It also contains great power. It is the most powerful talisman I carry. Brother, I know that I am possessed by an evil spirit. But if I do tomorrow what the consortium asks of me, then the evil spirit will be exorcised. I am certain of this. Please!"

Balám sobbed openly now, crying on Kaan's shoulder. From his place at the door, hidden behind the tapestry, One Eye clearly saw the look on Kaan's face. His features were tight, pale, his lips compressed into a thin line. And then Kaan said, "I cannot let such disaster befall my brother." His voice was strained but steady as he added, "May the gods have mercy on us both."

One Eye backed slowly away, stunned, and then stumbled blindly through the house to the servants' quarters, suddenly gripped with fear. He had laid heavy wagers on tomorrow's game, secure in the knowledge that Mayapan's team would win. But he had wagered a fortune that he did not have! If he lost, he would not be able to cover his debts and, dwarf of not, they would surely sell him into slavery.

Stepping over the snoring housemaids, cooks, stewards, and gardeners, One Eye found Tonina sleeping with Brave Eagle. Gently shaking her awake, he beckoned her to follow.

Out in the garden, beneath a gibbous moon, he recounted what he had overheard. Tonina yawned and rubbed her eyes. She could not grasp what he was saying. The people of Pearl Island wagered all the time. What was the problem?

"It is different on the islands!" One Eye hissed, pinching her arm. "Wake up! We have terrible trouble on our hands."

He recited the conversation again, and this time Tonina's mind cleared as she grasped the significance. "Can you leave the city? Run away?"

He shook his head miserably. "There is no escape. Men who accept heavy wagers have eyes and ears in all towns and villages. And truth be told, I am a distinctive-looking gentleman. There is no disguise on earth that will save me."

"Then what can we do?"

He looked up at Tonina. There it was again, on her face, the worry for his welfare. She had said "we." It was another first in his life. And suddenly an idea came to him. "There is a way we can set things right."

"How?"

"You must have Kaan sip from the prophecy cup, and then you will tell him that Mayapan wins tomorrow's game."

"How will that help?"

"You tell Kaan that his team wins," he said eagerly, suddenly seeing his salvation. "That means the gods have already ordered it so. He would not dare go against the wishes of the gods."

Tonina chewed her lip. She had vowed to tell no more lies. Were the lies piling up against her? Did each untruth she spoke keep her from finding the flower?

But she wanted to help One Eye. She also did not want Kaan to incur the gods' wrath by throwing the game. And Jade Sky had shown Brave

Eagle such kindness. "I will read Lord Kaan's fortune," Tonina finally said. "I will tell him he will win the game tomorrow, and in that way he will not dare force his team to lose."

But when they were summoned the next morning to tell fortunes, it was only Jade Sky. Kaan was gone.

17

Crowds had traveled great distances to attend the Thirteenth Game. The *koxol* were busy accepting wagers and handing out gambling pledges. Lookouts stood on the sloping walls of the ball court, ready to shout out the moves and action to the excited throng. And vendors sold everything from locks of hero players' hair to tortillas dipped in honey.

Standing behind Jade Sky at the open end of the field, Tonina wondered if Kaan was going to sacrifice his honor to save his friend, while One Eye was thinking that if Mayapan lost, he would get out of the city as fast as he could, head for the nearest coast, buy a canoe, and paddle into oblivion.

As the nobles and favored spectators took their places at the ends of the playing field, with much jostling for space, arguing over who was allowed to sit where, Lady Six Dove surreptitiously slipped a special mug into Jade Sky's basket of *kawkaw*-filled goblets. The brew in this new mug was laced with extract of pennyroyal, an herb that stimulated menstrual flow.

The royal botanist, H'meen, was at the game, small and frail, seated in an honored place, her fat little dog, Poki, curled in her lap.

As the two teams lined up before the priests, and the low rumble of their voices filled the air, Tonina wondered if Kaan was confessing his intention to purposely lose the game.

Today's game, though exciting, seemed to Tonina to be a reenactment of the Twelfth Game and she wondered how people could watch these same games over and over. She kept her eye on Kaan as One Eye quietly whispered in her ear if he had made a good play or a bad one. Through the long morning, the teams appeared to be equal, and by the mid-day break, the score between Mayapan and the southern city of Chacmultún was even.

There was a break for answering the call of nature and stretching legs, and then the game resumed.

Six Dove watched Jade Sky out of the corner of her eye as, one by one, she drained the *kawkaw* cups. Finally she reached for the cup that Six Dove had slipped among the others and raised it to her lips. Six Dove smiled in secret anticipation. When the pennyroyal had done its job and expelled the fetus from Jade Sky's womb, even the mild-tempered Jade Sky would have to be enraged at a fortune-teller who could not predict a miscarriage. She would throw the girl out and Six Dove would snap her up.

Balám missed a play and the crowd jeered. When Kaan flew in to make a recovery, he also failed, earning a tremendous roar of disapproval from the spectators.

Startled by the sudden sloppy playing, Six Dove forgot Jade Sky and focused her attention on the game. Incredibly, the Mayapan team was losing! The onlookers voiced their fury, and the king was conferring with his courtiers, a dark frown on his face.

Tonina saw Lady Six Dove lean forward, the two stools beneath her groaning with the weight. She placed a plump hand on her generous bosom, her lips parted. Tonina realized that Balám's wife was not aware of the secret pact her husband had entered into with Kaan.

Everyone was tense now. Back and forth the ball and the teams went, passing, receiving, intercepting. Jade Sky grew worried. Six Dove developed a thunderous frown. Something strange was going on. Three sloppy plays from Kaan. Tonina's heart raced as the game neared its conclusion, with the Chacmultún supporters already celebrating a victory.

"Great Lokono," Tonina whispered in prayer, "shed light into the heart of the man named Kaan."

Two Chacmultún players now had possession of the ball and were passing it back and forth as they ran toward their goal, with teammates keeping Mayapan away. Kaan ran alongside Balám, looking for an opening to intercept, and he took his eyes off the game for an instant, glancing ahead at the Chacmultún goal line behind which sat players' wives and families. In an instant he saw Jade Sky, and behind her, the tall island girl who had said his wife was carrying a son.

Balám maneuvered close to the Chacmultún pair for an intercept, and then suddenly, before thousands of startled eyes, Kaan jumped sideways *in front of Balám*, intercepted the ball with his elbow, and knocked it into the air. And then, in a maneuver that the spectators knew would be talked about for years to come, he sprang up, spun like a whirlwind, and hit the ball a second time with his other elbow, to shoot it onto the stone wall where it ricocheted at a narrow angle and flew through the scoring ring.

The crowd went wild. No man in the history of the game had sent the ball through the stone hoop *twice* in his career. Spectators swarmed onto the field. Like a tidal wave they washed over the bloody ground, swallowing up players and priests, lifting Kaan and Balám onto their shoulders with jubilant roars.

The two players did not smile, but no one noticed. They were sick with fear, as they knew what was going to happen. They had seen it happen before, to other men. Balám's world was about to come crashing down. He was about to lose everything and, by losing, by falling from heroic status, become the most reviled of men.

Hired guards immediately encircled the families of the winners, to protect them from zealous supporters, and as Tonina, One Eye, and Brave Eagle closed in on Jade Sky and her attendants, the dwarf whispered, "Great Lokono!" dumbfounded. He was suddenly a very rich man.

Lady Six Dove rose from her stools and offered a gracious but sour smile to Jade Sky, who had not drunk the special cup of *kawkaw*. There would be other opportunities, Balám's wife told herself as she fixed a greedy eye on the island girl, still determined to get the fortune-teller under her own roof. And then she turned her attention to her hero husband, who was being paraded around the field on the shoulders of his fanatical worshipers. She had been worried during the game, he had played so poorly, but she realized now he had been putting on an act. He and Kaan must have choreographed that final amazing play, and what a clever idea it was, because the people had loved it. Prince Balám was now adored more than ever, and he was richer, too, for Six Dove knew he had wagered heavily on this game. From now on, there was nothing Six Dove could not have.

The girl with the prophecy cup would be hers by nightfall.

Although supporters of other Mayapan players carried their favorites on their shoulders, it was Kaan and Balám who had the largest crowd following them as they were transported through the city streets amid deafening cheers. The men who held the heroes aloft were privileged; they had drawn lots and won. In Kaan's case, he was carried by an elite club who called themselves the Nine Brothers, whose members were passionate about ball games and hero players. They wore Mayapan's colors and chanted a song dedicated to the game, the field, the ball, and the winner.

As Kaan was carried off one way toward his villa, Balám's group struck off down another lane, where a celebration was to take place at Balám's villa. But when the rowdy procession entered the narrow street, they found guards barring the way. The gate in Balám's high wall stood open, and men were coming out with goods in their arms—pottery, statuary, tapestries.

Shouts of protest erupted from the crowd, but Balám called for calm. They lowered him to the ground and watched in confusion as he strode toward an important-looking man consulting an accounting book "What is the meaning of this?" Balám bellowed, although he already knew—he had to make a show in front of his hundreds of admirers.

The blue-robed official barely looked at him as he said, "We are here to collect debts."

Then Balám saw the heavy-lidded man from the consortium standing near the wall. "Give me time," he said quietly to the stone-faced man. "I can pay it all!"

But the man from the consortium said nothing as valuable items were carried past his inscrutable gaze.

"What is going on here?" came a familiar voice as the crowd parted for Lady Six Dove. She pushed her great weight through the onlookers and went straight to the gate, where men were dragging out a wooden chest filled with clothing, sandals, and headdresses. Reaching for the nearest man, she yanked him so hard he flew off his feet and landed on his backside.

Guards were immediately on either side of the outraged woman, taking her by fleshy arms. "How dare you!" she screamed. Turning to Balám, she said, "Husband, explain this!"

Before Balám could respond, a soldier came out of the crowd, with Ziyal crying in his arms. "Is this the girl?" he asked of the man with the accounting book.

"The daughter," the man muttered as he made a mark in the book.

As Six Dove reached for her daughter, ropes were tied to her own wrists and neck, making her shriek in protest.

"Take me instead," Balám said to the man from the consortium, realizing in sick fear what was happening. "Leave my family alone. Sell me instead."

The flat eyes slid to him. "They are worth more."

"It was not my fault that we did not lose," Balám protested, trying to keep his voice low. "I tried! I *did* persuade Kaan to help me throw the game. But he changed his mind. This is all *his* fault. You saw how I lost points for my team. I was honoring my agreement with you. It is Kaan's lands and wealth and wife you should take!"

But the man said, "Kaan is a man of honor. We respect him for what he did—or did not do. The responsibility is entirely yours, Balám." He pointedly omitted the honorific "my lord," letting Balám know that not only his possessions and family were being stripped from him.

As men started to lead Six Dove and Ziyal away, Balám reached for them, to embrace them, but his wife spat in his face and turned away so that he could not touch his precious daughter. Balám looked into Six Dove's hateful eyes and saw no forgiveness there. With loathing, she said, "When our daughter is old enough to understand, I am going to tell her how evil her father was, and that she is to curse your name every day of her life."

Four armed soldiers led the proud Six Dove through the crowd, and Balám's last glimpse of his family was Ziyal in her mother's arms, reaching out for him, crying, "*Taati!*"

W hen slaves went to the front entrance to help their master, Jade Sky ran to greet him. It was the middle of the night, and Kaan looked wretched.

"I could not find him," he said, gratefully accepting a cup of water. "I searched everywhere. Balám has disappeared." Kaan hurt all over, still covered in scratches, scrapes, and bruises from the game. They had not been able to celebrate the victory, as word quickly reached them of what had happened at Balám's house.

"It is my fault," Kaan said. "If I had done as Balám asked, he would now have his house and his family."

"No, beloved. You did the right thing. The games are sacred. Balám has doomed his soul to Hell for agreeing to commit such a sacrilege. Kaan, you must buy his wife and daughter tomorrow."

He had already arrived at that decision. No matter how much it took—all their own wealth and lands if need be—he would make sure that Six Dove and Ziyal were not sold into slavery.

18

The slave auction was held once every twenty days, on the first day of the month. But a special session was called due to the uniqueness of today's goods. Not just Six Dove and Ziyal, but personal effects as well, so that neighbors came to bid on books, statuary, and jewelry they had long coveted.

Kaan did not stand in the general crowd but occupied a special place near the auction block. People jockeyed to be near him; he had sent the ball through the stone hoop, he would be exuding good luck. Tonina, Brave Eagle, and One Eye found places near the front of the crowd. One Eye's head throbbed. Immediately after the victory he had collected his winnings and then had found two ladies with whom to celebrate over much *pulque*.

Household slaves and goods finally sold off, Six Dove was brought out with great drama, the slave auctioneer calling out her attributes in a ringing voice, extolling her noble bloodline. She was robed in scarlet cotton that seemed to emphasize her prodigious weight, and she held her head high, refusing to acknowledge the crowd or the situation.

Little Ziyal was then brought out, and around her neck hung the jade emblem of Uxmal that her father had worn on his belt to identify him as a prince of the royal line, proof now of the girl's own royal blood. Ziyal's face was red and puffy from crying, and she looked frightened as she was made to stand next to her mother on the platform that rose over the heads of the onlookers.

Kaan felt wretched. He blamed himself. He had looked at the goal end of the field and had seen his wife sitting there, and, behind her, the fortune-teller who had said Jade Sky carried a son. In that moment, Kaan could not throw the game.

But there *was* one thing he could do for his friend: purchase the wife and daughter. He prepared to call out his bid, with the intention of bidding until the last customer backed down, when the auctioneer announced that the pair had just had been purchased by an anonymous buyer in a special transaction called *tu'ux-a-kah*—"pleasure of the gods."

The crowd grumbled disapproval, as the bidding would have proven great sport, and then, as the mother and daughter were about to be taken away, before Kaan's horrified eyes, Six Dove broke free of the guards who held her, and lunged for her child, screaming, "Ziyal!"

The girl turned and bolted for her mother. Six Dove used her weight to push the soldiers out of the way, knocking one off the platform, bringing a roar of laughter from the crowd. Six Dove scooped the child into her fleshy arms and spun in a circle, searching for an exit.

More guards appeared on the platform as the auctioneer called for order. Ziyal was torn from her mother's arms. Both shrieked, and the onlookers either cheered or booed, and wagers broke out. Kaan tried to make his way to the platform, where guards were attempting to bring Six Dove into submission. But she was remarkably fast for one so heavy, and her weight was a weapon. Flinging out her arms, she struck two guards with her fists, and kneed another in the groin.

"Ziyal!" she cried as more guards closed in on her and the girl was carried away. As Kaan pulled himself up onto the platform, the guard who had received Six Dove's knee recovered and, bellowing his outrage, lifted his club high and brought it down on her head, sending a sickening *craack* up to the sky.

She slumped. The crowd fell silent and watched in fascination as her great form slipped gracefully to the platform, to deliver brains and blood onto the ancient boards.

~ 19 ~

Behind the north wall of Mayapan rose a giant, stinking mound created by the refuse of Mayapan's many inhabitants—broken pottery, rotten fruit, entrails, menstrual cloths, and dogs' business swept up from the lanes and alleys—taboo objects that could not be kept inside a house. It was a mound of such bad luck that, once every twenty days, it was set afire by city officials so that the smoke carried the spiritual poison away.

This was where Prince Balám, a man once worshiped by thousands, stumbled as he clutched a rope and looked for a place to hang himself.

He could not get the visions out of his head—standing outside his house as his wife and daughter were taken away, feeling the hundreds of eyes upon him, to witness his shame and degradation. Word had quickly spread that Balám had bet *against* his own team, which could only mean that he had planned to make sure they lost. It also explained his shoddy playing that day. Already, his name was taboo and he was the most despised man in the land.

Of all the forms of suicide, hanging was the only honorable one. Did he deserve that? Or did the gods demand that he sacrifice himself by poison or dagger, and thus send his soul to the Ninth Level of Hell?

Dropping to his knees, Balám sobbed loudly and bitterly. *The way little Ziyal had held her arms out to him, crying,* "Taati!" That cry would forever ring in his ears. For as long as he lived, Balám knew that he would be deaf to all else and hear only his precious daughter's plea to save her.

Balám collapsed and, as he lay among the muck and filth, felt a dark poison begin to swim through his veins. Closing his eyes, he relived the final play of the game, when Kaan had intercepted the ball, saying so that only Balám could hear, "I cannot throw the game, I have to think of my son." And then, in a brilliant move, he had shot the ball through the hoop.

And now Balám was the most wretched man on earth.

He wanted to die. But as the new poison swam through his veins, and he felt the throb of life in his neck, it occurred to him, among the odors of feces and urine and garbage, that before he left this world, others must die first.

Kaan and Jade Sky. This was all their fault. The fortune-teller's, too. Because she had told Jade Sky she was going to have a son, Kaan had decided not to help his brother. It was *her* fault they had not lost the game.

Balám's sobbing subsided. He sat up and ran a dirty hand over his face. Sitting among the garbage and refuse of other people, he grew coldly quiet. Thoughts left his mind. He felt only primal instinct. Hatred. Hunger for revenge. When the men from the consortium had stripped Balám's house, they had stripped the man, too. In front of a street full of gawkers, the fallen prince had been divested of his handsome loincloth and cloak, all jewelry—bracelets, ankle cuffs, earrings, nose and lip plugs—even his sandals. They left him barefoot like a commoner, wearing only a plain loincloth such as the poorest peasant wore, and two necklaces that they dared not touch because they were taboo: the small pouch that held Ziyal's baby tooth, and the jade amulet Balám had received on the day of his manhood, when he suffered the painful rite of genital piercing and bleeding.

But Balám gave no thought to any of that now. Nothing mattered anymore, only that those responsible paid for what they had done. He didn't care what happened after that, did not care what happened to himself, only that the three were punished. . . .

J ade Sky wished Kaan had not gone out yet again in search of his friend, not at this late hour when sane men did not go abroad. She was troubled by ill-ease and misgivings, and wanted her husband close. But Kaan was riddled with guilt and anguish, and she knew that if only he could find Balám, if they could be brothers again, peace might return to their house.

She moved about her spacious bedchamber, lighting incense, chanting sacred prayers. Lady Jade Sky was a member of the Cult of the Returning God. Generations ago, Kukulcan—whose pyramid dominated the main plaza of Mayapan—walked the earth as a wise king and healer. And when he left, to sail across the eastern sea on a raft made of snakes, he had promised to return and bring about an age of peace and harmony. It was to his effigy that Lady Jade Sky now prayed, hoping that the incense would carry her plea to the lofty ears of the feathered serpent, Kukulcan.

Other gods also resided in Jade Sky's bedchamber. To these she prayed and lit incense, pausing frequently to listen to the night, waiting for the sound of Kaan's familiar footfall beyond her door. But all she heard was a low murmuring in the outer corridor. One voice carrying on a two-sided conversation. Jade Sky had asked the fortune-teller to sleep there. The girl had agreed, providing the mute boy could keep her company. So the two were just outside her bedroom door—a prophetess and an enchanted boy—who together surely would keep evil spirits away.

But while evil spirits might be kept out, another sort of demon scaled the back wall at that moment and dropped softly into the garden.

Balám paused, looked around, and listened. Then he crept toward the house, crouched like an animal, alert for sounds. He knew they would all be asleep. He would run swiftly, he decided, striking throats and breasts, slaying as many as he could with the obsidian knife he had purchased with his sacred jade amulet of manhood.

He would start with the puny wife. She would be slumbering sweetly on her mat, Kaan's son cradled in her belly. Those two would be the first.

To his surprise, however, when he slipped through a rear door and made his way down the corridor, he saw that lamps glowed in Lady Jade Sky's bedchamber. And there she was, offering sacrifice to household gods.

When she heard a sound, and turned to see a shadow on the wall, Jade Sky started to call out for help. But then, to her shock, she saw that the silhouette, moving and shifting in the flickering light of oil lamps, was that of a hunchback.

Yes! A man bent over, his back curved! The fortune-teller's prophecy had come true!

Jade Sky hurried to the door to admit the good-luck man, wondering what it could mean, but deliriously happy that predictions from the prophecy cup did come true, which meant she was indeed carrying a son.

But when the crouching visitor came into the light, she gave him a startled look. "Balám!" She took in his wretched appearance, his filthy body and unkempt hair. "Kaan is out looking for you."

And then she saw the dagger in his hand.

Jade Sky backed away slowly, hands up. "Please," she began. He lunged. The obsidian blade flashed in the torchlight. Jade Sky opened her mouth to scream, but Balám's dirty hand went over her mouth. She twisted in his grasp. Eyes wide with fear, she saw the knife come close. Jade Sky opened her mouth and sank her teeth into his hand. Balám grunted and dropped the knife. She spun away. He grabbed her arm. As she tried to break free, he punched her in the stomach. She folded over, clutching her waist, and staggered away while Balám searched for the knife. Jade Sky knocked over a large urn, sending it crashing noisily to the floor.

"My lady?" a voice called from beyond the doorway.

Balám froze, turned in the direction of the door. When the voice called out again, he dashed from the room.

Tonina parted the hanging and looked in to see Jade Sky on the floor, curled up in a ball. Telling Brave Eagle to fetch help, Tonina ran to the lady's side.

Jade Sky was in too much pain to move. And then Tonina saw the first trickle of blood.

"Help me," Jade Sky whispered. "I am losing my baby. . . ."

Balám had not left the house but hid nearby in shadow. He watched as Tonina called out for help and then dropped to her knees next to Jade Sky, lifting her head into her lap.

Jade Sky struggled to say something.

"I do not understand," Tonina said.

Jade Sky whispered the words again in a tight voice, haltingly.

Tonina recognized only one word: *k'iinaam*, which she knew was Mayan for "agony."

As Balám watched Lady Jade Sky die, a new idea came to him. Let Kaan live, he thought, so that he, too, would know the pain of losing a wife.

As Balám slipped out into the night, Kaan ran in ahead of the servants who had met him at the villa's front entrance to tell him something was wrong with Lady Jade Sky.

Tears streaked Tonina's face as she looked up at him and said, "She must have tripped on the rug. She fell against the urn. . . ."

Kaan dropped to his knees in disbelief.

Brave Eagle and the servants stood silently in the doorway.

He raised haunted eyes to Tonina. "Did she . . . say anything before . . . ?"

Tonina did not understand him. She looked over her shoulder and was relieved to see One Eye pushing his way through. When he joined them, Tonina smelled the alcohol on him, and saw smears of a woman's cosmetic on his neck and face.

Kaan repeated his question, and the dwarf translated, waiting for the response.

Tonina did not want to lie, but she also could not bear to tell Kaan the truth. The people of Pearl Island feared a lingering death and had a custom of dispatching someone who was dying a prolonged death. This way they were sure to enter paradise, otherwise the spirit became confused. And sometimes demons stole the souls of the dying.

Nor could she tell him that his wife's final word was "agony."

"Your wife's death was instant," Tonina said softly. "Lady Jade Sky did not speak. She was not aware she was dying."

Kaan's features twisted in pain, a strangled sound came from his throat. "I should have been here! I might have saved her! This is my fault!"

All in an instant, he knew: The gods were angry that he had agreed to throw the game. Never mind that he had changed his mind, he had agreed to alter the divine plan! Now he was being punished. Worse, Jade Sky had died without benefit of confession, and so her soul and that of their unborn son would disappear forever.

Kaan shot to his feet, blind with pain and anger, and, in front of the startled onlookers, flew into a rage, smashing idols that were supposed to have protected Jade Sky. When Kaan reached for the statue of Kukulcan, Tonina ran to him and seized the effigy before he could dash it to the floor.

A neighbor came running in, wrapped in a cloak. He was Hu Imix, a wealthy lawyer and a good friend of Kaan and Jade Sky. Through open windows and over garden walls, sounds of violence had wakened him. He now looked upon the scene in shock and horror: Jade Sky lying dead in a pool of blood, a dwarf kneeling at her side, smashed idols scattered everywhere, Kaan and the fortune-teller holding Kukulcan between them.

What had happened here?

M ore friends and neighbors arrived, word having traveled swiftly through the elite neighborhood. They found Kaan kneeling beside Jade Sky, rocking back and forth with her body in his arms. There were urgent whisperings in the corridors, and the lawyer Hu Imix sending the villa's chief steward on a swift, official errand, until shortly, city guards arrived in the company of special priests whose duty was to protect the populace from sacrilege and blasphemy. When the servants were questioned, they said that Kaan and the fortune-teller had destroyed the household gods.

It took four men to pry Jade Sky's corpse from Kaan's hold. They dragged him to his feet, and he did not protest as they bound his wrists with rope. But Tonina cried out when they seized her, and she looked imploringly at One Eye, who stood in shock as she, too, was taken away.

They were placed in a holding cage adjacent to the palace. Kaan did not speak, but sat with empty eyes, and Tonina did not understand what was happening because no one translated for her. Outside, a crowd gathered, despite the night, bringing flaming torches to ward off ghosts and evil spirits. When One Eye heard that a tribunal was to be held, he hurried back to the villa, where all was in chaos as the servants feared punishment because they had served a blasphemer.

With Brave Eagle making desperate sounds in his throat, One Eye slipped into the servants' quarters where their possessions were still intact beside their sleeping mats. Rummaging through Tonina's travel pack, he brought out the small pouch of pearls, counted them, and wondered if they would be enough of a bribe to gain him audience in the palace. "The king might listen to me," he said to Brave Eagle. "Maybe I can offer him an arrangement. I am, after all, a one-eyed dwarf. His Exalted Goodness would be a fool not to admit me into his entourage in exchange for Tonina's·freedom. As for Kaan, I don't— What's that?"

He turned toward the doorway, where kitchen staff were talking excitedly. One Eye listened. His eyebrows rose. And then he smiled.

"You can calm yourself, my young friend," he said, patting Brave Eagle on the arm. "I am suddenly in possession of the most valuable information I have ever chanced upon. Information that is going to be very profitable to us."

And then he proceeded to tell Brave Eagle the most astonishing thing.

~ 20 ~

Nothing happened by accident. The Maya believed this most deeply. The cosmos worked according to a divine plan, from the movements of the stars to the bowel movements of a farmer. If anything went awry, it was a sign that the gods were not pleased. And so a problem was analyzed, its cause and solution found, and the gods' appeasement set into motion.

After much deliberation among priests and astrologers, scrutiny of the heavens, and study of ancient texts, the most auspicious day for the tribunal was chosen, to determine the extent of Kaan's crime against the gods, and the necessary appeasement to put the world back into balance.

Everyone was frightened, from the king to the lowliest slave. Sacrilege had taken place. What on earth had happened in the house of the great Kaan? How could such terrible luck befall so worshiped a man? His supporters had still been celebrating the Thirteenth Game victory when the gods had struck down his wife and unborn child. First Balám's unfortunate wife, and then Kaan's. And then Kaan had done the unthinkable: By lashing out at Mayapan's gods and cursing them, he had questioned the divine plan. What did it mean for the people of Mayapan?

Kaan would not speak in his own defense, would not retract his blasphemous words. He stood mute before the public tribunal in the plaza while, beyond the ring of soldiers guarding the proceedings, the populace watched in nervous silence, and the elite club of Nine Brothers wailed and beat their breasts.

"Speak up, man," Hu Imix whispered harshly next to him. Although Mayapan was a theocracy and governed mainly by religious law, there was still a need for secular laws. Hu Imix specialized in cases that did not require the involvement of the gods: inheritance, divorce, property ownership, and personal disputes. Although this was a case involving sacrilege, he had volunteered to be Kaan's advocate. "Recant, and we shall sacrifice a prisoner in your place. The gods will be appeased."

But Kaan remained resolutely silent.

However, when Hu Imix said, "Sacrificing the girl is not enough," Kaan blinked and briefly came out of himself to look at Tonina and murmur, "She did nothing wrong. She is innocent."

But no one cared about the girl. Though she must die, she would be a paltry sacrifice, being of low birth. Noble blood was called for.

His Exalted Goodness, seated on a high throne and dressed in his most dazzling raiment, was displeased. Kaan was Mayapan's best ballplayer. They had already lost Prince Balám—no one even knew where the wretch was. And now Kaan! Unfortunately, the compound where sacrificial victims were housed was currently empty. Mayan rulers made it a practice of regularly capturing and holding members of another city's nobility, for only these could be offered to the gods. So Mayapan must lose Kaan and therefore future ball games.

"Speak up!" Hu Imix hissed one last time, realizing that His Exalted Goodness was being forced into a decision no one wanted.

But the hero ballplayer had retreated within himself, as if already dead.

Judgment was passed and word was sent out into the city: The blaspheming pair were to be sacrificed to the gods.

21

For three days the royal court of Mayapan, the various priestly groups, soldiers, city officials, and persons of note prepared for the holy festival, filling the air within the city walls with scented smoke, the blaring of trumpets, and steady thumping of drums. When all were gathered in the main plaza, and prayers and incense had been offered to Kukulcan, the great procession of royalty and courtiers, nobles and merchants, followed by a ragtag populace, left the city to march sedately through the silent marketplace, through fields that had once been forest, past limestone quarries and farms, to finally set foot upon the wide, flat White Road that led to Chichén Itzá, where the ancient gods of the Maya would receive the souls of the two victims.

Tonina and Kaan were carried on small thrones that rested on the shoulders of specially chosen priests. While Kaan sat as silent and unmoving as a statue, Tonina looked for ways to escape. But she was surrounded by priests and guards.

They made camp that night in a clearing at the side of the road, trekked solemnly all the next day, and arrived by evening at the deserted city where a massive encampment was erected in the ancient plaza that spread below the Pyramid of Kukulcan to the ball court.

Although One Eye had done his best to comfort Brave Eagle, the youth was fraught with worry. Agitated, he could not eat and refused to sleep, but kept looking at the small tent where Tonina was imprisoned. "Do not worry, my mute friend. For the moment, Tonina is unharmed. Say one thing for the Maya, they treat their sacrificial victims well."

One Eye sighed. So well were they treated that men and women of noble blood in distressed circumstances often volunteered for the honor to be sacrificed, in order to escape a life of hardship and to experience, if only for a few days, luxury and ease.

Tonina did not feel she was experiencing luxury. Although women came to dress her hair, massage her body with sweet-smelling oils, and robe her in cotton so soft she barely felt it against her skin, she kept her eyes fixed on the tent opening, covered only by a cloth flap, certain that, at any moment, Brave Eagle and One Eye would burst through to rescue her. She was going to be beheaded, a dishonorable and ignoble death among the people of Pearl Island.

Tonina was not afraid to die. Islanders believed that the soul left the body after death and wandered for a while feeding on mammee apples until it was miraculously carried to Heaven to join other souls. Death was something to look forward to and not to be dreaded. What Tonina feared was not being able to live long enough to fulfill her promise to Grandfather.

I have let them down.

She could not help the tears that streamed down her cheeks, smudging the sacred symbols the attendants had painted on her face. Now that Tonina faced death, life suddenly became more meaningful, more precious. She would give anything to live just one more day among her people . . . to dive one more time, to taste Guama's stew, to sit at Huracan's feet and listen to one more story.

She thought also of Kaan, and could not put from her mind the sight of him kneeling on the floor, weeping as he cradled Jade Sky's body in his arms. I let him down, too, Tonina thought. Jade Sky had asked her to sit guard outside her room for just the one night, and it had ended in tragedy.

22

The next morning began with prayers and dancing, soldiers marching in intricate formation, trumpets blaring, and the great camped populace excitedly getting ready for the ritual.

Finally it was time. Beneath the noon sun, people took their places on the ancient plaza in front of the Kukulcan pyramid, drums struck a steady beat, and the procession set out upon a road called the Sacred Causeway, moving through dense forest, past abandoned dwellings and farms gone to seed. Musicians played lively music and people clapped their hands to alert the gods that a happy event was about to take place. Tonina stumbled along, her legs weak, frequently looking back for rescue that did not seem imminent. Ahead, Kaan walked in the center of a group of elite priests.

The parade emerged through the forest into a large open space ringed with trees. Tonina could not see what occupied the center, but as she was led up a limestone stairway and brought to the top, her eyes widened in astonishment.

They had come to the edge of an enormous sinkhole in the limestone floor of the lowland forest, filled with dark green water spotted with scum and mosquitoes, and the scattered dried leaves of autumn. It looked haunting and forbidding, and Tonina wondered if the beheading was to take place here.

Silence fell. Kaan and Tonina were left to stand side by side on a small outcropping. Tonina scanned the faces of those crowding the lip of the cenote and was shocked to see Kaan's mother there, her mantle over her head as if to hide herself. Tonina looked at Kaan. He, too, had espied his mother and Tonina was astonished to see emotion on his face for the first time since Jade Sky's death. Anger? Disdain? How terrible for the poor woman, to witness her son's dishonorable execution.

Tonina frantically searched for One Eye and Brave Eagle, who she had been so certain would rescue her. But they were nowhere to be seen.

One witness to the human sacrifice, Prince Balám, hid in the trees. In blind despair, he had followed the procession from Mayapan, keeping back, staggering along the White Road like a man possessed. Kaan was to be sacrificed to the gods, which meant his soul would fly straight to the Thirteenth Heaven.

This was not what Balám had intended. He had wanted Kaan to live forever, wretched and bitter, his soul eaten by remorse and guilt.

A lone trumpet sounded. Priests came forward with smoking censers as Tonina and Kaan were solemnly laden with heavy jade ornaments and stone weights. Tonina was puzzled. What had this to do with decapitation? She looked down at the water. Were they to be pushed into the well? That made no sense because all a person had to do was swim to the edge and climb up.

Or did terrible monsters lurk in those dark depths?

Fresh fear broke over her as she slowly drew in deep breaths. Was it the same monster whose bones lay at the bottom of the lagoon? This was worse than beheading. To be torn limb from limb—

She felt a rough hand on her back, and then she and Kaan were pushed.

They tumbled together through open space and hit the water, immediately sinking. Tonina quickly freed herself of the heavy weights and began to swim upward to the surface. But then she saw Kaan thrashing frantically, great bubbles of air exploding from his mouth. Although he had managed to free himself from the weights, Tonina realized in horror that he could not swim. As he sank deeper, she swam down to him and saw, littered on the bottom of the well, the skeletons of countless past victims.

Fear shot through her. The ravenous monster would appear at any moment, swallow them whole, and spit out their bones.

She knew she must reach Kaan before he tried to take in air. She reached for him and pulled him to her. Fixing her mouth over his, she released a small breath from her reserved air, and began to move her legs back and forth to drive herself and Kaan to the surface. But he struggled against her in panic, trying to pull away, to open his mouth and draw in air. She kept her lips on his as her strong legs propelled them upward toward the light.

He went limp in her arms and she was terrified that he had died.

When they broke the surface, Tonina's mouth was still on Kaan's. She held him above the water as she breathed into his lungs, then drew back and compressed his chest with her free hand. Water trickled from his mouth. He hung lifeless in her hold, his eyes closed, face pale. She breathed into him again, mindless of the crowd watching from above, stunned and silent.

When Kaan finally coughed and sputtered, the noise resonated off the limestone walls of the well and was then joined by another noise, the spontaneous roar of the onlookers when they realized that the sacrificial victims had survived.

Tonina gave no thought to what was going to happen next as she swam with her arm under Kaan's chin to the water's edge, to search for natural handholds in the rugged limestone. Before her startled eyes, rope ladders fell, held by sturdy men above, as onlookers cheered and urged them to climb up. Tonina went first, reaching for Kaan, pulling him by his wrist as, by instinct, he clasped the rope rungs and held on. When she reached the top, she was received by shouts of joy, people crowding close to touch her, until One Eye and Brave Eagle pushed through to seize her and pull her away. Tonina was instantly forgotten as it was Kaan whom everyone wanted to honor. His Exalted Goodness strode toward the drenched and breathless Kaan to drape a scarlet mantle around his shoulders and declare him to be blessed by the gods.

Balám fell back into the trees, stunned that Kaan had survived. He was now a greater hero than ever.

23

There is no monster in the cenote," One Eye said as he stirred the campfire embers. It was night and the massive crowd was celebrating beneath the stars above the Kukulcan pyramid. This lucky day would be talked about for years to come.

"That is not what kills the sacrificial victims," the dwarf continued. "The Maya don't swim. At least, the ones who live in inland cities don't. Victims rarely come out of the cenote alive. The Maya are terrified of bodies of water in the first place, and then the victims are weighted down. When they hit the water, they panic and ultimately drown. When I heard that the sacrifice was to take place at Chichén Itzá, that you were to be thrown into the great cenote, I knew you would survive." He grinned. "I placed wagers on your survival. You are an island girl." This last he said with a trace of pride. "I knew you would swim back up. But no one believed me and so they readily accepted my wagers as those of a fool."

Tonina barely listened as she sat close to the fire, bundled in One Eye's spare cloak while her tunic and skirt hung on a post to dry. Her mind was filled with a haunting image: the look on Kaan's face when he was lifted out of the cenote. As One Eye and Brave Eagle had spirited her away, Tonina had glanced back to see Kaan looking at her, and was shocked to see his face dark with fury.

He is angry that I saved his life.

"Tomorrow I shall collect my winnings and we will have a modest fortune," One Eye was saying.

She looked at him. "We?"

He shifted his eyes. "I, um, wagered your pearls. I was going to use them as a bribe," he added hastily. "I thought if I could gain an audience with the king I could strike a deal with him to set you free. And then I overheard the kitchen staff talking about the great cenote at Chichén Itzá. So I used your pearls instead to make wagers on your survival and now we will be comfortable."

Tonina did not care about comfort or winnings as her attention drifted to a large beautiful tent glowing with light. Kaan was, at that moment, the guest of His Exalted Goodness, enjoying a feast. Tonina had not been invited. She did not mind. What did trouble her, however, was that look of rage on Kaan's face. Twice now, she had saved a life, and both times the men she had saved had hated her for it. She combed her fingers through her long, damp hair, trying to sort her tangled thoughts.

Bringing her attention back to One Eye, she said, "Am I free to go to Quatemalan now?"

"Yes, yes," said One Eye, who had new plans of his own.

"I will leave in the morning, then. You do not have to come with me," she added, wishing she could already be on her way to the southern coast, sensing also a vague desire to be alone. But her mind was cloudy. At this late hour, her body ragged with fatigue and the aches of swimming again after so many days out of the sea, after the terror of thinking she was to be beheaded, and then Kaan's reaction to her rescuing him . . . she wanted to be alone and on her destined path once again.

She looked at Brave Eagle, who sat withdrawn and motionless, his golden eyes staring into the fire. One Eye had told her how frantic the boy had been when they had thought she was going to die. Looking at his beautiful features, at the sensuous mouth that was quick to smile, and thinking of what a comfort it was to sleep in his arms at night, she thought: No, I do not wish to travel entirely alone. With Brave Eagle, yes. He so needs taking care of. It will be just the two of us. . . .

But One Eye had every intention of staying close to this girl who had survived the cenote at Chichén Itzá, an extremely rare event. People would pay handsomely just to stand in her lucky shadow. It had also occurred to the wily trader that instead of selling Brave Eagle to hunters or men who collected human oddities—and what proof did he have that the boy was indeed a shape-shifter?—why not try to find the boy's real people, and sell *them* the information of his whereabouts? "I would like to travel with you," One Eye said. "I am curious about this red flower you seek. However, we must return to Mayapan, for I hid your travel pack at Kaan's villa, along with the winnings I gained from the Thirteenth Game victory. And anyway, we will need special supplies for such a trip."

Tonina nodded numbly in agreement. Two days' travel back to Mayapan, a one-night stay in Kaan's villa, and then she would be on the White Road heading south.

T he gods are smiling upon my people once again," the king of Mayapan said expansively.

The royal pavilion was brightly lit with oil lamps while musicians kept up a lively tune, dancers came and went, and platters of food appeared in an endless procession as the fat monarch, his equally fat wife, and his well-fed courtiers stuffed their faces. The center of attention was Kaan, splendidly attired in a jade-encrusted loincloth, vermillion mantle, necklaces and garlands of flowers about his neck, his long hair combed up and high in a handsome jaguar-tail. The girl who had saved his life was forgotten.

But not by Kaan.

Despite the charming distractions within the king's tent—now that Kaan was a widower, young women vied for his attention—he dwelled on the fact that he had gone willingly to the sacrifice, as he no longer wanted to live. But now, because of Tonina, he was still alive, and worse, back in favor with the gods!

The guilt that had burdened him since the night of Jade Sky's death grew. What right had he to enjoy such beneficence while her poor spirit wandered tragically in the realm between Heaven and Hell? He should have been there, protecting her. What had made her wake up and stumble against the urn? If he had been there, he would have summoned the midwives and they might have been able to save her and the baby.

But Kaan had not been there. Jade Sky and their son had died. He hated Tonina for doing this to him, for reviving him so that he must continue to live with this torture.

And yet . . .

Try as he did to focus on the lovely, nearly naked dancers who performed seductive movements for his pleasure, Kaan could not put something else out of his mind: the moment of regaining consciousness on the water's surface, Tonina's arm around him, holding him against her body, her mouth covering his as she breathed life into him. It had been a strangely intimate moment, despite the hundreds of witnesses ringing the cenote above. Some of her facial paint had washed off, giving him a glimpse of what she really looked like. Tonina was not beautiful—not by Mayan standards—but neither was she homely.

There was something else about the girl . . . something he should be considering, beyond the physical and emotional . . . but His Exalted Goodness was not giving him room to think. "We will have a month of celebrations!" the monarch expounded. "One for each day for twenty days! This will become known as the Year of Kaan. It will be recorded in the . . ."

Kaan rubbed his temples and turned a deaf ear to His Exalted Goodness. Tonina flitted at the edge of his mind, as if she herself were trying to get a word in, to tell him something. But Kaan's mind was too confused. He had almost died and now he was alive.

"Why did you not speak up in your own defense at the tribunal?" the king asked. "Had you publicly recanted, and then offered a blood sacrifice to the gods, you might not have had to suffer drowning in the cenote." The king popped a plump red berry into his mouth and munched juicily. "Losing a wife and child is tragic, but why curse the gods? I am curious."

Kaan finally spoke. "Jade Sky did not live long enough to confess her sins. Not," he sighed, "that I suppose she had many, she led such a virtuous life. But the prayer of confession was not spoken, and so she is denied Heaven. That is why I was angry with the gods."

His Exalted Goodness shrugged in a dismissive way. "Then why not make the pilgrimage to Teotihuacan and ask the holy sisters there to pray for the resurrection of her soul?"

Kaan stared at his king. "The City of the Gods? It *exists*? But I had thought it was only a myth!"

"The city exists, my friend. In truth, Teotihuacan lies in ruins, for the gods departed many generations ago. But they say the spirits of the gods still reside there."

Kaan blinked at His Exalted Goodness. Then he sat up, disengaging himself from two lovely females. "It is true?" he said, animated for the first time since the night of the tragedy. "I can save Jade Sky's soul?"

"Of course. I know of men who have made the pilgrimage. It is not an easy one, mind. There are bloodthirsty tribes between Mayapan and the City of the Gods. Mountains, hellish jungles and ferocious beasts, mythical creatures and much strange magic. But if you make it to Teotihuacan and perform the requisite ritual, Jade Sky's soul will be resurrected. However," the king cautioned, "you must not waste time. As you know, the spirits of the dead roam the nether realm for only a short time and then they vanish forever."

"How long do I have?"

"You must use the *tzolkin* calendar of nine months," the king said, referring to the most sacred of Mayan measurements of time. "Calculate from the moment of your wife's death two hundred and sixty days. That is the amount of time you have."

"Nine months, like a pregnancy," Kaan murmured.

"Just so! Because your wife died unconfessed, her soul cannot be resurrected without a period of gestation so that she can be reborn sinless in Heaven. In the City of the Gods you must seek out the Sisterhood of Souls, priestesses who are dedicated to the salvation of unconfessed sinners. They have an ancient holy shrine in the Temple of the Moon. And they are the only ones who can intercede on behalf of the unconfessed dead."

"I will succeed!" Kaan said with passion, suddenly filled with purpose again. "I shall set out at once for Teotihuacan. I will enter the city in a manner that will honor the gods, with slaves and attendants—"

The king held up a finger. "You must go alone."

"Alone?"

"No servants, no guards, no companions. Otherwise, what have you proven to the gods? You must endure solitude and hardship to prove your worth."

Kaan frowned. He had never been alone in his life. Even back before he was a wealthy ballplayer, when he lived with his mother in the palace kitchen, Kaan had always been surrounded by people. After he had moved into the ballplayer academy, he lived in the constant company of trainers, servants, teammates. The only time he had been alone was in the sweat bath. He did not relish the idea of being alone.

❧ 24 ❧

The three were in the busy marketplace purchasing supplies for
their journey.

As soon as they arrived in Mayapan, Tonina had gone directly to the
villa to collect her buried possessions. She had seen Kaan carried tri-
umphantly into the city and straight to the palace, where a celebration
was to take place. She had not been invited, nor had she wished to be.
She was in a hurry to strike for the southern coast.

While Tonina was perusing ladies' cloaks and One Eye was haggling
over the price of a pair of sandals, Brave Eagle discreetly separated himself from his two companions, slipping through the crowd to be gone before his friends knew it.

On the night Kaan and Tonina were arrested, quick-thinking One Eye
had had the wits to hide her travel pack. Brave Eagle now crept through
the villa's garden to the small stone statue of a god beneath a pepper tree,
and, moving the idol, found the secret cache. He removed only one item:
the glass cup of prophecy. Replacing the statue, he hurried back into the
house, making sure he was not seen.

Brave Eagle was not impelled by clear thought but rather by inchoate
emotions, fragments of dream-memories, and a growing urgency to join
his people. The youth did not question the compulsion to come here and
perform this inexplicable task, accepting it as something he must do.

Inside the villa, the setting sun sent pillars of golden light slanting into
spacious rooms where servants were busy cleaning, tidying, getting ready
for the return of their hero master. Brave Eagle found Kaan's bedroom. It
had already been cleaned and decorated with flowers in readiness for its
master's return. There he placed the glass cup, in the center of Kaan's

sleeping mat, so that it would not be overlooked. Brave Eagle left then and returned to the marketplace, where Tonina and One Eye had not noticed his absence.

The endless rituals and chants over, the censers empty of incense, the trumpets silenced and the priests retired to the inner precincts of the temple, Kaan was finally allowed to go home. He approached the villa with a heavy heart. He did not want to go inside, where painful memories awaited.

The moment he set foot through the door, the servants and slaves came running, throwing themselves at his feet and blessing the day that brought their lord home. As everyone clustered around him, following him from the villa's front entry to his bedroom in the rear, touching the edge of his richly colored mantle for luck, Kaan wondered if he would ever have peace of mind again. He had a thrumming headache and all he wanted to do was sleep, and be on the road northward to Teotihuacan by dawn.

But a sacred duty called.

With wooden feet he approached Jade Sky's bedchamber and swallowed painfully before parting the heavy drape over the doorway.

He scanned the spotless chamber, where servants had taken care to restore order. He saw the baskets of feathers, the unfinished bracelets with tender little bird tufts sewn on, the threads and sewing thorns waiting for their creator to return and take them up again.

He looked at the spot on the stone floor where her blood had flowed. Someone had thoughtfully placed a small rug over it. Jade Sky's death seemed to have happened so long ago. Her body had been cremated at Kaan's request. The lawyer Hu Imix had seen to it. The urn containing her ashes had been placed in a special vault beneath the Pyramid of Kukulcan, as was her right, and although it was certain that Kaan would die in the cenote sacrifice, Hu Imix had had the foresight to cut a small lock of Jade Sky's hair before the cremation, just in case. He had given the lock to Kaan at the celebration this evening. It was all Kaan had left of her.

He could not breathe. As if he were drowning again, his chest tightened, the room swam. Reaching for the door frame, he steadied himself. Jade Sky was dead. Their son was dead. He sobbed, and covered his face with his hands.

When he was able, he withdrew from the doorway, letting the tapestry fall into place, and he knew that never again would he set foot in this room, that it would remain untouched and unchanged for as long as he lived.

Focusing his thoughts on Teotihuacan and the hope of resurrecting Jade Sky's soul, Kaan walked now with purpose to his own bedchamber. Here, he sorted through his possessions, deciding what he would take on his solitary journey, what he would leave behind. Consulting with priests about the pilgrimage to Teotihuacan had confirmed what His Exalted Goodness had said: that he must go alone to the City of the Gods—no servants, friends, or guards—and that for the sake of the resurrection of Jade Sky's soul, he must reach Teotihuacan before the fiftieth day after the next summer solstice.

He stopped and stared at his sleeping mat. An object had been placed there.

The transparent goblet of prophecy.

He frowned. What was it doing here?

Suddenly furious—was the island girl mocking him?—Kaan carried the cup through the house to the servants' quarters, where he found Tonina and her two friends preparing travel packs with purchases from the marketplace.

"How did this get into my room?" he demanded of One Eye.

The dwarf spun around so fast he almost fell over. When he saw the object in Kaan's hand, he stammered, "I, um . . . my lord, I—"

"Why was this in my bedchamber?" Kaan repeated in his characteristic low voice that was nonetheless filled with meaning.

Tonina gave Kaan a studied look. There was the fury again, in his tone and darkening his handsome features. And once again she thought: He hates me for saving his life.

And then she saw what he was holding. "How did you get that?"

He looked at her outstretched hand and memories flashed in his mind: Jade Sky's head cradled in this girl's lap, those same hands pulling him up from the depths of the cenote, her mouth on his—

He relinquished the goblet and said to One Eye, "Who put the prophecy cup in my private room?"

"My lord, I swear upon the bones of my great-grandfather, I do not know." Like all members of his tribe, One Eye wore around his neck a small leather pouch containing the relics of an ancestor. In his case, they were the bones of a distant grandfather, and they possessed strong magic.

Tonina carefully wrapped the glass in a spare tunic and skirt, and tucked it into her travel pack, already crammed with supplies.

Kaan frowned. "You are leaving?"

Tonina had hoped their paths would not cross. Now that he was here, standing tall and imposing in the doorway, she felt a chaos of emotions wash over her. "I leave Mayapan in the morning," she said, understanding his words and so not needing One Eye to translate.

As Kaan watched her, the flitting thought returned, the elusive something that had nagged at him in the king's tent and that he had forgotten when His Exalted Goodness had told him about Teotihuacan. But it was coming back now, and starting to coalesce into a clear thought.

Tonina turned to face him and Kaan stared at her, taking in the curious white symbols hiding her features, and remembering. She had been here that night. It was she who had been Jade Sky's companion in her final hour. *It was she who had stopped him from destroying the statue of Kukulcan, Jade Sky's personal god.*

And suddenly—

Kaan raised his hand to his chest and fell back a step. A gasp, a look of shock, and then without another word, he turned abruptly and left.

Inside the dark, smoky chamber within the Temple of Kukulcan, the ancient priest nodded. "You are right, my son. It is one of our most ancient laws. It is written in our holiest of books. As you can see here." A knobby finger with a long black nail tapped the yellowed page upon which faded glyphs had been painted.

Kaan's suspicion was confirmed, what he had been trying to grasp immediately after his rescue from the cenote: the ancient spiritual law regarding the saving of lives.

"But His Exalted Goodness told me it was the *gods* who saved my life," Kaan argued now, dreading what this new revelation portended, "that the girl was merely their instrument."

"True," creaked the ancient voice. "But you are still bound to her. It is a sacred tie that cannot be broken until balance is achieved. A life for a life, my son. The girl saved yours, now you must save hers. If you do not, the world is out of balance, which can bring bad luck not only to yourself but to the city."

"What must I do?" Kaan asked in a tight voice, hoping the aged holy man would offer a swift solution, such as giving the girl money, or granting her any wish—a surrogate "life saving" similar to the surrogate victims used in blood sacrifice.

But the priest said, "You must do as she did for you. When she is in peril, or on the brink of death, you must bring her back. Nothing else will do. And until you save her life and restore balance, you and she are bound mortally and spiritually upon this earth."

Kaan was horrified. To be shackled to the island girl! In a last, desperate attempt to be absolved from this covenant, Kaan explained to the priest about his journey to Teotihuacan, adding, "His Exalted Goodness told me I must make this journey alone."

The old head, weighted by a feathered headdress, nodded. "That is true. The man who travels to the City of the Gods with well-armed soldiers and in the comfort of servants and slaves has not made a true sacrifice. You must be alone. But the girl is part of you, my son, and therefore her accompanying you is not only permitted, it is required. Until balance has been restored."

Kaan was gripped with panic. He did not want to be bound to the girl. She reminded him of the night Jade Sky died. She reminded him of other things, too, although what they were he could not say. From the first moment he had set eyes upon the fortune-teller, days ago when he and Balám were walking through the outer marketplace and Kaan had seen the tall, honey-skinned girl with island tattoos, she had haunted his thoughts in a way no other woman had.

The idea of taking her with him was unsupportable.

Yet the gods decreed that he must.

The priest's eyes were small and nearly hidden beneath folds of skin, but they were sharp and glinted with intelligence. In a voice that sounded like rustling dry leaves, he said, "You had forgotten this, Kaan. Had you gone to Teotihuacan without the girl, disaster would have befallen you. Remembering this sacred duty is proof that your good luck continues."

Kaan marveled at the way the gods worked, for surely it was by a supernatural hand that the transparent cup of prophecy had materialized in his bedchamber, as it had sent him to Tonina so that he would remember his sacred duty to save her life.

He sighed. Very well. He would take her with him. But that did not mean they would interact. He would establish rules. And they would travel swiftly. As he thought of the perils along the way that His Exalted Goodness had described, Kaan drew comfort from the fact that, if the gods were indeed with him, he would save her life after only a few days of journey, and be rid of her to continue on alone to Teotihuacan.

❦ 25 ❦

Tonina awoke with a start.

Blinking in the darkness, she tried to discern what had wakened her. And then she realized she was alone on the sleeping mat. Brave Eagle was not there.

She sat up and looked around. The household staff slumbered and snored beneath mantles and night, crowded together in the villa's dormitory. She saw One Eye asleep in the arms of a plump laundress.

"Tonina . . ."

A whisper. A voice she did not recognize.

"Tonina, come here. . . ."

Rising from her mat, she stepped over snoozing slaves and servants, passed through the door that opened onto a vegetable garden, and saw a man standing in the moonlight. He looked familiar. His body was draped in a magnificent feathered cloak—white on the shoulders, and black the rest of the way to the ground.

"Brave Eagle?" she said as she stepped closer, feeling the night breeze chill her flesh.

He held his hands out to her.

Close up, he looked different, older, his face matured with lines, and a thick brow over his golden irises. "I must say good-bye now," he said.

"You have found your voice!"

"I was asleep," he said. "I was dreaming, and I dreamed that my voice returned to my throat. I woke up and came out here, to listen to the wind."

"But . . . you look so different! What happened?" Even as she studied his face, the features shifted and changed subtly, as if the hand of an invisible sculptor were busily at work.

"My memory came back," he said with a smile. "It has all come back to me. I remember who I am, Tonina, who my people are, where my home lies. And I know now that it is time for me to leave. I can go no further with you."

"But who are you? Where do you live, who are your people?"

His face glowed in the moonlight, his cheekbones moved, changed. The brows grew heavy. "I cannot tell you everything, Tonina. But I can say that my home is far from here, high in the mountains. I was brought here for a purpose, and now it is time for me to go."

"Why?" she implored, her hands still in his as she squeezed his fingers, not wanting to let go. Her feelings for him ran deep. Not in a romantic way, but in the way, she suspected, that sisters felt toward brothers. He had been so helpless, and she had taken care of him.

"I cannot tell you. But you will understand, someday." He smiled gently. "You took very good care of me, Tonina, but I do not need looking after anymore."

She frowned. He no longer bore any resemblance to young Brave Eagle. He was now a man. But even then . . . Not quite a man, but continuing to change, his face sharpening, his shoulders narrowing, the feathered cape quivering. Tonina sensed the enchantment of the moment.

"I thank you, Tonina, for rescuing me from the hunters, and for this I will be eternally grateful. Do not fear, you will see me again. When you are most in need, I will come."

He released her hands and spread out his arms, the feathered cloak shimmering in the moonlight. Tonina watched spellbound as he slowly vanished, disappearing before her eyes. She searched the garden and saw that she was alone. And then she saw an eagle overhead, magnificent wings spread wide as it wheeled against the stars, crying *scree scree* until it flew up toward the moon and was gone.

Tonia stared up in dismay until she saw something drift down and land at her feet. She bent to pick it up, and saw that it was the blue healing feather Jade Sky had given to Brave Eagle.

❧ 26 ❧

One Eye came in as she was arranging her travel pack.

"We will be needing these," he said, setting the walking staffs down. "The whole city is talking about Kaan. They say he, too, is leaving Mayapan. Making a holy pilgrimage to a city far in the north. By himself, the rumor is. No servants. No guards. I was thinking, Tonina, that since we can afford a guard or two, you and Brave Eagle and I would benefit—"

She turned to him and said, "Brave Eagle is gone." Her throat tightened. She had awakened that morning to find herself alone on the sleeping mat, with the blue feather where Brave Eagle had slept. Not even a proper good-bye. Although . . . had he spoken to her while she slept? She seemed to remember a dream. . . . *"Do not fear, you will see me again. When you are most in need, I will come."*

One Eye was not surprised. He had kept quiet about his secret belief that Brave Eagle was a shape-shifter. Now his suspicion was confirmed. Such beings, everyone knew, belonged in a mystical realm and only walked among humans for brief periods, and for special reasons. Perhaps Brave Eagle had been a messenger. They might never know.

"I thank you for your help," Tonina said in a tight voice, not wanting to prolong the good-bye. "You were kind to me when I needed it. I shall be always grateful to you. But I must travel on my own from now on."

One Eye wrinkled his nose. "What are you talking about?"

"I must go to Quatemalan by myself."

"You mean, without me?" His one eye goggled her. "Are you mad? A girl traveling alone?"

Tonina could not explain it; she had no words to describe how Brave Eagle's departure had affected her—the feelings of sadness and disappointment, and even a trace of anger, a sense of betrayal. So she said, "I have been on my own since the day I was set upon the sea in an ark of reeds. Though Guama and Huracan loved me, I was not of their blood. I have belonged to no one, only myself. Dear One Eye, you have been good to me and I bless you, for what it is worth."

One Eye panicked. He could not let this happen. He had *plans*. "But who will translate for you?"

"I have learned much Mayan already, and will learn more along the way."

He nodded sadly. "Yes, I believe you will. At least let me travel with you part of the road." But when he saw the resolute look on her face, he silently cursed all strong-minded women and said, "Very well." Although his plans would need to be adjusted, One Eye prided himself on being resilient.

And then, in the next instant, his stocky malformed body was struck by such a new and unfamiliar emotion that he was physically jolted.

He did not want to be parted from Tonina.

The island trader had never married, but he had known the pleasure of many women. He might say he had never loved, or that he had loved a thousand times. But this new emotion shocked him even as the words formed in his mind, although he did not voice them out loud: *I* would never leave you.

"I am sorry we must part, but I understand," he said with a heavy heart. "Tonina, dear girl, I hope you find the magic flower, and I pray that you make your way back home to Pearl Island. I ask Lokono to bless you in the hope that perhaps we shall meet again someday."

Gathering his two travel packs and a walking staff, and the small pouches of his winnings, which formed a modest fortune, the dwarf dramatically dashed an imagined tear from his single eye, sniffed, then turned and walked away with as much dignity as his ungainly gait would allow.

As Tonina resumed packing, she fought the impulse to call him back. She knew that saying good-bye to him now would be less painful than to find him gone, as had happened with Brave Eagle, leaving her abandoned once again. She was thinking of Macu's betrayal—attacking her canoe when she had thought he had marriage on his mind—and wondering if this was to be her lot in life when she heard One Eye return, clearing his throat as he stepped back into the room.

"Have you forgotten something?" she said, and, turning, was startled to see Kaan standing with him in the doorway, dressed in a plain white traveling cloak. The long hair swept up and tied neatly on the top of his head in a jaguar-tail added height to his already imposing stature.

"The great Kaan wishes me to tell you something," One Eye said.

She looked at Kaan expectantly. His plain appearance mystified her. His loincloth and mantle were like those of a peasant, his arms and ankles were bare of adornment, his earrings were gone. Kaan spoke to One Eye in Mayan, and then the trader said to Tonina, "The great Kaan says you are to go with him."

She looked at the dwarf, then at the hero of Mayapan. "Go with him where?"

A brief exchange between One Eye and Kaan, and then: "A journey westward and northward. He says you both are to depart at once."

When Kaan made to leave, Tonina said in Mayan, "Wait! I do not understand."

Kaan turned to face her, mildly surprised at her use of his language. He spoke to One Eye, who said to Tonina, "The gods have decreed that you are to travel with him."

"The gods! But why?"

Making a sound of exasperation, the dwarf said, "I think it has to do with their obsession with keeping the world in balance. When a Mayan saves the life of another, the other is then committed to his rescuer until *his* life is saved. A life for a life. Balance. You saved his life so I suppose you must stay with him until he saves yours."

Tonina wondered if the Maya had more laws than there were stars in the heavens. "Please tell him he is free to go. I do not hold him to any obligation to me."

One Eye translated for Kaan, who looked at Tonina in frank perplexity.

"Did you tell him what I said?" Tonina asked.

"I did, but he can't believe you are not going with him. He is the great Kaan and he is used to people obeying his wishes. He also cannot imagine that you have a plan of your own. To him, you are an itinerant fortune-teller who roams the land in search of opportunity. You are also just a female, and I believe he expected you to be eager to join him."

She gave Kaan a thoughtful look, recalling the night of Jade Sky's death, recalling also their dramatic moments together in the cenote—intimate moments that had bound them together. "Why is he going on this journey?" she asked, wondering why Kaan, now a bigger hero than ever, would leave a city that worshiped him like a god.

"I know only that it is to be a holy pilgrimage to the City of the Gods, far in the northwest."

"And *I* must travel south," she said crisply.

Kaan did not need the dwarf to translate. Tonina's attitude was clear: She was refusing to go with him. He was both surprised and puzzled. When he asked One Eye the reasons for her refusal, and was told she was on an urgent, personal errand in Quatemalan—to find a flower—his puzzlement deepened. She was not just an itinerant entertainer looking for a free meal? Then why had she performed in the Grand Hall with the dancers and musicians?

Kaan briefly considered forcing her to go with him. But how? Certainly kidnapping would be offensive to the gods. And without personal assistants or guards he could never keep an eye on her. He instructed One Eye to tell her again that she must go with him, emphasizing that this was something the gods had decreed and that she would be free to search for the flower after they reached Teotihuacan.

Growing impatient with the awkward three-way conversation, Tonina said to One Eye, "How do I say 'I must go my own way' in Mayan?"

One Eye told her and she repeated it to Kaan, who, though impressed, nonetheless reiterated his insistence that she go with him. Kaan was growing anxious to be on his way. "Tell her that after we reach Teotihuacan in the north, she will be free to travel south."

By now Tonina had memorized the words that One Eye had been saying, and so she said directly to Kaan in Mayan, "I cannot go with you. I must go south. It is *my* gods whom I must obey."

"My lord," One Eye interjected, sensing that a stalemate had been reached, and suddenly also seeing an opportunity to serve his own purposes—traveling with so famous a hero could be profitable, "if I may make a suggestion? The way to Quatemalan is fraught with risks and dangers. Should you travel with the girl and see that she arrives safely at the southern coast, surely the gods will regard this as a life-saving act."

But Kaan said, "No, she is to come with me."

One Eye's mind raced. He knew now that he wanted to stay with Tonina, and that the only way to achieve this was to have Kaan travel with her, for they would need a translator. Since Tonina would never go with Kaan, One Eye had to persuade the hero ballplayer to go with the girl. Sorting through the facts he knew about this man, and remembering that although Kaan himself was not deeply religious, he had high regard for those who were, and most especially that Kaan lived by a code of honor, One Eye said, "You need to know, my lord, that she must reach the coast very soon." He explained about Huracan and his sickness, and the magical red flower, and how it would save her people. One Eye added, "She spoke a sacred oath. She is bound to honor it."

Kaan stared at the dwarf. The girl was on a holy quest? He had assumed she was in a hurry to be on women's business, such as a dying mother, or a pregnant sister soon to deliver—the usual reasons most women traveled. But a holy quest was something else. And One Eye had spoken of honor.

Kaan retreated into thought. He would never forget his wife's cry of delight when this girl had told Jade Sky that she was to have a son. This girl had brought happiness to his wife, who had despaired of ever having children.

And now he had learned she was on a sacred errand, as was he. But his lay in the north, hers in the south.

Kaan understood now why dwarfs were considered wise, for what the little man said about the journey to Quatemalan made good sense, that in delivering the girl safely into the care of her own gods, Kaan's bond with her would be broken. Working rapid calculations in his mind, Kaan determined that he could get her to Quatemalan and still have time to turn north and reach Teotihuacan before the next summer solstice.

"Very well," he said at last. "Tell her that I will take her to Quatemalan."

To his surprise, Tonina said no, that she wished to journey alone. He stared at her. Why would anyone *choose* to be alone?

One Eye was also surprised by her response. "Why did you say no?"

Tonina could not explain it to herself, let alone to these two men. It had to do with Kaan and her fear of him, or rather something within herself that she feared.

One Eye said unhappily to Kaan, "She will not even let *me* go with her, my lord, and I am her oldest friend."

"You would go alone?" Kaan asked Tonina. "You are not afraid?" He had never known a woman brave enough to willingly travel by herself.

With a calm she did not feel, Tonina said, "I made a promise and I intend to honor it."

Kaan retreated into thought again—honor was something he understood—and made another quick evaluation of this girl who he had thought was an opportunist. Not only brave, but loyal to a promise.

He studied her as she bent over her travel pack, rearranging the items within, her hair clicking with the many small shells threaded in the long locks. The sound annoyed him. And she gave off the scent of coconut— not unpleasant, just different. He did not relish traveling with her. But he had no choice. "What do you want?" he finally asked.

When she gave him a blank look, he held out his arms and said, "I am a wealthy man. I can give you whatever you want if you will come with me to Teotihuacan."

"I want only to go home," she said.

Realizing that fear and bribery were not going to influence her, Kaan said, "It is decided then. *I* shall go with *you*."

When she persisted in saying no, One Eye did some rapid thinking. Knowing what he knew of the girl, that she was one of those naïve women who placed the welfare of others before her own, he told her more of the nature of Kaan's pilgrimage. To pray for his wife's soul.

Tonina gave Kaan a startled look. She had thought his journey was for selfish reasons. And then she understood: Jade Sky was murdered. There was, no doubt, a Mayan ritual that must be conducted to remove the bad luck from so heinous a deed.

Finally, remembering the blue feather and Jade Sky's kindness to Brave Eagle, Tonina said, "Very well, he can come with me to Quatemalan."

"It is agreed, my lord," One Eye said as he cheerfully rubbed his stubby hands together. "I know some good roads, and I have friends along the way for I am known far and wide—"

"No," Kaan said. "The girl and I must go alone."

"But my lord," One Eye began, suddenly panicking.

"The gods have decreed it," Kaan said, and, without another word, strode away.

They did not speak as they left the villa, wearing traveling cloaks and sturdy sandals, and shouldering their packs. They pushed through the crowd of adorers and good-luck seekers who had gathered in the outer lane, and headed in the direction of the city gates.

Tonina was glad One Eye was not permitted to travel with them. Without a translator, there would be little for her and Kaan to say. They would journey silently through forest and village, along roads and fields until they reached her destination. She would not think of the man who walked at her side, but keep her thoughts on finding the flower and then sailing home. Once in Quatemalan, she would tell him that he had saved her life, she would declare it out loud so that his gods would hear and be satisfied, and then watch him go his own way.

Kaan was also relieved that the dwarf was not to travel with them. Without him to translate, Kaan would be under no obligation to talk to the girl. As they made their way wordlessly across the peninsula until they arrived at the coast, he would not even think about the girl sitting across the campfire, but keep his focus on reaching Teotihuacan and rescuing Jade Sky's soul. And when they arrived in Quatemalan, Kaan would make sacrifice to his gods and let them know he had escorted the girl through hazard and peril, and that the world was in balance again.

From the end of the lane they crossed the congested plaza, ignoring the throng that wanted to touch their hems. When they arrived at the street that led out of Mayapan, Kaan paused and turned toward the palace, blinding red in the noon sun. With no explanation to Tonina, he struck off in that direction. She hurried after him, wondering about the sudden, urgent errand.

The guards at a rear entrance took one look at Kaan and stepped aside, bowing formally as he and the girl passed. Tonina had decided he must want to say farewell to the king, but Kaan turned away from the direction where Tonina knew the Grand Hall and royal apartments were located to follow instead a narrow corridor that led to delicious cooking aromas.

She knew before they arrived that here was the vast kitchen of the royal residence of Mayapan. And then she remembered: His mother worked here, the mother he was ashamed of.

What was the root of that shame? Tonina wondered. Her lowly station in life? Why had he not elevated her when he became a hero? Or was it her bloodline, because that was something he could never change?

Tonina did not need to be told to stay back while he dropped his travel pack by her feet and strode into the kitchen. Instantly, the place fell silent as all work ceased, the servants and slaves staring open-mouthed as the most famous man in Mayapan materialized in their humble midst.

Tonina watched, deciphering body language, the visible emotions, and the few Mayan words she could pick out, to put them together with what she already knew about Kaan and his mother. The woman was dismayed to see him there; she waved her hands, turning away. But then Kaan said please, holding his hands out as if he were a supplicant. And Tonina realized that Kaan wanted to go to her, but that *she* was turning her back.

One Eye had said Kaan was ashamed of his bloodline, and Tonina had assumed that he was ashamed of his mother also. But it seemed now that he was not. He embraced her in front of all the people in the kitchen, holding her to him and speaking endearments until she softened against him, called him "Son," and wept against his chest.

Tonina watched in confusion. Had the estrangement come from *her*? Perhaps for her son's sake, so that his Mayan friends and admirers would not be reminded of his lowly blood? The mother appeared to be proud of her son, the way she now beamed up at him with a brilliant smile, stroking his cheek. And when she turned to the others in the kitchen, telling them that this was *her* boy, the mother turned into a proud woman herself, tall and straight with head held high, not the humble creature Tonina had seen hurry away from the villa's garden.

She wondered now about the emotions she had seen on Kaan's face on those prior occasions when he had looked at his mother, wondered if she had misread them, because he wore the same expression now, but Tonina saw no disgust or shame there, but a private agony and a deep longing.

She was stunned. How wrong she had been! The mother had made the self-sacrifice so that her son could have a good life. The son had tried to obey, but ultimately he could not. And when he dropped now to his knees to weep into his mother's apron, Tonina fell back against the wall, breathless and overcome, unable to witness more.

When Kaan had entered the kitchen and reached for his mother, unaware of Tonina's observance of this reunion, and oblivious to all who watched them, he had said, "Do not spurn me now, for there is no longer a reason for the charade. I am leaving Mayapan and do not know when I will return. Grant me this one embrace."

His mother had turned tear-filled eyes to him, this humble woman who had begged him to reject her—out of great love for him, he knew, knowing that it would embarrass him, perhaps even hamper his rise in society if people were reminded of his blood. It had been her idea that he dress Mayan, marry a Mayan woman, and live according to Mayan ways. Because of this, people could overlook his difference in appearance—his tallness among the Maya, his sharper facial features—and embrace him as a beloved hero.

But at what cost?

He recalled the morning she had come to the villa after hearing the news of Jade Sky's pregnancy. He had been overjoyed to see her, but she would not speak to him, would not step inside the house, had turned and hurried away.

And now she was grieving because she had lost a grandchild.

"Dearest Mother, you ordered me to stay away from you," he said now as he gathered her into an embrace. "You made me promise against my will. I can no longer honor your wishes. I ache for your love and your blessing. And your forgiveness, for I have caused my brother's death. All the city is saying Balám has killed himself. I am to blame!"

She stroked his head and murmured, "It was not your fault. Balám tried to cheat the gods."

"I am leaving Mayapan and I do not know when or if I shall ever return." He fell to his knees and embraced her, weeping against the coarse cloth of her apron. "I must go to Teotihuacan. I cannot go without your blessing."

She gently laid her rough hands on his head. Tears rolled down her cheeks and splashed onto his black hair. "My days are numbered, my son. Be content to know that I will die happy and at peace, for I saw how the gods cast their good luck upon you."

"You are dying?" he cried, shooting to his feet. "Then I will not go! My place is at your side!"

"No, my son. Your duty is to your wife and child, to see that they reach Heaven. I have made my peace with the gods. And if they grant, perhaps someday you and I shall be together again."

Hearing these words, and understanding them, Tonina drew away from the door and backed away down the corridor, unable to hear more. She felt a strange new ache in her heart—not for the arms and love of Guama and Huracan, but for a woman who had no face, no substance, the woman who had carried Tonina in her womb and given her life, and who had possibly been the one to set Tonina on the sea in a tiny ark.

For the first time in her life, Tonina wanted to know her mother.

Finally, Kaan came from the kitchen, his features stonelike, unreadable. Without a word he picked up his travel pack, and Tonina did the same, and they made their way through the crowded city until they arrived at the main gate. The sun stood high overhead. A crowd cheered and waved good-bye.

They stepped through the gates, Kaan the hero ballplayer and Tonina the island pearl diver, from two different worlds, facing two different destinies, each guided by personal talismans: Kaan, the lock of his wife's hair, and Tonina, the medallion she had worn since birth.

W atching them go was a man with a filthy mantle drawn over his head to conceal his identity—Prince Balám, the most wretched man on earth. A prince with no kingdom, no wife or daughter, no property, no wealth, and worst of all: no honor.

As he watched Kaan and Tonina blend into the marketplace crowd beyond the city walls, Balám pictured his precious daughter being taken away from the slave block, to be delivered into the hands of a stranger.

Balám staggered away from the wall and fell to his knees, sweating so copiously that he thought blood must have sprouted on his forehead. "The gods be my witness," he whispered with bile in his throat. "Kaan will pay. The island girl will pay. They will pay and pay, and then pay some more."

BOOK

TWO

～ 28 ～

Too late, Kaan realized he had made a mistake.

Not yet a full day out of Mayapan, and already he was regretting his decision to travel with Tonina to Quatemalan.

As he strode ahead through the dry forest, maintaining a distance from her, he tried not to think about the island girl walking behind him, but her long hair, strung from crown to ends with tiny shells so that it clicked whenever she moved, constantly reminded him of her presence. He did not like it. Mayan ladies did not draw attention to themselves by making noise with their hair.

As he plunged through trees and hacked a path with his knife, Kaan wished they could follow the White Road, which would make traveling easier and faster. But that morning, even in common attire, Kaan had been recognized and accosted by people wanting his good luck. So he had turned off the cement highway and delivered himself into the woods, Tonina following. There were farms and encampments there, too, where people called out and waved to the hero, but after a while human habitation thinned until the two traipsed through virgin wilderness.

Now it was sunset and Kaan pressed on despite the coming darkness, unaware that, behind him, Tonina was sharing his sentiments: She wished she had not agreed to let him accompany her.

He had taken the lead from the start, deciding which way they would go. Tonina wanted to make her own decisions. Now, when she called for him to stop, he ignored her. Finally she announced, "I am tired," in Mayan, and without waiting for a response, stopped where she was, dropped her travel pack, and surveyed the woods.

Kaan turned in surprise. They could continue for another good distance before needing to stop, but he saw that she was already clearing a place for a campfire. In irritation he dropped his packs and weapons. Having no desire for her company, he found a spot for himself and prepared to settle in for the night. They were far from the road, far from the camps of other travelers, with tree branches for shelter and plenty of dried wood to burn.

Tonina fashioned a circle of stones in the dirt and, using a fire-starter kit Guama had packed in her bag, soon had flames sending sparks to the stars.

Kaan, on the other hand, discovered that he had no idea how to start a fire. When he had packed for the journey, it had not occurred to him to prepare for this contingency. Cook fires had been ubiquitous in his life. He had never needed to start a fire on his own. He looked at Tonina in annoyance. He wasn't about to ask her for help. So he created a small circle of stones, filled it with bits and pieces of wood and dried brush, and labored with two rocks to create a spark.

Darkness fell, the forest came alive with sounds, and only one circle of stones glowed with light. Tonina considered inviting Kaan to share her fire, but she did not want his company, so she lit a twig and wordlessly came over to set it upon his small pile of kindling. As he watched her fan flames to life, annoying him with the sounds the many shells made in her long hair, Kaan wondered if the gods had not forgiven him after all, if perhaps *this* was his punishment for blaspheming.

Tonina returned to her own fire and the two ate separately and in silence, munching on food they had purchased in the marketplace: turkey eggs, deer meat, and salted sunflower seeds. Food and water would not be a problem for now. But both knew that beyond Uxmal lay unknown territory.

Tonina glanced over at Kaan to see his face illuminated in the fire's glow. He had a powerful profile—high forehead, strong jaw, large nose. Not the prominent nose of the Maya, enhanced with a clay appliance, but arrow-straight and forceful. Kaan's cheekbones were high, his cheeks sharply etched hollows. Tonina was stunned to find herself thinking how attractive he was. Stunned because Kaan was not at all good-looking— how could he be, when she had been raised to think of the round, soft faces of the islanders as the ideal of attractiveness? Yet she was thinking it all the same, and this puzzled her.

Kaan felt her eyes on him. Did the girl not know it was rude to stare?

He looked into the flames of his campfire and relived again the night Jade Sky's pregnancy was disclosed. The joy he had felt in that moment! Kaan's most cherished dream had always been to see his son play in the ball game and become the supreme hero of all the teams. Even as a child, Kaan had had this fantasy. In that dream, his son was always a true Mayan, not a boy shunned by the others because of his inferior blood.

A clicking sound brought him out of his thoughts. He frowned. Tonina's annoying shell-hair again. She had left her fire to survey the nearby trees. He watched as she retrieved the bedroll she had carried on her shoulders, shook it out, and then, to his astonishment, proceeded to tie the ends to sturdy branches. She was going to sleep in a tree?

When he realized it was a *hamac,* Kaan wondered if he should have purchased one, too. Sleeping arrangements had not occurred to him when he had rolled up the mat and cotton blanket he slept in at home. He watched her climb the tree and artfully slump into the palm-fiber sling, turn her back to him, and pull a cotton mantle over herself without so much as a good night.

Kaan was suddenly tired. Spreading out his mat, he lay down but could not get comfortable. There were pebbles on the ground, and the forest floor was uneven. And then the night grew cold and his fire died down. Jade Sky had always seen to his comfort. She had run the household so smoothly that he had been unaware of the effort. Although Kaan was an athlete and used to the rigors and punishments of the ball game, he was a stranger to other hardships in life.

He looked at the body in the *hamac,* illuminated by Tonina's campfire, and noticed the curves and roundness, how the *hamac* molded to her form. Her hair hung long over the side. When she sighed in her sleep, the *hamac* swayed slightly and Kaan felt an unexpected stab of desire. It shocked and ashamed him. He was dishonoring the memory of Jade Sky! But surely his body's reaction to the sight of a nubile girl had nothing to do with what was in his heart. He turned onto his side, his back to the curiously seductive creature suspended in the trees, and closed his eyes.

As he waited for sleep, Kaan consoled himself with the thought that, in all likelihood, his time with Tonina would be short. The territory between Mayapan and Uxmal was safe, as it was under the protection of both kings. But beyond Uxmal, Kaan and Tonina would enter a lawless region that would no doubt offer many opportunities to save the girl's life, and thereby sever their bond.

Comforted by the thought that he would be rid of her in a few days, Kaan recited prayers to the moon goddess of ballplayers, and drifted off to sleep.

Tonina tossed fitfully. The image of Kaan and his mother in the royal kitchen filled her mind, piercing her heart with a new ache: the desire to find her own parents. The prospect frightened her, as she wondered if she was going to come up against the temptation, once she had found the red flower, to stay and search for her people instead of returning straight-away to Pearl Island. If faced with the prospect of finding her mother and father, would she be strong enough to go back to Guama and Huracan?

Tonina finally fell asleep and dreamed of Brave Eagle. He had come back, and she was running to greet him, arms out, tears in her eyes. She awoke to find her face damp with tears. She heard someone crying, and thought she was still dreaming, until she looked down and saw Kaan wrapped in his mantle on his mat, sobbing in his sleep, calling for Jade Sky. Tonina was surprised when she heard him call out Balám's name next.

She was overcome by the urge to lie down next to him and take him into her arms as she had done with Brave Eagle. When Kaan finally quieted, Tonina tried to go back to sleep but was suddenly aware of strange sounds in the trees. Her skin prickled with fear as she thought of the wild animals that inhabited the forest, and ghosts and demons that prowled at night. She prayed to Lokono for protection, and hoped that the smoke from their smoldering campfires would be enough to keep danger away.

~ 29 ~

There was no opportunity to bathe, but broad-leafed plants, damp with night dew, served to clean away dirt and sweat, and mint-flavored *chicle* gum did a good job of cleaning the teeth. Afterward, while Kaan recited morning prayers to Mother Moon and Kukulcan, he watched Tonina out of the corner of his eye. She was applying the coconut paint to her face, once again concealing her features. He had not slept well. Disturbing dreams had made him toss and turn, and he had wakened several times to strange sounds in the forest and the pungent smell of smoke.

A wordless breakfast was followed by another day of walking. As Kaan slashed a path through the dense forest, Tonina could not take her eyes off his bare back—the sculpted muscles, the sinew and scars, reminding her of his action on the playing field, how powerful he was as he flew past his opponents, propelling the ball to the goal and victory.

Kaan's thoughts were likewise upon his companion. Her hair kept making that annoying sound. He wished he could walk faster and leave her behind, but the gods would not permit it. Through the forest they marched, over dried leaves and twigs, the smell of dust and dead wood in their nostrils, until sundown when they found a place to camp for the night. While Tonina searched for a place to tie her *hamac,* Kaan labored in vain to start a fire.

Tonina joined him, bringing her fire-starter kit made of two specially carved pieces of wood—a drill and a block. For kindling she scooped an abandoned termite nest from a tree. Spitting on her hands before beginning, she then showed Kaan how to spin the drill, keeping movements rapid and the pressure forceful. The ashes began to collect, and when she had an ember, she dropped bits of termite nest on it until a flame rose up and the fire began.

Tonina retrieved her travel pack and bedroll, and brought them back to the circle of warmth and light and, sitting down, searched among her things for something to eat.

Kaan stared at her. She was staying with him? Why did she not go off and create a fire of her own? Now she sat opposite, cracking open a cooked turkey egg and sprinkling it with salt. Without being invited.

They ate silently again, like two strangers passing on a road, not wishing to make each other's acquaintance.

The forest darkness deepened and came to life with the cries of nocturnal birds. Kaan produced a small figurine of Kukulcan and filled his thoughts with memories of Jade Sky. Before departing Mayapan he had joined the Cult of the Returning God, although in his heart he did not really believe.

Tonina likewise was thinking of someone she missed: Brave Eagle. She was surprised to find herself missing One Eye, too. His companionship had been a connection to the islands, to Guama and Huracan and home.

When Kaan brought out the bark-paper map he had purchased in Mayapan, Tonina moved next to him, to scrutinize the lines and symbols that made no sense. She gave him a questioning look.

Kaan wished she wouldn't sit so close. Tonina smelled faintly of coconut. It was in the white paint that covered her face and arms. Not an unpleasant fragrance, but not one a Mayan lady would use.

Tapping the center of the page, he said, "Mayapan." Lines radiated from there, with glyphs along the way, and symbols all around the edge. As Kaan did not know how to read or write, he had had to memorize the map as the mapmaker described it to him, pointing out the cities, roads, and regions. He knew which glyph identified Palenque, not because he could read it, but because the mapmaker had said, "There is the city of Palenque."

When Kaan pointed to more places on the map, reciting the names of cities that were unfamiliar to Tonina—"Uxmal. Tikal. Copan. Palenque."—she said, "Quatemalan?"

He indicated the farthest edge of the paper, but it made no sense to her as she had no idea of scope or scale. "Where," she asked, suddenly breathless by his nearness, "is Teotihuacan?"

She saw a shadow of grief darken his eyes before he looked down at the map and then pointed to a glyph at the opposite edge of the page from Quatemalan. When Tonina saw that the place where he was supposed to be was many more days away than Quatemalan, she felt a stab of guilt. He needed to go there to conduct a Mayan funerary ritual. But she needed to go south. And the gods had ruled that they must stay together.

She wished she could say to Kaan, "Very well, we shall go north to Teotihuacan." She wished she could explain how vital it was that she find the red flower and take it back to her people. If only One Eye were there to translate. But after Kaan had said they were to travel alone, One Eye had said, "It is just as well. I have been a long time from home. I will head to the coast and buy a canoe. I wonder if my mother is still alive."

Sharply aware of her nearness, Kaan shot to his feet. The situation was becoming intolerable. The girl was a constant reminder of the night Jade Sky died. He wished to remember Jade Sky when she was happy, her laugh, the curve of her neck as she concentrated on making a feather bracelet. Not as he had found her, dead in a pool of blood.

He was glad he and the girl couldn't communicate, glad the dwarf had not come with them. There was something about Tonina that made Kaan think that if she had the ability to make herself understood, his heart and soul would become vulnerable. He did not know what magic she cast over him, but from the day he had first set eyes on her, Kaan had known this was no ordinary girl.

He stopped pacing and looked down at her as she sat in the fire's glow. He still could not get a good look at her, as her features were hidden beneath the symbols painted in white on her cheeks, forehead, and chin. And her long, unruly hair often fell across her face, hiding her further. But he had seen the strong nose and sharply etched jaw. Features strangely like his own.

"We must sleep," he said in Mayan, and Tonina understood.

He tried not to watch her as she tied the ends of her *hamac* to two trees, but he was unused to seeing so slender and long-limbed a woman, especially when she stretched up on tiptoe to tie the strings. Her tunic rode up, exposing a curious belt underneath, one that she kept hidden. Decorated with cowry shells, it was not Mayan, and Kaan wondered at its significance.

Tonina was finally situated in her bed-sling, off the ground and protected by a canopy of branches and leaves. But sleep did not come. Kaan filled her thoughts. The red flower had not entered her mind all day. She was being distracted by him and she didn't know why. All she knew was that she could not go on this way. I will leave him, she decided as sleep stole over her. I will sneak away into the forest and he will never find me. . . .

Once again Kaan tossed and turned on his mat, unable to keep his eyes off the girl up in the *hamac*, mesmerized by the way the palm-fiber tree-bed changed her. She was slim-hipped and broad-shouldered when she walked, but slung between two trees, her body grew curvy, softer, more feminine. She was distracting him. He needed to go on his way alone. Tomorrow, he decided as he drifted off to sleep, unaware of the pungent scent of smoke drifting through the trees, he would come up with a solution.

They awoke abruptly. A forest fire! Yet the sky did not glow with flame, they did not hear the roar of a conflagration, nor did wild animals come running through their camp.

Kaan retrieved his spear and club, gesturing to Tonina that he was going to investigate. With her knife ready, she silently followed him through the dense woods, and when they reached a clearing, they both stopped short, unprepared for the astonishing sight that met their eyes.

Blessings of the gods!" One Eye called to them, waving his short arms.

Kaan and Tonina stared at the large camp, marveling that so great a group of people had been nearby, undetected.

"I told them to be quiet," One Eye explained as he approached in his familiar rolling gait that made Tonina's heart dance. She had missed him so! "I told them you must not be disturbed on your sacred journey."

"What is all this?" Kaan asked furiously. He could not believe the number of people milling in and about the trees where campfires burned. There were elders and children, with dogs and turkeys scratching in the dust.

"My lord," One Eye said, "I intended to come alone, but the royal *h'meen* asked to join me and I could not refuse her, and then word spread, you know how it is in a city, my lord, and before I knew it this great crowd was following us."

Kaan frowned. The *h'meen* of the king's royal garden was there indeed, the curious girl who looked like an elderly woman, sitting at a campfire, a little fat dog in her lap. She was flanked by two attendants bearing the symbols of the king of Mayapan.

Kaan then recognized members of the Nine Brothers, such ball-game fanatics that they neglected their farms and their families whenever games were being held. They had protested and lamented loudly at the cenote before Kaan was pushed in, and had cheered deafeningly when Kaan emerged alive. When they had heard that he was leaving Mayapan, they must have packed up their goods and their wives and children to follow him.

"My lord," One Eye said quickly, when he saw the anger on Kaan's face, "you and Tonina are the luckiest man and woman in the world, for you both survived the cenote sacrifice. Some of the people here wish to follow you to Teotihuacan and receive redemption from the gods, and others want to follow Tonina in the hope that the magical flower will cure their ailments. The royal *h'meen* herself," he added pointedly, "hopes the flower will stop the strange aging illness that wastes her body."

"We must go alone," Kaan said quietly, forcefully.

"Oh, we do not go *with* you, my lord. We are merely travelers on the same path. You lead, we follow."

"And you think the gods can be fooled?"

"I would never presume so, my lord! After all, this is not my fault." When word had spread that Kaan was planning a journey to Teotihuacan, H'meen had sent for One Eye and asked if she could accompany the great Kaan, expressing the wish to see the world before she died. The dwarf had agreed, suspecting that Kaan would never say no to the respected caretaker of the royal garden. Sniffing a profit in the operation, One Eye had then spread the word that Kaan was leaving the city at noon, making sure the Nine Brothers heard.

One Eye prayed that Kaan did not ask why One Eye himself was following him. How many lies could he tell in a day? The truth was simple. As people had come to the city gate, asking to join One Eye's now well-advertised caravan that would follow Kaan the Hero, he had charged a modest payment—for food and services, he had said—plus a small commission for himself, as it was only fair. One Eye calculated that by the time they reached Quatemalan, he would be rich enough to purchase not only a canoe, but an entire island and all the people on it, where he would live like a king for the rest of his life.

The peaceful camp was disrupted by a sudden shriek. The wife of one of the Nine Brothers was lobbing fruit at her husband, a giant of a man who cowered and protected his head with his arms. "I will not go one more step with you!" she screamed as she volleyed another fruit that bonked him on the head with a hollow sound. "You and your ball games! You are *insane!*"

Kaan and Tonina stared in amazement as the woman, her anger

vented, picked up her smallest child, gestured to the other children, and marched back through the trees in the direction of Mayapan, other women joining her. When the cowering brother, covered in juicy pulp and seeds, finally stood up, everyone burst out laughing. He ignored them, but ran instead to Kaan, throwing himself at the feet of his hero to declare undying loyalty.

The leader of the Nine Brothers stepped forward—Hairless, a nickname given to him in the Mayan fondness for irony, as Hairless was the most hirsute man in the land. He was a prosperous beekeeper who had given his hives and his home to a cousin in order to follow Kaan.

When Hairless declared his loyalty to Kaan, others rushed forward so that Kaan had to fall back with One Eye interceding, shouting at everyone to stay away. Kaan was appalled at the enormity of the situation. He was to make a solitary, holy pilgrimage to the City of the Gods and suddenly he had this unruly crowd! Grabbing One Eye's mantle, he pulled the little man close and whispered hoarsely, "You cannot come with me! I must make this pilgrimage alone or my journey will be worthless."

One Eye pulled himself free, cleared his throat, and said quietly, "My lord, if I may point out? You are not yet on the road to Teotihuacan. You are escorting a friend to Quatemalan, nothing more. Once you leave Tonina on the coast, you will begin your sacred journey and then, I promise you upon the bones of my great-grandfather, you will go alone."

While Kaan considered this, One Eye added quickly, "With our help, my lord, you will satisfy the gods." He tilted his head toward Tonina to make his meaning clear.

Kaan sighed. It was true. Delivering Tonina safely to the southern coast would constitute saving her life, and with these people accompanying them through the dangerous country that lay beyond Uxmal, his goal was as good as assured.

"Very well," he said, and turned to plunge through the trees back to their own camp.

Tonina did not follow, but stayed instead, to say to One Eye, "I *am* pleased to see you," and she bent to kiss him, a soft, moist caress on his cheek as her long hair fell forward to brush his shoulder. When she added, "I need you," One Eye's heart soared to the stars.

"I need you to teach me Mayan," she said. "I must know this language quickly. I cannot travel with Kaan. I must go alone."

One Eye nodded, disappointed that her joy was from another source than the sheer pleasure of himself, but he hid his disappointment as he said, "I will teach you everything you want to know." He said this because she had kissed him, and because One Eye the Taino trader, the shortest man in the world, had just fallen in love with the tallest woman.

~ 31 ~

Hidden in the trees, Balám lifted the blowgun to his lips and took aim.

The camp in the forest clearing was so chaotic and noisy, with arguments going on, children running this way and that, men engaged in heated games of chance, and women gossiping as they cooked and nursed babies, that Balám knew it would only take one swift strike, and Kaan, who was sitting alone at the edge of the encampment, would fall. No one would notice until it was too late.

The poisoned dart would not cause instant death. There was just enough curare on the tip to cause paralysis. Kaan would topple, and then he would take a long time to die. First, his limbs would fail him. And then his breathing would slow. He would remain conscious, struggling for breath until the very end, when the spirit in the curare stopped his lungs altogether. Kaan would lie helpless, feeling his heart flip-flop in his chest, realizing that he was never going to reach Teotihuacan.

I will stand over him then, Balám thought in bitter satisfaction, to watch the fear in his eyes, to watch the life leave his body. I will bend over him and whisper, "This is for Six Dove and Ziyal."

Balám had followed Kaan from Mayapan, had watched unseen as the dwarf and his ridiculous entourage had caught up with Kaan and the island girl. Balám had then followed them to Uxmal, through the city, had waited while they rested and bought supplies, adding more fools to their crowd, and finally he had followed them out of Uxmal and onto the White Road.

No one knew that Balám stalked them. No one knew he carried death in his hands. Balám did not consider the crowd's reaction to the assassination. Perhaps they would seize him and tear him limb from limb. He did not care. He had nothing to live for.

While in Uxmal, he had used the cover of night to make his way to his ancestral home, a villa situated near the Pyramid of the Soothsayer. As news of his disgrace and downfall had already reached his family, Balám's father had had slaves throw him out. But as Balám cowered in the darkness of the garden, his mother had come to him, the elegant Lady White Heron, to give him food and water and to hold him in her arms. He stayed in the garden for three nights, hidden from his father, and when he had ventured into the city and had seen Kaan and the girl in the marketplace, preparing to depart, Balám had kissed his mother good-bye and left. He did not go empty-handed. She had given him jade and cacao beans, weapons and fresh clothing, and had ordered four nephews to travel with him, bored young men who jumped at the chance for adventure and who cared nothing about disgrace or bad luck. Balám had promised his mother he would return, but he had no intention of doing so. Once his vengeance against Kaan was complete, Balám would find a sturdy tree and hang himself from it.

He had no other recourse. Balám could never go back to Mayapan. When the final tally of his debts was done, it was found that he still owed the recompense that Six Dove would have brought on the slave block, and so those creditors, feeling cheated by the wife's death, were calling for Balám to do the honorable thing and put *himself* on the slave auction. There was even a reward on his head.

Nor could Balám search for his daughter, because to inquire among travelers and merchants about Ziyal's whereabouts would alert officials to the fact that he was alive, and he would be captured and taken to the slave block in disgrace.

He drew in a breath to shoot the poisoned dart, but stopped when he saw the island girl approach Kaan and say something to him. Kaan dismissed her with an impatient flick of his wrist. The girl did not obey. She bent closer and spoke a little louder. To Balám's surprise, Kaan spoke sharply to her, causing her to straighten and look down at him with an impatient expression. Then she turned and marched away.

Balám narrowed his eyes. He had never seen Kaan treat another so rudely. It was clear from Kaan's posture and manner that he was utterly miserable. And a new thought entered Balám's head.

As he withdrew into the trees and the dry greenery that camouflaged him, he thought: It is foolish to kill Kaan now. There is no satisfaction in taking the life of a man who no longer enjoys living. Let him live, Balám decided. Let him believe he will make it to the City of the Gods and receive solace there. And just when my former brother is beginning to think life is sweet again, as he surely eventually will, I will snatch that sweet life from him.

As for the fortune-teller, if she had chosen Balám's wife instead of Jade Sky that evening in the Grand Hall, everything would be different. She would have read Six Dove's fortune in the magic cup, would have seen the terrible fate that awaited her, and Balám could have changed things!

For the fortune-teller, Balám decided as he vanished back through the trees, he would devise a very special punishment.

Tonina surveyed the chaotic camp in trepidation.

It wasn't the restless young men seeking adventure who disturbed her, with their weapons and war paint and whoops of victory when they trapped an animal. Nor was it the older warriors without an army, pensioned off and feeling useless, likewise traveling with spears and javelins and tales of bloody conquests. Nor the strapping fanatical devotees of the ball game, who had brought along their lusty wives and robust children. What disquieted Tonina among this diverse group that followed her and Kaan were the sick ones, the crippled and the lame, the deaf and the blind, the women who could not bear children, the men stricken with impotence.

These were the dangerous ones, driven not by greed or ambition or a thirst for power, but by desperation.

As she sat at her solitary campfire, baking a small pumpkin in the hot coals, she surveyed the sprawling camp of many fires and many people that crowded the clearing and spread away into the trees—a noisy, rowdy

mob that filled the night with cacophony and smoke. Five days out of
Uxmal, and an alarming thirty days since she had left Pearl Island, they
were traveling due south, straight as an arrow, to the city of Tikal at the
edge of the rain forest, at which point Tonina and Kaan would turn eastward and head to the Quatemalan coast.

The journey was taking too long.

From a small crowd of dedicated followers, and those in need of good
luck and a change in life, an unruly mob had grown. Tonina had asked
One Eye to take charge, but he was interested only in amusing himself
with ladies and collecting fees for allowing people to tag along. When she
had asked him if Kaan might take control of this lawless entourage, One
Eye had replied, "Kaan cares nothing for these people. He withdraws
more each day. He is in his own world. Remember, girl, he lost more
than his wife and child. He lost his best friend. He and Balám were like
brothers. Kaan owed everything to Balám—his wealth, his fame, even
Jade Sky. The story goes that Kaan was being accosted by another group
of boys—they were stoning him!—when Balám intervened. Kaan now
carries the burden of causing Balám's downfall and possibly his death."

"But surely Balám brought it upon himself," Tonina had countered.

"It matters not. Kaan lives by a strict code of honor, and he feels he
has betrayed a brother, therefore betraying that code. And now the
brother is dead, for it is almost certain Balám hanged himself."

Tonina now looked at Kaan at the edge of the camp, isolating himself
as was his habit, his strong back curved beneath the burden of grief. She
had approached him just moments before, asking him to take control of
this lawless mob, and he had waved a dismissive hand at her, saying,
"They are following us. I have no say in how they lead their lives."

Tonina could not begin to imagine the depths of his despair and she
wished he could grieve in peace. Nonetheless, something had to be done
about this unruly mob.

Their worst offense was fighting over food. No one shared. Everyone
hoarded. Some were even going hungry amid all this plenty. Only the
day before, a Huastec tribesman had trapped an iguana, and as he sat
roasting it over his campfire, five men attacked him, stealing the roasted

animal and driving the Huastec from his own camp. No one had gone to the man's defense because he was the only Huastec in the group.

If they are this way about food, how are they going to react when the red flower is found? *They will descend upon the bush or tree where it grows and ravage it as they ravage all in their path, destroying the blossoms in their frenzy, leaving nothing for the people of Pearl Island.*

The night deepened and the camp settled down to sleep, the smoky air filled with the sound of murmured prayers, snores, and the grunts of sexual couplings. Tonina brought her two travel packs up a tree with her and slung them into her *hamac,* for she had seen the way people eyed her possessions, inquiring about the transparent prophecy cup. Knowing that she herself was not immune to the rampant thievery in the crowd, she now slept with her possessions close. After she prayed to Lokono, the Spirit of All, and her dolphin spirits, she waited for sleep and thought of the difficult decision she must make. For the sake of Huracan and her people, she must leave Kaan and this mob.

*D*o not go out tonight," Jade Sky pleaded. "Do not leave me for I am filled with terrible premonition."

"I must find Balám."

"My love, he is not your responsibility. It was he who gambled himself so far into debt that he could not be saved."

"Had I not thrown that final shot through the hoop—"

"You did the right thing. You did as the gods willed. You acted with honor."

And then Kaan was out in the night, following lanes and alleys, searching for his friend, the man he called brother. But Balám was nowhere to be found. Had he hanged himself as he had threatened?

Returning to the villa . . . Jade Sky lying on the floor, her head cradled in the lap of the fortune-teller . . . the blood pooling on the tiles— "Your wife's death was instant," the island girl said.

Kaan woke with a strangled cry. He was sweating, his mantle soaked.

He sat up and looked around. No one had heard him. The camp slept on. Then he searched the overhead branches where a few slumbered in *hamacs*. To his shock, Tonina was not among them. Her *hamac* and travel pack were gone.

The dark forest was menacing and fraught with danger, but it was the only way to escape Kaan and the mob. By the time everyone woke in the morning and realized Tonina was gone, she would be so far away they would never find her.

As they had traveled through Uxmal and the countryside beyond, Tonina had walked with One Eye, constantly asking, "What do you call this in Mayan? How do I say that in Mayan?" The key to independence lay in knowing the language. She was glad she had persisted. As she hurried through the dense woods, putting distance between herself and Kaan, she knew her language skills would help her to survive.

She moved swiftly through trees and brush, her knife gripped in readiness. She thought of Guama and Huracan, pictured them standing on the promontory over the lagoon, eyes westward in hopes of sighting her canoe. Did they know by now of Macu's treachery? Had anyone survived the fight at sea to report of the tragedy? Perhaps they thought Tonina was dead. No, Guama would not give up on her, and Tonina would not let her grandmother down. The red flower lay ahead, she was certain, growing in the high rugged cliffs along the Quatemalan shore. She would harvest them and use her few remaining pearls to purchase a canoe and sail home.

She stopped suddenly, catching her breath to listen to the night around her. She frowned. Why had she stopped?

She looked back through the trees. *Kaan.*

What would he do when he found her missing? Would he search for her? Or would he seize the opportunity and turn northward for Teotihuacan?

Tonina turned around to resume her flight into the forest but found she could not move. She was immobilized.

Go! she shouted silently. Do not stand here. Hurry!

But her feet refused to obey. Peering through the darkness, listening to the calls of night birds, the noisy chatter of monkeys, she imagined Kaan waking suddenly, realizing she was gone, and then going in pursuit.

Tonina did not know what rooted her to the forest floor, only that she was struggling with thought, with ideas and reasoning, something she had never had to do before. Decisions had always come easily: If last year's oyster beds were depleted, swim farther out. When she was told that Huracan's life depended upon a rare flower, no complex thinking had been required for Tonina to say, "I will go."

Now she was torn. She did not understand what it was about Kaan that prevented her from breaking free of him. It shocked her to realize that she wanted to go back to the camp. Yet she must continue on and fulfill her promise to Guama and Huracan.

The back of her neck prickled. She felt eyes watching her.

She turned to run, chastising herself for having lingered in this dangerous place. Suddenly Kaan emerged through the trees, his face dark with fury. He took her by the shoulders and demanded to know what she was doing.

She was barely able to speak; his sudden nearness robbed her of breath. "How did you know where—"

"Hairless, leader of the Nine Brothers, who have appointed themselves the night guards, saw you slip out of the camp. Why are you running away? The gods have decreed that we stay together."

"*Your* gods, not mine!" she said in a strangled cry.

Kaan's fingers dug into her flesh. He suddenly did not know what to do. Mingled with the scent of her coconut face paint was the aroma of bay leaves and mint. He felt cool skin beneath his fingers. Her eyes were luminous as they looked up at him.

"Let me go on my own," she whispered, struggling with newly learned Mayan. "I free you of your obligation to save my life."

Kaan inhaled her scent, searched her face in the dappled moonlight, and found himself confused about his reasons for going after her. He told himself it was because of the gods' decree that they stay together. And yet, when he woke up and saw that she was gone, his gut reaction had been something else, unexpected and indefinable. She annoyed and irritated him, he wished he could be free of her, yet he felt a strong need to have her near. A need that was deeper than any laws of gods or men.

"It is not within your power to set me free," he finally said in a hoarse whisper. "That is the purview of the gods." When he saw her frown, and he realized she had not understood him, he spoke more slowly, making his meaning clear. She had learned his language quickly, but was not yet fluent. "You must come back. We are bound together by ancient law. I cannot go to Teotihuacan until I have fulfilled my obligation to that law."

As Tonina looked up into a face that she had decided was strangely attractive, another curious thought occurred to her. Despite their many differences—in gods and language and customs—she and Kaan were alike in one way: Each had a promise to fulfill, promises that had been placed upon them and that they were forced to accept, no matter how reluctantly.

And so she sought another way to be free of him. "The crowd is"—she tried to think of the word—"*holding* me back."

He arched an eyebrow. "Surely you have a better chance of finding the flower with the crowd helping."

"They are not helping. They frighten me!"

His hands dropped from her shoulders. "Frighten you?"

"What do you think they will do when we find the flower? Those people are . . ." She cursed the language barrier between them. "They are desperate. They will surely kill one another over the flower."

"You exaggerate."

"Already the strong are stealing food from the weak."

Kaan blinked. "What are you talking about?"

"Some are not getting food at all."

His brow furrowed. "Why is this being allowed?"

"Allowed! Who is to stop them?"

Kaan stared at her. How was it that some went without food? He had seen plentiful meat and fruits in the camp. "It is no reason to run away, simply because of the food. We can do something about that."

While he stood so close that she could hear his soft breathing, Tonina suddenly needed to ask him something. "Why do you hate me?"

His eyebrows arched. "Hate you?"

"The way you looked at me at the cenote. You are angry with me for saving your life."

He stared at her for a long moment and realized he *was* angry with this girl, but not because she saved his life. For the first time since the night of the tragedy, Kaan realized something he had not known before. *I resent her because she was with Jade Sky when she died, while I was not. For that, I cannot forgive her.*

No, he thought, I cannot forgive myself.

She lifted her face to his and whispered again, "Please let me go."

As Kaan looked down at her with dark, turbulent eyes, he fought the urge to take the upturned face in his hands and gently wipe away the white paint to expose the features underneath. "I cannot," he said.

"I am far from home, far from my people and my gods. I am all alone."

The sudden tears startled him. This island girl was so strong and self-sufficient, and so determined to go her own way that it hadn't occurred to him that she was capable of crying. "This is *your* land," she said in a tight voice. "It is not mine. I do not wish to be here. I want to be by the sea again. I am far from my dolphin spirits."

Suppressed for so long, Tonina's emotions now poured forth. "I yearn to be back under the waves in the silent depths of my private world. I ache for the freedom of swimming. Without the sea I am nothing."

Kaan was taken aback by the passion in her voice. He had glimpsed the sea once, when the Mayapan team had traveled to Campeche for a tournament. But Kaan had not gone near the beach, remaining instead on a hilltop to stare at the terrifying expanse of water that stretched to the horizon. People drowned in such water, were devoured by savage sea creatures there. How could she love something so formidable and destructive?

And suddenly another voice, Jade Sky's, before they were married, came into his mind: "Why do you love a sport that causes you so much physical pain, that can actually kill you?"

He had never thought about his passion for the ball game before, had never analyzed his need to play, or how alive he felt when he was pitted against the skills and strengths of other men. On the playing field he was neither Mayan nor Chichimec, just muscle and blood and strength. He was *himself*. Was this how Tonina felt about the sea?

He was startled to realize in that moment that, despite their differences—she from the uncivilized islands and he a Mayan hero— they were alike in one aspect: their love for something that meant more to them than life.

He stepped back, shaken by the revelation. *We are* not *alike. Not alike at all.*

However, to persuade her to return to the camp, he would do as she asked—take control of the crowd. He would do it not for Tonina, he told himself, but for Jade Sky. If Tonina was right, and that unruly mob destroyed the red flower, then he would never be free to take the road north to Teotihuacan.

The next morning, Kaan called for attention. The smoky camp fell silent, all eyes on him.

As he looked at the expectant faces, he thought: I am no leader of men. And then he heard his mother's words from long ago: "Do not ever be a failure, my son."

Kaan had always known that he could not fail if he did not reach beyond himself, which was why he had never accepted the captaincy of the ball team. And he did not want to reach now, but he looked at Tonina, recalling their intimate encounter during the night—a moment of personal revelations—and accepted that this was something he must do.

But he was nervous. Kaan was not a trained speaker and was unused to addressing a crowd. I am a man of action, not words, he thought, as he drew himself up straight and tall. And then he reasoned that words were a form of action, and so he said in a commanding voice, "Though you are but following me, you must abide by my rules. There will be no more delays. We must travel swiftly. If you cannot keep up, turn back and go home."

He paused and looked at each face, the way his coach had at the academy, meeting each player's eyes to drive home a point. "Everyone must participate in hunting or gathering, everyone must contribute," Kaan said, forming his rudimentary rules out of the ballplayer academy's Code of Honor, which was based on trust and fairness, honesty and respect. "Food is to be communal. You will distribute the food accordingly: the elderly first, then the children, then mothers, and finally the men. We will pour libations to the gods before each meal, and sacrifice a portion of food to each campfire, also for the gods. There will be no blaspheming, no sacrilege. There will be no stealing. Anyone caught in the act of theft will suffer his hand cut off. Adultery will be punished by death. The Law of the Maya will apply here as in the city."

While he spoke, H'meen recorded his words in a new book. Before calling the crowd to attention, Kaan had respectfully asked the royal herbalist to write down the new laws he spoke here today, to provide a validity that would ensure their enforcement. She sat cross-legged on the ground, her brush dipping into ink and painting glyphs and symbols on clean bark paper.

Finally Kaan said, "These are the laws by which we will all abide," and then he waited, scanning the faces, expecting an uproar. When no one challenged him, but rather nodded and voiced murmurs of approval, Kaan felt a little amazed. He had reached beyond himself and had not failed.

He added one last instruction: "I am not your leader. You will elect a chief from among yourselves, one who is just and fair and before whom all grievances will be brought. Now prepare to resume the journey."

As the crowd stirred to life and began discussing this new turn of events, Tonina quietly approached Kaan and said, "I have been thinking. Would this not constitute paying me back for saving your life?"

He looked down at her, as he stood a head taller. The white symbols were fresh upon her face this morning, obscuring her features, making him wonder again what she really looked like. "How so?"

"As you yourself said, dangerous country lies ahead. I could have been killed had I continued on my own, but you prevented it by bringing me back last night. I would say that our debt is cancelled."

He gave this some thought, said, "The gods are not so easily fooled," and walked away.

"A word of advice from a friend," One Eye said as he came up to her. "If you wish to be quickly rid of Kaan, Tonina, do him no more favors. Get him deeper into your debt and you will never be free of him."

❧ 33 ❧

H'meen's little fat dog, Poki, snuffled happily in the brush, scaring up rodents and other small creatures, unaware that the tip of a spear was aimed at his plump body.

Prince Balám smiled in anticipation. The dog would make for juicy eating.

When Balám heard voices through the trees, his smile widened. It was the island girl and the royal herbalist, on one of their forays into the woods while the great crowd that was accompanying Kaan made temporary camp for a noon meal and rest.

Balám had been trailing them, staying in the forest while they followed the White Road, waiting for the moment to execute his plan for revenge. The island girl was alone now, except for the strange old-woman-child and the male attendant who accompanied them. Balám looked up at the clear sky. The day was cool. The winter solstice had come and gone. It was the dry season, with little water to be found. And the city of Tikal lay yet days away.

He glanced back at his own small entourage, which had grown since his departure from Uxmal. Starting with the four cousins who had eagerly agreed to accompany him, more had joined—young Mayans thirsty for adventure, with no interest in farming or becoming woodcarvers. When they had heard that Balám, hero of the ball games, and a *prince*, was on a special journey, they forgot the rumors of his disgrace and whispers that he had wagered against his own team—after all, that had happened in faraway Mayapan—and allied themselves with him.

Bringing his attention back to the snorting little dog that had yet to catch his scent, Balám peered through the trees and—there she was, tall and slim, her hair hanging in long locks woven with shells, her arms and face decorated with white paint. He didn't like her looks. And he hated her.

Now, he thought in dark glee. Now . . .

"Have you ever been in love?"

The question startled Tonina so much that she nearly dropped the flower she had been inspecting.

It was H'meen who had asked the question. Tonina smiled at the strange-looking child, whose appearance made her forget that this was not a woman who had lived a lifetime of experiences and relationships. Short and thin, the royal *h'meen* of Mayapan possessed a narrow, wizened birdlike face with a small jaw and no eyebrows or eyelashes. With her wrinkled skin and wispy white hair, she looked as if she were a hundred years old, though she was not yet fifteen.

"I have only ever known the palace and its terraced gardens," the woman-child had explained when One Eye and his group had been found out in the forest between Mayapan and Uxmal. "Before I die, I want to see trees and flowers in their natural homes. I long to see the landscape as the gods created it. If the flower you speak of really exists, then perhaps it will reverse my aging illness and I can live a little longer. Because I have few years left to live, there are three apprentice *h'meens* already training to take my place. I will not be missed."

H'meen had then told Tonina, as they had sat together at the campfire and made each other's acquaintance during their journey from Mayapan, that she did not know what herbs the former *h'meen* had given to her as a child to speed up her mental abilities so that she would learn all the more quickly, but that had sped up her growth as well. "Not upward," H'meen had said with a laugh, "but *forward*. I did not grow tall, I grew old."

The question asked now about love saddened Tonina, because she knew this tragic girl would never know love and romance or the joys of marriage and motherhood. So she wanted to give her a satisfying answer. Looking into the heart of the red blossom in her hands—unfortunately not the flower she sought—Tonina thought first of Macu, with whom she had been infatuated, and then of Brave Eagle, whom she had loved as a brother. But romantic love? "No, H'meen," she said at last, "I have never been in love."

The herbalist lowered her small frame onto a fallen log and sighed. As she journeyed through the forest with the great crowd following Kaan, she traveled in a special basket strapped to one of her attendants, her legs dangling through openings in the wicker mesh. But when she could, she preferred to walk on her own, although she had to sit frequently.

"One Eye is very sweet, is he not?" H'meen said shyly, thinking of her gallant rescuer, who called her "my lady" when all others addressed her simply as H'meen. She would never forget the morning he came into the terrace garden, offering to take her out into the world. H'meen had burst into tears with gratitude. Calling for her assistants, her books, her traveling basket, she had been ready before the sun was high in the sky, and off they had gone, H'meen riding on the back of her brawny, loyal bodyguard, with her attendants happily walking behind, laden with books and writing implements, looking forward to the adventure. H'meen had not needed permission from the king. The *h'meen* of the palace garden was autonomous, like a high priest, answerable to no one but the gods. Still, she had sent His Exalted Goodness a message of thanks and blessings, informing him that her young apprentices were now the caretakers of the royal flora.

Tonina looked at the girl in surprise. H'meen had romantic feelings for *One Eye*? Seeing the blush on the wrinkled cheeks, Tonina smiled. The human heart went its own way.

Suddenly, Kaan appeared in her mind and it so shocked Tonina that she quickly turned away. Why had he entered her thoughts—and in such lifelike detail that it was as if he had joined them in the small clearing? It was not just a visual experience, but the smell of him—sweat mingled with the scent of green leaves and grass—and the sound of his voice, soft yet powerful, and the feel of his nearness, his hands on her shoulders, his breath on her cheeks.

Telling herself it was but a random flash of memory and nothing more, Tonina turned to face H'meen again and forced herself to concentrate on the topic the herbalist had raised—questions of love and romance, which had *nothing*, Tonina mentally insisted, to do with Kaan.

She knew why H'meen was asking about love. In the evenings, when the great traveling crowd stopped to camp, H'meen asked Tonina many questions about men and women. The small, frail girl-woman who possessed astounding knowledge of plants, medicines, the stars, and the supernatural had led such a sheltered life that she knew nothing of the practical world. And so the two had entered into an exchange of information. As Tonina searched for the red flower, H'meen taught her about botany and herbals, and in return, Tonina imparted what she knew of the ways of people and life. "I myself am still learning," she had warned, and H'meen had said, "I am still learning, too, for now I am seeing trees and flowers that I never knew to exist."

Poki started barking in the tight, squeaking sound of his breed, his short hairs bristling, his little ears erect.

"What is it, naughty boy?" H'meen said with affection. But her attendant, a burly Mayan with crossed eyes, shot to his feet, suddenly alert.

Unsheathing the knife at her belt, Tonina walked slowly to the thicket that had Poki's attention. She exchanged a glance with the royal attendant—he, too, sensed something behind the trees—then Tonina gestured for him to move to the right, and she would move to the left. Soundlessly they approached in a wide arc, while H'meen sat on the log, talking to Poki as if nothing were out of the ordinary.

Tonina made a swift move through the trees and was met by a startled shout and a man jumping up, hands in the air. "Do not hurt me!" he cried.

Tonina and the attendant stared at the intruder, a Mayan with a sloping forehead, big fleshy nose, and characteristic overbite. Not very tall, and stocky rather than sinewy. He wore a plain loincloth and mantle tied at the neck, with bow and arrows slung on his back, along with two spears and a club. His long hair was drawn up into a jaguar-tail that cascaded between his shoulder blades.

Tonina frowned. He looked vaguely familiar.

"Prince Balám!" H'meen said as she joined them, Poki silent now as he sensed the danger had passed.

Balám nodded respectfully and said in embarrassment, "I thought you were bandits."

Tonina stared at him. The few times she had seen Balám—in the marketplace, in the Grand Hall, on the playing field—he had been richly attired and heavily adorned, or wearing his ball gear, his body painted entirely in red. She had not recognized him at first.

H'meen said in astonishment, "Everyone believes you are dead, Lord Balám. Are you a ghost?"

"To my shame, honorable H'meen, I am still alive."

Tonina's expertise in the Mayan tongue was sufficient for her to follow the conversation as Balám said anxiously, "Please do not tell anyone I am here. I have kept my presence secret for all these days. I did not mean for you to find me."

"But why do you follow us? Why not join us?"

"Surely you know this, honorable one. I am in disgrace. The gods have cursed me. I would not bring my bad luck to those respectful people who are accompanying my brother, Kaan."

"You must let Kaan know you are alive!" Tonina blurted.

When he shifted his eyes to her she thought she saw, for an instant, a dark look sweep across his face. And then his features were clear again as he said, "Kaan most of all must not know I am here. He is on a holy pilgrimage. My presence would be a desecration."

"Why then *do* you follow?" H'meen asked gently in her old woman's voice.

"I am filled with everlasting shame, honorable one," he said as he hung his head. "But it is my hope that I might redeem myself at the City of the Gods. I pray that, when my brother arrives at Teotihuacan, I might throw myself upon the mercy of the holy men there and find redemption."

"Kaan believes you are dead," Tonina said in halting Mayan. "He mourns for you. He would rejoice that you are alive."

"Yes," H'meen said eagerly. "Surely the gods see into your heart and know that you are penitent."

"Honorable one," Balám said with bowed head, "I fear Kaan knows that I am responsible for his wife's death and that he will kill me out of revenge."

H'meen and Tonina gave him a shocked look. "We have heard nothing of this, Prince Balám," H'meen said. "We know only that Kaan is in deep anguish over your tragedy. He would never kill you."

He peered at her from under his eyelashes, a sly look that Tonina and H'meen mistakenly took for one of humility. "You think not?" he said.

"How can you possibly be responsible for Jade Sky's death?" Tonina asked. "It was an accident."

Again, a quick dark look before his features cleared. Balám did not like this creature addressing him so directly and with such familiarity. But her time would come—this fortune-teller who had robbed him of his wife and daughter. "It is something I must tell to Kaan myself."

"Then come with us," H'meen said.

"No, no. I cannot show myself to others. Please bring Kaan here to me. And tell him to come alone."

"I will go," Tonina said, and in that instant, One Eye's voice sounded in her head: "If you wish to be quickly rid of Kaan, Tonina, do him no more favors. Get him deeper into your debt and you will never be free of him."

And suddenly she thought: If I tell Kaan that Balám is alive, thus relieving his conscience, it will place him more deeply in my debt. But if I do not tell him Balám is alive, he will remain in pain, thinking that Balám is dead because of him.

Tonina was briefly conflicted, and then she said, "I will fetch him."

K aan was sitting at the edge of the camp as was his habit, staring into nothingness. He had not even built himself a fire, and had allowed no one else to do it for him. He had stopped eating.

Tonina recalled Guama once saying, "Time soothes all grief." Yet Kaan's grief seemed to be growing. He no longer consulted the map. He seemed not to care where they went or how long it was taking. Had he forgotten Teotihuacan?

She approached him quietly and said, "My lord."

His head snapped up. Tonina had never addressed him that way before.

"My lord," she said again, softly. "I have news."

He waited, shadowed eyes watching her.

"Prince Balám lives."

Kaan blinked. Frowned. "Lives?"

"He is through those trees and wishes to talk to you—"

Kaan was on his feet and running. It was a moment before Tonina could gather herself and go after him, arriving to see Kaan and Balám fall into an emotional embrace.

"Blessed Mother Moon!" Kaan cried. "Am I dreaming? You are alive! Forgive me for what I did! Forgive me for winning the game!"

"I hold no grudge against you, brother," Balám said, wiping tears from his eyes. "The fault was mine."

Tonina and H'meen and the attendant watched in astonishment as the two men talked at once.

"But you lost your wife and daughter because of me!" Kaan said.

"No, brother, because of *me*. And they kissed me before they were taken away. My beloved wife and precious Ziyal kissed me and forgave me and asked the gods to bless me. So I have sought you out to ask *your* forgiveness, that I might find favor with the gods and peace in my soul."

"Of course I forgive you, and I bless the gods for bringing you to me!"

Balám drew back and grew somber. "But now I have something disturbing to tell you, brother. It is my fault that Jade Sky was murdered."

"Murdered! It was an accident. She fell."

"No."

The sunlight in the glade seemed to shift and darken. Monkey chatter and birdsong seemed to recede, as if all of nature knew that a momentous turning point was at hand. Kaan swallowed painfully. "Tell me," he said.

Inside Balám's head, the fateful encounter with members of the consortium stood in stark relief as he heard himself once again telling them that it was not his fault. But the man from the consortium had said, "Kaan is a man of honor. We respect him for what he did—or did not do."

Suppressing the hateful memory, Balám now said, "My brother, I told the members of the consortium that I had asked you to throw the game but that you refused, that you did the honorable thing. But they said it did not matter. They said you were not honorable. All they cared about was winning or losing, and you did not lose the game as they had asked. And so they had your wife and unborn son killed to teach you a lesson."

A cloud appeared in the sky, sunlight vanished, and the world was cast in shadow. "I cannot—," Kaan began in a tight whisper.

"It is true, brother. The consortium hired an assassin; it was they who killed Jade Sky," Balám said, thinking how Jade Sky fought him that night, and how he felled her with a lethal punch to the stomach.

Kaan struggled for breath. His hands curled into fists. "Give me their names."

"Why?" Balám asked, knowing why, struggling not to smile at how easily Kaan had entered the trap.

"The men of the consortium," Kaan said through clenched teeth. "*I want their names!*"

And Balám told him.

"Listen to me, my brother," he added, "do not entertain the thoughts that I believe you are entertaining. Let all this go and proceed to Teoti-huacan. Nothing good can come of your returning to Mayapan and ex-acting revenge, for I know that is what you are thinking. It was my poor mishandling of gambling debts that led to the murder of your beloved wife and child! *I* am the one who entered into a contract with the con-sortium. I am also the one who put you in the unthinkable position of having to choose between the game or our friendship. I am the cause of it all!"

But Kaan's thoughts were already centered upon a swift return to Mayapan, and the justice he would seek there.

H'meen and Tonina watched the emotional reunion as Kaan now said, "My brother, the only reason I kept myself alive was to save the souls of Jade Sky and our son. I no longer cared about myself. But now I sud-denly care very much whether I live or die. My brother, you have brought purpose to my life, and you have renewed my faith in the gods, for here you stand, in flesh and blood, when I thought you were gone forever. Come and join our camp. Let us pray to Mother Moon together."

But Balám hung back. "I am under a vow of penance. I vowed that I would deny myself the pleasures of meat, alcohol, tobacco, and women until I have been redeemed at the City of the Gods. Gambling, too, this above all will I give up, and that is the biggest sacrifice of all." Balám did not add that he no longer worshiped the patron goddess of ballplayers, but had turned his devotion to another god, one of darkness and blood: Buluc Chabtan, Mayan god of war.

"Surely you can travel with us."

Balám said, "There is a reward upon my head. The consortium is demanding that I should put myself for sale on the slave block. I will remain hidden until I can return to Mayapan with honor."

One Eye climbed down from his *hamac* and made his way into the forest to answer the call of nature. Dawn was not far off and he had slept little.

Most in the group were city-dwellers or farmers used to sleeping on the floor in a protective shelter. But when the hazards of sleeping in a forest were discovered, many had purchased the more practical *hamac* in towns they had passed. One of the Nine Brothers, sleeping for the first time in a tree-slung bed, had decided to pleasure his wife. They had gotten into a vigorous rhythm when the *hamac* had suddenly flipped over. Because the webbing had been pulled taut, the pair had been caught in it until the *hamac* flipped upright again, so that around and around they went, spinning and yelling until one of the ropes broke and the lovers were dumped unceremoniously to the ground.

It had woken One Eye, who could not then get back to sleep. Amateurs! he thought as he searched for a tree to urinate against. It took years to develop the skill of pleasuring a woman in a *hamac*—

He stopped suddenly. *Voices in the darkness.* Peering through the trees, he saw Balám laughing with his friends.

Like the superlative spy he was, when One Eye had seen Kaan suddenly run from the camp after Tonina had said something to him, One Eye had followed and had witnessed the emotional reunion with Prince Balám. Balám had declared he was under a vow of abstinence, yet One Eye saw now that Balám was drinking alcohol, while the bones of a roasted animal were scattered nearby, and he and his friends passed around a pipe, and rolled colored beans in a game of chance. All that was missing, One Eye thought in disgust, was the women.

As he turned to leave, he stepped on a dry twig and the snap sounded loudly in the night. Balám shot to his feet and growled, "Who's there?"

One Eye froze, hoping they would think it was just an animal and return to their gambling. But in the next instant he felt a rough hand at his neck and suddenly his feet were off the ground.

"Are you spying on me?"

"No, my lord," One Eye croaked. "I swear upon my great-grandfather's bones!"

Balám leaned close and hissed, "Listen to me, monkey man. Stop spying on me with your evil little eye. If I catch you watching me again, I will run your ugly little body through with a spit and roast you like a dog."

~ 34 ~

The city of Tikal—at last!

As soon as they emerged from the thick jungle and set foot upon the stone causeway that led to the city gates, Kaan murmured hasty instructions to Hairless, then he broke into a sprint toward the city.

Tonina, walking at the head of the crowd, understood the urgency of Kaan's errand. "I must go back to Mayapan," he had said after his reconciliation with Balám. "I must confront my wife's killers and see that they are brought to justice." Tonina had once again told him he was free of his obligation to her, but Kaan had insisted he see her safely to the coast. Inquiries among local farmers had told them that the coast was still many days away and Kaan was feeling the pressure of time. A solution, however, could be found in the city of Tikal, where Kaan was told he could hire the services of trusted guards and guides who would take Tonina the rest of the way to the coast.

Therefore, he had veered from their original track, due east, to turn southward for Tikal. Gradually they had entered Quatemalan, where dry forest had changed to damp rain forest, trees were strangled by vines, and everything grew close together—ferns, plants, fungus, and moss—an arduous trek requiring advance scouts with knives to hack through the growth. The terrain had grown hilly with small streams and marshy patches, and now the air was hot and humid, and filled with insects.

Tonina and her followers were weary and looked forward to the comforts and security of a city, but as they followed the main causeway into Tikal—a paved road embraced on either side by towering trees and thick, green brush—they saw no people, no guards standing sentry, no lights glowing in windows.

Where was everyone?

The newcomers fell silent as they followed Tonina and the Nine Brothers over the broken paving stones. Hairless marched with his broad face forward, watching his master vanish between the city gates, wishing he could sprint ahead to make sure the great Kaan was safe. But he had been given orders to protect the throng.

Walking at Hairless's side, Tonina also watched Kaan run into the strangely silent city up ahead, and pictured him scouring the lanes and alleys for trustworthy men to take her to the coast.

Behind Tonina came H'meen's robust attendants, one of them carrying the royal herbalist, the other carrying One Eye. Though he had tried to keep up, the Taino trader had finally had to suffer the humiliation of riding on a man's back. It was H'meen's idea, when it was obvious the dwarf would never keep pace with Kaan's new urgency. Since the night of his miraculous reunion with Prince Balám, Kaan had moved with speed.

One Eye had grudgingly accepted H'meen's offer and now rode into Tikal on the brawny shoulders of one of her attendants while H'meen rode in her special back-basket strapped to another attendant. She smiled at One Eye, but he did not return it.

He wanted to die.

One Eye had told no one about spying on Balám and finding the prince indulging in all the things he had sworn to forgo. One Eye did not care about Balám's lies and duplicity, or that he might have made amends with Kaan for less noble reasons. *"If I catch you watching me again, I will run your ugly little body through with a spit and roast you like a dog."*

It wasn't the threat that bothered him. One Eye had been threatened more times than he could count. It was the word "ugly" that stuck to him like a spiny burr.

One Eye had always thought himself handsome, and many women had said so. But Balám's words had caused him to lie awake until finally, one night, One Eye had wakened his latest sleeping partner and asked her if she thought he was handsome. She had laughed and said, "No."

"Am I homely?" he had pressed.

She had hesitated in a way he did not like. "Am I ugly?"

"Yes, that's it," she had said with a sleepy smile. "You're very ugly."

"Then why do you sleep with me?"

"Because it is good luck."

And so he knew the truth, that women gave themselves to him only because he was a dwarf and they wanted his luck. It had nothing to do with One Eye himself, his looks or his charm, as he had always thought. All his life, he had been deluding himself. And now he wanted to die.

"People at last!" H'meen said as she and One Eye rode past ramshackle houses with vegetable plots, men and women coming out to stare at the passing crowd.

Not a completely deserted city after all.

The procession passed through an arched gate where no guards stood sentinel, and finally reached what they guessed was the heart of Tikal, where a modest marketplace occupied a plaza embraced by massive stone temples—edifices that rose to the sky in levels and terraces. Three appeared to be abandoned, while two others were clearly still in use, with people coming and going from colonnades and doorways. But there was evidence of lack of maintenance, with weeds and vines encroaching upon the gray stone walls.

Not the welcoming population center everyone had been imagining.

Tonina and Hairless decided that here was where they should make camp, for it was safe and protected, and there was a small water reservoir nearby. They found room in one corner of the plaza and immediately territories were staked out upon the damp, mossy paving stones.

Finding space for herself near the steps of a deserted temple, Tonina got a small fire started and looked around the camp, where people huddled in the shadows of massive stone monuments.

She was familiar with pyramid-temples by now. Many dotted the route from Uxmal to Tikal. All had been built centuries ago by people long forgotten so that many were no longer in use, some in such an advanced state of neglect that they were completely covered in vegetation and looked like natural hills. But a few were still used, in populated religious centers, and kept in good repair. However, none of the hundreds of those structures resembled the astounding pyramid-temples of Tikal.

These rose gracefully from the jungle, like plumes of water rising from the sea, Tonina thought, with impossibly steep walls and stairways, and were so high that surely they touched Heaven. At the summit stood strange square crowns that seemed to serve no purpose. Who had built such monuments, and why? And *how*, she wondered, recalling the dense green jungle they had just traversed, had they managed to carve out enormous blocks of limestone, haul them to this place, and then pile them up, block upon block?

Bringing her attention back to the plaza, she searched for Kaan, who was no doubt, at that moment, arranging for guides to escort her to the coast. Tomorrow, all these people were going to have to make a decision: to continue with Tonina, or remain in Tikal. Traveling back to Mayapan with Kaan was not an option. And judging by the dilapidated state of Tikal's buildings and the miserable state of its few inhabitants, Tonina did not suppose her people would opt to stay here. She was not looking forward to continuing the journey with this great crowd without Kaan's presence to keep them in order.

Tonina saw One Eye, haggling with a local merchant over a gourd of *pulque*. For some reason, he had stopped inviting women to share his bed, and had stopped teaching Tonina the Mayan language. She did not know why One Eye had grown silent and petulant; when she had asked, his reply had been a grunt. And when she had inquired if he was going to the coast with her, or remaining here, or possibly even returning to Mayapan, she had received stony silence.

Through the smoky atmosphere that was growing gloomy with the dying day, she saw the *h'meen* kneeling next to a pregnant woman, offering a drink. H'meen wore all white, and bound her white hair in a scarf. She was like a glowing beacon in the darkness. It had become her nightly habit, while her attendants saw to setting up her private camp, to gather her medicine supplies and deliver herself among the people to see who needed help.

Over a hundred people traveled with Kaan now. There were some new faces among them, but many who had joined them at Mayapan were still there. Along the way, three had been buried, two had been born. As they passed through settlements and small towns, and camped overnight near farms, some left the group and new ones joined. Word of the red flower was a powerful draw, and the fact that a hero of the ball court was on a holy quest. Families brought crippled children, loved ones suffering from wasting sickness, the blind and the deaf.

Such a crowd needed the services of a healer.

Tonina knew that H'meen's duties at the Mayapan palace had been restricted to tending the garden and maintaining the herbal books. But along the journey she had collected healing plants, and each evening she and her attendants had transformed leaves and stems and petals into powders and elixirs and teas. Now she had a medicine kit, and as night descended over the half-deserted city of Tikal, H'meen took up her newest occupation of healer, an endeavor she discovered she loved, as she dispensed oil of castor beans to colicky children, applied a paste of black beans to painful boils, and poured dandelion wine on sores that would not heal. Everyone she ministered to blessed her and called her "Mother," not knowing she had just turned fifteen.

Tonina wondered what H'meen's decision was going to be tomorrow: continue to the coast, or stay here with those who elected to stay behind.

Tonina's anxiousness grew. Where was Kaan?

Hairless, the hirsute beekeeper, along with the six Nine Brothers (who had never really numbered nine, but merely assigned the lucky number to the name of their club in support of the hero player, Kaan) and their wives, were seeing to the making of Kaan's camp, as they did every night.

But Kaan was not among them.

Finally she saw him, on the far side of the plaza, engaged in animated conversation with two strangers. Even from this distance, across the smoke-filled plaza now glowing with campfires, Tonina could see the tension in his body as he seemed to be arguing with the men. She watched as words were exchanged, with shaking heads and gestures, until Kaan turned on his heel and struck off between two dark temples.

Tonina frowned. Where was he going?

W e are being watched," Balám's cousin said quietly as they sat at their campfire.

"I know." He had been aware of the unseen eyes since morning, as they had neared the perimeter of Tikal. It had happened before. First, Kaan and his great parade would pass by a farm, a settlement, and people would come out to gawk and wonder, ask themselves if this was a caravan, excited over the prospect of novelty and entertainment. It was always Kaan who received the attention. But occasionally Prince Balám and his smaller group, following by half a day, received attention as well, mostly from young men who were intrigued to see this contingent, so different from the larger group with its women and children, old people, and those being carried in litters. The second group was comprised of youths with weapons, long hair drawn back into tails decorated with feathers, bodies painted with the stripes of warriors.

Balám was not concerned about the unseen watchers. He had more important things on his mind as he and his companions climbed the gradual hill toward the city. In the days since reuniting with Kaan, Balám had thought of nothing but his plans for revenge against Kaan and the island girl. Every morning, mid-day, and evening he would ask himself: What is the worst thing that could happen to Kaan? Do I lay a trap for my dear brother in the jungle, far from his friends, slash his hamstrings so that he can never walk again, and then slay the island girl before his eyes? Do I inflict him with a slow wasting disease for which there is no cure? Bury him and the girl alive together, with no food or water, and no hope of escape?

The resentment and hatred grew inside Balám as he watched the mass of adoring people who followed Kaan so trustingly. Balám despised the crowd that forgave Kaan for cursing the gods. He had lost his wife, they said. He had been thrown into the cenote, they said. Poor Kaan, they said.

Balám wanted to shout: Where is the sympathy for *me*?

His rancor grew by the day, so that its depth and breadth now encompassed the universe. Balám had been swallowed up by his hatred. The thought of what his daughter was going through plagued him. Horrific visions made him feverish; Ziyal's cries of pain and terror filled his ears. But only Balám was aware of his personal torment as he pressed on through the jungle with his coterie of energetic young men looking for adventure.

Balám had not brought his cousins and the others into his confidence. None knew, in fact, of his private plans for revenge. They believed, as he wished them to believe, that he had truly made amends with Kaan. His moment for revenge, Balám decided as he stared into the flames of his campfire, was at hand. He knew that Kaan was at that moment seeking guides to take the island girl to the coast, after which he would turn back for Mayapan.

Balám had chosen a camping spot in the rain forest outside the city, far from Kaan's great encampment. While his companions started a fire and produced food, ready to spend the evening rolling colored beans in games of chance and waiting for the women to come—as they always did, from Kaan's group or from the city or nearby farms, women seeking food or jade or cacao in exchange for sexual favors—Balám sat at the fire and morosely rubbed the spot on his cheek where his wife's spittle had landed. No matter how much he scrubbed his face, the spit would not come off.

Balám had heard of Tikal. Six Dove had had a passion for the mint-flavored *chicle* gum that was manufactured in this region. So Balám had expected to find a thriving, industrious city. But as he and his companions had followed the main causeway into Tikal, they had seen that although the gray stone buildings went on forever, and the metropolis was many times bigger than Mayapan, half of it was in ruins. Balám had realized in dismay that only a small population lived here, while, clearly, generations ago this city had been mightier even than Mayapan or Chichén Itzá.

Forcing the troubling thought from his mind—that Tikal was a dying city—Balám curled his fingers around the small pouch that hung from a thong about his neck. Ziyal's baby tooth.

Although there was a price on his head, Balám had been unable to keep silent any longer. He had put out word of a reward for information on the whereabouts of a certain Mayan child purchased at the Mayapan slave market. Everywhere they camped, through every kind of habitation—if it was but a single monk maintaining the roadside shrine of a forgotten god—Balám asked about Ziyal, describing her, giving the date of her purchase, and asking that people spread news of a reward. He imagined his net growing, and soon it would be cast far and wide enough for someone, somewhere, to have the information he needed. And he would rescue his daughter.

The spies who had been watching Balám and his comrades finally showed themselves, emerging shyly from the jungle like cautious young ocelots—healthy youths with strapping bodies and eyes filled with curiosity. They would be farmers, or woodworkers, or young men who hauled water from cenotes. Their story would be the same as all the others across the peninsula: With no more wars and combat, with kings growing peaceful and fat, there was nothing for young men to do but follow in their fathers' footsteps.

And they hated it.

"Blessings of the gods," they said with trepidation.

"Blessings," Balám's companions murmured.

The young men came forward, eyeing the rabbit roasting on the spit, and licked their lips. When one of them started to sit at the fire, Balám's spear moved so swiftly the man did not see it coming. The sharp point sliced into his thigh and he cried out, shooting to his feet and cupping the bleeding wound.

"I am Prince Balám of the royal house of Uxmal," Balám said in a throaty growl, "hero of the Thirteen Games. You do not sit in my presence."

As they backed humbly away, Balám gauged their reaction. They seemed not to know who he was or to have heard of his shame. Perhaps the news had not traveled this far south yet. "Why do you follow us?" he asked.

The eldest of the strangers, a young man in his twenties wearing a stained loincloth and no mantle, said, "We live nearby, noble prince. We are *chicle* harvesters. Where are you going, noble prince? May we travel with you?"

Balám sighed. He had not planned to journey with an entourage. He wanted to travel alone. But restless young men were drawn to him. He had tried to explain that he had no plan, he was not on a valiant quest. They did not care. They wanted to run away from farms and strict fathers, to find adventure and women.

"We are being slowly invaded," the young man said in a plaintive voice. "People are coming from the far north—such dogs as Chichimecs, Huastecs, Zapotecs—to settle on our land and steal our women. Our chief is weak. He does nothing about the invaders who squat here like toads. Let us go with you, noble prince."

Balám grunted and wiped the blood off his spear. He had seen these so-called invaders—miserable, ragtag refugees running from the constant warring in the north, straggling southward in the hope of a new life.

"You may join us," he said, and gestured to one of his cousins to take over supervision of the newcomers. "Except that one," Balám added, pointing to the man with the wounded thigh, who had now slumped to the ground. "Let him bleed to death for his disrespect."

"You will not regret your decision, noble prince," said the one who spoke for the *chicle* workers, glancing nervously at his fallen friend. None made a step toward the injured man, who was now slipping into unconsciousness. "We are strong and fearless, like warriors. Our work is very dangerous and we must be brave."

Balám squinted up at the young man. "Dangerous, you say? How?"

"We must climb very tall trees and make cuts in the bark. We do this with rope, thusly. . . ." The young man made motions, showing how difficult the climb was and how high from the ground. "It is a solitary job, each man on a different tree, sometimes far apart. If a man slips, he is caught in the rope and he hangs there until someone comes for him. Sometimes for days."

"For days?" Balám asked, picturing it.

"It happened to my brother. When we realized he had not come back to camp, we searched for him. But the sapodilla forest is large and by the time we found him, he had hung in the tree for three days. I climbed as swiftly as I could, but he died before I could reach him."

"He died before you could reach him," Balám murmured, a plan forming in his mind.

"It is a terrible, painful death, noble prince."

Balám nodded, familiar with terrible, painful deaths. He looked at the bleeding man, unconscious but still alive, and suddenly lifted a smile to his cousins. "Five pieces of jade says you cannot keep him alive until dawn!"

They immediately bent to scrutinize the dying man, murmured among themselves, and then, eagerly accepting the wager, fell upon the poor wretch with bandages and tourniquets, determined to win their cousin's jade.

Balám leaned forward, elbows on his knees, and said to the *chicle* harvesters, "Now, tell me more about these dangerous trees. . . ."

Tonina knew where to find him.

During their journey from Uxmal, they had encountered hundreds of ball courts, some enclosed in parallel masonry walls, others simply open fields. Every village had its team; even the humblest farm cleared space for the ball game. Although many in their crowd, including the Nine Brothers, joined local players in vigorous matches, Kaan never did.

Tonina found him at the great ball court of Tikal, at one end of the moonlit playing field, pacing, deep in thought. She saw agitation in his body as he took six strides, snapped about, went back six, turned, and paced six more. Back and forth, a man with devils at his heels.

"I found men willing to take you to the coast," he said when he saw her approaching, "but I do not trust them. And the city is not safe." There was frustration in his voice. "I cannot leave all those people here. I am not yet free to turn back to Mayapan, and I wasted precious time with this detour to Tikal. Now that I must return to Mayapan before going to Teotihuacan, days are as precious as pieces of jade."

She wanted to say that he had fulfilled his promise to her; he had brought her to Quatemalan, and his duty was done, he was free to leave. But she knew he would not agree. "I'm sorry," she whispered.

"It is not your fault," he said in agitation. "It is mine."

Tonina sensed the tension in his body as he stood stiffly at the edge of a playing field that had once been his life, but which he now denied to himself. His troubled gaze swept the towering trees that seemed determined to march into Tikal and conquer the city. Monkeys and birds kept up a steady cacophony in the dark branches.

"I am not used to solitude," Kaan finally said. "All my life I have lived in a noisy, crowded place, from the palace kitchen when I was a small boy, to the academy, to my wife's villa—I have always been surrounded by people. It is very strange to be alone like this."

"I like being alone," Tonina said, surprised at his unexpected admission. "When I dive for pearls, I work alone. I love the silence of the sea."

He nodded, thinking how there had been a time when he would not have separated himself from the main group so willingly, and yet now he found the solitude strangely alluring. What was it like, he wondered, to swim in the silence of the sea? "You will be by the sea again, soon enough," he said, turning to look at her, thinking the white symbols on her face seemed brighter in the moonlight, obscuring her features all the more. What was the true shape of her eyes? "You will be glad to be rid of all of us."

But she shook her head. Tonina had found herself growing to enjoy the company of others, the feeling of belonging and acceptance, of being part of a greater whole.

A breeze came up, rustling the tall trees at the end of the ball court, and carrying on it the aromas of cook fires, voices from the nearby camp. "I cannot stop thinking about my son," Kaan said after a moment. "Even when I was a boy, I dreamed of having a son. Is that a strange dream for a boy? I never knew my father, he died when I was a baby, so perhaps I wanted to *be* a father, to know what it was like. I looked forward to the day when I could teach my son the game, train him to become a hero player. It was my only dream. Jade Sky was going to make it come true. And now it is all gone."

As Kaan returned to staring down the length of the massive ball court, as if picturing all the tournaments that had been held there, Tonina wondered why he had not engaged in games with the others. She knew that playing the ball game was, for him, like swimming was for her.

"Why do you not play the game?" she asked. "If I were to encounter a large body of water, I would not hesitate to plunge in."

He turned dark eyes to her then, filled with sorrow and pain, and Tonina wished he would let her talk about Jade Sky, to reassure him once again that she had died a swift death. It was not the truth, but for the sake of easing his pain, she would lie.

"Have you ever lost anyone?" he whispered.

"I have," she said, but would say nothing more—she would not speak of her grandparents on Pearl Island, of Macu and Brave Eagle, of the family who had put her on the sea as an infant. Tonina wanted to tell him that her life was one of constant loss, yet she would not give up hope of one day finding happiness. "But even in loss, there is hope," she added. "Nothing is permanent."

"How can you be so sure?"

"Have you ever seen the ocean surf? The waves coming onshore?"

"Once," he said softly. "Overlooking the Bay of Campeche. Why?"

"The ebb and flow of the sea is not constant; it is never the same. When the tide recedes, we are terrified because we think the water will never come back. But it always does, just in a different pattern, a different wave. Life is like the sea."

Kaan stared at her as softly spoken words, drifting on the night breeze, rooted him to the spot in a way more powerful than if he had been tethered by ropes. As he inhaled the coconut fragrance that covered her body, and heard the gentle clicking of the many shells that decorated her hair, as he recalled the feel of her shoulders beneath his hands when she had run away and he had caught her, as he thought of the kiss of life she had given him in the cenote, and as he now looked into her dark brown eyes and saw warm moonlight there, he heard the truth and wisdom in her words.

"I think," she said softly, "I have something that might help."

He watched as she reached beneath her tunic and dug into the waistband of her skirt. He glimpsed bare skin underneath, the color of dark honey.

"Here," she said with a smile, and he saw that she was offering a small blue feather.

"What is it?"

"Your wife gave this to my friend, Brave Eagle. He had lost his memory and she said this would help. Brave Eagle has gone to his people, and so maybe the magic feather will help *you*."

Kaan held out his hand and the feather landed so softly in his calloused palm that he didn't feel it. He shuddered with emotion.

Kaan looked from the feather to Tonina, and felt another, newer emotion rock his heart, and he was overcome with the impulse to pull this girl to him and press his mouth to hers.

"I will treasure this," he said, tucking the small feather into the waistband of his loincloth. And then he said, "Tomorrow we start eastward for the Quatemalan coast."

Tonina was shocked to feel a small leap of her heart, and realized she had not wanted to part ways with him so soon, that she had, in fact, been dreading having to say good-bye. Now, they would have more time together.

Kaan, too, was experiencing a strange, secret elation. He should be focused on returning to Mayapan and exacting revenge. Instead, he found himself suddenly pleased that none of the guides in Tikal had measured up and that he must continue his journey with Tonina.

"Master!"

They spun around to see Hairless trotting breathlessly toward them. "Master!" he said. "The advance scouts have just come back. We have arrived at the coast!"

"What!"

Hairless pointed excitedly toward the south. "That way, a day's journey. There is the sea! We are already there!"

Kaan and Tonina looked at each other. Their journey together had come to an end after all.

Kaan had first consulted his map, wondering if the scale was wrong, and then he had conferred with H'meen, but she knew nothing of this region. And when he asked One Eye, who had been silent and morose for days, the island trader had shouted, "Why would you ask advice from the ugliest man in the world?" Finally, two men in the marketplace, whose acquaintance Kaan had already made, verified that the coast did indeed lie in that direction, a mere day away, and that for a fee they would be happy to escort Kaan and his followers through the hilly terrain.

No one chose to stay behind in Tikal, and many of its citizens had requested to be allowed to join the traveling throng—they had heard by now of the quest for the healing flower, and that Kaan was a hero. The new members—old and young, single people and families—did not know where they were going, only that good luck lay ahead while Tikal was dying. Before long, they assured one another, the lame would walk, the blind would see, and barren women would be with child.

They followed an ancient trail through the dense forest as monkeys chattered in the overhead canopy, throwing fruit and sticks at the procession below, and toucans and parrots flew suddenly across their path in bright flashes of color.

When Kaan brought his people through the trees to a sandy shore, a hundred voices fell silent, a hundred pairs of eyes stared.

They had indeed arrived at a shore—but it did not lead to an ocean, rather to a lake, for they could see the shore on the far side.

Confused, Kaan turned to the two Tikal guides, to find them gone, along with the cacao beans he had paid them. And then his confusion turned to outrage. They had taken advantage of his ignorance of the region, and of the fact that his advance scouts were inland Maya to whom any large body of water would be a "sea."

The lake was vast, stretching away to a barely seen shore on the other side, surrounded by hills and forest, and reflecting the gray winter sky. Kaan was deciding what to do next when, to his surprise, Tonina dropped her travel packs and started to remove her clothing. Seeing the shocked look on his face, she remembered Mayan modesty and kept her clothes on as she ran for the water, where, to everyone's surprise, she dived in and disappeared under the surface.

The onlookers watched in tense anticipation as the water grew calm over Tonina's head and the ripples ceased and the late afternoon grew still. Even One Eye, having grown up among swimmers, became tense. She was down there too long. Perhaps all that cumbersome clothing . . .

And then she burst from the water and everyone cried out with relief.

Kaan started to call her back, to inform everyone that they must keep on the move, but he watched how she swam, cavorted, and flew out of the water to dive back in. It reminded him of the Bay of Campeche when he had looked out over the water and had seen dolphins at play. There was joy in Tonina's movements, and it made him think of his own joy on the playing field, when he was free to run and dodge and sprint.

Finally she ceased her water antics and rose out of the lake like a statue, her wet tunic and skirt clinging to the contours of her body, the many shells in her hair glittering with water droplets. A veritable sea goddess. To Kaan's surprise, she gestured to him to join her.

Was she challenging him?

Kaan did not want to accept the dare. He was furious with himself for having been duped by the Tikal guides. He wanted to get the throng moving again to make up for lost time. But Tonina was beckoning, daring him. And he felt hundreds of eyes watching him.

And then a strange thought jolted him: Mayans are afraid of water, but what if *my* race is not?

Slipping out of his sandals, he untied his mantle and let it drop to the ground, along with his travel packs and weapons. As he took his first steps, his throat tightened, his heart pounded. Kaan's muscular, powerful body was covered in the scars and marks from the combat of the playing field—he had been wounded more times than he could count—and yet they were nothing compared to the feel of the first swirls of water around his ankles.

He stopped. He could not go in.

And then the breeze shifted, carrying distant voices across the lake, and he recognized the disdainful laugh of his friend Balám. It did not surprise him. Kaan wondered now if Balám had ever really regarded him as an equal, if, behind the words of affection and brotherhood, Balám still thought of Kaan as the son of a lowly kitchen worker. But here, because of Tonina, was a moment in which he could show Balám who he really was and what he was made of.

Kaan progressed farther, cautiously, bare feet planted on the muddy bottom, the cold water engulfing his ankles and calves, then knees and thighs, as he drew closer to Tonina, finally delivering his hands into hers. She drew him out until he was waist-deep and he felt the gentle tug of a tide, as if the lake were welcoming him. He heard gasps and murmurs of wonder on the shore.

Now, closer up, with some of the face paint washed away, he saw the fullness of her lips, the high cheekbones, the firm jaw. Neither islander nor Mayan, he realized, but something else. . . .

B alám watched with an impassive expression. This mistaken sidetrack to a lake was unexpected, but it did not spoil his plan—the scheme for exacting revenge at last, that had come to him while talking with the *chicle* harvesters. As he watched what he thought was a disgusting spectacle out in the water—the hero Kaan being seduced by a common island girl—Balám's thoughts went back to the city of Tikal, which he had explored that morning. "Tikal is said to be over a thousand years old," he murmured now to his cousin at his side, a young man who shifted restlessly on his feet. "Centuries ago, more people lived there than anywhere else in the world. The kings were rich and powerful. The gods blessed this place. And now the gods and the kings have left."

The cousin grunted and scratched his groin. He cared nothing for past greatness or derelict cities. He had lain with a local woman the night before, and now he had a terrible itch.

Balám shook his head to dispel his dark thoughts. He did not know why the city's decay troubled him, and so he forced his thoughts back to his plan for revenge.

From the sandy bank, One Eye watched the pair in the water.

Tonina had coaxed Kaan farther out. He was chest-deep now, still holding on to her hands. They spoke not a word as they looked into each other's eyes. One Eye wondered if he was the only one aware of what was truly going on out there.

Two days out of Mayapan, One Eye had fallen in love with Tonina, and had since harbored the hope that someday they would share a *hamac*. But he knew now that it was a futile hope. Tonina would never look favorably upon so ugly a man as One Eye the dwarf.

She was at that moment looking at Kaan with an expression One Eye knew only too well and of which, he would wager all his possessions, Kaan was oblivious. What a sad state of affairs, the dwarf thought as he wallowed in his misery. He loved Tonina and Tonina loved a man who clung to a dead wife.

Poki, the fat little dog, dashed by just then to run to the water's edge and bark happily at the frogs in the reeds. One Eye looked up and saw H'meen, her large, aged eyes smiling, her white wispy hair dancing in the breeze. He could hear her aged bones, just fifteen years old, creaking. Sweet child, he thought, if a bit annoying, always trying to cheer him up.

She sat next to him without being invited and said, "Why do you call yourself the ugliest man in the world?"

He gave her a look. Did she not have eyes? "Because I am."

"It is not so."

"You don't have to be nice to me, I know the truth."

She plucked a blade of grass and mused, "The more I have been hearing about the red flower, I think it has powerful magic indeed. And if it can cure illness, and make barren women fertile, then certainly it can turn an almost-handsome man into a truly handsome man."

One Eye studied the curiously old yet naïve face and said, "Great Lokono, do you think so?"

"I have seen ordinary plants work miraculous cures. How much more miraculous when the cure is from so magical a flower?"

He blinked. He had not thought of that. If red petals could cure blindness or fertilize a recalcitrant womb, why *not* cure his troubles as well? And even if the flower could not transform him into a vision of handsomeness, at least it could enchant women's eyes so that when they looked upon One Eye they *saw* a handsome fellow.

He felt his spirits lift. "My lady," he said to H'meen, "do you think the flower will make me tall, too?"

The eagerness in his voice, the sudden hope in his eye, his sudden *need* of her, made H'meen's heart do a funny little tumble it had never done before. "Is that your wish? To be tall?"

"Well, look at me! My feet barely reach the ground!"

She started to laugh, and One Eye joined her, and then, feeling so much better after days of depression, he grabbed his stomach and rocked back and forth until a shadow suddenly blocked the sun.

Gulping back their laughter, One Eye and H'meen looked up to see the most remarkable stranger standing over them.

❧ 36 ❧

They camped that night on the lake, and for the first time Kaan did not separate himself from the main body, but built a fire and invited a few to join him: Tonina, One Eye, H'meen and her attendants, Hairless and his wife.

And the stranger.

"I am a message-carrier!" he boasted between mouthfuls of roasted turkey. "I travel the White Roads taking communications to people. You have noticed what a big head I have. It can hold much more than a normal head. I memorize news, announcements, statements, declarations, and even love notes." He tapped his temple. "At this moment, I carry twice thirteen messages to people all over the land, even as far north as the isthmus. Once I recite the message, it vanishes from my head, leaving room for a new one."

A swallow of *pulque* and he continued: "Families become divided and scattered. You would be surprised. Daughters leave to marry elsewhere. Sons leave to find employment elsewhere. A man joins a king's army. A merchant is delayed in a city. Whatever separates kinfolk. When they need to announce a birth, a wedding, or a death, or any news that families exchange, sending a letter on paper is too costly and risky. So they send me!"

"It seems a lonely occupation," H'meen observed, thinking what a strange-looking man he was—tall and bone-thin, with a broad skull and widely spaced eyes. His mantle was decorated with symbols that identified his profession.

"Not at all, honorable herbalist! I have wives in the four corners of the earth, with healthy children and fine homes and plenty of food. I visit each regularly, and in between I am a free man. Few brigands impede my way for I have nothing of value to them, and even brigands need a way to communicate, do they not? Rarely am I accosted. It is a good life."

He polished off the turkey bone and threw it into the fire. "And may I ask what you good people are about?" He scanned the camp. "You seem not to live here permanently, and you are diverse. Elders, children, not all of you are Mayans. . . ." His eyes settled thoughtfully on Tonina.

"We are searching for a flower," she said.

He picked his teeth with a twig. "What kind of flower?"

"One that heals."

He shrugged. "Many healing flowers in the rain forest. What does this one look like?"

Tonina started to reply but Kaan held up a hand. Since Uxmal they had encountered many people only too eager to say, "Yes, I know where the red flower is," and then demand payment. As a result, they had bought many false leads. "What kind of flowers do you know?" Kaan asked cautiously.

The man went on to describe various blossoms and their unique habitats, while H'meen listened and nodded as she recognized each.

He fell silent, squinted into the fire, then said thoughtfully, "There is another one, I think. But I saw it only once. Scarlet," he said, "like the feathers of a macaw. But it does not grow upward to the sun, rather it greets the ground, thusly," and he placed his wrists together, fingers downward. "It grows on a tall bush with very few blooms."

"And is it found in Quatemalan?" Tonina asked, suddenly excited.

"Quatemalan? No," he said with a shake of his big head. "This flower grows close to the gods, which is why it has magical powers. High in the mountains of the Copan region."

"Where is that?"

"Far to the south," One Eye interjected. "Where mountains touch the sky." He had never been there, but had heard the terrain was perilous.

"Does this flower cure all ills?"

The man shrugged. "Who can say? I have seen the flower but once. It is beautiful, to be sure. But I never availed myself of its healing properties. Nor do I know anyone who has."

"*How* far to the south?" Tonina asked softly, glancing at Kaan.

The traveler wrinkled his nose. "You say you came from Uxmal? The distance from Uxmal here to Tikal is how far it is from here to Copan."

"Another twenty days of travel," Kaan murmured.

"Alas, no, my friend, for it is very mountainous, very hard traveling. Steep slopes, inaccessible passes, rivers and waterfalls, strange beasts and savage tribes. Two lunar months at least, perhaps more."

"And the flower grows nowhere else?" Tonina asked.

"The honorable royal herbalist will tell you that some plants thrive only in certain climes."

Tonina looked at H'meen, who nodded, and a strange mood settled over the gathered company. The news was both good and bad. They now knew where the flower grew, but it was farther away than they had thought, and through hazardous country.

Finally Tonina said, "I will go to Copan," for there was no other choice.

She saw a look of displeasure darken Kaan's face. She knew what he was thinking: that escorting her to the Quatemalan coast was one thing, but taking her the greater distance to Copan was impossible. He needed to turn back for Teotihuacan in order to reach the Sisterhood in time for the special ritual, and he needed to stop first at Mayapan. It could not be done, she knew, if he continued south to Copan.

She wanted him to reach Teotihuacan and perform the funerary ritual for Jade Sky's soul. She did not know the rite's purpose, but suspected that it had something to do with Jade Sky being the victim of murder. Kaan must complete his pilgrimage before a certain day, and *she* must obtain the flower before the start of the next hurricane season.

While his companions mulled over this new wrinkle, wondering why the gods always seemed to bring bad news with good, Kaan rubbed his jaw and stared into the flames of the campfire. He was bound by religious law to help Tonina achieve her goal, and yet he owed it to Jade Sky to mete revenge upon the men who killed her. He could not, now, do both.

"I will go alone," Tonina said decisively, and waited for Kaan to object. Once again, she found herself anxious to be away from his influence. She wished she had not coaxed him into the lake that afternoon. What had possessed her to act so recklessly, when she knew her heart was starting to betray her? Guama and Huracan, Pearl Island, Brave Eagle—even the red flower—were taking up less time in her thoughts while Kaan was beginning to take up more. She had merely wanted to share with him the joy of the water, and to show him there was nothing to be afraid of. Instead he had come toward her and trustingly placed his hands in hers and she had felt a jolt go through her that had almost made her cry out.

Before Kaan could protest Tonina's announcement to go alone, H'meen said, "I will go with you. I must see what grows in the mountains of the gods."

One Eye added, "I will go, too." H'meen had given him hope again. The magic flower with its power to make him appear handsome to women. . . .

"Noble Kaan," Tonina said, addressing him across the campfire, "you have escorted me across perilous terrain, you have brought me to this place that begins my path to the red flower. Surely the gods are satisfied that you have repaid your debt to me and the world is in balance again. I cannot ask you to sacrifice more."

He met her eyes with a turbulent expression, his thoughts and emotions in turmoil. *The way she had guided him into the water, the play of a smile about her mouth, the wet cotton tunic clinging to the contours of her breasts, the nipples alluringly hard—*

But Tonina was not his destiny. Their paths had been joined only temporarily. Greater duties demanded his attention—the consortium in Mayapan, then Teotihuacan and Jade Sky's soul.

37

K aan was finally free.

Having agreed at last that the gods would deem his debt to Tonina paid, he had traveled with her as far as the village of Ixponé, where a modest market had provided food and supplies, and where guides into the Copan region could be hired. Kaan had asked Hairless and the Nine Brothers to stay with Tonina until she found the flower, to protect her and the great throng that had opted to follow her into the mountains, and from there escort her to the coast and see her safely on her way to Pearl Island.

They had spoken emotional good-byes and now he was on the road northward, alone and free, the morning sun in his eyes. Up ahead lay the encampment of a traveling merchant whom Kaan had met the evening before, a trader bound for Uxmal who had invited the noble Kaan to journey with them, and Kaan had accepted.

"We leave promptly at noon," the man had said pointedly.

Kaan told himself now, as he followed a path between flat green pineapple fields, that he was pleased with this turn of events, to be free of his obligation to Tonina. But his conscience was troubled. Despite her insistence that she could take care of herself, and despite Hairless's promise to protect her, something bothered him. . . .

The great crowd camped outside Ixponé, already starting to break rules, before Kaan had even said farewell.

Without him, would they become an unruly mob again?

Hearing heavy footfalls, he turned to see Balám sprinting along the path, wearing a mantle and sandals, weapons strapped to his back. Dressed for travel, Kaan noted in surprise. When he had asked Balám to return to Mayapan with him, Balám had declined. "There is a bounty on my head. They will put me on the slave block the instant I step through the gates. No, brother, I will head for Teotihuacan. Perhaps you and I will meet there in a grand reunion."

Yet here he was, running toward Kaan, waving an arm, and shouting, "I have changed my mind. I would travel with you part of the way."

"Where are the rest of your men?"

"They are enjoying a sport. For me, it holds no interest. They will catch up later."

"Sport?"

"Your people are having sport in the marketplace!"

Kaan frowned. "What are you talking about?"

"Some local Chichimecs cheated your men and now there is a fight and my cousins have stayed to lay wagers." Balám shrugged, adjusting the quiver of arrows on his back. "As you know, I myself no longer gamble."

Kaan bristled at "Chichimecs," a word he once ignored but that now stung like a thorn.

He squinted in the bright sunlight to survey the vast fields that had replaced thick jungle. Locals had told him of refugees from the far north, with tribal names like Zapotec, Mixtec, and Mexica, escaping strife in their homeland to stream into Maya territory, then slash and burn the jungle to plant pineapples.

Kaan understood the resentment of the locals. But he also remembered his own parents' plight, as they had made the difficult decision to leave their homeland and strike eastward into Maya land when he was a baby, hoping for a better life.

And then he recalled the "Chichimec" pineapple vendors in the Ixponé marketplace, simple people with paltry offerings. They were Nahua, he had noted, members of a tribe who spoke Nahuatl, the tongue his mother had spoken, the language of Kaan's boyhood. Humble folk, like his parents, struggling to survive.

Kaan brought his gaze back from the pineapple fields, and looked up at the sun. The traveling merchant had said he would not wait. With the caravan, Kaan would enjoy safe passage back to Mayapan. On his own, he would face dangers and possibly not survive. Judging the sun's position, he decided that if he hurried, he could return to Ixponé, remind his people of the laws he had set down, and get back to the caravan in time.

"Where are you going?" Balám called after him. "Brother, they are but miserable Chichimecs!"

The fruit sellers occupied a small space between a man selling ocelot skins and a merchant selling rope. Kaan strode into the marketplace before the startled eyes of people to whom he had earlier said good-bye, and saw that the fruit vendors, squatting behind their humble mat where pineapples were spread out, appeared to be a family consisting of an old man, two younger men, three women, and a child. They looked very poor, and they hadn't many pineapples to sell.

Kaan frowned. They were not being harassed by his own men, as Balám had said, but by a local Mayan wearing a red cotton loincloth and blue cotton mantle. He seemed very angry at the vendors, who cowered beneath his verbal onslaught. "Go back where you belong! We do not want dogs in Ixponé!"

When he kicked out at the fruit, sending pineapples flying, smashing them, Kaan lowered his travel pack to the ground and walked up to the angry Mayan to say quietly, "Is there trouble here?"

The Mayan looked him up and down, squinting, confused. He saw before him a man dressed like a Mayan, speaking perfect Mayan, and of noble bearing, with the tattoos of a man of rank. And yet . . . "These dogs come to our land and steal from us."

Kaan looked down at the huddled family, their smashed fruit. "How are they stealing?"

"I am a seller of pineapple. When people buy from these dogs, it impoverishes *me*!"

Kaan eyed the man's prosperous belly, the costly jade plugs in his ears, and said, "You do not look impoverished."

"Who *are* you?" the man growled, thrusting his face into Kaan's.

"It does not matter who I am," Kaan said quietly. "What matters is that these people have done no wrong. They want merely to survive. Surely there are enough customers for all."

"Are you one of *them*?" the burly man asked, jerking a thumb at the frightened family. "You look like them, somehow," he said, and he spat at Kaan's feet.

Kaan contemplated the droplets on the ground, thought of the noon sun, the caravan preparing to leave, and his urgency to be on his way to Mayapan. And he made a decision. "You should not have said that, friend," he said, lifting his eyes, facing the Mayan squarely.

"I'm no friend of yours!" the other man said, and he drew himself tall, curling his hands into fists. Three other Mayans moved close to their friend's side, challenging the newcomer.

In an instant, Hairless and the Nine Brothers joined Kaan, lining up with him, showing greater numbers and greater strength, ready to fight. But Kaan gestured for them to step back. They did so reluctantly, leaving their master to face the angry Mayans alone.

By now a small crowd had gathered, and more were arriving as word of a conflict spread. Already, bets were being placed. One Eye hurried as fast as he could, with H'meen at his side, wondering why Kaan had come back, and worried for his sake, fearing he was about to do something reckless. One man against four.

But Kaan did not appear to be intimidated as he calmly repeated his request. "Leave these people alone."

Again the other man spat at Kaan's feet. Kaan calmly untied his mantle, handing it to Hairless, who reluctantly accepted it.

Laughing, the Mayan did the same, ordering his comrades to stay out of the fray, that he could take on this dog alone. Wearing only loincloths, the two men squared off. And then the Mayan threw the first punch.

Although Kaan had not played the ball game in many days, he still had his edge. The fist flew past his head as he easily dodged it, while his own hand met with a solid target as it shot out and caught the big man in the neck.

With a grunt, the man staggered back, then flew at Kaan, who sidestepped and chopped the man on the back of his neck. The crowd cheered. The wagers grew. And the odds shifted in favor of Kaan.

But the Mayan, realizing he had underestimated the stranger, came back with renewed force, flying at Kaan, this time anticipating the side-step so that he made body contact and both men crashed to the ground.

The crowd grew. People pushed and jostled for a better view. Hairless and the six Nine Brothers closed protectively around Tonina, One Eye, and H'meen.

Kaan and the man grappled on the paving stones until they both shot to their feet and threw punches. The Mayan, though a sloppy fighter, was slightly taller and heavier, giving him an advantage. Kaan forced his mind away from the fight and onto a ball court. He was not fighting, he was playing the game. *Look for the hoop. Get the ball through. . . .*

The Mayan drew his arm back for what everyone thought would be the decisive punch, when Kaan startled everyone by dropping low and swiping out with one leg—a classic move on the playing field but never witnessed in a fight. As if to send a ball flying to his teammate, Kaan swept his leg against the Mayan's ankles with such force that the Mayan fell backward. As he stumbled, flailing his arms, Kaan flew up in the air and shot his leg out again in a move so sudden the crowd cried out in wonder. The heel of Kaan's foot connected with the man's jaw and sent him flying, to land unconscious in the middle of a pottery display.

Suddenly the fallen man's comrades were in the fight, not bothering to remove their mantles, coming at Kaan with fury.

"Help him!" Tonina said to Hairless. But the hirsute Mayan was mes-merized. This was the Kaan he had worshiped for so long. This was the man he had built his life around, following the Mayapan team from town to town. Hairless had not seen Kaan play in months, yet here he was, not exactly on a playing field but on the paving stones of an ancient plaza, and not exactly playing against a ball team, but proving himself against these bullies nonetheless, as he evaded their fists, danced around them, feinted and dodged, kicked out, confounding them, one man against four until the last man was knocked down and Kaan was the only one standing, sweating, heaving for breath, trickles of blood streaming down his body.

A hush fell over the crowd. No one moved or spoke. And then the first Mayan, coming to and shaking his head, struggled to his feet and, wiping the blood from his jaw, staggered away and out of the plaza, his comrades limping after him.

As the crowd erupted in cheers, gathering around the victor, Kaan retrieved his mantle from Hairless, knotted it around his neck, and then approached the pineapple vendors' stall. As they stared at him in awe, Kaan looked over the smashed fruit, hopelessly destroyed, and quietly said, "I wish to buy your fruit." He handed the old man five cacao beans, and as the elder blessed Kaan in Nahuatl, invoking the names of gods that Kaan remembered from his childhood, the excited crowd suddenly picked him off his feet and hoisted him onto their shoulders.

As Balám watched his former friend being carried around the plaza on the shoulders of frenzied admirers, he gripped his spear in fury. This was not why he had lured Kaan back to Ixponé on a false pretext! The ruse had backfired and now Kaan was a greater hero than ever—Kaan, who had blasphemed, desecrated statues of gods, and caused the ignominious death of his beloved Six Dove.

Balám readied himself to run out onto the plaza, to push his way through the crowd, thrust his spear upward in a swift move before anyone could see what was happening, and impale the great Kaan before the eyes of his foolish admirers. Balám would dash away before they could seize him, and run his spear, still red with Kaan's blood, through the body of the fortune-teller who could have spared Six Dove's life.

But as Balám tightened his grip on the wooden shaft and started forward, his mother's voice whispered in his head words he had forgotten. Or had not listened to at the time. Back in Uxmal, when he had hidden in the garden because his father had barred him from the house, the elegant Lady White Heron had come to him and said, "Son, you *can* redeem yourself. And you do not have to go to Teotihuacan to do it."

So deep had been his despair at the time, his fury with Kaan, his grief over the loss of Six Dove and Ziyal, that he had not listened to his mother's reply. It came back now, as crisp and clear as if she stood next to him.

And as he listened, Balám felt himself grow strangely calm. The plaza quieted. The noise, the people, the jungle—everything vanished until all Prince Balám of Uxmal was aware of was a white light that collected around him. He closed his eyes and absorbed the light, as if it were air in his lungs. Never had he felt so serene. Tranquility washed over him as if he stood beneath a refreshing waterfall.

As he absorbed the wondrous light, Balám felt it fill him with a strange new power, and an *understanding* that was so astonishingly clear and sharp, he had to hold his breath to contain it.

Behind his closed eyes he saw a vision of himself on a future day, and he knew the gods were showing him his destiny. As the ragged crowd continued to celebrate and *pulque* was being passed around, Prince Balám stood like a statue at the edge of the marketplace and suddenly he knew what he was born to do.

38

Tonina gazed down the length of the farmers' ball court illuminated by the full moon. Kaan was back in the encampment outside the village, conferring with Hairless. After the fight in the marketplace, Kaan had said it was too late for him to start for Mayapan, but he would do so in the morning.

Why had he come back?

Tonina thought about the fight. She had seen men fight before. On Pearl Island, they fought with clubs, or they wrestled. She had never seen a man fly up in the air as Kaan had and deliver a crippling blow with his foot. But the confrontation had also revealed more to her about the man who was increasingly occupying her thoughts: his deep-rooted sense of moral justice that made him stand up for others at personal sacrifice. Despite his urgency to be on the road to Mayapan, the plight of the poor pineapple sellers had made him set aside his own needs and go to their rescue.

She heard that they had given Kaan a special gift afterward. She wondered what it was.

Tonina herself had a gift for him. She did not know what had possessed her to part with her few remaining pearls, but a compulsion had driven her to the stall of a certain merchant who specialized in one product. When she had told him who the gift was for, he had brought out an item not on display for the casual buyer, but set aside for someone unique. And now she had it, and did not know how she was going to present it to him.

———

Kaan watched her in the moonlight, wondering why she had come to this humble, weedy ball court. He was torn, wanting to join her, and yet not. He had said good-bye once; he was not relishing doing so a second time.

"I have spoken with my men," he said as he walked up. "They assure me that law and order will be kept under tight control after I am gone."

She spun around, startled. "Then you leave," she said, "in the morning? Without the protection of a caravan?"

"I can waste no more time. Mayapan is not on the way to Teotihuacan, and so I must hurry." He glanced down at her hands and, when he saw what they held, raised his eyebrows.

"I bought this for you," she said, handing the ball to him. "The seller said it is the finest. I thought—," she began, and then did not know how to finish.

Kaan looked at the rubber sphere in his hands, felt the hardness and heft of it. "Mother Moon," he said softly.

"Why did you come back to Ixponé?"

He looked into her eyes, which were wide and clear. "Balám told me it was my people who were harassing the pineapple sellers. I felt responsible."

"But it was not our people."

"Nonetheless, the vendors needed defending."

One Eye had told Tonina after the fight that it was possible Kaan was actually defending his own people, for they were speakers of Nahuatl, which Kaan's own mother had been. It occurred to Tonina now that Kaan was not as ashamed of his race as he claimed to be, for he had fought for them at great risk to himself.

In the silver moonlight, she saw on his arms, chest, and jaw places where he had been wounded in that afternoon's fight, small injuries covered in H'meen's ointments. "But why did you stand up to the Mayans alone?" she asked. "Why did you not let your friends fight with you?"

Kaan thought of another group of bullies long ago, when he was a boy and older boys had ganged up on him. He had not been able to defend himself then, and Balám had come to his rescue. This time, for reasons he could not define, Kaan had decided that it was something he must do for himself.

"The pineapple sellers gave me a gift," he said, not answering her question. "I didn't want to take it but they insisted. Out of respect for their humble pride, I accepted it." Setting the ball on the ground, he reached into his waistband and brought out a small object wrapped in cloth.

"The old man told me the legend of a deity called the Earthbound Goddess. Long ago, she came to earth to see what we humans loved so much about our land. A local king captured the goddess and demanded she make him wealthy and powerful. When she refused, he buried her alive in an underground chamber, promising to keep her there forever until she granted his wishes."

Kaan unwrapped the cloth to reveal a small rock in the moonlight.

"The old pineapple seller told me that when he was a young man, he made a pilgrimage to the city of Palenque in the west, to pay homage to Kukulcan in the famous Time Temples there. On his way home, he came upon a traveler at the side of the road, dying. The pineapple farmer stayed with the man and took care of him in his final days. For this kindness, the man rewarded him with this."

Ghostly moonlight washed the object in silver light, but Tonina could not discern what it was. It looked like an ordinary rock.

"The dying traveler told the pineapple seller that he had gone to Palenque in search of the Earthbound Goddess in order to set her free. It is said she lives there still, underground, and possesses limitless powers, with the exception of setting herself free, and that she will grant any wish to the person who releases her."

"What is it?" Tonina asked, taking the rock, turning it around.

"I do not know. But the pineapple seller said it is the key to finding the Earthbound Goddess. He said that many men have tried, but none have succeeded. This stone, he said, will show the way."

How wondrous, Tonina thought as she replaced the rock in Kaan's hand and he rewrapped it, to tuck it back into his waistband. To rescue a goddess! If I were that person, what wish would I ask for?

The night breeze shifted and they caught the scent of cook fires and roasting food. Kaan knew he should get back to his camp, for he had an early start in the morning. Yet he could not move.

"Thank you," Tonina said, "for reminding the people of your laws. I had feared they might become unruly again, once you were gone."

"They will obey," he said.

"You take command so easily and the people do listen to you. Why are you such a reluctant leader when it comes so naturally to you?"

Tonina stood close to him; he could smell the fragrance of coconut, which he no longer found offensive but rather alluring, and the clicking sound of the many shells in her hair just added to the music of the night— monkeys and frogs in the trees, crickets in the underbrush—as all joined in a noisy chorus that surely must be heard as far away as the full moon.

"It is because of what my mother told me as a boy," Kaan said at last. "Do not ever be a failure, she said. It was her biggest fear for me, and soon it became *my* biggest fear."

"You try to win ball games," Tonina pointed out. "And most of the time you do."

"It is different with a team. It is all of us striving, all of us winning. But on my own . . ." He shook his head. "For as long as I can remember, I have avoided situations where I might fail."

" 'Do not ever be a failure,' " she murmured. "Are you sure that's what she meant?"

He looked at her, at the white paint on her face standing out in the bright moonlight. This, too, he no longer found annoying but in fact beautiful, in a strange way. "What else could it mean?" he asked softly.

Tonina did not answer.

Kaan studied the lines and dots and circles that decorated her features, realizing that they were not haphazardly applied as he had once thought, but carefully drawn to match the contours of her face. In astonishment, he realized that her face paint enhanced what he suspected was a natural beauty underneath.

"I have a recurring nightmare," he said, speaking words he had never thought he would, for this was his most private secret, one that he had never revealed even to Jade Sky. "In the nightmare I score the winning goal. But instead of the crowd cheering, they are laughing at me. And I suddenly realize that even though I am called the Great Kaan, the people actually despise me because I am a lowly Chichimec—a barbarian. They laugh and mock me, and one by one my teammates and friends turn their backs on me. Finally Jade Sky turns her back so that I am all alone in the world, and I wake up in a sweat."

"But you know that would never happen," Tonina said softly.

"Yes, I *know* it, but my heart fears that someday I am going to be discovered to be a fraud, someone is going to say that Kaan is not a hero after all. And that is why I have always avoided taking on leadership. Because what if I accept and then lead the people to disaster?"

Tonina did not know what to say. She was suddenly breathless, aware that he was revealing personal fears, aware, too, that they were alone on the deserted playing field, surrounded by dark jungle and a star-splashed sky.

Needing to say something, she looked down at the ball by her feet and tapped it with her toe. "How is the game played?"

His eyes flickered. He had said too much. This girl had no interest in his nightmares and personal fears. What was it about her that loosened his tongue? Clearing his throat, he assumed a professional air, as he did when new recruits arrived at the academy. "First of all, you do not touch the ball with hands or feet. Like this," he said, and moved to stand behind her, placing his hands on her hips. "Pretend that someone has sent the ball to you. Now thrust sideways as if to send it to another player."

Tonina swung her hips and Kaan was astonished to feel the muscle beneath the fabric of her skirt. She was not soft and fleshy. He sensed power in her, and knew she would be a worthy opponent in a ball game.

His thoughts shocked him. The longer he was away from Mayapan, the dimmer his memory of Jade Sky grew. Tonina was creeping into his thoughts and dreams, and now she threatened to steal into his heart.

As Kaan placed his hands on her hips, Tonina felt a jolt shoot through her. She mentally scolded herself. She had made a sacred vow to Guama and Huracan to find the red flower and return to her people, yet here she was enjoying the touch of a man she had known but a short time.

Stepping away so that his hands could not reach her, Tonina snatched up the ball and threw it at him, creating distance, challenging him, surprised to hear herself laugh.

He threw the ball back and Tonina ran to catch it with her hip, but her long skirt hampered her and she missed the ball. Muttering an oath in her native tongue, she paused to draw up the material and anchor it in the waistband.

Kaan was taken aback at the sudden sight of her bare legs, her creamy thighs and calves in the moonlight—strong legs, he noticed, realizing that a swimmer's legs would be like a ballplayer's.

Suddenly the ball was sailing back to him. He intercepted with his hip and shot it back to her. Tonina ran, laughing, to strike the ball with a shoulder, cheering when she saw how far it went. Kaan ran to the ball and jumped high, meeting it with his thigh and propelling the ball in another direction, forcing Tonina to run. As Kaan watched her, waiting for the return, he realized he was exhilarated, that he had not felt this way in months, for not even in the fateful Thirteenth Game had he felt so alive.

Catching the return ball with his hip, he gave his body an unexpected twist, to shoot the ball in a direction Tonina was not expecting. She dashed forward but miscalculated. The hard rubber ball struck her in the temple and sent her flying backward.

She landed on her back and lay still.

Kaan stopped abruptly, his chest heaving. "Tonina?" he whispered.

She did not move.

He broke into a run and dropped to her side, gathering her into his arms. "Tonina! Are you all right?"

She moaned. Rolled her head. Her eyelids fluttered open. *"Guay,"* she whispered. "I saw stars."

"Can you see me?" he asked, studying her eyes. But her pupils were equal and, after a moment, focused on his face. She smiled. "You are supposed to *save* my life."

"Thank the gods," he murmured in relief. Impulsively he pressed his lips to the place where the ball had struck her, then he lifted her in his arms and carried her off the field. Tonina moaned and curled her arms around his neck, her head on his shoulder as she floated in a sweet netherworld. Kaan's warmth permeated her clothes; she felt the power of his arms, and thought she could ride in them forever.

As he walked with her, Kaan was overcome by the feel of her in his arms, the sensation of cool, bare flesh on the arm that supported her legs. He lowered her onto a soft patch of cool grass and once again anxiously searched her face. "How do you feel? Shall I take you to H'meen?"

"I am all right. Just give me a moment. . . ."

Kaan reached out and ran a thumb over her forehead, near the place she had been hit, and smudged a white symbol. "Why do you never remove the face paint?" An impulsive question, spoken before he could call it back.

"To hide my plainness," she said in a soft voice, startled that the confession of her secret had tumbled so easily from her lips.

"I doubt you are plain." Kaan almost said, "I think you are very pretty," but caught himself, although it was the truth, even though he was only just now realizing it. He had never really given thought to the Mayan ideal of beauty—the sloping forehead, elongated eyes, receding chin, and protruding teeth—but now he realized he did not find such features beautiful at all.

"On the islands I am plain," Tonina said. "In fact, to them I am homely."

" 'Them'? Your people?"

"I am not an island girl." She told her story briefly; Huracan finding the basket in the shallows, he and Guama raising the child as their own. "Since Guama and Huracan told everyone I was brought to the island by the sea gods, it made me an outsider. Islanders wear much face paint, and so I used it as a shield, to hide my differences, and at the same time to look like them."

Kaan was momentarily speechless, then he said, "You do not know who your people are?"

She shook her head and wished he would lift her in his arms again.

"Have you ever thought of searching for them?"

"I had a childhood dream that I would one day meet my mother. But the dream died long ago. Until . . ."

He waited. Tonina struggled to sit up, and Kaan supported her with one arm, bringing her face close to his.

"I watched you say good-bye to your mother in the palace kitchen," she said. "You were so tender with her, and she was so loving to you. I want to experience that."

"You have no idea who your parents are? No clue?"

"Just this." She lifted one of her necklaces from beneath her blouse: the medallion still encased in Guama's woven jacket of palm fibers. "My grandmother concealed it because she feared its power, she said, and she was also afraid someone might steal it."

"Have you ever looked inside?"

"Guama said I would know when the time was right. But it has never felt like the right time." Tonina said nothing more as she slipped the pendant beneath her tunic. But there was more: her fear of what she would find when the wrapping came off. *I would no longer be Tonina of Pearl Island.*

"I also have the small blanket I was swaddled in," she said. "Guama said the embroidered design might be significant."

"Tonina, you must search for your mother," Kaan said, unable to imagine such a thing, for he had lived with his mother during his early years, and after that, only a few streets away from her. Never to have known her, to not even know her name or her face—he could not imagine it.

"No, I must return to Pearl Island," she said. "I promised them. But I do want to know who my mother is," she said with sudden passion. "And where I come from. My heritage. My culture. If I had not been placed upon the sea in a basket, who would I be now; my name, the language I speak, the gods I worship? How different would my life be? I long to sit among people who share my bloodline and no longer be an outsider."

Kaan thought about the irony of their situations, a girl who did not know her bloodline but yearned to know, and a man who did know his bloodline and wished he did not.

"Kaan, what is the name of your people?"

Her question startled him. "I do not know. I was told long ago, but I have forgotten." He drew aside his mantle and pointed to a mark on the left side of his chest, over his heart, which Tonina had assumed was an old game scar. "I received this tattoo when I was a boy, and so it has grown distorted and unidentifiable. I believe it signifies my mother's tribe."

Tonina wanted to touch the tattoo that decorated a firm pectoral. Wanted to put her lips to it and kiss it.

Kaan suddenly could not breathe. Sexual desire swept over him in such an unexpected and overwhelming wave that he leaned away from Tonina and looked up at the full moon, dipping behind the towering cedars. "We should be getting back to camp. We both have much to do before going our separate ways."

As he helped her to her feet, Tonina lifted her face to him and said, "You are so fortunate. You have a people to be proud of. I have no one. You ask me if I will search for my mother, but I am afraid. I was set upon the sea for a reason. Was I a sacrifice? If I find my people, will they sacrifice me again?"

Taking her by the arms, Kaan said with sudden passion, "And what if you were taken *from* them? Torn from your mother's arms by ruthless men, to be put on the sea out of her reach. What if she saw you drift away on the current, helpless to bring you back? What if she has been grieving for you every day since? Tonina, this is something I feel most strongly and with all my heart. No matter how I feel about my true people, about the race into which I was born and of whom, yes, I am ashamed, I honor my mother."

"Then why—," she began, biting her lip. It was none of her business.

"Why do I allow her to toil in the royal kitchen while I live a life of luxury? Tonina, that is not my choice! I begged her to live with us, I tried to set her up in her own villa with servants. But my mother is proud of the work she does, preparing feasts for the king. Tonina, a mother is to be placed on a pedestal. She is a part of you. You lived the first months of your life in her body. And when you were born, she loved you. That is why, no matter where she is or what she has done, above all else, you must find your mother."

Electrified by his words, Tonina suddenly saw a vision: running down a path toward a hut, a woman in the doorway, arms outstretched, tears in her eyes. The details were unclear. What were the clothes? The jewelry? How did the woman wear her hair? What language did she speak?

Tonina grew dizzy from the astounding prospects that Kaan had suddenly opened before her. It was as if all her hopes and dreams had been sealed in a clay jar, and Kaan had broken that seal, to let the contents out. Like butterflies, they flew around her, and Tonina wanted to pluck them all from the air and hold them close to cherish them.

And she wanted to kiss this wondrous man named Kaan, to embrace him in gratitude as she thought in excitement: Yes, I *will* find my mother.

As Kaan bent to retrieve the ball from the damp grass, fresh emotion shot through him. Tonina had given him this. She had given the game back to him when he had thought he would never play again. Impulsively taking her by the arms he said, "Tonina, you are right about the mob. For some reason they see me as their leader, and I fear that when I am gone they will relapse into lawlessness. I see now that my debt to you is not yet repaid, for if I leave you now, I leave you in peril."

"But Mayapan—"

"If I do not return to Mayapan now, there is still time for me to go to Copan, and afterward carry on to Teotihuacan. Vengeance follows no calendar, Tonina. I can conduct my personal justice with the consortium *after* my pilgrimage to the Sisterhood of Souls."

His grip tightened. He wanted to kiss her, to pull her to him and hold her forever.

Tonina looked up at him, spellbound as she sensed his inner struggle. He said, "Tomorrow, Tonina, I will go with you to Copan."

39

Kaan slashed at vines and creepers when suddenly, out of the mist, a man rose before him on the trail.

Kaan brought his people to a halt. As he took the measure of the silent sentinel that barred his way, he saw eyes made of stone, a face partially broken away, and one hand missing. The statue had been carved centuries ago, Kaan realized, and now was claimed by the jungle.

He sent for H'meen to see if the markings were significant. They had encountered many of these upright stone slabs—called stelae—at Tikal and other places, erected by kings to mark territory or to record momentous events. While H'meen had been able to read most, on this one she could interpret only a few of the glyphs, as the engravings had been weathered smooth. "It says his name was King Rabbit, but his accomplishments, listed here, are too decayed to decipher. Whoever he was, his memory has been lost in time."

"Does this stela mark a city's boundary?" Kaan asked, squinting ahead through the silent mist, seeing only ghostly trees and phantom shrubs.

"It does, honorable Kaan. We have arrived."

At last, the fabled city of Copan.

Kaan gave the signal and the trek resumed, at a quicker pace now, with people talking excitedly among themselves. Surely the red flower was near at hand!

In the forty-two days since they had left Ixponé in Quatemalan, the great crowd that followed Kaan and Tonina had continued to shift, reshape, and grow, like a living organism. Six people had died en route; four babies had been born. Some original members decided to settle in peaceful villages, while new hopefuls took their places. Mayans left, members of other races joined. Couples married and divorced. Families broke up, new families were formed, and because the people looked to Kaan to administer justice, he had reluctantly sat in judgment on six accusations of theft, one of rape, three of adultery, five of wife-beating, four of cheating in games of chance, one of murder, and two of blasphemy. He had meted out punishments while H'meen had recorded the proceedings, adding new laws to the growing list.

Hairless, the hirsute giant, was now a widower. Three days out of Ixponé, his wife had dropped into an unseen sinkhole, with a dead log falling in after her, crashing down on her head. When the men hauled her out, they found that her neck had snapped, separating her skull from her spine. Amazingly, she was still alive—skin, muscle, and spinal cord were undamaged. But she could not control her head, so that it fell every which way until Hairless devised a wooden brace to prop it up. But even though she could breathe and talk, she had lost the ability to swallow, and so she died a few days later. With her wits fully about her, sitting upright, she said good-bye to her friends. She then asked Hairless to remove the uncomfortable brace. He tearfully did so, and her head fell back so that it rested between her shoulder blades and she looked up at the sky. With a whispered blessing to everyone, the woman died.

Now they were in a land of misty mountains, descending a trail through leaves and vines, their eyes open for the first sign of the great city described by the message-carrier outside of Tikal. It had been an arduous trek over hills and valleys, cutting their way through giant ferns, ropy vines, and snakelike tree roots that curled up out of the soil, with only occasional sunlight breaking through the overhead canopy. And unrelenting *green*.

In all that time and in all that vegetation, they had not found the red flower.

But as Tonina walked at Kaan's side, hacking at vines and growth with her knife, she was able to bite back her disappointment. Because, ever since the night she and Kaan had stood in the moonlight at the Ixponé ball court, she had been driven by a new hope. "You must find your mother," Kaan had said. Five simple words, and yet necklaces and bracelets of jade and gold would not have been a greater gift.

Finally the jungle trail ended and the group came upon a wide valley through which a river flowed, its bottomlands dotted with farms and huts.

But no city.

Kaan signaled for his people to lay down their burdens, which they did gladly, eyeing the pole-huts thatched with corn husks, the farms green with crops. People came out of doorways, or ceased work to stare in fear at the huge mass of newcomers.

A bald-headed man appeared from the largest hut, flanked by two young men and a gray-haired woman. The man was draped in filthy ocelot pelts stiffened with dirt, grease, and blood. He wore a bone through his nose and bones through his earlobes; his cheeks had been pierced with the long stiff whiskers of a large cat.

Kaan approached with hands held out in a gesture of peace. "Blessings of the gods," he called in Mayan. "We are weary travelers who come seeking only to rest. We will trade for food and space. We will not disturb your community. We will honor your gods and your ancestors."

The bald man identified himself as Chief Ocelot, and he wrinkled his nose at the ragtag collection of children, old folks, and sick people. "Where do you come from?" he asked warily.

"We came from Quatemalan, noble chief," Kaan said. "We have climbed many mountains to reach this place."

Ocelot laughed and said, "You came from Quatemalan? Then those were not mountains you crossed, my friend." He turned and pointed eastward. "*Those* are mountains!"

Tonina and Kaan stared in awe at green peaks rising to the sky to disappear in mist.

"That is the great Cloud Forest," the chief said boastingly, as if he had created it himself. "Any man who climbs that high never comes down."

"Where is the city?" Kaan asked.

"City? You mean Copan?" Gesturing for them to follow, Ocelot led his visitors to the other side of the settlement, to the bank of the river, and he pointed again. "There is Copan."

Kaan and Tonina could barely glimpse, through vines and creepers, a stone wall embraced by monstrous leaves and tangles of giant roots. As their eyes adjusted to the confusing overgrowth, they made out collapsed lintels and caved-in vaults, tumbledown walls and buildings entirely overgrown by vegetation.

Chief Ocelot said, "For one thousand years great kings lived in that city. It is said that two times thirteen thousand people once lived there. And then, for reasons known only to the ancestors, the last king erected the last stone stela and those great people built no more."

Kaan looked at the ruins claimed by a greedy jungle, and surmised that the last man to leave Copan had done so hundreds of years ago.

Tonina eyed the wide river that stood between them and the city. "Is there no access?" she asked, thinking that a rare flower could grow in those neglected ruins and thrive unharmed.

"An old rope bridge lies upriver. But the city is taboo. The gods do not allow us to trespass there. But come now and enjoy our hospitality! You will see that we are civilized people."

When Kaan and Tonina entered Ocelot's large hut, they received a shock. They were walking upon a man's face.

The chief puffed out his chest. "It took thirty men to haul this stone from the ruins. Whoever he was," he said, pointing to the stone carving with vacant eyes that served as the hut's floor, "whether god or king, his spirit watches over my house."

The gray-haired woman turned out to be Ocelot's wife. Her plump body was draped in a long cotton shift with many beaded necklaces, and, although she was Mayan and wore her hair drawn back in the traditional long tail, her forehead was not sloping. Her head rested on a goiter the size of a melon, and her eyes bulged. While her husband went off to make preparations for a feast, she pointed to a wide mat on the floor and said with a smile, "Here is where guests sleep. You will be comfortable."

Tonina eyed the mat. "We sleep together?"

The chief's wife gave them a blank look.

Kaan said, "We are not married."

As the woman's protruding eyes looked from Kaan to Tonina, her two guests saw in her expression what they had seen on the faces of other strangers encountered during the journey: the scrutiny to determine what tribe these two belonged to, as they were obviously neither Mayan nor islander, body adornments and clothing notwithstanding. Both tall, too, the chief's wife noted. *He* looked like he came from the north, Mixtec perhaps. Hard to tell about the girl beneath all that face paint. But they must be a couple, there was enough similarity.

While there was a time when Kaan would have jumped at an invitation to sleep indoors on a proper sleeping mat, he now said, "Thank you for your hospitality, honorable mother, but I will make my own camp outside."

Tonina watched him leave, recalling the first night of their journey, when Kaan had not known how to start a fire. In the days since, he had learned wilderness survival so that he was no longer a sheltered city-dweller depending on servants for his needs.

As Kaan set up his own small camp against the south wall of the chief's spacious hut, he surveyed his people as they found places between huts and fields to light fires and spread sleeping mats. Somewhere along the way, this amorphous mass of humanity had organized itself into an orderly entity, with artisans and various professionals instinctively grouping together. It was like a traveling town, Kaan thought, with its Street of Weavers and Lane of Potters. Once a camp was set up, and the idols of gods and the bones of ancestors placed on makeshift altars, the skilled workers produced their looms, carving tools, clay and paints, feathers and string, and set about to create goods to be traded with those in the camp who hunted and gathered food, or with people encountered en route.

Although Kaan had led them and lived with them for many days and nights, and although they came to him with their disputes, complaints, and woes, he did not feel a part of them. He did not feel a part of anyone or anyplace. So long now out of Mayapan, he was experiencing a growing sense of alienation. His only link to that city was his mother, who had said she would not live long enough to see him again. He had not been born there, had no blood ties to Mayapan, nor to anyone that he knew of in the whole world. Where his mother's people were, he did not know. The name of her tribe, which she had told him long ago, Kaan had since forgotten. And so on sturdy foot did Kaan, the hero of the ball game, who was not Mayan or Mixtec or Zapotec, walk past farms, villages, and towns, and nowhere could he stand and say, "Here is where I belong."

"Blessings!" Chief Ocelot called out as he joined him, offering Kaan a freshly rolled cigar, lit and smoldering. "I see you have a dwarf among your people. I would like to buy him. We have a dwarf, of course, but he has two eyes! I am willing to pay many skins for yours."

Kaan accepted the cigar but did not smoke it. "He is not for sale."

Ocelot grunted. "You are the leader of all these people?"

"No. I am on a solitary quest. They are following me because they think I have good luck."

"Who then *is* their leader?"

"They have none."

Ocelot scanned the vast encampment that had transformed his sleepy settlement, his own people now engaging in commerce and friendly gossip with the newcomers. "But where are they going, all these people?"

"I do not know."

Ocelot pursed his tobacco-stained lips, making the stiff cat whiskers quiver on his cheeks, and he decided that he would not mind being the chief of so large a group, especially one that contained skilled craftsmen, expert hunters, and, according to reports, a royal *h'meen*! They had brought many gods with them, which was also a good thing; he could already feel the good luck in the air and the promise of new prosperity. If he could persuade these people to stay, perhaps he could put them to work building a new settlement here. After all, if a hut could have a stone floor, why not stone walls? Why not have more stone brought from the ruins to build a new city here? Ocelot could have himself a fine house of stone—a palace even!

Visions danced suddenly before his eyes: a throne, a crown, people bowing to him, warriors standing at attention, emissaries from other kingdoms bringing tribute. It was so grand and perfect a vision that Ocelot could not believe his luck. All he had to do was think of a way to convince these people to settle here, and then set himself up as their chief. His greedy eyes slid sideways to the tall man at his side. Officially elected leader or not, obviously Kaan was the people's chosen chief.

Ocelot smiled. A small obstacle. Poison should do it.

"You will join us in a feast tonight, my new friend," he said, and went in search of the local shaman.

The interior of Ocelot's spacious hut was like all others Tonina had entered: woven mats on the floor, strings of garlic and peppers hanging from the rafters; an altar for the gods, one for the ancestors; clothing draped on pegs; spears, bows, and arrows propped against the wall; sandals, eating bowls, and waterskins organized on wooden shelves.

As Tonina unpacked her travel pack, answering the many questions the chief's wife had about lands to the west, she showed the woman her embroidered baby blanket. It was a habit Tonina had gotten into after Kaan had sparked her new desire to find her mother. Along the way, at farms and settlements, she would show the small blanket around, asking if anyone recognized the embroidery. But no one had, just as the chief's wife now shook her head over the melonlike goiter, saying it was no embroidery she was familiar with.

"If it is a clan symbol," she said, "those are kept only within the clan. Cloth that is embroidered for export would not bear a private symbol, and so few people outside of this particular region would recognize the pattern."

Tonina detected an accent in the woman's Mayan. "You are not from here?" she ventured.

"I married Ocelot as a young girl. But I was born far to the north, on the Quatemalan coast. I have island blood in me," she said with pride. "But I suspect you do not, even though you are painted with island symbols."

"I come from a place called Pearl Island. Have you heard of it?"

"The name is familiar. When I was a girl, many island traders came to our village. I remember pearls and oyster shells."

Tonina grew excited. "Do you know how far Pearl Island is from the nearest coast?"

The woman sniffed and rubbed her nose to coax childhood memories back to life. "It would be many days' sailing, straight northeast. But it can be done, I think. Just avoid the stormy season, as you would know."

The stormy season, Tonina thought anxiously, lay just four months away. "And the coastline?" she asked. "Are there any inlets or safe harbors?"

"Eh? The coastline? Of Quatemalan, you mean? Don't need harbors, it's all flat and swampy, end to end, dotted with lagoons."

Tonina frowned. Grandfather had described craggy cliffs and dangerous rocky shores. Was there another coastline? Had she misunderstood?

"I am searching for a rare flower," she said, describing it, demonstrating with her hands, but the woman shook her head above the protruding goiter.

"I have seen no such flower, have never heard of it, not in this area."

Tonina thought of the towering mountains to the east, disappearing into clouds, and the area north, the Quatemalan coast, and she thought: I could spend months—*years*—looking for the flower.

Thanking the chief's wife, she left the hut to go in search of Kaan, whom she found across the busy compound, talking to H'meen.

He consulted daily with the royal botanist, one of whose duties was to keep track of the days, calculating by using the Mayan measure of twenty-day months as well as island time, which went by lunar months. There were local calendars as well, among people who lived outside the influence of the Maya to the north and the islands to the northeast. H'meen included all of these in her calculations and had been able, only the night before, to assure Kaan once again that the point of no return— when he could no longer turn around and reach Teotihuacan in time— still lay days away.

Tonina watched him as he squatted before the fifteen-year-old girl, his big hand patting little Poki's head. Kaan was always tender and patient with H'meen, as if she were truly a woman of advanced years.

Kaan thanked H'meen and straightened, turning Tonina's way. When their eyes met across the smoky encampment, her heart leaped. Though she fought with all her might, she could not suppress her growing desire for him. She told herself repeatedly that they could never be together, that an insurmountable obstacle stood between them.

254 🦎 BARBARA WOOD

The sole purpose of Kaan's pilgrimage to Teotihuacan, Tonina reminded herself, was to pray for his wife's soul. She knew that his love for Jade Sky left no room for anyone else.

As Kaan approached, he wondered when he had stopped thinking of Tonina as a responsibility decreed by the gods. It had been a while since he had thought of the religious law that bound them together. He truly wanted to help Tonina find the flower.

He reminded himself that such feelings were dangerous. He should not be thinking of another woman, only of Jade Sky. He tried, every night, to keep her memory alive, to keep his love for her strong. The Kukulcan statuette and lock of hair were reminders, but when he looked at the blue feather Jade Sky had given to Brave Eagle, all he could think of was when Tonina had given it to him in Tikal.

It seemed to Kaan that his body and heart were determined to betray him, for when he reached Tonina, he could not help but look at the spot on her head, near the hairline, where the ball had struck her, and he had pressed his lips there, tasting the coconut of her face paint, wishing he could taste more.

"I have a plan," he said. "And H'meen has given me a timetable in which to work it. I promise you we will find the flower."

Tonina was surprised to feel a pang of disappointment, when she should have been elated. But she could not help think that, once the flower was found, she and Kaan would go their separate ways.

"Afterward," he continued, "I will see to it that Hairless and his brothers escort you to the coast, hire a canoe and oarsmen for you, and that you are safely on your way home."

Kaan hated speaking the words. He found himself dreading their parting. As he looked at her in the deepening dusk, with cooking aromas filling the air, along with the sounds of laughter, music, shouting, arguments, and children crying—as the two stood alone in the midst of a sea of humanity, it occurred to Kaan that, just as the pilgrimage to Teotihuacan had been thrust upon him, so had the duty of finding the red flower been thrust upon her.

The more he stayed with her, the more he realized how much they had in common. What was next? he wondered, already suspecting what was next—that beneath the white face paint and symbols of the islands, he would find racial features similar to his own.

"I will organize searches," he said perfunctorily. "I will appoint each of the Nine Brothers to head a team, and they will go off in all directions. H'meen has obtained a map of this region. We shall cover every piece of ground, examine every tree and bush. Do not worry, Tonina, we *will* find the flower."

It was a good plan, Tonina thought. But she was still worried. If Kaan were to unleash this great crowd upon the surrounding jungle, and the delicate, rare flower were found, what then? So many were desperate, and as the journey had lengthened, their desperation had grown. They could descend upon the fragile blossom and utterly destroy it.

She surveyed the encampment in bewilderment. How had it come to this? Guama had sent her to find a medicine to cure Grandfather's sickness, but somewhere along the way the red flower had taken on mythic proportions. Camped near the river was a mother whose listless baby would not eat; beneath a mahogany tree sat a man with useless legs, carried by his family all the way from Uxmal; nearby was the young woman who had gone deaf suddenly and had left her farm to follow Tonina. So many filled with desperate hope, all wanting the flower's magic for themselves.

Tonina knew she must find the flower before the mob did.

❧ 40 ❧

The young woman squirmed impatiently beneath Prince Balám's thrusts.

He was not the skilled lover she had expected and so she had to force herself to be patient as he went about his business. She was only submitting to him because he was of royal blood. And if this hasty coupling resulted in pregnancy, so much the better. Her child would be the offspring of a prince of Uxmal.

Balám finally released a low growl, shuddered, and slumped. The young woman waited a polite moment, then pushed at his shoulders so that he rolled onto his back. Rising to her feet, she let her skirt fall—he had not even bothered to undress her—and hurried away through the trees, back to the women's camp where she would report to her friends a more romantic and flattering version of the event.

Balám gave no thought to the young woman as he retied his loincloth. He never thought about them. The prince had developed a voracious sexual appetite, choosing a woman almost every night. The couplings were hurried and with only fleeting gratification. Balám was driven by a hunger that could not be sated, and he knew its roots lay in Six Dove. No amount of female flesh could compete with the great bosom and magnificent thighs of one of the fattest and lustiest women in Mayapan.

And she was dead.

His one consolation was that one day he would find his daughter.

During the blinding epiphany in the Ixponé market, when he had seen his destiny, Balám had known that he would be reunited with Ziyal. It was this certainty that drove him, that kept him to the trail blazed by

Kaan and his pitiful followers. When Balám led his men through the jungle, one desire glowed in his mind like a beckoning torch: to hold his daughter again.

At the heart of Balám's secret plan were the destinies of Kaan and the island girl. Although they did not know it, *they* were going to be the instruments that would lead him to Ziyal.

O ne Eye could not help being nosy. It was his nature. And now that Kaan had brought the crowd to a temporary settlement, One Eye felt the call of his profession: to collect information and then find buyers for it.

Life was good. He was sleeping with women again. While he knew they only did it to catch his good luck, and while he yearned for a woman to love him for himself, he saw no reason to be denied the pleasure of a warm body sharing his *hamac*. Before leaving Tikal he had gotten a haircut—island fashion, using a coconut shell to trim his hair into a "bowl" style—and a new leather eye patch with a blue cotton ribbon to tie it to his head. Wearing a bright orange mantle and a handsome red loincloth, One Eye the dwarf felt like his old charming self once more.

Having made acquaintances in the river settlement, getting himself known, being the congenial fellow that he was—and no one would suspect so colorfully attired a gentleman of being a spy—One Eye decided to see what Prince Balám and his cousins were up to. Kaan's people had seen little of the small knot of warriors who traveled half a day behind. "I will follow you to Copan," Balám had declared in Ixponé, "for those who follow you are weak and they are many, and you have few warriors. My men and I will offer protection. And then you and I will travel together to Teotihuacan." But when Kaan had invited Balám to share their camp, the prince said, "I will keep a distance so that my accursed presence will not pollute you."

One Eye did not believe him.

Suspecting that the Uxmal prince was up to something, the crafty dwarf decided on this cool winter's evening to see what he could learn of Kaan's erstwhile "brother."

Balám's contingent had grown so that his camp was now spread over a large area, and included women, many of whom had the sole occupation of making tortillas—a daylong, ceaseless labor—as there were now many men to feed. Balám did not ask questions of those wishing to join him. These were not like the people in Kaan's group, the sick and the lame who traveled with their gods and hope. Balám attracted bored young men, husbands deserting families, and criminals running from justice. There were no weaklings in his group, and there was a lot of anger and bitterness, which Balám knew would one day stand him in good stead. All he asked of his followers was obedience.

And patience.

As he sat at his noisy campfire, he thought of what he was going to do next, but chatter invaded his head. Balám never ate alone. He had found within himself a deep need for constant human company. He told himself it was because of the loneliness resulting from losing his family and being away from home and the familiar.

He could not face the real reason: The ruined city of Copan had filled him with a nameless dread. He could not think of the crumbled buildings and vacant causeways without a cold horror chilling his soul. Unlike Tikal, where some of the structures were still in use, Copan was completely dead. The locals said that at the city's height as many as twice thirteen thousand people lived here—warriors, priests, scholars, astronomers, scribes, nobles. Where did they go? Why did they leave?

And so he surrounded himself with animated young men, filled with life and ambition, and who liked to joke and talk and laugh until the ruins and the ghosts left Balám's uneasy thoughts.

"Cousin," one of the young men across the fire called, "you said that when we arrived here you would let us in on a secret."

At noon, hunters had trapped and slain a tapir, giving it to the women to gut and divide among the groups at various campfires. A haunch had gone to Balám's personal fire, and it slowly roasted now as the prince and his cousins waited in hungry anticipation. Giving the juicy meat a poke with his knife to test for readiness, he told them the secret, and when they heard the story, they laughed.

"But why, Cousin, would you ask the big-headed message-carrier to spin this false tale of a red flower in Copan?"

"I have my reasons," Balám said tersely. He had first planned to hang the island girl from a *chicle* tree, alerting Kaan to her whereabouts only when she was on the brink of death, so that Kaan would have the pain of watching her die. But then the *chicle* harvesters had mentioned a traveler staying in their camp, a message-carrier, and Balám had come up with a better idea: to drive Kaan yet farther south so that he would never reach Teotihuacan in time.

"So there is no red flower here, Cousin?"

"No red flower anywhere—and certainly not the one the island girl so foolishly searches for."

He drove his knife into the roasting haunch, and pink juices flowed. Declaring the meat done, he hacked a small piece first, for Buluc Chabtan, his new god, and, dropping the chunk into the fire, recited a prayer to the deity of warriors. Balám then carved a slab of rare flesh for himself and sat back to eat as his comrades descended upon the meat.

"I propose a wager!" one of the cousins declared after a spell of silent chewing, instantly sparking Balám's interest. "Up there," the cousin said, pointing with a greasy finger to an overhead branch, "there sits an owl. I will bet that when I throw this rock, the bird will fly away to the east. Who challenges me?"

"I do," Balám said with a grin. Nothing got his blood up like a wager. "I say the bird will fly west. What are the stakes?"

"This ocelot pelt," the cousin said, slapping the handsome spotted hide he wore over his shoulders, "and all the jade I possess."

But Balám said sportingly, "You have to make it more interesting than that, otherwise where is the excitement?"

"What do you propose, Cousin?"

"A hand," Balám said with a grin, throwing down leftover gristle and wiping his fingers on his mantle. "The loser sacrifices a hand, but he can choose which, right or left."

His companions fell silent. It would be cowardly for the man who had proposed the wager to back down. And yet he did not relish losing a hand.

Blessed Lokono! One Eye thought as he watched from his hiding place, marveling that Balám would risk losing a hand over so trifling a wager. There was no telling which way the owl would fly!

One Eye was amazed that Balám could still gamble after everything that had happened to him. A sane man would have learned his lesson. But One Eye knew it was a sickness in Balám, who would no doubt wager his own soul if the stakes were tempting enough.

"Agreed," the cousin said, but with less heart than when he was risking a pelt.

With all eyes on the treetop, the cousin threw the rock and the owl flew off the branch—eastward!

Balám had lost.

Rather than cry out in jubilation, the challenger fell silent, wondering if his princely cousin was truly going to pay up. But Balám was grinning as he reached for a club fitted with sharp obsidian blades. He reached out his left arm—his companions' eyes widening in disbelief, and One Eye's throat running dry—and in a move so quick no one saw it coming, grabbed the right hand of the cousin sitting next to him and hacked it off in one swipe.

The man howled, gave Balám a startled look, and then slumped to the ground in a dead faint. While others rushed to his aid, Balám held the bloody hand aloft and said merrily, "I did not say I would pay with one of my *own* hands!" and he threw the severed member into the fire.

His companions roared with laughter, filling the night with yelps of delight. But as they were warriors and hunters, with keen senses and cat-like reflexes, they nonetheless heard a sound that did not belong—the snapping of a twig underfoot.

Balám was immediately on his feet, his cousins joining him to scan the surrounding forest. "There!" cried one, and they ran for the trees, reaching the spy before he could get far on his short legs.

One Eye shrieked in terror as he was seized by his neck and lifted from the ground.

Balám brought his face close and said, "I warned you about spying on me, little man."

"Forgive me, honorable prince," One Eye gasped as his mantle grew tight at his throat. "I swear upon the bones of my great-grandfather—"

Balám raised the dwarf over his head and hurled him as hard as he could, slamming One Eye against the broad trunk of a mahogany tree so that he fell with cries of pain.

Balám was on him again, picking him up by his heels, to swing him around and bash him against the tree.

One Eye howled and sobbed for mercy.

Again he was taken by the heels, swinging around, slamming the tree so hard that One Eye felt his teeth rattle.

Balám finally dropped him to the ground and put his sandaled foot on One Eye's barrel chest. "I am going to skin you alive," he growled, "and roast you like a dog."

But one of the cousins stepped up and, placing a hand on Balám's arm, warned, "It is the worst luck to kill a dwarf."

Balám squinted down at the small form sobbing beneath his foot. One Eye's left arm lay at an unnatural angle, and one of his legs was broken.

Kneeling next to him, Balám said, "Now listen to me. If you repeat anything you overheard here tonight, or if you tell anyone that I did this to you, I will make the girl suffer. I will slowly torture her to death while you watch. Do you understand?"

One Eye nodded through a haze of pain, and was wondering how he was going to get back to the main camp when, instead of rising and telling him to go, Balám unsheathed the obsidian knife at his waist and proceeded to carve four slashes into One Eye's face.

When the dwarf shrieked, Balám stuffed the corner of One Eye's mantle into his mouth. He then carved two more sets of four on One Eye's chest. They were not deep enough to be lethal, or to make him bleed to death, just enough to throw off suspicion.

When he was done and One Eye had stopped shrieking, Balám

resheathed his knife and hoisted the unconscious dwarf onto his shoulders. Balám's camp was upriver from Kaan's, north of the ancient suspension bridge, and so he broke into a trot, the lifeless body bouncing on his back.

As he strode unceremoniously through the vast encampment that had swallowed up Ocelot's peaceful village, people fell silent. One by one, at each fire, people stared at the prince with the bloody dwarf on his shoulders, until Balám reached Kaan's camp and deposited One Eye on the ground, saying, "I found him outside my camp. He must have been attacked by a giant cat, judging by the claw marks."

H'meen was immediately at One Eye's side with her medicine kit. "It is so," she said to Kaan. "These are the marks of a jaguar."

"Can you save him?" Kaan asked.

She raised tear-filled eyes. "The gods willing," she whispered.

❦ 41 ❦

The day was ominous, with a strangely overcast sky, the air crisp and chill, and wind blowing from the northeast, carrying the threat of rain. The grass hut was poor shelter against the elements as the group huddled around the fire, wrapped in cloaks, waiting for H'meen to finish her astronomical calculations.

Two cycles of the moon had passed, and no red flower had been found in the vicinity of the ancient city of Copan. It was time, Tonina had decided, for her to hurry north and search there for the red flower. The start of the islands' storm season lay but two months away. She had told Kaan that their bond was broken, that he was no longer indebted to her. Although he was reluctant to agree, he knew it was time for him to turn back and travel to Teotihuacan.

As all eyes remained fixed on H'meen while she examined her books, One Eye clutched his mantle tightly at his throat, unable to forget another time when his mantle had choked him—when Balám had lifted him by the neck and thrown him against a tree. H'meen had nursed One Eye back to health. She had set his bones and sutured his wounds, then stayed by his side night and day. She had slept with him, warmed him, cried over him, and begged his spirit to come back. No one knew the truth of his injuries, that the scars on his face and chest had not come from cat claws. No one knew the horrible secret that ate away at his soul—that this journey to faraway Copan had been for nothing, a ruse created by Balám. Yet he could tell no one. Every day he watched the search teams go out and return empty-handed. One Eye knew they would find nothing, but he could not tell them. Balám would torture Tonina if he did.

One Eye had briefly wondered why Balám should want to drive Kaan as far from Teotihuacan as possible, why he would go to the trouble of paying the message-carrier to tell a falsehood about the red flower. And then, in pain and sick at heart, One Eye had decided he did not care.

Finally H'meen, having consulted her books and charts and noted the current placement of the moon, sun, and planets, arrived at the precise time and date of the most auspicious time when Kaan should start for Teotihuacan. "You still have one hundred and thirteen days to reach the City of the Gods."

"Do you know the best route?" Kaan asked. "Should I retrace my steps to Tikal and turn west from there?"

"May I see your map?" the fifteen-year-old asked, holding out a hand that could be a grandmother's, with knobby knuckles and prominent veins.

Kaan reached into his travel pack and unfolded the paper he had purchased back in Mayapan, where the map seller had identified the glyphs for him, as he could not read. As a safety measure, Kaan had shown the map to One Eye outside Uxmal, and the much-traveled dwarf had confirmed what the map seller had said. Mayapan in the north, Tikal due south, Palenque in the west, and Teotihuacan just northwest of that.

H'meen studied the map by the flickering light of the campfire. She nodded in satisfaction as she read the notations alongside lines that indicated the White Roads. Her eye traced the route from Copan to Tikal to Palenque, mentally adding up the number of travel days between each. And then she froze.

"What is it?" Kaan asked anxiously.

"Is *this* the map you have been following since Mayapan?" she asked, and suddenly everyone's blood ran cold. The look in her eyes, the tone in her voice . . .

"Yes," Kaan said. "Why? I *will* reach Teotihuacan in time, will I not?"

She held the map for him to see. "According to notations along the White Roads, it should take you sixty days to reach this point," she said, her arthritic finger touching the glyph containing the symbol of Teotihuacan. "But, noble Kaan, this is not a glyph for the *city* of Teotihuacan. It identifies the beginning of the One Hundred Days Road *to* Teotihuacan."

His thick black brows came together. "What does this mean?"

"It means, noble Kaan, that from this point it is one hundred days to the City of the Gods." She lifted sorrowful eyes to him. "You have run out of time."

Chief Ocelot stood in the doorway of his spacious hut and watched the group huddled over books and maps. He did not trust people who could read. They kept secrets. And their heads were together now, planning Kaan's departure. Ocelot was not at all pleased.

Two months prior, his wife had talked him out of poisoning Kaan because she had heard about the healing flower and believed it would cure her goiter. But the flower had not been found, and Ocelot was at the end of his patience. He did not want this great crowd of people to leave. He intended to be their chief and live well while he governed them.

He looked up at the strangely cloudy sky. The air felt heavy with rain, and yet it was still the dry season. Bad portents. It was time to act. Having stirred poisonous cinnabar into a cup of *pulque,* he handed it to his wife and said, "Take this to Kaan."

Kaan was so stunned by what H'meen had just said that he absently accepted the cup without thinking. The chief's wife said, "Drink up, noble Kaan. It will keep you warm." Then she left the shelter and hurried back to her husband, feeling the first cold drops of rain on her bare arms.

Kaan frowned at the map, and then at H'meen. Surely he had heard wrong. "Are you sure?" he said again, lifting the cup to his lips. "A hundred and thirteen days seems sufficient time."

"Sufficient time to reach the *start* of the road," H'meen said. "Even if you hurry and travel at your fastest pace, it will take you sixty days. From there, Kaan, Teotihuacan is a journey of an additional one hundred days."

The cup paused at his mouth, the heady aroma filling his nostrils.

Then he lowered the cup, letting it drop so that the drink seeped into the hut's earthen floor. "You are saying there is no way I can reach Teotihuacan in time?"

"Sadly not," H'meen said, feeling terrible about this shocking mistake. She should have looked at the map long ago, but she had assumed he knew where he was going.

The others in the silent group were thinking the same thing. And as the wind whistled through the flimsy shelter, tugging at cloaks and chilling bare skin, the horrible truth began to dawn on them.

Releasing a strangled cry, Kaan shot to his feet and ran from the shelter.

They watched him go, delivering himself into the deepening dusk, the wind and the increasing raindrops, each feeling a terrible sickness in his stomach. They loved and respected Kaan and each believed himself responsible in some way for this disastrous turn of events: One Eye for misreading the map in the first place; H'meen for not looking at the map sooner; Tonina for having caused him to stray from his path to Teotihuacan at the very beginning.

She left the shelter and caught up with him. "Can you not say the prayers for Jade Sky here?" she ventured.

The words came out as a strangled cry. "It requires a special sisterhood of priestesses; only they can save her."

"But surely one of the temples at Tikal will have the priestess you require. We could reach Tikal in time—"

"You do not understand!" he boomed. "Because of me, Jade Sky's immortal soul will vanish forever!"

He turned away and strode to the edge of the camp, where he fell to his knees and lifted his arms to the lowering sky.

H'meen came to stand at Tonina's side, speaking above the rising wind. "It has to do with the way Jade Sky died," she said. "It is a very ancient, very special ritual that Kaan must perform, and it can only be performed by the Teotihuacan priestesses, and by a certain holy date. But now it is too late and her soul will be lost forever."

"I did not know this!" Tonina said. "I had thought it was merely . . ." Her voice trailed off as she was struck by the enormity of Kaan's loss. Was it true that a murdered person, according to Mayan belief, could have no afterlife if special prayers were not spoken at Teotihuacan? "And nothing can be done?"

H'meen shook her head, tightened her cloak about herself, and returned to the shelter.

Tonina looked at Kaan on his knees, silently crying to the heavens. She wanted to help him, ease his pain. But she did not know how. He had done so much for others, and yet now that *he* needed help—

Suddenly, the pineapple sellers in Ixponé came to mind, how Kaan had fought for them, and how they had given him a gift in return, saying something about an earthbound goddess who would grant any wish if she were set free. Tonina had learned more about the Earthbound Goddess since. She lived underwater, and it was said that many had tried to rescue her but all had failed. Tonina now thought: Perhaps those who had tried and failed were Mayans who did not swim well. Had an islander ever tried? Had a *pearl diver* tried?

But no one knew exactly where the goddess was imprisoned. "Somewhere near the city of Palenque," was what everyone said, referring to a large region riddled with many subterranean rivers and streams. Men had spent lifetimes searching for the goddess. But there was the curious gift the pineapple sellers had given to Kaan—an ordinary lump of stone that seemed to have no value or purpose, yet which they claimed would "point the way."

Recalling that Kaan had given the stone to H'meen for study, Tonina ran back to the shelter and asked for it. H'meen found the stone tucked into her medicine kit and, puzzled, gave it to Tonina, who asked, "How far is it to Palenque?"

H'meen looked at the map. "Fifty days."

Tonina rushed back to Kaan, where, ignoring the rain that was now falling steadily, she fell to her knees and held out her hand. "Here is the answer! Kaan, we can go to Palenque! It is only fifty days from here. We will rescue the goddess and she will grant any wish we ask for."

But Kaan had reached his limit. He shot to his feet and shouted, "Why do you always think there is a solution? Why do you never give up? Do you not see this is hopeless? The gods have been mocking us! Tonina, you are the most stubborn, relentless woman I have ever met. But even you must see that a time comes when it is all hopeless!"

Rising to her feet, she said, "Kaan, there is always hope."

He took her by the shoulders and cried, "I let her down, Tonina! For the second time! The night Jade Sky died, she begged me to stay home with her. But I insisted on going in search of Balám. Had I stayed, she would not have been murdered. And now, for the second time, I have failed. It was but a simple trek to Teotihuacan and yet I could not do even that!"

She held out the stone. "The goddess—"

"There is no goddess!" he cried, snatching the rock from Tonina's hand and hurling it into the trees.

"No!" she screamed, and started after it. But a fierce wind came up suddenly, pushing her back, and before they both knew it, the storm was upon them.

The cloudburst was stunning and spectacular, the heavens parting suddenly in a violent downpour that caught everyone by surprise. Within moments, the ground was sodden and running with water, rooftops were flying off, trees were bending in the wind.

Everyone dashed for shelter, but the storm picked up and the flimsy huts blew away. The rain was freezing, pelting bare skin with icy drops, drenching clothing, turning fingers and toes numb. People ran every which way, screaming, carrying children, calling the names of loved ones. Hairless scooped up One Eye and H'meen, one under each arm, and ran with them. Trees were toppled, roots exposed. As the downpour increased and the wind gained strength, everyone realized that there was no shelter on this side of the river. They ran for the footbridge that led to the forbidden city.

When Kaan and Tonina reached it, they stopped to let those already on the bridge make it to the other side. But others came behind, pushing. Kaan turned and shouted through the downpour, "Wait! The bridge cannot hold everyone. A few at a time! We can all get across—"

But he was shoved aside and the panicked crowd raced forward.

The ropes were sodden and the boards slippery. Tonina lost her footing and slid off, screaming. Kaan knelt and, holding on to the swaying rope, pulled her back up. At the halfway point, the bridge, overloaded with people, swayed in the fierce wind and tipped over, sending men, women, and children into the raging river below.

Grabbing Tonina's hand, Kaan shouted, "We must run for it!" And together they dashed across, holding on to the ropes as the wind threatened to send them to their deaths.

On the other side, where giant leaves and ferns whipped and lashed about, Kaan fought his way to a stone shelter. Hacking away the vines, he fell inside, bringing Tonina with him. Soaked and shivering, they watched in horror as more people tried to cross the bridge, packing on too tightly so that it tipped over again, sending more to watery deaths.

The wind howled and shrieked past the small stone shelter as Kaan and Tonina saw huts fly past. Small trees were plucked up and carried away. Sheets of water came now, in such a deluge that the river began to rise.

Kaan gauged the distance from their shelter to the banks, and saw that they would soon be flooded out. Taking Tonina's hand once again, he dashed out into the tempest, and they fought their way toward another structure. Trees crashed down in their path, branches toppled from above. They stopped to hold on to a giant mahogany as the wind blew with such force that they felt their feet lift from the ground.

"There!" Kaan shouted, pointing ahead to an opening.

Tonina let go of the tree. "*Guay!*" she cried, as the wind started to carry her away.

But Kaan had her, his fingers gripping her wrist while his other arm went around her waist. He ran with her as she held tightly to him, realizing in terror that a hurricane was upon them, and that it was blowing from the northeast. From the direction of Pearl Island.

Near the shelter they saw a man lying on the ground, his head crushed by a heavy branch. They heard cries on the wind; people in distress, in pain, being swept away. Kaan groped the stone wall and reached the opening where they both fell in, panting and heaving.

"Are you all right?" he asked as he made a quick assessment of their shelter. In the dim light he saw a woman towering above them, stony blank eyes gazing over their heads. He hoped she was a goddess and still retained some power.

"You are hurt!" Tonina cried.

He looked down at his thigh, where a gash was running with bright red blood. "It is nothing," he said, but suddenly he was in pain and he saw that the blood ran too freely.

Cupping the wound, he looked about for something to bind it with. Suddenly Tonina was out of the shelter and gone.

"Tonina!" he shouted. "Come back!"

But all he heard was the unearthly howling of the devil wind.

And then she fell inside the shelter, clutching leaves and vines.

Kaan covered the wound with the large waxy leaves and bound them tightly with the vines, tying them about his thigh until the bleeding stopped. In his days on the ball court he had learned how to manage serious wounds, and so he knew not to tie them too tightly.

Night fell and the storm raged on. In the darkness, Tonina and Kaan were blind and so they sought each other out by feel, needing each other's touch and warmth. Their clothes were cold and wet; they shivered against each other. Kaan drew Tonina into his arms and she sank against his chest, closing her eyes against the horrific visions that lingered there—people screaming as they plunged into the river, their heads seen above the torrent as they were carried away. "Do you suppose everyone is all right?" she asked, meaning their friends.

"I pray to Mother Moon that they are," he murmured, his hand on her damp hair, finding strange comfort in the feel of the tiny shells. It amazed him that he had once found such adornment annoying.

"Forgive me," she murmured against his chest. "I did not understand the urgency of your pilgrimage to Teotihuacan. I thought it was merely a routine ritual for the dead. I had no idea the very existence of Jade Sky's soul was at stake."

He buried his face in her hair and held her tight, and they spoke no more. As the wind howled and whistled around them, and the stone building shook until they thought it was going to come down on their heads, Kaan the hero ballplayer and Tonina the pearl diver thought of no one else in the world except this warm body, this firm flesh, this soft breath that was a comfort through the storm.

Tonina knew that she was falling in love with Kaan. But she had been let down, abandoned, or betrayed for so long that she would never again commit herself to another, especially not to a man who was in love with his dead wife, and whose destiny was not the same as hers. She would keep this love a secret and she would carry it forever in her heart.

Remembering the feel of her mouth on his as she had breathed life into him in the cenote, Kaan pressed his lips to Tonina's wet hair, marveling at this miracle of a girl who had come so unexpectedly into his life, and whom the gods had bound to him by ancient law—whom he now wished never to be parted from. But he was not free to love, to give his heart to another woman. It was his fault that Jade Sky and his son were dead. It was his fault that their souls would vanish forever and never know eternal bliss. He knew now that he must dedicate his life to the atonement of his sins, and let this remarkable girl go her own way.

❧ 43 ❧

By dawn the storm had died, and light flooded the shelter. Kaan and Tonina crept out and looked around at the dripping vines and branches, the ground covered in puddles. They heard only birdsong and the chatter of monkeys, but no people.

Kaan saw in the watery light that much of Tonina's white face paint had washed away. Now for the first time he could see the true curve of her jaw, the line of her cheek, the shape of her brow. Not all her features, not clearly, but more than he had seen before, and he suddenly yearned to see more. "Luminous Mother Moon," he whispered. Overcome by a storm of emotions—relief, worry, anger, and sexual desire—he impulsively cupped her face in his hands and kissed her on the lips. She curled her arms around his neck and kissed him back, deeply and for a long, desperate moment.

And then they heard shouts.

Tonina and Kaan tore away from each other and broke into a run.

Miraculously, the suspension bridge was still intact, although missing a few boards. As people crept from their stone hiding places, blinking in shock and dismay, they formed a weary and silent procession back to the river where Kaan and Hairless oversaw an orderly crossing to the other side. It was a slow and dangerous process, as the river had now swelled to its banks and raged just below the bridge.

The scene on the other side was one of utter devastation.

Beneath a cloudy morning sky, people milled about in shock to discover homes gone and crops vanished. Men called out to wives; mothers to children. There were joyous embraces as loved ones found each other, and cries of anguish as bodies were discovered.

Kaan and Tonina went straight to where their hut had been to look for everyone's travel packs. The night before, One Eye had secured them against theft with rope and stakes. They were there still, buried in mud but intact.

"Have you seen Poki?" H'meen asked, her arms filled with her rescued books. "He ran away when the storm hit."

Tonina shook her head.

Then H'meen saw Kaan's wound and brought her medicine kit. But he said, "Take care of my people first."

Tonina looked at him. *My people.* A change was taking place in him.

She knew that a change had taken place within herself as well—that, in fact, a change had occurred in her life, for she wondered now if Pearl Island had survived the storm. The hurricane had hit with such ferocity on the mainland that surely its greater strength over the sea must have destroyed small islands. Had Grandfather been able to warn the people? Or had he died and the islanders received no warning of the coming storm?

Separating herself from the silent crowd that was coalescing on the site of devastation, searching for loved ones and possessions, Tonina returned to the river, where she looked across at the ancient, abandoned buildings.

I let them down, she thought. I did not search hard enough for the red flower. I allowed myself to be encumbered by the people who followed me. And I was hampered by my feelings for Kaan. Oh, Guama! Are you dead because of me?

She felt a presence at her side and knew without looking that it was Kaan.

"You were right," he said quietly. "When you said we should look to the Earthbound Goddess for hope." He squinted toward the trees where he had hurled the rock. The forest looked different this morning; trees ripped up, snapped in half, the vegetation rearranged by force of nature. If he searched for the stone, he would not even know where to begin. "I will go to Palenque," he said. "I cannot give up. While there is still a chance to save Jade Sky's soul, and that of my unborn child, I must do what I can." He smiled sadly. "Who knows? If I can survive the cenote of Chichén Itzá, which they say no man survives, perhaps I can survive an underwater search for a goddess."

Kaan's eyes met hers as he thought of their nightlong embrace, which, although chaste, had been one charged with passion and new desires. Wishing he could draw her into his arms again, he said, "Where will you go now?"

"I do not know. Should I keep searching for the red flower? Or hurry home to Pearl Island? I feel responsible for my people. Perhaps I should find the red flower first and then go back to Pearl and look for survivors. If none are there, then go to other islands until I have atoned for my mistakes. But how do I decide?"

"Perhaps the decision has already been made for you."

"What do you mean?"

Kaan pointed to the medallion that lay upon her breast, still encased in a jacket woven of palm fibers.

"I have always been afraid to open it," she said quietly. "Once I unwrap this medallion, I will no longer be Tonina of Pearl Island. When I see what is inside, there can be no going back. I must be what this medallion says I am. And it frightens me."

She looked at Kaan with wide, timorous eyes. "How do I know that I can be this other person? What if my true place is so far inland that I never again hear the ocean surf or the call of the dolphin?"

"You can do it, Tonina."

She looked into his eyes and saw a dare. No, a challenge.

But she was torn. Part of her wanted to go home. She longed for the familiar, for the sea. She might have been an outsider on Pearl Island, but it was the life she had known. Maybe the island had been spared in the storm. Perhaps Grandfather had warned the people in time and life would continue there as it always had.

But she also wanted to know who she was and who her parents were.

She looked into Kaan's dark eyes and thought: And I want to stay with this man.

Drawing a deep breath for courage, she lifted the medallion and picked at the dried fibers that, over the years, had been weathered by saltwater and sun, so that it was difficult to shred. When the round, flat stone was finally exposed to the gray morning light, she saw—

Tonina gasped. Kaan frowned. And then he whispered, "Mother Moon!"

The stone was vibrant pink and translucent, and inlaid with brilliant red and green ceramic to form a picture.

"So there *is* a red flower; it isn't a myth," Kaan murmured in wonder.

"But what does it mean? I still do not know what I am supposed to do. Keep searching for the flower here, or up along the Quatemalan coast?"

"It is a message," Kaan said. "It is meant to show you the way back to where you came from. To your people. Tonina, when you find this flower, you will find your true identity."

She looked at the engraved flower—the green stem and red petals—and suddenly she understood: When Guama had lifted the baby from her little ark, she had seen this red flower embedded in stone, and had known it connected the child to her people. Guama had also known that someday Tonina must return to those people. Grandfather was not ill. Guama had invented the story of a healing flower as a ruse to get Tonina to leave Pearl Island of her own volition. It explained why Grandfather's description of the Quatemalan coast did not match what Ocelot's wife had said.

And I am not meant to return to Pearl Island.

"But I have no idea where to start looking."

"Perhaps the Earthbound Goddess can tell you. If you set her free—" A dark look swept over Kaan's face and he said suddenly, "I am sorry I threw the rock away. The pineapple sellers had said it would show us the way to the goddess. What a fool I am!"

They heard weeping then, and, turning, saw H'meen sitting on a boulder, her hands pressed to her eyes. "I should have held on to him!" she cried as One Eye awkwardly tried to console her. "Poki got away from me and now he is dead!"

Suddenly, a little figure darted from the distant trees, as if answering to his name—Poki, soaked and muddy and barely alive. H'meen cried out with joy, but the dog ran past her to Kaan, whining and snuffling at his feet.

"Poki!" H'meen called, clapping her hands.

But the little dog made sounds at Kaan's feet until they noticed he had something in his mouth. As H'meen pried the object from between Poki's teeth, sodden earth fell from it, and they all realized it was the rock from the pineapple sellers. It had lain for hours in soaking rain so that it had been washed clean of years of accumulated detritus.

"How could Poki have found it?" Tonina said in wonder.

"It is a miracle," Kaan said.

"He caught your scent on it," H'meen said pragmatically as she rinsed the object in a puddle. "Poki remembered your kindnesses to him."

She brought the object to light and they saw that it was a stone, but not in its natural state. There were carvings on it. Glyphs.

"What do they mean?" Tonina asked in sudden excitement.

H'meen could not read them, but she declared that it was a sign from the gods. "When we decipher these glyphs we will know where to find the Earthbound Goddess."

She looked at Tonina and said solemnly, "It is not by chance that this stone came into *our* possession, for the gods saw to it that this key to finding the Earthbound Goddess was given to people who have a brave swimmer among them, for that is the only way she can be rescued."

When she saw the skeptical look on Tonina's face, H'meen said, "Nothing happens by accident. What did the old pineapple seller say? That never had anyone defended him and his family before, as Kaan had. That this stone had been in their possession for years. And so the gods brought the two of you to the Ixponé marketplace that this stone should end up in your possession. To rescue the goddess."

Tonina gazed in awe at the small stone in her hand, engraved with mysterious symbols.

"The goddess," H'meen said softly, "will grant any wish to the person who sets her free."

Tonina lifted her eyes to the elderly girl, looked into the cloudy cataracts beneath the thin, delicate brow of an old woman, and she thought: We all have a wish to ask of the goddess.

Turning to Kaan, she said, "Why do you need priestesses to intercede on Jade Sky's behalf when you can pray directly to a goddess?"

The small group stood in silence as the enormity of this gift sank in, and hope blossomed once again in despairing hearts.

"Keep it safe for us, honorable H'meen," Tonina said, pressing the glyph stone into the arthritic hands. "You have the favor of the gods."

Once again, Tonina marveled at the mysterious workings of fate. When she thought she had reached the end of her road, when she thought she had gone as far as she could, the gods had opened a new path. She realized now that it was meant to be, that here, in this aftermath of destruction, she should finally unwrap the medallion she had worn all her life and discover that, while she had been searching for a flower, it had been with her all along.

She looked at Kaan. He had truly saved her life at last, when she had slipped on the suspension bridge, so that their debt was finally erased, the world was in balance again. Westward they would go, to Palenque, in the hope of saving Jade Sky's soul, and Tonina finding her people. She felt a strange, exciting warmth swim through her veins as she wondered where her new road was going to lead. She was filled with the sense that one stage of her life had ended and a new one was beginning, and it filled her heart with fresh purpose.

"Thank the gods, brother, that you are alive!"

They turned to see Balám emerge from the forest. Kaan strode to him and enveloped him in a joyous embrace.

"We took shelter in a cave," Balám said. "Unfortunately, we lost four men. What a storm!" Then he grew somber, rubbing his hands, and he looked around. "What now, brother? Do we turn back for Teotihuacan?"

When Kaan explained about the error with the map, that he could no longer make it back to Teotihuacan in time, Balám had to check his impulse to cheer, for his clever ploy to drive Kaan as far from the City of the Gods as possible had worked.

Kaan outlined his new plan to find the Earthbound Goddess, and Balám thumped his chest, crying, "Let me go with you! I shall help you search for this goddess and if she is generous, perhaps she will look kindly upon my miserable self as well, and tell me where my precious daughter is."

Balám and his men camped with Kaan's group, lighting fires with what dry material they could find, and eating cold rations amid a gloomy atmosphere. The storm survivors slept in *hamacs* far above the ground, away from the snakes and lizards that now slithered in the mud, and awoke the next morning to bright sunlight and a blue, cloudless sky.

And found the camp half deserted.

Tonina climbed down from her *hamac* in puzzlement. People had left during the night. Who? And then she realized: Balám and his companions were gone.

Kaan came striding up, with One Eye and Hairless on his heels. "Did you hear them leave?" he asked.

Tonina shook her head. She started to say, "Why would he—," when the morning air was shattered by a shriek.

They found H'meen kneeling over her medicine box, frantically going through its contents. She looked up with tear-filled eyes.

The glyph stone was gone.

Kaan heard the word "betrayal" whispered in his mind but he refused to listen. It was too painful to believe—that Balám should have betrayed a friend. He is desperate, Kaan told himself. Balám lost everything; his wife was dead and his daughter sold on the slave block. Kaan refused to allow himself to be angry for what Balám had done. But he *was* alarmed.

"He will do anything," Kaan said to his friends when a weak fire was going and they roasted corn on a flat stone. "Balám is so desperate to find his daughter that he will act recklessly with the key that points the way to the goddess. They might destroy it forever."

There was no time to waste. Kaan knew they must reach Palenque before Balám did, or at the least catch up with him. He did not voice the unspoken fear that they all shared: Balám was already a day ahead, and his men were strong and healthy; they would cover more ground than their own people, who were weak and slow.

They hastily broke camp, with Hairless and the six Nine Brothers moving among the families to assist, to urge them to hurry. Few chose to stay and many more had asked to join. It would be a larger group leaving than had arrived.

Chief Ocelot, now a widower, approached Kaan and said, "I am to blame for what happened here. I stole stone from the forbidden city. I took statues and relics and sold them to travelers. I grew rich on death. And now my wife is dead and the crops are ruined. The gods punished me for my wrongdoing."

"You are welcome to join us," Kaan said, thinking the man looked less formidable without his feline whiskers.

Ocelot shook his head. "I will stay here and rebuild my village. But I shall do so humbly and with no further offense to the gods." The chief nodded, to reaffirm his last words, but as he turned toward the stone slab that was all that remained of his hut, he recalled smaller cuts of stone he had seen in the city, and thought they would make nice sturdy walls. . . .

As the camp broke up and families prepared to embark on the trek westward, Kaan felt his heart race with new hope—that the goddess would see to the resurrection of Jade Sky's soul—but with fresh fear, too, that Balám would get there first.

Tonina took care to restore her face paint. She had replenished the coconut paint and now she carefully traced the symbols of the island people on her cheeks, chin, forehead, and arms. Not until she knew who she really was would she wash them off forever.

As she did so, she thought: I have walked the deserted roads of ancient cities, I have dwelled briefly on farms and in the huts of people who were not my own race. I think of the place where I was raised, and it is an island where I lived but did not belong. From the day I was set upon the sea in a basket, I have been alone. I do not know who I am, or where I am supposed to be. Perhaps I will never know, perhaps I am not meant to know. But I will search, if it takes me all the days of my life.

She picked up her travel pack and her spear and, taking her place at Kaan's side, she turned in the direction of the sea one last time and silently said good-bye to Guama and Huracan and Pearl Island.

Then, facing westward, Tonina took the first step toward her new, unknown destiny.

BOOK

THREE

❧ 44 ❧

L eave me, master!" cried Hairless. "Save yourself! Find the goddess."
He was stuck in mud up to his waist while men on the bank
were frantically throwing ropes to him.

Snapping impatient orders, Kaan ignored his friend's pleas. Although
time was running out and they had yet to find Balám, Kaan was not going to leave this man behind.

They had finally reached the region of the fabled city of Palenque and
had been searching for the Earthbound Goddess for days. While they
heard many stories from the local people who insisted she *was* there
somewhere, no one could offer precise information. Without the glyph
stone that Balám had stolen, they had no way of finding her.

"Save him, please!" wailed a young woman in the crowd that encircled
the swamp. The daughter of a pumpkin farmer, she had taken up with
Hairless when the group had camped near her farm.

"Catch this!" Kaan shouted as he threw a rope weighted with a small
rock. It landed on the surface of the mire close enough for Hairless to
catch. Then Kaan wrapped the other end around his waist and, digging
his heels into the damp ground, pulled back. He silently thanked the
gods that it was still morning, otherwise they might not be able to rescue
the poor man.

Halfway between the spring equinox and the summer solstice, when
the great traveling crowd was passing through the ancient city of Yaxchilan, the dry season had ended and the rainy season had arrived in full
force. Although the days always began dry and bright, heavy rainfall
struck by afternoon. If the accident had not happened in the morning,
Hairless would most certainly have been carried off in a river of mud.

Kaan's people had found themselves battling ferocious rainstorms and calf-deep mud ever since Yaxchilan, where they had purchased waterproof mantles—cotton cloaks coated in rubber that, though heavy and cumbersome, kept a person dry—and straw hats with brims so wide that shoulders did not get wet. But there was no relief from the heat and humidity, or the clouds of mosquitoes and giant, biting flies.

Not to mention sudden, unexpected swamps like this one.

At the edge of the marsh, well away from the deadly quagmire, One Eye watched the desperate operation, noting in particular Tonina's part as she worked at Kaan's side, pulling the rope with her feet dug in, as strong as any man. He recalled the day back in Mayapan when she had watched her first ball game. She had expressed skepticism over the value of teamwork.

But look at her now, One Eye thought as he admired the strength and tautness of her body, in love with her now more than ever, with a love that was more futile than ever. Was she aware how this journey was changing her? When One Eye first met her, Tonina had told him she was an outsider and preferred to be alone. Kaan, too, had insisted he must journey alone, and in those early days each had made a solitary camp and kept apart from the rest. But during the difficult trek from Copan to Palenque, each evening Kaan and Tonina had moved through the camp, speaking with the people, listening to their woes, bolstering spirits. Kaan regularly sat in judgment now to hear complaints and accusations, and he created new laws, based upon his personal code of honor. Wife-beating and public drunkenness were now punishable, with H'meen recording the new rules in her chronicle. Were they aware, One Eye the observant dwarf wondered, that these two who had always insisted they were alone upon the earth were now part of a great family of their own creation?

He was brought out of his thoughts when a woman tried to dash out into the quagmire and men caught her to hold her back. She was the mother of the child that had caused this disaster in the first place. The boy had wandered off and Hairless had found him trapped in the mud. Hairless had jumped in to save him, but the quagmire proved too strong. The child was pulled under and Hairless was now stuck.

"Pull!" Kaan shouted, and the air was filled with the grunts of men struggling with ropes. It was not that Hairless was so heavy—although he was—it was the mud sucking him down. Despite extraordinary efforts, the hapless leader of the Nine Brothers was now up to his chest in the mire.

"Leave me, master," he wailed again. "Let me go. I am unimportant. Find Prince Balám. Find the goddess!"

"Do not release the rope!" Kaan shouted at him when Hairless threatened to cut himself free. "If you do I shall curse you for all eternity!"

Tears streamed down Hairless's broad face and he could be heard murmuring the prayer of confession.

"Kaan," Tonina said, dropping her rope and drawing deep breaths, "we cannot do it this way. But look!" She pointed up to the crowns of trees surrounding them. While many of the nearby trees were heavily branched and leafy, those that grew to the very top of the rain forest canopy had smooth, thin-barked trunks. "If we chop one of these down and attach ropes—"

"You there! You with axes, follow me!"

Soon the rain forest was filled with the sound of stone blades hacking away at wood. Six men pushed at the sturdy trunk until it fell across the pond of brown muck. Kaan ran along its length, and when he reached Hairless, dropped to his knees and shouted, "Grab on to the tree!"

The mud was now up to the man's armpits. Hairless was having difficulty breathing. But he had had the wits to keep his arms free, so he was able to reach the tree and, with Kaan's help, gain a solid grasp. Kaan then plucked up the ropes that had been thrown for Hairless to grab, anchored them to the trunk, and shouted back to those on shore to start pulling.

Everyone watched in breathless anticipation as bit by bit the fallen tree turned and began a laborious drift back to shore. The mud now covered Hairless's shoulders and he was sobbing noisily, realizing that it looked as if he would be sucked under before they made it to dry land.

"Pull!" Kaan shouted to those on shore.

When the mud reached Hairless's chin, he sobbed with fear and self-pity, allowing watery muck to run into his mouth. Kaan jumped down from the tree, sliding into the quicksand up to his chest, but he felt the solid bottom beneath his feet and with tremendous effort, his hands under his friend's arms, strained to take a step backward, and then another, and another, until they both slowly rose from the bog. Men rushed forward to grab Kaan and Hairless and drag them back onto high ground.

Hairless fell into a dead faint and H'meen was instantly at his side with her medicine kit.

Kaan's eyes met Tonina's in silent communication: another life saved, but another day lost. They had not reached Palenque in the predicted fifty days. It had taken them sixty. Tomorrow was the summer solstice.

The region was dappled with marshes and bogs, but also with clear ponds and streams, so that Kaan and Hairless and the men who had worked the ropes were able to wash themselves. Hairless received doting attention from the young woman who was in love with him, while the mother of the lost child wailed amid the close company of her friends and family.

Unfortunately, it was a common sight.

During the journey from Copan, twelve had been lost to snakebite, fever, festering wounds, swamps, and old age. But there had also been ten births, in the timeless way the gods kept balance in the world. Nine divorces and eleven marriages had also taken place. Forty-three people had left the great traveling group, and sixty-two had joined. There were fewer Mayans now and more from the myriad tribes that occupied this southwestern edge of Mayan influence. H'meen kept a daily tally of these fluctuations and recorded it in her chronicle.

Also recorded were new flowers they had discovered in Tonina's relentless search for the red blossom that she believed would lead her to her people. Having accepted her new fate, and the reality that she was never returning to Pearl Island, Tonina walked with new purpose and determination. At every farm they passed, every village they visited, Tonina talked with people, examined their local textiles and embroidery, and asked if any knew what the design of her baby blanket signified.

These were the actions observed by those who traveled with her. What they did not see, and what she kept close to her heart, was her growing love for Kaan, her aching desire for him, her longing to be part of him. It was a love she could never express, for the spirit of Jade Sky stood between them.

As Kaan dried off from his dip in a pond—less terrified of water now—he absently rubbed the scar on his thigh. It had given him trouble the first days out of Copan, but luckily no spirits of infection had taken up residence in the injury he incurred during the hurricane. But it had caused great pain, and Kaan had walked with a limp. The pain and limp were gone, but the scar remained, a reminder of the night he had spent with Tonina in his arms.

Kaan's desire for her grew daily, his longing to embrace her, to kiss her. But he had to hold himself back. What if the Earthbound Goddess demanded a reckoning of his life? What if, like the Sisterhood of Souls, she posed a list of questions in order to judge his heart and weigh his worth? What if she asked: Have you remained faithful to the memory of your wife?

"Master! Master!"

The man who came running through the trees was one of the Nine Brothers—an advance scout exploring the area. After being the butt of many jokes since the night his wife threw rotten fruit at him, calling him foolish and turning back to Mayapan, he had met a new girl and married her. The couple had recently announced a pregnancy. "Master," he said in a hushed voice when he reached Kaan. "Three dead men! Through there!" He pointed back the way he had come.

Gesturing to the others to remain quiet, Kaan retrieved his spear and club and followed the scout, Tonina falling into step behind them.

On the other side of the dense forest, they came upon a green hill covered in thick vegetation. They saw a cave with three men lying at the entrance. Pausing to assess the situation, Kaan listened for sounds of wild animals. Hearing nothing out of the ordinary, he crept forward, his companions close, spears at the ready.

When they reached the corpses, they frowned. The men were lying on their backs, almost peacefully, as if asleep. There were no wounds on their bodies; no signs of a fight. But their clothes were soaking wet. And then Tonina saw the foam on their lips and knew that they had drowned.

Suddenly they heard voices inside the cave, echoing off the walls. Two men emerged into the daylight, dragging another corpse.

Kaan cried out. They had found Balám.

B rother!" shouted Balám. "Thank the gods you found us!"

Kaan exploded in a mixture of relief, anger, and joy. "Why did you leave Copan in the night like a thief? Why did you steal the glyph stone?"

Balám gave him a wounded look. "Thief! Brother, did Chief Ocelot not tell you? I gave him a message for you."

"I received no message," Kaan said darkly.

"And I trusted that numbskull!" Balám said, amazed at how easily lies came to his lips these days, enjoying the change in Kaan's facial expression from anger to perplexity. Manipulation of others was a form of power Balám discovered he enjoyed. "I did it for you! From Mayapan to Copan, you did all the work, brother, finding the trails, creating new ones, while my comrades and I followed with ease. It was time I reciprocated. I left you a message with Chief Ocelot, so that all this time I thought you were following my trail. But thank the gods you are here!"

When it was apparent that Kaan was not entirely convinced, Balám quickly said, "Brother, I have found the Earthbound Goddess!"

Kaan's face instantly cleared.

"These men," Balám said, pointing to the four dead, "sacrificed their lives trying to save her. But it is all water, brother! The goddess lives in an underground river."

"How do you know this?" Tonina asked, stepping forward.

Balám shot her a look. He would have liked to seize her throat right then and squeeze the life out of her. But he had secret plans for her and Kaan.

"I asked among the local farmers," Balám said. "The corn growers here are very friendly folk," he added, thinking of the man he had tortured to death to obtain the information he needed: the location of a stone stela, like the ones they had seen in Tikal and Copan, very old and hidden in jungle growth. "Just there," he said, pointing, and the others saw the slab of stone, as tall as a man, tilting in the brush. "The farmer said that legend speaks of a stela that marks the hiding place of the goddess. It was a matter of inspecting all the stelae in the area—there are many, brother—until we came upon this one."

Kaan and Tonina saw where a chunk of the engraved stela had been cut away. "You see?" Balám said as he nestled the glyph rock into the stela, completing the portrait of a woman seated on a throne.

Kaan looked toward the cave's entrance. "She is down there?"

"Most definitely so, brother, but it will not be easy reaching her."

They went inside and found a stream running through the small cave. "It runs under the hill there," Balám said, pointing to the dark water, his voice echoing in the dank cave. In the dim light they were able to make out an underwater opening in the rock wall. "My men tried to swim into that opening, but all four got trapped and we had to pull them out, too late."

Tonina saw that, from where they stood, it was difficult to determine the width of the opening, or its depth. "I will get through," she said.

A disdainful look swept across Balám's face. He hated her more than ever. A mere girl who boasted she could do what his strongest and bravest warriors could not.

Kaan took her by the shoulders and said, "If you do not come back soon, I will go in after you."

"You cannot swim," she whispered, looking up into his eyes.

His fingers tightened on her shoulders. "I can if I have to."

She thought he was going to kiss her, right there in front of everyone. He brought his face closer and she *hoped* he would kiss her, but feared it also, and then Kaan drew back, suddenly aware of Balám and the others.

Before entering the water, Tonina thought of the great crowd that was now gathered outside the cave, watching anxiously; the people who had so trustingly followed her, first to find the red flower, and now in hopes of meeting a goddess. She knew the question that stood on everyone's mind: Will the goddess grant more than one wish, and if not, whose wish should be granted? In every heart, the answer was *mine*.

Tonina paused to murmur a prayer. "Spirits of the cave, I come in peace, I mean no harm. I wish to speak with the Earthbound Goddess." Then she delivered herself into the swiftly running water, keeping her head above the surface as she allowed the current to carry her to the opening in the wall. Drawing in deep breaths, she dived under, felt for the opening, and swam in.

As Kaan stood at the edge of the subterranean stream, anxiously watching the dark water, Balám took his men outside and readied them to snatch the goddess as soon as Tonina returned with her. "Kill the others if you have to, but the goddess must be ours."

Swimming in the underground channel was nothing like swimming in the lagoon back home. Tonina had never experienced such darkness underwater, where there was not the slightest dapple of sunlight. Trying not to think of the solid rock all around her, or that there was no surface over her head where she could take in air, she pulled herself along with steady, determined sweeps of her strong arms. Progress was slow and difficult, as she encountered jutting rock and narrow passages. There seemed to be no end to the tunnel. Her lungs started to ache, but there was no room for her to turn around, and the current was swift. She was going to drown!

And if she did not come out, Kaan would come in after her. . . .

And then suddenly and without warning, she was out, tumbling down a waterfall and plunging into a black lagoon. Tonina immediately shot up to the surface, gasping for air, and swam to the edge, where she held on and caught her breath, allowing her eyes to adjust to the dim light of what turned out to be a large, domed cavern.

When she had caught her breath, and the panic had subsided, she pulled herself out of the water and came shakily to her feet. More features became visible: rocky walls, a cold earthen floor, cone-shaped stalagmites rising to meet hanging stalactites. The source of light appeared to be an opening in the dome, high above, through which sunlight filtered down, illuminating the cold lagoon, the waterfall, and—

Tonina's eyes widened. Directly beneath the ceiling hole, laid out in squares on the dirt floor of the cavern, was a garden, green and thick and flourishing. She could make out tomatoes, berries, honeysuckle. Trellises and arbors were covered in flowering vines. Against the far wall, Tonina identified a sleeping area, complete with mats and blankets and a small altar. A separate cooking area was distinguished by a blackened fire pit and rows of gourds and clay bowls.

Hearing a small gasp, she turned and saw an apparition standing before her. Reflexively, Tonina traced a protective sign in the air until she realized she was looking at a woman, who stared back at her in wide-eyed shock.

The moment stretched as they looked at each other across dust-moted shafts of light, the waterfall filling the air with refreshing music. Above the sound of the water, Tonina thought she heard the melodious call of a bird, but could not take her eyes off the woman in white. She was about eighty years old, by Tonina's reckoning, and immaculately clean. Her long white dress, though frayed and tattered, was spotless, as was her white hair that streamed past her waist in two long braids.

"Are you a ghost?" the old woman finally asked. She spoke Mayan, and her voice was smooth and warm.

Tonina could barely speak. How did one address a goddess? "No."

"But . . . your face . . ."

Tonina realized that the paint must have run and smeared, giving her a stark white countenance. "I have come to set you free."

Another soft gasp. "Is it true?"

Tonina nodded, while her hair and her clothes dripped onto the cavern floor. "My friends are waiting to rescue you."

The woman broke down weeping. "I have waited for so long," she sobbed into her hands.

Awkwardly, Tonina went to her and placed a comforting arm around thin shoulders. The goddess was shockingly bony and frail.

She lifted a face that was lined and aged, and for a moment Tonina thought of H'meen. Then the woman asked, "Is Cheveyo with you?"

"Cheveyo?"

"Perhaps the king sent you?"

"What king?"

"Pac Kinnich, who sits upon the throne."

Tonina and her people had heard that the nearby city of Palenque had been abandoned long ago. "There is no king," she said gently, her mind shifting to the problem of getting out of this cave.

The old woman looked at her spotted hands, her long white hair. "I was down here for many years. I suppose my beloved Cheveyo is dead by now. Everyone is gone. Even the evil man who put me here has long turned to dust. What is your name, child?"

"Tonina."

"I am Ixchel. The gods bless you, Tonina, for rescuing me. Whatever I can do to repay you, I shall."

Tonina searched the cavern. How to get *out*? "We cannot leave the way I came," she said, pointing to the waterfall. "Is there another escape route?" she asked, knowing it was a futile question since the goddess would have used it long ago.

Then Tonina said, "We must hurry," thinking of Kaan's promise to dive into the subterranean river if she was gone too long. He would never survive. When she heard a melodious birdcall again, Tonina finally saw the creature on a perch, his feet tethered to a rope.

Tonina stared in astonishment. She knew of the magnificent quetzal bird, a small green and red parrot with long, iridescent green tail feathers worth more than gold or jade—the quetzal was associated with Kukul-can, one of the supreme deities of the Maya, therefore killing the sacred bird was punished by death—but although Tonina had traipsed through many a jungle, she had never been rewarded with a glimpse of the fabled bird.

He sat quietly on his perch, fat little red breast puffed out as his long, dramatic tail feathers reached the floor of the cave. Ixchel stroked his head as she said, "He was sentenced with me to this living death, and he has been my loyal companion all these years."

Tonina noticed that the bird's tether was very long so that he could fly up and flit about the dome of the cavern without escaping through the hole at the top. What if she were to set the bird free? Would Kaan and the others see him fly out and know to come looking on the crest of the hill?

When she suggested this to Ixchel, the goddess said, "Then we must do it. But let me tie something to him, so that your friends will know he has come from me and is not just a wild bird."

Tonina watched as the quetzal allowed Ixchel to tie a ribbon around one of his legs. Tonina then used her knife to cut the tether, and they clapped their hands to send the bird flying upward.

They watched as he flew up and out of the hole and—in the wrong direction! Too late, it occurred to Tonina that the quetzal's breeding season was spring to summer. Might his instincts cause him to fly off in search of a mate?

Together they watched the opening in the dome, their eyes fixed on a sky growing dark with clouds.

Nothing.

Time stretched.

Suddenly—the bird flew back in! "No!" Tonina cried when he alighted on his perch. Ixchel spoke to him, stroking his crest, and then she clapped her hands and he was up and out again, as if understanding his mission this time, for he flew in the correct direction when he cleared the opening.

At the cave's entrance, Kaan was becoming alarmed. Tonina had been in there too long. How deep into the hill was the goddess's prison? What if Tonina was caught in an underground river that ran all the way to the Bay of Campeche? She would be swept out to sea! Cursing himself for having let her go—surely there must be other ways to rescue the goddess—he whipped off his mantle and started for the cave.

"No, master!" cried Hairless. "You will not survive!"

But Kaan was determined.

And then One Eye shouted, "Look! What is that?"

They all looked up, shading their eyes against the last of the sunlight, and saw the beautiful quetzal flying in a great circle above them, his long shimmering green tail quivering like a pennant.

"There is something tied to its leg," Kaan said. "It is no wild bird."

When the quetzal swooped suddenly down to the crest of the hill, Kaan took off running, the others following.

They scaled the hill, keeping an eye on the bird as he flew down and then up and around, until they came to the top where, after searching frantically through dense brush, they found the hidden opening in the ground.

Dropping to his knees, Kaan called down and heard Tonina call back: "I am here! And I have found her!"

A makeshift sling made of ropes and a *hamac* was lowered, and as Tonina helped Ixchel into the seat, sitting with her and holding tight, Tonina knew what she was going to ask of the goddess when she reached the surface: that she grant the one wish to Kaan. I can always search for my family, Tonina thought as they rose slowly from the cave's floor. But Jade Sky has only fifty days. . . .

As Tonina and Ixchel were being lifted from the cavern, Balám's warriors stood tense and waiting to grab the goddess. Balám knew the others would offer little resistance, as they would be caught unaware. He would have the goddess and be off with her before Kaan could draw his knife.

But as soon as the white-haired woman appeared, Balám's men fell to their knees and pressed their foreheads to the ground. And then Balám himself could not move. They were in the presence of a living goddess.

Kaan hurriedly helped Tonina out of the harness, saying, "Thank the gods you are all right." Tonina's face paint was smeared and her clothes were wet from the dangerous swim. "Tonina, the wish to be granted shall be yours. You were the one who saved the goddess while I stood out here in safety."

But she smiled and laid her hand on his arm. "Kaan, this is Ixchel, and she has said she will reward us however she can."

"Precious lady," Kaan said as he knelt before Ixchel. "We honor you—" His voice broke.

Ixchel's eyes filled with tears as she looked at all who had come to rescue her—brave and noble souls! And then she looked up at the sky, the clouds, the trees that swept away like a great green sea to the horizon, and she trembled with joy. "Am I truly free?" she whispered.

"We are your servants!" Balám cried, finally remembering himself, and seeing at once that seizing the goddess was going to be no easy matter. "How may we serve you?"

"I wish to be taken to the Time Temples. But I fear I am unable to walk that far."

Balám slapped his chest. "Permit me to carry you."

She looked at him for a long moment, assessing the sloping forehead, slanting eyes, receding chin, and great arched nose fitted with an appliance.

Then she looked at Kaan, who knelt before her, and she took in facial features she found attractive—the straight nose and square jaw. Although the long hair drawn up into a jaguar-tail, the jade earplugs, and the tattoos were Mayan fashion, yet . . . he was not Mayan. She said, "I wish for this man to carry me."

As Balám stepped away, scowling, Kaan gently lifted the feather-light woman in his strong arms and started down the hill. With Tonina walking at their side, and the quetzal bird circling overhead, they led an excited procession through the forest toward the fabled city of Palenque.

~ 46 ~

The ancient city dominated a region known as Eastern Chiapán, where rugged highlands overlooked a heavily forested coastal plain. Here was the western edge of Mayan influence. Beyond, in the snowcapped mountains of Chiapán, people did not speak Mayan, they kept different calendars, and worshiped foreign gods.

The city itself, comprising myriad buildings, structures, and dwellings, occupied a unique setting at the base of thickly forested hills that rose suddenly from the flat coastal plain. Massive stone buildings appeared abruptly against a backdrop of dense green trees, with morning mist hanging low to add an atmosphere of mystery and otherworldliness. That the city, like Copan and much of Tikal, had been deserted for centuries was apparent, and while the original blood-red stucco and bright blue ornamentation remained in but a few places, Ixchel voiced her surprise to find the plaza and temples in such a state of neglect. Was she *that* old?

"The city was abandoned long ago for reasons no one knows. But a small population occupied a portion of the city in my time," Ixchel explained as her companions stared wide-eyed at the stepped pyramids rising into the mist. Howler monkeys and parrots raised the alarm at the arrival of a human throng numbering in the hundreds.

"Centuries ago," Ixchel said, her eyes filling with tears at the sight of the city she had so long despaired of ever seeing again, "King Pacal's engineers found a way to funnel water uphill, so that the palaces and temples received running water from these underground streams. And there were fountains! Oh, beautiful fountains." She dropped her fragile head on Kaan's strong shoulder and wept softly.

The visitors were eerily silent as they followed the main thoroughfare, passing building after building, silent sentinels of an era long past. Even children and babes in arms were hushed as hundreds of pairs of eyes scanned the broken edifices, now grown over with aggressive vegetation. The hundreds of human feet and sandals shuffling over the damp pavement sounded like the whisperings of ghosts.

Balám felt his stomach tighten. Ruined cities were becoming a common sight, and it troubled his Mayan soul. What had happened to the great men who built this place? Where were their descendants?

Was this the future of Uxmal and Mayapan? The future of *all* Maya?

"There," Ixchel said, pointing with a shaking hand, "those three pyramids are the Time Temples. Take me to the central one, the tallest."

When they arrived at the base of the pyramid, Kaan gave the order for the people to remain in the plaza, where they immediately laid down their burdens. He instructed Hairless and the Nine Brothers to organize teams to fetch water, find dry firewood, and assist H'meen with those in need of healing care. With Balám on his right, Tonina on his left, and One Eye close behind, Kaan cautiously scaled the many steep steps, which were wet and slippery, the frail goddess in his arms.

Below, the crowd did not make camp as was their habit, but remained strangely silent and watchful. What was going to happen now? What miracles was the goddess about to perform? In each heart, the same question was asked: Will I be cured/find fortune/achieve happiness today?

When they reached the massive stone sanctuary at the top of the pyramid, Kaan felt Ixchel's thin body shiver with excitement. He, too, was tense with anticipation, his heart racing as he wondered what miracle was going to occur. At his side, Tonina could barely breathe as she thought of the wishes the goddess was going to grant. And Balám, grim and angry, tried to think of a way to persuade the goddess to grant *his* wish.

But as they delivered themselves into the dank, dreary interior, Ixchel cried, "Where are the priests? Where are the offerings and incense?" Suddenly her rescuers were worried. Was she going to be furious that no one had maintained her shrine? Instead of granting wishes, was she going to place curses upon their heads?

They made their way down the narrow stone passage, with its damp walls and moist floors, until they arrived at a sanctuary made up of a low stone altar with a massive stone stela behind it, intricately carved with a giant cross flanked by a god and a king. Kaan and Balám recognized it as the World Tree, as such shrines existed also in Mayapan and Uxmal. The cross, they knew, represented the sacred cottonwood—the Tree of Life— the foundation of all Mayan belief. The main trunk of the cross rose from the Underworld, with the outstretched crossbeam supporting the heavens. At the base of the cross-tree, the horrific face of a monster depicted the suppression of evil in the world.

Tonina also recognized the symbols. She had seen a mural of the strange tree with the crossbeam branches in the shelter at Chichén Itzá where she and Brave Eagle had spent the night.

Kaan gently set Ixchel on the damp stone floor, easing her down until she stood on her own. As the ancient woman mutely surveyed her surroundings, her companions tried not to show impatience. One Eye did not relish being in such close company with the man who had almost killed him, and who still might, while Balám gave no thought to anyone or anything except asking the goddess to restore Ziyal to him.

Finally she turned to a dilapidated wooden chest tucked against one wall, its lid in splinters on the floor. She looked inside and murmured, "Thank the gods it is still here."

Kaan looked in. "There is nothing there, sacred lady," he said.

"Pry up the bottom of the chest."

He did so and exposed a curious bundle underneath. "May I have it, please?" she asked, and Kaan retrieved a feathered blanket wrapped around a few hard objects. The blanket appeared to be ancient; its colors were faded and feathers were missing.

Ixchel smiled as she clasped the bundle to her breast. "My treasure." She looked at the faces around her and quickly said, "Oh, not treasure as you would think. This contains no jade or cacao beans, no gold or amber. Just paper," she said softly. "Very old paper. . . ."

She turned to Kaan. "Will you carry me down the steps, please? After that, I can walk on my own."

Kaan exchanged a glance with Tonina. "Walk?" he said. "Where?"

"I would like to go to my house now."

"Your house!" barked Balám. "Is this shrine not your house?"

"This shrine? But why would you—" Her eyes widened. "Ah, I see. You think I am the Earthbound Goddess. That is why you rescued me," she said, looking at Tonina. "Although I am old, my age is not measured in eons. I am not a goddess. I am a mortal woman."

Kaan frowned. "Are you a priestess, then?"

"I am no one special, my son, just a humble servant of the gods."

Balám wanted to spit with disgust. An old woman! All this time and effort gone to waste.

But Kaan held on to one last straw of hope as he asked, "How far is it to Teotihuacan?"

"The City of the Gods?" It was Ixchel's turn to frown. "Let me think. If I remember correctly, Teotihuacan lies a hundred days in the north. The road begins west of here, after a journey of seven days."

The final hope died. Kaan had run out of time.

Tonina asked, "But if you are not a goddess, then how did that beautiful underground garden come to be?"

"The man who buried me in that cave did not intend for me to die for a long time, and so he placed supplies in there with me—seeds and cuttings that I might sustain myself and thus know loneliness for many years."

One Eye could not keep silent any longer. "But what of the goddess?"

"The legend of the Earthbound Goddess was here years before I was placed in that cavern," Ixchel explained. "I do not know the origin of the legend. Perhaps, long ago, a woman like myself was buried alive down there, as was I, but no one rescued her and she died there, and a legend grew around her."

When she saw their crestfallen faces, she added, "But I *will* pray for you and ask the gods to grant you the deepest wishes in your hearts. May we please go now to my house?"

Kaan lifted Ixchel into his arms again and they left the sanctuary, a somber group descending the steep, slippery steps, no longer excited and joyful, but silent and dispirited. When they reached the bottom, word spread quickly among the crowd that this was not the Earthbound God-dess and she could grant no wishes.

It was a puzzled crowd that followed Kaan through the deserted, weed-grown streets of Palenque. They could not understand how they had come so far for nothing, leaving behind homes and loved ones to fol-low an empty dream. What was going to happen to them now? And then the germ of an idea sprouted among them, perhaps emanating from one mind, one mouth, whispered to his or her neighbor, spreading through the throng like fire: the sudden realization that the old woman must be very lucky.

She was certainly the oldest person anyone had ever seen. And she said she had been underground for many years. How had she survived? An elderly person was rare to begin with, life being so hazardous, and therefore people of lengthy years were revered for their good luck. How much luckier was this frail woman for surviving so long underground?

Someone pointed to the quetzal bird that followed, circling overhead, a rarely glimpsed creature known in myth and legend to be a messenger of the gods. That was how the woman had done it, the people told themselves now as they grew excited with renewed hope, deciding as they reached the outskirts of the city that surely the old woman's good luck must be the most powerful in the world! Perhaps this was better than finding the Earthbound Goddess, they assured one another, for it was said she could grant only one wish, whereas this woman's luck could be shared by all.

Balám, however, was developing a different kind of interest in the old woman. As he strode past temples shrouded in melancholy mist, where dark doorways were festooned with vines and creepers dripping mois-ture, he thought of the item she had retrieved from the Time Temple. "Paper," she had said. A book?

The Maya were fanatical book lovers. No wealthy house was without its library, to be boasted of by the owners. Old and rare books were espe-cially valued, as they contained lost and forgotten stories. Balám did not care about Ixchel's book per se, or the story it contained, rather what he could get for it. A collector would pay handsomely for such a rare tome.

Since his blinding vision in the marketplace of Ixponé, when he had seen his new destiny so clearly, the prince of Uxmal had been slowly and secretly accumulating wealth, which he carried on his person in the form of a thick, wide belt. Tucked into the jaguar-skin pockets were jade pieces, gold, cacao beans, amber, all saved against the day when he would need it to execute his brilliant plan.

Balám decided now that the old woman's book was to be his, and he knew it would be no problem, once Kaan and the others had left her at her home, to take the feather-wrapped bundle from her.

Ixchel led them to a two-story house made of stone and cement, with a walled courtyard, doors and windows, and a solid roof, nestled in the embrace of thick green trees and broad-leafed ferns. But the structure was deserted and overgrown with vines and creepers.

As dark clouds gathered overhead and a damp wind blew through the empty rooms, Ixchel stood with strangers in a home she remembered from yesterday, but with tapestries and statuary, flowers and laughter. "What happened?" she whispered.

From among the large crowd clogging the lane outside, a cotton mantle was sent forward. And then came a sleeping mat. Gourds and pots were offered. Eggs and salt fish and dried berries. Offerings for the luckiest woman on earth, that she might share some of her good luck with those in need of it. As Tonina and Kaan placed these gifts in her house, sweeping out the littered leaves, pulling up vines and weeds, lighting a fire to ward off the damp, and as Ixchel watched the sudden generous industry, with even the one-eyed dwarf moving from room to room, casting about his own unique luck, it came to her what had happened here. "The king was evil," she said, and the others stopped to listen. "When he committed an act so vile that even the gods could not turn a blind eye, everyone must have fled, for they knew the city was cursed."

As she continued to clutch the feather bundle to her chest, Ixchel looked at the great crowd of strangers coming so unexpectedly to Palenque—a caravan of pilgrims, hoping for miracles from the Earthbound Goddess. She drew in a shaky breath, sighed deeply, then turned a shy smile to her rescuers. "Although I am not the goddess you sought, nor have I any wealth, I thank you for bringing me out of my prison, and for that I bestow upon you whatever good luck the gods have given me."

Tonina knelt for the benediction, and then Kaan, and then One Eye, Hairless, and anyone who could crowd into the courtyard—all kneeling to receive the ancient hand upon their heads. All telling themselves that they did not mind that she was not a true goddess after all.

≈ 47 ≈

While the people made camp in and around the deserted houses, with everyone lining up to be brought into the presence of the good-luck woman—H'meen and One Eye having volunteered to help Ixchel dispense her benedictions—Tonina went in search of Kaan.

After receiving Ixchel's blessing, he had marched out and disappeared into the crowd. Now it was late evening and the air was heavy with heat and humidity. Although the rain had eased up, it had left behind a sultry night that made it almost impossible to breathe. She found him in a glade outside the city, standing at the edge of a pond where a small waterfall bubbled. She held back while the moon performed a slow dance with the scudding clouds, shedding silver light and then withholding it, so that the jungle landscape changed moment to moment.

Tonina studied the bend of Kaan's neck, the slope of his shoulders, and she thought: He is a man without hope. She wanted to comfort him. She wished she had the words, the magic. They had been through so much together, had shared such high hopes, and now it was over.

He cupped something in his hands and was staring at it intently. Something that had belonged to Jade Sky, Tonina suspected—the lock of hair, the Kukulcan statuette, the blue feather. Was he speaking to her one last time, before she vanished? Was he asking her for forgiveness? Tonina wished she knew how to pray to the Mayan dead, for she would explain to Jade Sky that Kaan had done his best, that his heart was good, that if he had it to do all over again, he would make sure she was not murdered.

As the moon withdrew and then suddenly emerged again through a break in the clouds, spilling silvery light over vines and creepers, broad-leafed plants, and small creatures with glowing eyes, an idea came to

Tonina. It was a small hope, and an even smaller chance, but to the drowning man even a straw can look like a life raft.

Kaan shivered despite the warm night. He was in a dark place, where the chill came not from the air but from deep within his despairing soul. He stared at the small blue feather cupped in his hands, his thoughts and emotions confused. Did he cherish this little feather because it had once belonged to Jade Sky, or because Tonina had given it to him? Was this why the gods were punishing him, because he had allowed his heart to open to another when he was not free to do so?

Kaan did not know the answers, but he did know one thing: He must never tell Tonina how he desired her, how he longed to wash the paint from her face and see her for the first time, to kiss those lips that had breathed life into him when he had drowned. This would be his penance. To desire without fulfillment. To love without reciprocation. He did not know how Tonina felt toward him—there had been the one desperate kiss after the hurricane at Copan, but none since—although, sometimes, when he caught her looking at him, his heart would leap and then whisper, *She feels the same.* But he would never know. And that, too, was part of his penance.

He heard the clicking of a hundred tiny shells woven into long hair, and his heart jumped. He dreaded Tonina's company, even as he welcomed it. He wished their paths had never crossed. He wished he could spend eternity with her. As she approached, he had to force himself to look at her, knowing he could drown in her eyes, and when he saw that she had restored the paint on her face, that island symbols concealed her once again, he both cursed the practice and was thankful for it.

"Kaan, I have been thinking," she said as she drew near, stepping from deep shadow into silver moonglow. "How do you know Jade Sky was murdered?"

He tucked the little feather into the waistband of his loincloth. Kaan wore no mantle, so that his torso glistened with sweat. "Balám told me. He said it was the members of the consortium."

"What I mean is, although the consortium *said* they were going to murder Jade Sky, is it not still possible that she died by accident, that an assassin did not arrive in time?"

He frowned. "What do you mean?"

"Kaan, I was there and I did not hear anyone in the bedroom. I thought Jade Sky had tripped and hit her head. What if that was really the case?"

He thought about it, then said, "What does it matter?"

"Because then her soul would have been saved, would it not?"

He gave her a puzzled look. "I don't understand."

"Is that not why you were going to see the Sisterhood of Souls? Because you thought your wife was murdered?"

"Murdered?" He blinked. "Murdered," he repeated. And then he understood. "Tonina, that is not why I needed the Sisterhood. It does not matter how a person dies, whether by accident, illness, or old age. What matters is reciting the prayer of confession before death. Either way—if Jade Sky was murdered or it was indeed an accident—you said that she died swiftly, and so had no time to recite the prayer."

Tonina stared at him, his attractive features illuminated by moonglow one moment, cast in darkness the next. The sound of the little waterfall bubbling over moss-covered rocks seemed to grow louder as Tonina took in Kaan's words. She looked down at the surface of the leaf-strewn pond, the moon and clouds reflected upon its surface as if another world existed down there. Then she lifted her eyes and looked at Kaan in sudden realization. *What had she done?* "Oh, Kaan, I am so sorry!"

"It is not your fault," he said with a sad smile. "Perhaps the gods did not mean for me to reach my goal. They joined my path with yours from the very beginning, and then they tricked me with a false reading of the map—"

"No, no," she said, stepping close to him, "that is not what I am sorry about. I did not know about the need to recite a prayer. I thought that, like islanders, Mayans prefer a swift death. On Pearl Island, everyone dreads a lingering death, for the dying are vulnerable and are prey to evil spirits that can snatch a soul away. I lied to you, Kaan. I lied to bring you comfort when now I see it has only brought you anguish."

His brow furrowed. "Lied?"

"Jade Sky's death was not instant. I told you that to give you peace of mind. Kaan," Tonina said quickly, "she spoke before she died. I understood little Mayan then, but I remember the words."

"What did she say?" he whispered, the breath caught in his throat.

"She said several words, but the one I clearly understood was 'agony' and so I did not want you to know that her last moments were in agony."

His frown deepened. Tonina was saying *k'iinaam*, but he wondered if she had heard Jade Sky correctly. "Are you sure that was the word? Could it have been 'sun'?" he asked, saying the Mayan word *k'inn*.

Tonina thought for a moment. "Yes," she said, realizing now that the words "sun" *(k'inn)* and "agony" *(k'iinaam)* might be mistaken for each other, especially as Jade Sky was having difficulty speaking.

"Could she have said 'beautiful'?" he asked, pronouncing the word *kiichpan*.

Tonina's eyes widened. Thinking back and reliving that fateful night with her greater understanding of the Mayan tongue, she realized she had indeed mistranslated the words. She had thought Jade Sky was saying *k'iinaam*, that she was in agony, when in fact she had said *k'inn kiichpan*—"beautiful sun."

"I believe that is what she said. Is it significant?"

"Tonina, the words 'beautiful sun' are in the prayer of confession!"

"*Guay,*" she whispered, bringing her hand to her mouth.

"How long," he began, licking his lips, his excitement building, "how long did she speak? Was it but a moment? Only a moment?"

"No. She had started speaking before I reached her. And then I knelt and brought her head into my lap. She kept talking. I did not understand her. I tried to comfort her. I called for help and in all that time she spoke many words—"

"Blessed Mother Moon! Jade Sky's soul was saved that night!" Kaan cried, nearly shouting. "As was my son's!"

"I am so sorry," Tonina said again.

"Sorry! No! There is nothing to be sorry for."

"I should have told you the truth."

"It was my fault. You tried to talk about Jade Sky, but I would not allow it." He took her face in his hands and studied her cheeks, brow, lips, wanting to taste the coconut paint. "I feel as if a thousand weights have been lifted from me."

She was unable to move, enthralled by his touch, the heat of his passion.

"I want—," he began, but he could not finish. Strange new emotions flooded him—a joy he had never felt before, elation that made him feel as if he were soaring, and a sudden, intense need to reward Tonina.

He spun away from her, turning in a circle to scan the lush green moonlit glade. Where were the treasures he could lay at her feet? He thought of the riches that filled his villa in Mayapan—jade necklaces, amber bracelets, gold earrings—and how he wished he could summon them all here right now.

He stopped and settled his eyes on Tonina, backdropped by the rippling pond and bubbling waterfall. I wish to give her the sea. I wish to give her all the oceans in the world.

As he gazed at the tall girl he had once thought was a punishment from the gods, at the oval face and narrow nose and long hair braded with a hundred tiny shells, Kaan felt his relief and elation and feelings of intense gratitude shift to something else.

Reality settled in. Jade Sky was saved. He was free.

Kaan knew Jade Sky would always occupy a special place in his heart. He would always love her, and the memory of her. But she was with the gods now.

And Tonina was *here.*

The humid air was ripe with aromatic hints of life and fecundity. Exotic flowers hung heavy on drooping stems, thick petals opening wide to the moonlight. Kaan felt sharp new desires stir in his loins. He had suppressed his growing attraction for this girl for so long that, finally set free, the sexual desire hit him with the intensity of a physical blow.

With Kaan's dark eyes fixed on her, Tonina felt the atmosphere shift and change, like a warm, salty tide, as if she and Kaan swam in a sultry lagoon. Her heart raced. She felt strange new sensations awaken deep within her—*physical* sensations, a sweet ache that was at once agonizing and delicious.

She knew that Jade Sky would always be special to him, but she no longer stood between them. She was a spirit with the gods, whereas Tonina was here and now, planted firmly in this world of sensation and earthly pleasures.

When he came toward her, the breath caught in her chest. She thought her heart was going to stop.

"I marvel at the miracle," he murmured, drawing close, his eyes searching her face, placing his hands on her cheeks.

"Miracle?" she whispered breathlessly, lost in his eyes, in the warmth of his hands on her face.

"That night, when I returned home and found Jade Sky dead . . . Had you not been moved by my grief, Tonina, to lie and tell me she died instantly—had you spoken the truth that night, I would not have cursed the gods. I would not have been arrested and sent to the cenote for sacrifice. I would have wept over my wife's body, attended her funeral, and you would have left Mayapan forever. And yet, because of that single act of compassion we are here tonight, in this strange place, in a different world from what we once knew, two different people from who we once were."

Finally he tasted the coconut, as he bent his head and gently kissed her forehead, cheeks, mouth. When Tonina parted her lips, the kiss turned from gentle to urgent, and Kaan drew her into a hard embrace. Tonina curled her arms around his neck to anchor herself to him as the moist night swam about them. Kaan could not draw her tightly enough to himself. She moaned. The fragrance of fertile soil and lush, green growth filled their nostrils.

He drove his hand into her shell-woven hair. Tonina dug her fingers into his hard back, feeling old scars and knotted muscles. Kaan explored her body, slipping under the cotton tunic to find a tender breast and hard nipple. Tonina felt his manhood straining at his loincloth. She reached up and untied the hemp string that tamed his jaguar-tail, allowing long black hair to tumble over his shoulders and down his back. Tonina gasped. It gave him a wild, untamed look.

They grew frantic, pulling at cloth, mouths together as hands flew to knots and waistbands, desperate to feel skin against skin. Tonina bent a knee and slid her leg up Kaan's strong thigh. His hand shot down, exploring heat and moistness.

Tonina dropped to the grass, drawing him down, wanting his weight on her, the press and excitement of his firm body on hers.

Kaan covered her, kissing her hard, lifting her skirt. Tonina closed her eyes in ecstasy. Yes, she thought. Yes. . . .

He drew back to gaze at her face in the moonlight. Tomorrow, he thought, the paint will come off once and for all.

She opened her eyes and smiled. "Do not stop," she whispered.

His hand went to her waist to pull her skirt away. He stopped when his fingers met the slender hemp rope that rested above her hips—the belt she wore beneath her tunic, crafted in the islands and decorated with cowry shells. Kaan had learned its meaning.

"Tonina," he asked in a hoarse whisper, "you have never been with a man, have you?"

"No. . . ."

He groaned. Fingers plucking at the virginity belt, Kaan wanted to rip it away and delve into this enchanted creature, lose himself entirely in her. When Tonina parted her thighs, Kaan wanted to shout his protest to the sky. Another ragged groan and then, with intense effort, he raised himself up.

He could not treat Tonina with dishonor.

Her look was questioning, and it filled him with pain and frustration. But he respected her too much to give in to his desire.

It would not be for much longer, he assured himself as he touched her hair, traced the line of her chin with a fingertip, saw the pulse throbbing at her throat. From here to Mayapan it is a White Road all the way, he told himself, policed by the soldiers of local chiefs, with no mountains to impede us. We can be in Mayapan in twenty days, and I can make sacrifice at the Temple of Kukulcan to end my period of mourning. Before I enjoy the pleasures of life again, both Jade Sky and Tonina must be respected.

He kissed her sweetly and tenderly, on the lips, eyebrows, beneath her earlobes. "We must wait a little longer," he said, hating the words, wishing he could disregard the strict code of honor by which he had always lived. But Tonina was a virgin, and Mayan law and custom compelled him to take her only in marriage. "We will leave at once, tomorrow morning, and once we are in Mayapan I will visit the temple of—"

"Mayapan?" she said.

"My journey is over, Tonina. I can go home now."

She stared at him, and his words from long ago, spoken in Mayapan, came back: "I am going to Teotihuacan and you must accompany me." Thinking only of himself and his needs.

"*My* journey is not over," she said, experiencing a sharp pain of disappointment. She straightened her clothing as she found her way to her feet. "Why must you go to Mayapan?" she asked, already knowing—dreading—the answer.

Kaan rose to his feet and faced her. "Tonina, you have known since Balám told me about the consortium that I must go back. Murder must be avenged. Honor demands it."

"I thought you had . . ."

"Changed my mind?" He shook his head. "I have been focusing on resurrecting Jade Sky's soul. Now that it's no longer necessary, I must address the second half of my duty. I cannot rest until my wife's murderers have been held accountable for their crime." And then he added quickly, "But, Tonina, you and I will be married there. It is only for a short while longer."

She remained still for a long moment as the clouds played tricks with moonlight, and jungle sounds grew deafening. Night birds and monkeys and cicadas competed to be the loudest, until the waterfall was drowned out.

She struggled with her emotions as she said, "Kaan, I cannot go to Mayapan. I owe it to my people to find them. When this medallion was placed about my neck, someone knew I would use it someday to find my way back. Perhaps just over the next hill, in the next valley, I will find my people. I cannot turn away now."

He took her by the shoulders and said with passion, "You could search for years and never find them. Tonina, there are people in Mayapan who can help you—archivists, historians, merchants who travel the width and breadth of the land. *Come back with me.*"

She looked at him with pleading eyes. "Oh, Kaan, can you not come with *me*? What good can come of revenge?"

"My wife was murdered and her killers walk free. I must see that justice is served." But even as he spoke the words, Kaan heard other words, a deeper truth, whisper in his heart, one that he did not wish to hear. Palenque stood at the westernmost border of Mayan influence. Beyond lay a vast land of mountains and lakes, coastal shores and valleys, a land that was rumored to have no end. And in all that area there lived many tribes who knew nothing of Mayan ways. Kaan's mother had told him he came from one of those tribes. Journeying there frightened him, for it would mean losing his Mayan identity, the only identity he had ever known.

And a deeper, more frightening fear: that he would discover that his people truly *were* godless barbarians.

Leave now, his mind whispered. Hurry from this place and this girl's influence, and you will still be Kaan the Mayan ballplayer.

He looked at Tonina's moist, parted lips and wished that he could take her now and quench his burning desire. But she was not just a woman to be used for carnal needs. He wanted to be with her in every way, spiritually as well as physically. And taking pleasure with her now, he knew, would not douse the fire that raged in him. Intimacy with Tonina would only stoke the flames and make him burn all the more.

He thought of the wondrous news she had just told him—that Jade Sky and their son were saved. Yet the joy he had felt upon hearing this had turned to dust in his mouth. "I understand now," he said in a low voice tight with pain, his hands gripping her arms, his face close to hers. "I do not have the right to love you. I have no right to joy. It is the will of the gods. Jade Sky begged me to stay with her that night, but I went in search of Balám instead. The blame lies with me. Although she died by the hand of another man, I alone am responsible, and I must pay the price."

Tonina looked up into dark, turbulent eyes and knew that if Kaan kissed her now, merely the brush of his lips on hers, she would surrender completely. Her hunger for him was greater than any she had ever known, and once she gave herself to him, she would follow him to the ends of the earth, at the sacrifice of her own destiny.

But she knew that he was driven by a deep moral sense and the need to see justice served. This was his strength. In Ixponé she had seen how this worked for good when he defended the pineapple sellers. But his need for justice was also his weakness, for it was an obsession that could destroy him.

"Kaan," Tonina said as tears rolled down her cheeks, "I cannot return east for I have already been there, and nowhere in Uxmal or Mayapan did I see the distinctive embroidery of my baby blanket. I have been told to look westward, beyond Palenque, and perhaps even farther than that. Kaan, I have a duty to my people."

His eyes locked with hers for a brief, charged moment, as clouds parted to allow moonlight into the glade. Then Kaan's hands fell away from Tonina's shoulders. "In the morning I will start back for Mayapan," he said. "I will seek out every member of the consortium, and make them pay for what they did. If it takes the rest of my life."

S harpen your spears," Balám had told his men at sunset. "For soon we engage in battle."

Now it was the dark hour before dawn, when everyone slept except for the troubled prince of Uxmal. The evening before, Kaan had come to him with surprising news: Jade Sky's soul was not lost after all. And so Kaan's pilgrimage had come to an end. "I leave at dawn for Mayapan," he had said grimly.

"Then here is where you and I part ways, brother," Balám had said, the lie rolling glibly from his tongue, "for I am off to Teotihuacan to pray for forgiveness and to ask the gods to grant me a reunion with my beloved daughter." Balám had given up on stealing Ixchel's feather-wrapped book. The old woman was surrounded by too many people.

Kaan did not say what the island girl was going to do now, or what was going to happen to the hundreds who had followed them. Kaan had said very little, in fact, which made Balám wonder what had happened. Not that he cared. All he was concerned with was when and where Kaan would be at noon tomorrow. For that was when the new plan would be executed.

As the disgraced prince of Uxmal now moved among his men, quietly waking them, ordering them to prepare for a silent predawn departure from Palenque, he thought about the blinding vision he had experienced in Ixponé when he heard his mother's voice whisper to him, "Son, you *can* redeem yourself. If you return as the victor of a defeated enemy and march into Uxmal at the head of captives and slaves, you will redeem yourself in the eyes of gods and men, and you will earn the right to demand the return of your daughter."

His mother's powerful words had changed Balám that fateful afternoon in the marketplace, for upon hearing them in his head, he had grown calm, a white light had embraced him, and a stunning vision had come to him. He had seen himself leading an army through the streets of Uxmal, and behind him, prisoners shackled together, gifts for the king. He had known then that what he saw was his destiny; his great violent god Buluc Chabtan revealing to him what he had been born to do. Since that day, throughout the long trek to Palenque, Balám had been slowly and secretly amassing manpower and wealth. And he knew who his captives would be—Kaan and the hundreds who so blindly followed him.

With fewer wars between the Mayan kingdoms, suitable sacrificial victims for the gods were becoming rare. Balám's uncle would regard the captives as more valuable than all the jade and gold in the world, and he would reward his nephew by restoring his honor and granting him the right to reclaim his daughter from whoever had purchased her. Balám was certain of victory, for his plan was to leave Palenque before sunrise and lie in wait at the White Road. The ambush would take Kaan and his men by surprise. Not precisely a combat of war, but a fight nonetheless. And Balám knew that his warriors, like soldiers everywhere, would exaggerate in the retelling of the battle, making it sound like a grand and honorable clash indeed.

Soon, Ziyal would be returned to him.

As they prepared to leave Palenque, Hairless eyed his master from beneath bushy brows. Kaan's manner this morning was distant and cold, like the mist that hung low over the ancient city. He seemed to be without emotion, when he should be rejoicing. Hairless had learned that Kaan's wife had indeed recited the prayer of confession and so her soul was saved. They were all happy for Kaan. He should be happy. Yet he was not.

Perhaps it is this journey of revenge, Hairless told himself as he rolled up the last of the *hamacs* and strapped them to his hairy back. Kaan is not by nature a violent man. He is not a killer. And yet that is what he must become to avenge his wife's death.

Or perhaps, Hairless thought as he glimpsed Tonina across the smoky camp, silently bundling up her own possessions with crisp movements, Kaan's grim mood has more to do with the fact that he and the island girl are about to part company.

Hairless noticed that the two had not exchanged words that morning, despite sharing a camp, and both looked as if they had not slept. There was but one trail out of Palenque, which they must travel together, but beyond the final stela lay the White Road. On that spot, Tonina and her small group would turn west, Kaan and his companions, east. Hairless suspected that their hearts did not wish the separation, yet both were under obligations beyond their choosing.

Hairless sighed and signaled to his young wife that he was ready to go. Whatever troubled his master's heart, Hairless would not inquire. A man's demons were his own business.

The majority of the great crowd that had accompanied them from Copan had chosen to stay in Palenque. Many were too weak or tired or ill to continue a journey. And many saw no advantage to returning to Mayapan, or going westward with Tonina, while here at least was an old woman filled with incredible good luck. Perhaps living in Ixchel's proximity would cure illness, heal wounds, bring unfaithful husbands back, and stimulate fertility.

H'meen had elected to stay. "Ixchel is weak from her ordeal in the cave," she said to Tonina. "She needs someone to take care of her and nurse her back to health." H'meen's knowledge of medicine had expanded, and she now had a rich collection of healing herbs: the bark of the cinchona tree to reduce fever, the leaves of the purple foxglove to ease ailments of the heart, yam roots for treating arthritis. People came to H'meen with headaches, earaches, chest congestion, bowel problems, menstrual irregularities, and impotence, all of which she treated with botanicals, amulets, spells, and prayers. And now she hoped to restore strength and years to the poor woman who had lived most of her life underground.

"I can learn a great deal from a lady of such advanced years," H'meen explained to Tonina. "Perhaps within Ixchel's vast knowledge and wisdom lies the cure for my aging illness. I thank you, Tonina, for showing me the world. Should I die tomorrow, it was all worth it."

Tonina was going to miss the strange elderly child, a girl of fifteen who looked as ancient as Ixchel. They embraced and wished each other luck.

When Tonina privately asked One Eye to stay with Ixchel and H'meen, for a while at least, he agreed. He was tired of hardships and constant traveling, and was in the mood to stay put for a while. With women coming in from the nearby corn and cotton farms to receive blessings from Ixchel, One Eye found himself once again the object of feminine attention, for a one-eyed dwarf who had survived a jaguar attack was double luck indeed.

And so the dwarf stood on a low stone wall in order to embrace Tonina in a tearful farewell, relishing the feel of her arms around him, the warmth of her bosom against his chest, swearing that he would love her forever.

Y ou know what to do," Balám said to his cousins. They were at the end of the trail, where it met the east–west White Road, and his men were taking their places behind trees and bushes, readying the trap for Kaan. "I want as little killing as possible," Balám said, squinting at the sun breaking through the mist. "Kaan and Tonina especially are to be taken alive."

His cousins readily complied, for they were excited young men, eager to fight at last. Their spears were about to drink the blood of enemies, and in just a few days, they would enjoy a hero's welcome in Uxmal.

T wo groups departed Palenque—one large, one pitifully small. No one had chosen to go with Tonina. Why should they? everyone said. She was heading directly west, up into the snow-covered mountains of Chiapán. There was nothing there for them. However, there were those who wanted to go with Kaan, for they were homesick for Mayapan, or curious to see a city, or hopeful of a change of fortune.

Nonetheless, Tonina would not travel alone. Kaan had found local men who were willing to take her into the Chiapán mountains, reliable guides who knew the region and spoke the dialect. Even so, it was a small contingent, and Kaan was not pleased with this. Therefore, he ordered Hairless and his fellows to accompany Tonina until she was no longer in need of their protection, no matter how long it might take. Of the Nine Brothers, who now numbered five, three were married and all three wives refused to go west into hostile territory, and so they joined Kaan's group back to Mayapan, leaving their husbands to travel with Hairless.

Finally they left, all good-byes having been said, tearful embraces over. Kaan and Tonina did not speak as they walked at the head of the combined crowd through the coastal forest. Tonina was afraid to look at the man at her side. She knew that her willpower hung by a fragile thread. *Ask me to go with you and I will say yes.* Kaan strode with a resolute step as he remembered the day Tonina coaxed him into the waters of Lake Peten near Tikal. If you hold out your hands now, he thought, I will do as I did then: deliver my own hands into yours and let you lead me anywhere.

They come, my lord!" Balám's scout reported with excitement. The prince of Uxmal, devoted acolyte of the bloody Buluc Chabtan, gripped his spear and smiled grimly. The hour of sweet revenge was at hand.

There was something strange about Ixchel. H'meen could not put her finger on it. The notion had come to her when she had first set eyes upon the white-haired woman, on the crest of the hill as she had tearfully thanked everyone for rescuing her. Even now, as Ixchel spoke softly about her underground garden, H'meen could not shake the feeling that something was wrong.

The morning mist had burned off and the sun shone brightly. Soon, clouds would come, followed by the inevitable downpour. With her friends having departed earlier that morning, H'meen had taken up residence in Ixchel's house, and they now shared a lunch of nourishing broth. The quetzal bird had stayed instead of flying away to freedom, and now sat upon his perch, pecking happily at a piece of fruit, while Poki, as fat and content as ever, napped on an old blanket rich with subterranean smells. Kaan had sent Hairless and his men down into the cavern to retrieve Ixchel's possessions so that her stone house was furnished with the familiar items of her long imprisonment.

"Honored lady," H'meen said as she handed Ixchel a gourd of hot soup, "how were you able to grow such a wonderful garden underground, with poor soil and so little light?"

Ixchel lifted the bowl to her lips and sipped delicately. The taste was heavenly. "Through the opening in the cavern's ceiling there was enough sunlight each day to raise plants that do not require complete light, or that flourish in shade. And of course I had plenty of water. There were small river fish in the lagoon as well. I used them for fertilizer."

As H'meen watched Ixchel chew on a piece of onion, closing her eyes to enjoy a flavor she had not tasted in years, she asked, "Honorable Ixchel, forgive me for asking, but why did the king put you in the cavern?"

Ixchel brought herself back to the small house and the company of the curious girl who had aged beyond her years. "Pac Kinnich wanted something that belonged to my family." Ixchel's eye flickered to the feather-wrapped bundle that she kept close by. "He threatened to kill us all, to kill my beloved husband Cheveyo if I did not give him the sacred book that has been in my house for generations."

A shadow passed over the little stone dwelling, blotting out the sun, presaging the storm that was soon to come. "It was the Year of the Five Hurricanes," Ixchel said, the soup ignored as she recalled the painful memory. "Pac Kinnich was an evil man. When my family went into hiding, he laid dangerous traps in the western hills, the sort hunters use for catching tapirs and deer, with sharp stakes pointing upward. He hoped we would fall into them. . . ."

H'meen added herbs and spices to the pot, listening to Ixchel's story as she told how they were warned of the traps and fled in different directions, she and her beloved Cheveyo becoming separated in their escapes.

H'meen suddenly looked up, her hands frozen over the soup. She blinked at the old woman, and then suddenly she cried out, startling Poki, who was immediately on his feet, yapping his squeaky bark.

Ixchel said, "What is it?"

"We have to stop them!" H'meen said, jumping to her feet. "One Eye!"

He came running in. "What? What's the matter?"

"We must get word to Tonina! We must call her back!"

"Back! But that is not possible! They are at the White Road by now."

"Runners!" H'meen said, pushing One Eye toward the door. "Find men to go after them."

Ixchel dropped her bowl of soup as her hands flew to her mouth. "You think the traps are still there?"

"Runners will never reach Tonina in time," One Eye said. Traps? What was this about traps? "The sky darkens. Soon it will be raining and then the trail will be like a river. By the time we send someone—"

"One Eye!" H'meen cried frantically. "It is urgent!"

"I don't know how—"

"The tower," Ixchel said suddenly.

They looked at her.

"If it is still standing," she said, struggling to her feet, "you can climb up and signal to people on the trail."

"Where is this tower?" One Eye said.

"I will show you."

The tall wooden structure stood at the edge of the city and rose higher than the tallest tree in the rain forest canopy. "There is an obsidian mirror at the top," Ixchel said, pointing up where the tower disappeared through the trees. "It was placed there many years ago, for lookout scouts to watch for invaders. When the mirror is positioned just so, in conjunction with the sun, it flashes bright warning lights to those on the plain below, alerting them to come into the city for protection."

She fell silent and they all looked up at the darkening sky. Typical for this time of the year, after the morning mist had burned off, bright sunlight shone. But by mid-day, clouds had begun to gather so that soon the downpour would begin. Someone must get to the mirror and manipulate it while there was still sunlight.

A small crowd had gathered at the base of the rickety watchtower, and a few old farmers remembered the working of the mirror, saying that it required a strong man with a keen eye, for the obsidian surface had to be aimed precisely in order for those on the trail to see the flash of light.

One brawny man volunteered to go up, but as soon as he took hold of the first rung, the tower creaked ominously.

"Stop," H'meen said. "It will not take your weight. I shall go up."

The big-armed farmer said, "You won't be able to move the mirror. It's very heavy."

H'meen gnawed her lip. If what Ixchel had said was true, it was vital that Tonina be called back. But once the rains came, they would lose their chance of signaling her. After that, it would be impossible to know which trail into the Chiapán hills she had taken. It was now or never.

When One Eye saw the fear and worry on H'meen's face, he made a decision all in an instant. "I will go up," he said, speaking with a bravado he did not feel. "The tower will take my weight, and I have the strength in my arms to move the mirror."

"But it takes a keen eye," the farmer warned. "A man with good vision in *both* eyes," he added significantly. "If you aim wrong, they will never see the signal."

One Eye thought of the comfortable life he had planned for himself in this paradise where a one-eyed dwarf could be king. It was a new experience for him to weigh his own fortune against the good of the others. In order to climb the tower and call Tonina back, he must reveal a secret about himself. Once that secret was revealed, he would no longer have the good life here in Palenque.

Ah well, he thought, you're only young once and never old twice. And this life is all there is. Untying the ribbon from around his head, he removed his eye patch and said, "There is nothing wrong with my sight."

Everyone gasped to see the healthy, brown-irised eye look right at them.

The idea had come to him long ago in a town where there had been such a concentration of dwarfs they had had their own guild. Because they were so numerous, people didn't find them special. And then it had come to the wily island trader that a dwarf who had lost an eye and still survived was a lucky man indeed!

Understanding his sacrifice, H'meen touched his arm and said, "The gods bless you."

As he started the climb, One Eye prayed it was not too late, for then his sacrifice would have been in vain.

T hey were near the White Road, from where it was a straight journey back to Mayapan. Tonina, however, would soon reach the western terminus of the Mayan highway and must turn onto trails that would take her into the pine forests of Chiapán.

As Kaan and Tonina turned to each other to speak a painful and emotional farewell, Balám, hidden nearby, raised his arm to give the signal for attack.

O ne Eye cursed his shortness.

He had reached the top of the tower and, once he regained his equilibrium—he had never been so high off the ground—he struggled to reach the edge of the massive slab of obsidian that served as a signaling mirror. The wind blew fiercely at this height, with no protection from trees. The tower swayed and he almost lost his footing.

Rising on his toes and stretching his arms, One Eye cursed the Mayan obsession with mirrors, cursed all Mayans in general, and cursed his cavalier soul for having volunteered for this suicidal gallantry.

Finally, a tenuous grip on the heavy, slippery disc, and then: *"Guay!"* The sun had slipped behind a dark cloud, and the first raindrop fell.

K aan's heart thumped as he dared to take Tonina's hands in his and delve deeply into her eyes while their companions looked the other way. "I pray that the gods keep you," he said in a husky voice as he struggled for control. "I pray you find your family."

Tonina parted her lips, but no voice came out.

Through the trees, Balám prepared to bring down his arm in the attack signal when Hairless suddenly said, "What is that?"

They turned in the direction he was pointing and saw a bright light flashing above the trees near the city.

Kaan frowned. "What is it?"

One of Tonina's guides said, "It is an alarm, master! Something is terribly wrong at the city. We must go back."

"Go back!" Tonina said. "But why?"

Two of her hired men were already running back along the trail while a third said, "There is trouble! We must return!"

Hastily giving orders to Hairless to stay with the people, Kaan took Tonina's wrist, and together they sprinted back toward Palenque.

When One Eye descended the tower, having signaled as best he could until the rain came down in earnest, he was prepared for the reproach that was sure to come, everyone cursing him for his fakery with the eye patch. Instead it was a cheerful crowd that met him, with women crowding around him, saying what a hero he was, and men clapping him on the back for his bravery.

Beneath a warm downpour, the happy procession returned to the city and ended at Ixchel's house, to await the return of Kaan and Tonina. H'meen handed around gourds of soup while someone produced *pulque* and cigars, and One Eye soaked up his sudden notoriety. "How clever you are," H'meen said to him, her heart swelling with love and pride, adding playfully, "Next you are going to tell us you are not really a dwarf!"

Kaan was the first to enter the courtyard. "What is it? What happened?" he asked breathlessly. Tonina was behind him, also out of breath. Both were soaked from the rain. When she saw One Eye, her brows arched and she said, "Where is your eye patch?"

He was about to reply when Ixchel said, "There are dangerous traps in the hills, placed long ago by an evil king. That is why we called you back. Come here by the fire and dry yourselves."

They sat around the small fire while the rain fell outside. People in the courtyard preferred to huddle beneath waterproof mantles rather than return to their own homes, for they were curious about why Kaan and Tonina had been called back.

"Pac Kinnich captured me," Ixchel began in a soft voice, uncertain how she could help these young people. She had no idea where Pac Kinnich had dug his traps. "He lowered me into the cavern from which there was no escape. And every day he came to the opening in the dome and asked me where I had hidden the sacred book. He lowered food down to me, and clothing. He wanted me to survive, to live in that tomb for as long as possible. And then one day he stopped coming and I heard from him no more. That was many, many years ago."

"Honorable Ixchel," H'meen said gently, "tell Tonina and Kaan the first part of your story. Before Pac Kinnich captured you."

"My family would not give King Pac Kinnich our sacred book, and so he slew my parents and my sisters. Cheveyo and I hid the sacred book in the Time Temple, and then we ran. But we became separated. I do not know where Cheveyo went. Pac Kinnich came after me. I fled eastward with a few loyal friends. I ran to the end of the earth, until I could go no further."

Ixchel looked around at her companions and said, "Surely this does not interest you. H'meen called you back because of the traps and I cannot tell you where they are."

"Honorable Ixchel," said H'meen, "please tell us the rest of your story—what you told me over soup, about running to the end of the earth."

"I knew that if Pac Kinnich caught me, he would use my child to force me to reveal the whereabouts of the book. And so I fled eastward to the legendary place where it was said the great god Quetzalcoatl had set sail on his raft of serpents to traverse the eastern sea. There I wove a small ark out of reeds—for my family are basket weavers—and placed my baby daughter on the sea, praying that the tides and winds and currents would carry her to the land where Quetzalcoatl dwelled, praying that he would take care of her and bring her back to me someday."

Tonina gave a cry. She stared at Ixchel for a moment, then she reached for the string around her neck, lifting it over her head and bringing the medallion into view. "Honorable Ixchel," Tonina said in a cautious tone, "have you seen this before?"

The old woman examined the round amulet in the firelight. "Bless the gods! I placed this necklace around my baby's neck when I set her on the sea! Where did you find it?"

"Twenty-one years ago—," Tonina began, glancing at Kaan, then at One Eye and H'meen, finally bringing her eyes back to Ixchel, "an elderly couple on an island far to the east found a basket caught in a mangrove forest. They said dolphins had guided the basket to shore, and inside they found a baby girl. She had this necklace on her."

Ixchel's eyes were fixed on Tonina.

"I was that baby," Tonina said softly. "I was wrapped in a blanket," she continued, reaching with trembling hands for her travel pack. "I was told that the embroidery would lead me to my people." She found the small blanket and handed it across to Ixchel.

The white-haired woman turned wide eyes to the small square of cotton, its border decorated in a familiar pattern, in familiar stitches because they had been wrought by her own hand. "I embroidered this blanket while I was pregnant with my child." Ixchel lifted her head and whispered, "Can it be? Are you my little Malinal?"

✎ 49 ✐

As Tonina stared in shock at the woman whose white hair glowed in the firelight, and the others sat in stunned silence, H'meen said, "This is why I called you back, Tonina. Not because of dangerous traps in the hills, but because of Ixchel's remarkable story. When I heard it, I realized you must be that baby."

"But," Kaan interjected, "forgive me . . . isn't honorable Ixchel too old to be Tonina's mother?"

H'meen said to Ixchel, "While you and I were eating, honorable mother, something troubled me. Whenever you spoke or smiled, you revealed healthy teeth, with none missing. I was wondering how that was possible, when it suddenly came to me that you might not be as old as we had thought. Honorable Ixchel," H'meen said, "how old were you when Pac Kinnich placed you underground?"

"I was in my nineteenth summer."

"And in what year did Pac Kinnich put you underground?"

"It was the Year of the Five Hurricanes."

"Honorable Ixchel, the Year of the Five Hurricanes was twenty-one years ago, which means you are only forty years old."

"*Great Lokono!*" whispered One Eye.

"I remember that year," Kaan said, looking at Tonina in amazement. "I remember the hurricanes, five in a row. I was seven years old, and so it was indeed twenty-one years ago."

Ixchel frowned. "But look at me. I *am* an old woman."

"I believe," H'meen ventured, "that living in darkness for so long, and eating food that rarely saw the sun, caused this aging in you, as it was once caused in me."

Ixchel's eyes grew large and luminous as she turned to Tonina. "Can this be true? Are you my daughter? Pac Kinnich sent men in canoes to fetch my baby, but they came back to say that the sea had swallowed her. He lied!" Ixchel broke down sobbing, covering her face with her hands. Tonina was immediately at her side, her arm around the frail shoulders.

They wept softly together, mother and daughter, too overcome to speak, while One Eye sniffed and ran a hand under his nose, remembering his mother who must have died long ago, and Kaan touched fingers to his damp eyes as he recalled his farewell to his mother in the palace kitchen.

When Ixchel's gaze fell upon Tonina's travel pack, lying open, she whispered, "Signs and wonders!" And then, remembering their companions, drew away from Tonina and struggled to compose herself.

She paused for a long moment to marvel at this tall, strong young woman at her side, knowing that it would be a while before she could fully accept the reality of this miracle, then she said, "When Pac Kinnich took me to the crest of the hill to lower me into the cave, he said that since I had put my child on the water, out of his reach, so would he put me *under* water, out of reach. And yet it is precisely because I *was* underwater that you were able to rescue me. I put you on the sea and the gods made you a swimmer."

She laid a quivering hand on Tonina's painted cheek and said, "The underground river that flows through the cavern empties into the Bay of Campeche, and so I prayed to the gods of the sea to find you and bring you back to me. I wept as I prayed, so that my tears were carried out to sea. The sea gods tasted my tears and heard my prayers and answered them."

Suddenly Cheveyo came into her mind, beloved and handsome. And another thought occurred to her: If she was indeed much younger than she had thought, was it possible her husband was still alive? As Pac Kinnich had lowered her into the cave, the king had said he had shown something of hers to Cheveyo, smeared with blood, and told him she was dead. Cheveyo believed him and left Palenque. Ixchel knew this must be so, for if Cheveyo had thought she was alive, he would have spent his life searching for her and possibly would have found her.

But now Ixchel felt a thrill of hope. Cheveyo still alive!

"Honorable Mother," Tonina said, realizing that the honorific title now took on a literal meaning, "I have searched everywhere for this flower. But no red flowers hang from trees. Not that look like that." She pointed at the stone that still lay in Ixchel's palm.

"From trees? The flower grows upward, in the shape of a cup." She held up the string so that everyone saw the petals growing upward.

And then Tonina realized that Guama had looked at the medallion upside down. Ixchel said, "You will not find this flower in any ordinary forest, for it is a very special flower."

"Where can I find it?"

Ixchel glanced at the others around the fire. The secret of the red flower was not for their ears. "I cannot speak of it now," Ixchel said. "And I am weary. . . ."

Tonina wanted to know more, but H'meen said, "You must all leave now. Honorable Ixchel needs her rest."

As Tonina tenderly embraced her mother and kissed her good night, Ixchel said, "We will speak again tomorrow, dear child. I have much to tell you. But know this: Very ancient and noble blood flows in your veins. And this," Ixchel said as she picked up the feather bundle and held it to her breast, "will one day be yours."

❧ 50 ❧

*V*ery ancient and noble blood flows in your veins."
       Ixchel's words reverberated in Kaan's mind like a never-ending
echo. Though she had spoken them five days ago, and had elaborated no
further on the subject except to say that Tonina belonged to a tribe that
lived in the northern highlands, in a place called the Valley of Anahuac,
Kaan could not stop thinking about it.

Noble blood . . .

He was happy for Tonina, but troubled at the same time. As he
walked through the plaza encampment, giving orders to his men as
they prepared for transporting so great a company of men, women,
and children—all of whom now wanted to go to Mayapan—his
thoughts revolved around Tonina and the startling change in her circumstances.

As he watched her approach, he felt a stab of fresh pain, for the chasm
that seemed to have stood between them from the day they first met was
now wider than ever.

"Is it true you leave tomorrow?" she asked as she drew near. Since she
had spent the past few days with her mother, and because the growing
crowd demanded Kaan's attention, they had seen little of each other.

Kaan could not take his eyes off her. Although she now knew that she
was of Nahua blood—meaning that she belonged to one of the many
tribes that spoke Nahuatl—Tonina still wore her island face paint. Kaan
wondered why. When she saw how his eyes roved her face, she heard the
silent question, and said, "I am not yet ready to say good-bye to Tonina.
My mother says my real name is Malinal. But I do not know who Malinal is.

I am still Tonina the pearl diver. And I think . . . to remove the identifying marks of Pearl Island would be to dishonor the two who raised me from infancy, and whom I still love as my grandparents."

Kaan understood, and admired her for it.

"You leave tomorrow?" she asked again.

He nodded.

"We seem to be always saying good-bye." She shifted the travel pack on her shoulder. She had come to trade in the marketplace.

"So it would seem. What do you do now?"

"My mother," Tonina said, relishing the words on her tongue, "wants to go in search of my father, Cheveyo. And to find our people. When she is strong enough, we will go west, and then north into the highlands to the Valley of Anahuac. She said that she has never been there, for she was born here in Palenque. But our tribe lives far to the north."

They fell silent, lost in each other's gaze, oblivious to the fact that they were surrounded by energetic and noisy humanity.

In the days since they had returned from the White Road, an even greater crowd had now become encamped in the ancient plaza of Palenque; a combination of Balám's group and those who followed Kaan, as well as hopeful people who had come from farms seeking a better life. Many were leaving tomorrow with Kaan, and a few new young men planned to go west with Balám.

Kaan looked around at the ruins, the empty buildings being gobbled up by the jungle. After tomorrow, this would be a city of ghosts once again. "Tonina, when my business is finished in Mayapan, I will come back."

But they both knew he did not have the power to keep such a promise, for the men of the consortium would fight him. Even if he were able to bring them before the king's tribunal, he had no proof of their involvement in Jade Sky's death. Tonina and Kaan knew that his duty in Mayapan and her own in Palenque could last them the rest of their lives.

"I wish I could go with you," Tonina whispered.

"I wish I could stay," Kaan said.

And the chasm grew wider.

Ixchel watched from a nearby basket weaver's stall. Her heart swelled with pride to see her beautiful daughter, tall and slender, like all the women in their family. Tonina's unusual honey-colored skin, like Ixchel's, was inherited from a distant grandmother.

They are in love, she thought as she watched Tonina with the handsome young man. But they fight it. Kaan is on a path of revenge. It is keeping him from giving his heart to my daughter. And Malinal—Tonina—is torn: She wishes to go with him.

But Tonina's destiny lay elsewhere. And now it was time for her to learn the true meaning of the red flower.

"Blessings of the gods," Ixchel called out.

Tonina and Kaan turned to see her approach. Ixchel had changed, walking now with a straighter spine and a steadier step; her dress was no longer tattered, and her white hair was done up in a handsome style and decorated with colorful ribbons. Flesh was returning to her cheeks and her body was filling out, as if the lost years had found her.

As Ixchel approached, she studied Kaan. He looks like he could be one of us, she thought, and yet he chooses to dress and act Mayan. He had rescued her, and Ixchel believed that nothing happened without a reason. The gods had sent him. But why?

"Noble Kaan, what is your tribe?"

"I do not know. My mother told me long ago, but I have forgotten. I suppose I am Chichimec."

A small furrow appeared between Ixchel's eyebrows. "Never call yourself that, my son, for it is a term of derision. I do not see before me a savage barbarian." Her keen eyes searched his face, studying his features, and Kaan saw intelligence at work behind them. Ixchel reached up and touched his forehead with cool fingertips, and when she said, "You have a noble brow," it startled him.

Ixchel looked across the noisy plaza at another young man, whom she instinctively distrusted—Balám, who claimed to be a prince. He and his warriors had left Palenque before dawn five days prior, but had returned when they saw the signal from the watchtower. They had been camping outside the city ever since, even though it was said Balám was in a hurry to travel north. Ixchel did not like him. He resembled Pac Kinnich; possessing the same sloping forehead, slanting eyes, grotesque nose, and receding chin. All were artificially produced, as if the features given to them by the gods were not good enough.

"I wish to talk to you both in private," she said to Tonina and Kaan. "The Mayans must not know what I am about to tell you. My parents were persecuted in the Valley of Anahuac and forced to flee because of this secret, and my family here in Palenque perished to keep the secret from Pac Kinnich. I was buried for twenty years because I would not divulge the secret. You both must now swear an oath that you will guard this secret with your lives."

She looked at Kaan with bright, keen eyes, and he knew she was giving him the opportunity to back away and carry on with his plans to depart for Mayapan. But he looked at Tonina, and then thought of his own mother, who had also left the Valley of Anahuac years ago, although for different reasons, and he said, "I swear by Mother Moon, honorable Ixchel, that your secret will be safe with me."

"Then let us go," she said, turning to lead them across the plaza, the mysterious feather-wrapped bundle clasped to her bosom.

B alám leaned on his spear as he watched the three scale the steps of the Time Temple pyramid and disappear into the shrine at the top.

Days prior, when he had been lying in wait at the White Road and had seen the signal flashing in the trees, he had followed Tonina and Kaan back to Palenque, to hear of a remarkable mother-and-daughter reunion. Word then began to spread that Tonina was descended from a noble bloodline and that Ixchel was the guardian of a rare and priceless treasure.

"Birthright" was the word everyone was using. Tonina was coming into a surprising legacy.

Balám spat on the mossy paving stones of the plaza and ran his hand across his mouth. What about *my* daughter's birthright? When does

Ziyal come into *her* legacy? She is a daughter of the royal line of Uxmal! She should be a princess!

And then he thought: Yes. And once again his vision grew. Now he saw himself not only at the head of a conquered people, but as the captor of a Chichimec noblewoman and her noble daughter. His uncle the king could do no less than reward his victorious nephew with a crown for Ziyal, a throne of her own, and a shrine where the people would pay homage to her.

Balám shuddered with pleasure. These visions, which had begun in the Ixponé marketplace, were coming more frequently and with more intensity as he saw the sparkling destiny the gods had laid out for him. And it was all so easy! The ancient plaza was packed with families who had come in from struggling farms. His warriors, numbering over three hundred and heavily armed, would vanquish this mob with no resistance. And then: everyone tied together—men, women, and children—to be marched on the White Road to Uxmal, Kaan and Tonina and the old woman in the lead, with Balám at their head, returning triumphant to the city of his birth.

As Ixchel and her companions slipped into the shadows of the Time Temple, an old man hurried forward and prostrated himself at her feet. Ixchel helped him up, saying, "The honor is mine, dear Ahau. It is I who should be paying homage to you."

To Kaan and Tonina she said, "This is Ahau. He was the caretaker of the Time Temple under Pac Kinnich's rule. I found him living with a family who had taken him in after the city was abandoned. They told me that Pac Kinnich had tortured him to learn the hiding place of the secret book. When Ahau would not tell him, Pac Kinnich cut Ahau's tongue out."

She smiled warmly at the bent old man whose face shone with joy and gratitude. "Although Ahau is Mayan, we were great friends, for he was the caretaker of Kukulcan, who is Quetzalcoatl, the god whom I serve. Honorable Ahau, I will be speaking with these two young people about the book. Will you light the sacred incense, please?"

Nodding vigorously, the old caretaker retreated into the darkness, and Ixchel invited Kaan and Tonina to sit.

As they took places on the cold stone floor at the foot of the altar, they heard mumbling in the shadows, and Ixchel said, "Poor Ahau cannot properly chant the prayers, for he has no tongue." She smiled. "The gods understand him nonetheless."

Soon the fragrant smoke filled their nostrils. "You have seen the Tree of Life," Ixchel said softly, "which rises there behind the altar. It symbolizes Lord Quetzalcoatl, and the monster lurking at the base of the tree demonstrates Lord Quetzalcoatl's power over evil."

She looked at Kaan. "Mayans know him as Kukulcan."

Kaan nodded. The Cult of the Returning God, of which Jade Sky had been a devout member.

Tonina stared at the carving on the wall and said, "When Brave Eagle and I were hiding from the eagle hunters in Chichén Itzá, we took shelter in a small chamber with paintings on its walls. They seemed to depict the story of a tall, fair-skinned man with hair growing from his chin."

Ixchel said, "It is the story of Lord Quetzalcoatl, a story that is known worldwide, whether he is called Quetzalcoatl or Kukulcan. In your father's culture, Tonina, he is called Pahana, and far to the south dwells a race of people called Incas who worship a god named Viracocha who once walked the earth as a man. He, too, was tall, pale-skinned, and had a beard, and promised one day to return and restore peace in the land."

They heard Ahau's shuffling footsteps in the antechamber as he mumbled wordless prayers to the gods.

"When Lord Quetzalcoatl walked the earth as a man," Ixchel continued, resting the feather-wrapped bundle on her knees, "he invented books and the calendar, and gave corn to mankind. He was born to a virgin mother, the goddess Coatlicue. Legend tells us that when Quetzalcoatl died, he descended into Hell and, by dripping his blood onto the bones of the dead, brought about the resurrection of human souls.

"But Lord Quetzalcoatl did not stay in Hell. He returned to life after three days and then he left our people by sailing away on a raft of snakes, across the eastern sea toward the rising sun, promising to come back one day and bring eternal peace. Many of our people awaited his return, but when the years went by, and then the centuries—for it is said Lord Quetzalcoatl walked this land over a thousand years ago—the people began to give up hope and they lost their belief in him. And then, three hundred years ago, a miracle occurred. Lord Quetzalcoatl sent proof that he would indeed one day come back to us."

Ixchel paused and stared at the feather-wrapped bundle in her lap. Although the day outside was bright, the light was dim inside the sanctuary, where pungent incense filled the air, and the only sound to be heard was the mumbled drone of old Ahau.

"Three hundred years ago," Ixchel said with wonder in her voice, "strangers came to this land from across the eastern sea to tell us that Quetzalcoatl had not forgotten his promise to return. My grandmother's grandmother sojourned awhile with those strangers and she recorded a chronicle of her life among them. You, Tonina, are descended from that distant grandmother, and so this book also belongs to you."

As Tonina listened with interest, she was aware of Kaan seated at her side. She wondered what he was thinking.

Ixchel reverently unwrapped the feather bundle to expose a thick book, yellowed and brittle with age. She called it the Book of a Thousand Secrets.

"As I have told you, Tonina, our tribe lives in the Valley of Anahuac, in the northern highlands near the city of Teotihuacan, on the shore of a lake called Texcoco. Our tribe is the Mexica. And just as Pac Kinnich coveted this book, so did another tribe, called Tepanec. My parents were forced to flee when the chief of the Tepanecs sent his warriors to steal the book. My mother and father found sanctuary in Palenque and settled in the Basket Weavers' Quarter. Here is where I was born, Tonina. And here is also where you were born. As my mother was guardian of this special book, when she died I became the guardian of the book. And so will you someday.

"This is no ordinary book," Ixchel said as she turned the pages for Tonina to see. In the ray of sunlight that reached the inner sanctuary, Tonina saw that Ixchel's pictorial manuscript was comprised of sheets of bark paper pasted end to end so that they formed a long panel, folded back and forth into uniform segments that were the pages, each covered in pictographic symbols, glyphs, and images outlined in black and filled in with various colors—human and animal forms in stiff poses, elaborately costumed, and all shown in profile.

The writing was like none Tonina had ever seen. Mayan books contained mysterious glyphs that could be deciphered only by those schooled in reading them. But Ixchel's book was based on Nahuatl, the language of the Nahua peoples, who employed clearly recognizable pictures to tell stories and record events.

"This book contains the history of our people. The chronicle was added to in each generation, and ended twenty years ago when I placed it here for safekeeping." As Ixchel turned the richly decorated pages, she explained some of the descriptive symbols: "This man dressed only in a loincloth depicts a year of famine. This yellow flower with many leaves indicates a year of good harvest." She returned to the earlier pages. "Here are symbols that record where our people stayed for a while in their early migrations. The Place of Many Fish. The Hill of the One-Handed Man." Tonina saw tiny footprints connecting the pictographs, and could imagine the tribe wandering from place to place, to settle for a while, only to move on.

While Ixchel turned the pages of the book and told Tonina the history of their people, Kaan listened, curious now about his own people, wondering where they were and what events filled their history. As Ixchel pointed to symbols and named the years, she and her companions were unaware of another way of counting years, on the far side of the earth in a land they could not imagine. For Ixchel and Kaan and Tonina, this was the year 11 Reed, and the day and month were 3 Chicchan. But on the other side of the world, the year was A.D. 1324 and the day and month were the twenty-seventh of June.

Ahau continued his mumbled chanting in the deep shadows, his feet shuffling over the damp stone floor as he carried out secret rituals. He did not disturb the trio sitting at the base of the altar, but moved as one of the silhouettes dancing on the walls.

"This book contains many secrets, Daughter: how the world came into existence, when the gods created human beings, what makes the stars and the planets move in the heavens. These pages contain magic spells, incantations, healing prayers, and prophecies. Here is the story of Quetzalcoatl, and the myths of other gods. Legends of our people, battles we won and lost, the deaths of important people, those who were crowned."

Tonina saw that the book was an unending chronicle, from the earliest, oldest pages, to the newer ones that had been pasted on.

"These secrets are for our family only, for now," Ixchel said. "And you will learn them all someday, my daughter, just as the day will come when we reveal these secrets to our tribe. I can tell you the greatest secret now, for this is why I brought you here into the safety of the Time Temple where no one can hear my words except for you." Her eyes flickered to Kaan. Though he was not of their family, Ixchel had decided that he must be brought into the secret, for her daughter's sake. Ixchel prayed that, once he heard it, he would change his mind about returning to Mayapan.

She turned to a page in the middle of the book and said, "This is one of our most precious secrets, for here is recorded the miracle of three hundred years ago, when Lord Quetzalcoatl sent proof that he will indeed return."

Tonina and Kaan saw, by the flickering light of the oil lamps, images of men and women, huts and hills and trees, and a serpent on water.

"Many generations ago, strangers arrived at the eastern shore of our land; pale-skinned and bearded men with hair like a golden-red sunset and eyes the color of the sea. Their legs were covered in strange skins, as were their arms. Their feet were clad in leather. And upon their heads were helmets fashioned from a strange gray metal. They arrived in a ship that looked like a serpent, such as the one that carried Lord Quetzalcoatl away."

The left side of the page showed brown-skinned men ornamented in loincloths, feathers, and jade, and on the right were men with lighter skin and wearing strange clothes. Out of the mouth of each rose the Nahuatl glyph indicating speech.

"They called themselves Northern Sea Men," Ixchel explained, "and said they were explorers who had been blown off course and shipwrecked on our shore. You can see that they were not killed by our people as other invaders might have been. This was because they bore a resemblance to Lord Quetzalcoatl, and they sailed a boat carved like a serpent. Our ancestors, Tonina, thought that Lord Quetzalcoatl had returned and so they welcomed the strangers with honor. By the time the mistake was learned, that they were mortal men who had lost their way, friendships had been formed—and even marriages—and there was no animosity between the races."

When a whispering sound filled the chamber, Tonina looked toward the entrance and saw that rain had begun to fall. Outside, in the plaza, people would be running for shelter. As the light within the shrine grew dim, new lights appeared—Ahau producing more oil lamps to ward off the darkness of the afternoon.

"The Northern Sea Men," Ixchel continued, "were astounded to learn that our people worshiped a fair-skinned, bearded man who had lived among us long ago, teaching and healing, who had died and spent three days with the dead, and who had then risen and left, traveling eastward on the sea on a raft of snakes. The strangers exclaimed that they, too, worshiped such a man, although they knew him by a different name, and they, too, anticipated his return. There was some argument then, among our people and the strangers, for the Northern Sea Men claimed that Quetzalcoatl had originated far to the east of their own land, that they had known him first, and that only afterward would he have come west to this land. But *we* believe, Tonina, that Quetzalcoatl lived among us first before sailing to the east to live among other races."

Tonina glanced at Kaan, his profile etched in darkness and light as Ahau's oil lamps created shadows and small pools of illumination. Kaan's face was fixed in rapt attention. He looked like a man, she thought, hungry for stories from his own past.

"Our ancestress—my grandmother's grandmother, Malinal, for whom you were named—lived in the village where the strangers sojourned for the time it took them to repair their boat. She spoke with them and recorded the details of their visits. These paintings were wrought by her hand."

As Tonina stared at the images of men and women, animals and houses, the incense filling her head, she thought she sensed another presence in the shrine—not just Ahau, who went unseen about his mysterious business, but something otherworldly.

Why is this called a Time Temple? she wondered. Tonina looked toward the entrance, which seemed so far away, a pale rectangle at the end of an impossibly long tunnel. Is the city still there? If I look, will I see only jungle?

Ixchel continued, "Malinal believed that Lord Quetzalcoatl had sent the Northern Sea Men to remind us of his promise to return, and to instruct us to prepare for that return. After a year and twenty-two days," Ixchel said, pointing to numeric glyphs on the page, "the strangers completed their boat repairs and set sail back toward the east, just as Lord Quetzalcoatl had done many generations prior, and our people never saw them again. But we remembered the promise and our duty to prepare for his coming. The Northern Sea Men told us that we would recognize Lord Quetzalcoatl by this sign. . . ."

Ixchel reached into the folds of the feather blanket and brought out a curious object. "They carried this with them wherever they went, and they said it was the symbol of the returning god."

The strange object, the length of a child's forearm and very heavy, appeared to be a crossbeamed tree with a circle surrounding the intersection of the upright post and the horizontal beam. "What kind of metal is this?" Kaan asked, for it was wrought neither of copper nor of gold, but of a dark gray element.

"I do not know, nor do I understand the symbols engraved in it. But the Northern Sea Men called this a 'cross' and it is further proof that their god and Lord Quetzalcoatl are the same, for the symbol is the same." She pointed to the World Tree rising behind the stone altar.

Ixchel replaced the cross in its protective pocket and said, "Tonina, the evening of my rescue, when you and I embraced, I saw an object in your travel pack, a vessel made of transparent stone. May I see it now?"

As Tonina retrieved the goblet from her travel pack, she told the story of Macu's near drowning in the lagoon and the transparent cup that was in his hand when she brought him ashore.

Ixchel said, "In the book, my grandmother's grandmother describes such drinking vessels that were used by the Northern Sea Men. They claimed to have the magic skill to create such objects from sand."

She turned the goblet around in her hands, marveling at the transparency, yet sturdy thickness, and the tracing of blue and green in the glass.

When she lifted tear-filled eyes, Kaan and Tonina read a silent question in them: Could the sea monster in the Pearl Island lagoon be one of the serpent boats, destroyed on the reef long ago? She said in a shaking voice, "Although it is not recorded in my grandmother's grandmother's chronicle, I have sometimes thought that my distant ancestress fell in love with one of those strangers from the northern sea. It saddens me to think he might never have made it back to his home, but that instead his boat sank in the lagoon of Pearl Island."

"Perhaps there were other boats," Kaan offered gently. "In Mayapan, historians speak of many visitors from strange lands—men with skin the color of black ink, who landed long ago in the Bay of Campeche and who could not return home. And a stranger race of men who landed on a mythical shore in the west, whose skin was yellow and who had the magic to make black powder explode. These are myths, honorable Ixchel, but they might be rooted in truth, and so the sea monster at the bottom of the lagoon could be the remains of another boat, sailed by other men."

She thought about this, then nodded in gratitude and drew in a steadying breath. When Kaan saw how she trembled, he took the goblet from her and, rising to his feet, walked down the corridor to the entrance that looked out over a rain-swept city. Holding the cup in the downpour, he filled it, watching how the warm tropical rain washed temples and buildings, walls and paving stones, its humidity promising the growth of more vegetation, so that tomorrow men would have to take to the jungle again with their knives and axes, to keep the city from being swallowed entirely.

The cup filled, Kaan brought it back to Ixchel, who gratefully took a long drink.

Thanking him for his kindness, she handed the goblet to Tonina, who, before drinking, looked into the water. And an image flashed suddenly before her eyes—a smoke-blackened sky, a plain strewn with bodies, and a man in the center, crying out for help.

"*Guay!*" Tonina dropped the goblet but Kaan, with his quick reflexes, caught it.

"What is it?" Ixchel said.

Tonina described the scene, the man calling for help, and Ixchel's hands flew to her mouth. "You saw your father! The long braided hair, the tunic and leggings of deerskin and fringe—you have described my beloved Cheveyo!"

Tonina looked at her with frightened eyes. Was the vessel a prophecy cup after all? And what did the vision mean?

Ixchel looked about for Ahau because the incense had burned down. Calling to him, and receiving a mumbled reply from the antechamber, she picked up the Book of a Thousand Secrets and said, "It is time now to tell you the most important secret of all. You have seen, Tonina, why this book is so precious, for it is proof that Lord Quetzalcoatl will return to his people. But there is more," she added cautiously, remembering the lengths to which the evil Pac Kinnich had gone to lay his hands on this chronicle. "What I am going to tell you next is the reason I was buried alive, the reason my family were slaughtered, the reason poor Ahau lost his tongue—and the reason," her voice broke, "why my beloved Cheveyo left Palenque long ago."

Tonina and Kaan paid earnest attention now, sensing supernatural powers at work in the sanctuary. The three were no longer alone. The gods had joined them.

"We believe," Ixchel said, "that when Lord Quetzalcoatl returns, he will not appear here in Palenque, or in Chichén Itzá or Copan or Uxmal, or in any Mayan city. He will come back to us in the northern highlands, in a place where our tribe had its beginnings. Our people's destiny, Tonina, is connected to our beginnings."

She turned to the first page of the book and pointed to what was clearly a red flower, its petals cupped and growing upward. "This flower indicates the place of our origins. And this chronicle will end, Tonina, when we find that red flower, for *there* is home."

Kaan frowned at the glyph, from which tiny footprints led to other glyphs, indicating places where the tribe had stayed during centuries of migration. "What is the name of this place?" he asked, and believed he already knew. Aztlan. His mother had told him about it.

"Our people were created in Aztlan," Ixchel said, "which means 'place of whiteness.' There are seven caves in Aztlan, and when the people emerged, they formed seven tribes and began spreading out over the land. Our tribe was one of the seven. Our enemies call us Chichimecs, which means 'barbarians,' but we call ourselves Mexica. We cannot speak our true name because our great creator god, Huitzilopochtli, forbade us to, in case it should give our enemies power over us. But I can tell you that name, Tonina, in this sacred place where we are safe. Our name derives from the place of our origin. Since we are from Aztlan, we are *aztecatl*. Aztec."

"Mother Moon," Kaan whispered, a long forgotten memory suddenly coming back. "My mother told me of Aztlan," he said, struggling to remember the stories, the myth, and the edict from Huitzilopochtli that the name Aztec was not to be spoken.

Ixchel smiled and nodded, knowing that she had guessed right. While Kaan might not be of their own clan, he was descended from one of the seven tribes of Aztlan, possibly even Mexica.

Tonina looked at Kaan and felt a new, palpable connection to him, as if Ixchel's words had combined with the sacred incense to weave a bond between them. She touched his arm. He looked at her with glistening eyes.

"You see that an eagle sits next to the red flower," Ixchel said. "I had always been taught that an eagle would lead us back to Aztlan. But I see now that the prophecy was misread, for I know now that the eagle represents the boy who brought you to Mayapan."

"Brave Eagle," Tonina whispered. Setting him free from the cage, being forced to go westward by the hunters who had pursued them—all of that was part of the gods' plan to reunite Tonina with her mother. Had Brave Eagle finally realized this, and that was why he left? Because his purpose was ended?

"The reason Pac Kinnich wanted this book, and the Tepanecs before him," Ixchel said, "was not merely for its many secrets, but because it tells us *where* Quetzalcoatl will reappear. In Aztlan. And on that glorious day we will be free to call ourselves Aztec at last, and we shall achieve greatness."

The three fell silent, marveling at the mysterious workings of the gods, while tropical rain fell softly outside, and Ahau, unseen, chanted.

"Where is Aztlan?" Kaan asked.

"No one knows. Our tribe left long ago, at the beginning of time. We have only clues and speculations. Here," she said, opening the book to the first page again and pointing to a glyph next to the red flower. "No one has been able to interpret the meaning of this glyph, but when we do, we will know we are near Aztlan."

He squinted at the curious little picture, unable to identify it.

Ixchel said, "It represents the Nahuatl word *iztaccíhuatl,* which means 'white woman.'"

"Who is she?"

"We do not know. We can only search for her. But we must go soon. Tonina, your father left long ago to go in search of Aztlan. And I fear that if he did not find it, then he will return to his own people far in the north, in a land of canyons and mesas where once, in centuries past, Toltec lords ruled."

"My father," Tonina whispered.

"His name Cheveyo means, in his native tongue, 'spirit warrior.' He belongs to the People of the Sun, who call themselves Hopi. Cheveyo is a shaman, a very wise and compassionate man. His people also await the return of a bearded white man, whom they call Pahana, which means 'lost white brother.' His shamanic office required him to leave his clan and go in search of Pahana, a duty handed down from father to son, back through the generations. Cheveyo was roaming the land in search of Pahana when we met. We fell in love and married. I told him about Aztlan, and he believed that the Pahana he sought would appear there, and so we decided we should search for Aztlan together. And then Pac Kinnich intervened and changed our lives forever."

Ixchel reached for Tonina's hand. "Daughter," she said with sudden urgency, "while I was buried in that cavern, I thought so many years had passed that surely my beloved Cheveyo was dead. But now that I know he might still be alive, I must search for him. The vision you saw just now, in the transparent cup, is a sign from the gods that we must hurry. And it is another sign as well."

Holding Tonina's hand between her own, Ixchel said with passion, "Finding Aztlan is up to you, my daughter."

"Me! But, Mother, *you* are the guardian of the Book of a Thousand Secrets. You are the one to find Aztlan."

Ixchel shook her head. "The vision of your father in peril came to *you*. Our people are without a home, Daughter. Not until they find Aztlan will Quetzalcoatl-Pahana come back to us."

"But why me? I am just a humble pearl diver."

"Because special blood runs in your veins. You have the blood of my people and your father's people. You are Mexica, who await Quetzalcoatl, and you are People of the Sun, who await the return of Pahana."

Tonina gave this some thought and then, looking at the hands cradling hers, said, "Mother, if I have been born to a special destiny, it is this: that I find my father and make restitution for the terrible things that happened to you both twenty-one years ago. I do not know about Aztlan or gods, but no matter what I do in this life, or where I go, I promise you this one thing, we *will* find Cheveyo."

A s they left the shrine and descended the slippery steps, Balám, hidden inside the sanctuary, released a strangled cry.

He had heard it all, from the first word about Quetzalcoatl, when he had taken Ahau's place to light the incense in the sanctuary, to the very last about a man named Cheveyo. Balám had mumbled and shuffled his feet as he had eavesdropped on the startling conversation, and now he stood frozen with shock, as if Ixchel's words had been arrows: "We will be free to call ourselves Aztec at last, and we shall achieve greatness."

No! he silently cried, and he fled the temple through the priests' corridor.

Down on the rain-drenched plaza, the threesome hurried to Ixchel's house, unaware of having been spied upon, unaware that old Ahau's broken body lay at the foot of the pyramid's south stairway.

Demons taunted him.

He felt burning firebrands behind his eyes. His stomach was a nest of hornets. While everyone in Palenque slept beneath a clear, starry sky, Balám stumbled into the jungle, driven by the shocking revelation he had overheard in the Time Temple—barbarians taking over the world.

No! screamed his tormented soul. Mayan supremacy is Ziyal's birthright. *My daughter was not born to see the sunset of our world.*

What should he do? His path had been so clear: take prisoners back to Uxmal. But now Kaan and Tonina were going to bring about the rise of Aztec power. If he took them back to Uxmal as gifts for his uncle, it meant turning his back on the rising threat in the north. Should he take his warriors north and vanquish the barbarian threat? Then what about Kaan and Tonina?

It was a decision no mortal man could make.

Balám had found a seller of *k'aizalah okox,* the "lost-judgment mushroom," so-named because, when ingested, the spirit residing in the mushroom overpowered the spirit of the man who ate it, imposing its own judgment and will upon him, thus making the impossible decisions.

Finding a solitary place among towering trees and ferns heavy with night dew, Balám unwrapped his loincloth so that he stood naked before the gods. Chanting a prayer, he inserted the small mushroom cake into his rectum and waited for the effects. Soon, visions came. Ziyal was the first, healthy and whole, showing no signs of abuse or grief, but smiling at him with glowing eyes. Balám knew this was a sign that he was back in favor with the gods.

But now he needed to hear a message. What did the gods want him to do?

Buluc Chabtan, ferocious god of war, rose before him next, a fierce being ornamented in jade, feathers, and jaguar skins. He demanded a sacrifice of Balám, to prove his worthiness. Balám knew what was expected. Seizing his sharp obsidian knife, he reached down, pinched his foreskin between finger and thumb, and thrust the knife tip through. Clenching his teeth so that he would not cry out, he inserted a knotted hemp string into the bleeding cut and drew it slowly through, nearly passing out with pain. As blood ran to the moist earth, Balám chanted prayers to his new god, promising loyalty and allegiance, until the pain became so intense that he vomited. And then he passed out.

When he awoke, naked and bloody, dawn was breaking over the rain forest. Balám staggered to his feet and retied his loincloth. The wound had clotted and no longer bled, but the thrumming pain was a reminder of his sacrifice. He vaguely recalled dreams and visions, voices and hallucinations. Buluc Chabtan had lifted his loyal servant from the loamy forest floor and carried him to the stars, where Balám had seen the sun's sleeping place at night, where the moon received her glow. And there, among the shining bodies of the cosmos, Balám had heard the message.

His true destiny lay on the high plateau in the northwest, in the Valley of Anahuac, where he was to carry out the will of the gods. In their gratitude for quelling the Aztec threat, the Mayan gods would restore Balám's daughter to him right there and then, on the field of victory and honor. And then they would make Balám himself one of them.

No longer a prince, but a god.

～ 52 ～

Dawn broke, illuminating ancient pyramids and mossy temples beneath low-hanging mist. The damp air was alive with monkey chatter and birdcalls, and soon the ancient marketplace was bustling with industry as hundreds of people prepared to decamp.

Ixchel and Tonina had gone out among the Nahua of Palenque, speaking to them of Quetzalcoatl and Aztlan, and while the people had been intrigued and had respected the story, and though they would have preferred to live in proximity of a good-luck woman, they were too afraid to take the journey. Some chose to stay in the city where it was safe, they said, while most elected to go with Kaan, which was also safe. But to venture into lands known to be inhabited by warlike, hostile tribes—Ixchel and Tonina could persuade no one.

And so it would be a small group that would trek westward to the Valley of Anahuac where it was said a ring of volcanoes spewed black smoke into the sky. There they would visit the place of Ixchel's birth, pay homage to her ancestors, and then continue northward out of the valley to search for the red flower that would lead them to the mythical homeland, Aztlan. The group consisted of Ixchel, Tonina, One Eye, and H'meen, with hired guides and porters, as well as Hairless and his men. Kaan was not going. Ixchel had hoped that by drawing him into the secrets of her sacred book she could persuade him to search for Aztlan with Tonina. But he had said he had responsibilities in Mayapan and must start eastward at once.

Ixchel, too, was anxious to leave. Ever since Tonina's shocking vision in the Time Temple, she was certain Cheveyo was in danger and needed her. And so it was with earnestness that, on this morning heavy with mists and worries, she oversaw the packing of food, medicines, and water.

As Tonina filled her travel pack with salted nuts and sunflower seeds, she thought of the wondrous things Ixchel had told her about Aztlan—that it was a paradise where the First Pair had been created by the gods. No one aged or sickened in Aztlan, food grew in abundance, and there was no war. And the red flower was indeed a magical healing plant. How had Guama known?

Tonina trembled to think that she was also going to meet her father. Or so she prayed. Cheveyo had been gone for twenty-one years. He could be anywhere on earth. Or dead.

As she made sure the transparent goblet was safely tucked into the bag, she wondered about the vision that had come to her in the Time Temple. Had it been merely her imagination, or a true prophecy? It must have been true, for how had she been able to describe Cheveyo so accurately— copper-skinned, with a broad face tattooed on forehead and cheeks, his hair plaited in two long braids. And his attire! The man in her vision had worn deerskin leggings and a fringed shirt. Tonina had never seen such clothing before, and yet Ixchel said that was how Cheveyo dressed.

She paused to survey the small group—One Eye was assisting H'meen while Ixchel gave instructions to Hairless—and wondered how they were going to survive. Twelve people in a hostile wilderness.

And then she peered through the opening in the courtyard wall where she saw, in the busy plaza, Kaan snapping orders to his men. She yearned to go with him, felt a sharp pain in her breast that she knew would never go away—she would ache for Kaan for the rest of her life. But she also wanted to find her father and see her parents reunited in joy.

Tonina realized that her journey was no longer her own, that her needs no longer came first. She felt responsible for this handful of people—H'meen who rode in a basket strapped to an attendant's back as she carried fat little Poki in her lap; One Eye doting on the elderly child, calling her "my lady" and telling her all would be well; Ixchel, no longer as frail or old as when she first came out of the cave, but still far from robust. Even Hairless, big strapping man that he was, possessed no sharper wit than the knife he carried. What chance had they against barbaric tribes who slaughtered any who trespassed upon their ground?

Tonina had never asked for help in her life, and she did not want to ask now. Yet, for *their* sakes, she must.

But she was afraid, for it was Kaan she was going to ask—and thereby lay her weakness and vulnerability at his feet. He had helped her once before, back in Copan when she had stood in indecision, wondering which way to go. Kaan had pointed to her medallion and said, "It is a message."

But this was different. He was in a hurry to return to Mayapan, burning with a need to bring Jade Sky's murderers to justice. *If I ask him to come with us, will he say no?*

A s Balám moved among his men, quietly giving orders, they exchanged wary looks. Their master had changed. Everyone noticed it. Prince Balám was subdued, less demonstrative—solemn, even. His cousins sensed a new power in him, making them wonder in excitement if he was going to lead them to glory at last.

Balám knew his men wondered about the change. But he would explain himself to no one. Nor would he divulge the real reason for his trek west, allowing them to believe he was heading for Teotihuacan to pray for his wife and daughter. Not until he was near Aztlan and met his foe on the field of battle would he reveal the final glorious plan to his warriors: to stop the barbarians from taking over the world.

The gods themselves had called upon him to take a stand and fight for Mayan sovereignty. And then all these people, including Kaan and Tonina, were going to bow down to him. He would travel to all the deserted cities of the Maya and resurrect them, bestowing his god's-luck upon the abandoned pyramids and overgrown temples and bringing them back to life. People would flock to the newly born cities and worship Balám as a god on earth.

He smiled to himself—a cold and secretive smile. He had wanted to give Ziyal the city of Uxmal. Now he was going to give her the *world*.

K aan studied the new map to Mayapan with the intensity of a cat watching a mouse hole. He forced himself to focus on his destination and to think of nothing else, especially his parting of ways with Tonina.

As he raised his eyes to the trail that led from Palenque, disappearing into the dense green jungle, and as he pictured its terminus at the White Road where, once again, painful farewells would be spoken, Kaan marveled at the time, back in Mayapan, when he had dreaded having to journey with the island girl. Now he dreaded leaving her.

Against his will, his gaze shifted from the jungle to the row of stone houses that comprised the Basket Weavers' Quarter. At Ixchel's house, where the courtyard was alive with preparations for a journey, he saw Hairless's great shaggy head rise above the rest as he surveyed supplies, gave instructions to his men, and consulted with the local guides. Loyal, simple Hairless, who had accepted Kaan's order to accompany the small group without question.

Kaan searched for Tonina. He did not see her. But there was Ixchel, standing straighter, looking more youthful each day, her face radiant now. *It is because she is on a holy mission.*

Aztlan—the mythical paradise. Kaan wondered if she would find it, wondered if such a place even existed.

But there was more to Ixchel's quest, Kaan reminded himself. She was going in search of the man she loved. And in doing so was willing to brave untold dangers. As was Tonina, accepting without hesitation the call to find her father and her people, giving no thought to her own safety.

He frowned. Their group suddenly looked small and vulnerable. Everyone said that in the upland plateaus there were savage, uncivilized tribes, constantly at war. Three women on their own, traveling with but a handful of men, would not survive.

Kaan felt wretched. How could he allow them to go alone? But they were venturing into the land of the Chichimecs and Kaan was terrified at what he might find there. *Ixchel touching his forehead: "You have a noble brow."*

His mother had told him long ago that her people came from a valley in the northern highlands, ringed by volcanoes. She had spoken a name that he had long since forgotten, nor could he now recall if it was the name of a place, a tribe, or possibly a man. By traveling with Tonina to that northern plateau, he risked encountering his mother's people—*his* people—and it terrified him.

A s One Eye examined H'meen's carrying basket to make sure she rode comfortably, she said again, "It was so brave of you to go up that tower."

"Yes, it was," he averred. Since his daring feat at the signal tower, One Eye had found a new confidence, one that gave him the courage to accompany Tonina and her mother to the upland plateaus, which H'meen now wanted to see. He still could not divulge the truth of his "jaguar" scars, or that it was Balám who had made Kaan travel to Copan and thus miss his appointment with the Sisterhood in Teotihuacan. But that seemed not to matter anymore.

However, One Eye did not like the idea that Balám and his small army would be traveling along the same route. Ixchel and Tonina needed protection from that devil. But Kaan was set upon going to Mayapan. How to persuade him to come with them?

One Eye decided he was going to try every kind of bribery and trickery to convince Kaan to go west. Maybe even threaten to put a dwarf's curse upon him. But as One Eye started for the gate in the courtyard wall, he saw Tonina walking across the crowded plaza toward Kaan.

One Eye held back, sensing that Tonina was going to ask Kaan to come with them for protection. But even if Kaan did agree to accompany them west, One Eye vowed to keep an eye on Balám nonetheless. As he inspected H'meen's carrying basket once more, One Eye the two-eyed dwarf silently vowed upon the bones of his great-grandfather that he would not allow Balám to hurt his friends.

B lessings of the gods," Tonina said when she reached Kaan. She saw that he was holding a map to Mayapan. "We are almost ready to leave." She surveyed his many porters and guides, his armed warriors, and the families grouped together, bent beneath their burdens. "And I see you are also."

"We are," Kaan said, a painful lump in his chest. He could not get over how beautiful she was, how each day she seemed to be born anew, fresher, lovelier, taller, and stronger. The realistic Kaan knew she was the same girl she had been that afternoon in the Mayapan marketplace, but the Kaan who was in love marveled at the miraculous transformation.

"Tonina—"

She held up a hand. She needed to speak quickly before she lost her courage. Here she was at last: facing her worst fear. For the sake of others, she must face it. The fear of being let down. *If he says no to me now, I shall not ask anything of anyone ever again.*

"Kaan, I know how important it is for you to go to Mayapan. I know the tremendous responsibility that awaits you there. But Ixchel and I cannot make the journey to the Valley of Anahuac with just our handful of companions. Kaan," she said, nearly breathless, "we need you. *I* need you."

He was instantly flung back to Mayapan, when he had said she must travel with him, and she had declared she was going to travel alone, that she was capable of doing things on her own. And outside Uxmal, when she had left during the night and he had caught up with her, and had said, "Don't you know it's too dangerous for you to go alone?" And she had replied, "I have always been alone. I do not need anyone."

And now she was looking at him with open, honest eyes, swallowing her pride, laying bare her weaknesses as she said, "I need your help."

"I had already decided to go with you," he said quietly, wishing all the people in the plaza would disappear, that he and Tonina could be alone on earth with no thoughts except for each other, free to love and to make love.

Her eyes widened and a small gasp escaped her lips. Her eyes welled with tears. "Thank you," she whispered. "I shall tell the others."

H ad Balám not undergone a life-changing experience in the Time Temple, were he not now the agent of the gods, he would have

swaggered when he went to Kaan and said, "Brother, I hear you have decided to go west. I suggest we all travel together, for there will be safety in
numbers." But the new Balám was a more cunning man and so did not
reveal the triumph he felt inside. The old Balám would have gloated. The
Balám of the gods, however, merely signaled to his men and they came
forward to join the combined groups of Kaan and Tonina.

And so they left the ancient, crumbling city of Palenque to abandon it
once more and for all time—hundreds of men, women, and children,
hoping for a better life. It mattered not to the throng that Kaan had
changed his destination, for now they were headed for the magical city of
Aztlan.

One Eye walked at H'meen's side, reaching up to hold her hand as
both prayed that Aztlan could be found, and that it was the paradise Ixchel had promised: a land where youth was restored to the old, and short,
ugly men were made tall and handsome. Balám marched with a firm
step, knowing that glory and the gods awaited him at the end of this
road, while Kaan and Tonina walked at the head of the crowd, with Ixchel between them, looking toward the west, where destiny awaited—
and a beloved husband and father named Cheveyo.

When they reached the White Road, Ixchel set the quetzal free. The
shimmering green bird was reluctant to go, and hovered for a long time
before finally wheeling in the sky and disappearing into the great jungle
canopy.

As they set foot upon the wide cement highway that flowed east to
west, they came upon a blind, footless beggar sitting under a tree. Filthy
and wizened, his cheeks sunken, his face covered in dirt, he heard the approach of travelers and held out a hand, calling down the blessings of the
gods on the passersby.

Kaan gave the poor man tortillas and a gourd of water, and the enormous crowd moved on.

As the blind man heard the stamping of many feet pass by, he sighed
wistfully and thought: You see before you a wretch of a man. But there
was a time when I was addressed as "your shining brilliance." I wore
jaguar skins and leather sandals. I was feared throughout the land. But my
people did not appreciate me. It was all the fault of those two worthless

Chichimecs, Ixchel and Cheveyo, who thought they were better than me, hiding their precious book.

But I won in the end.

I chased the woman to the ends of the earth and when I saw the dolphins carry the basket away, I told her the baby had perished. Then I put the woman in the ground. And when her husband came looking for her, I put him in a cavern, too. And that was when my ungrateful people revolted, attacked the palace, seized their king, and stripped me, chopping off my feet and blinding me.

But theirs was no victory, Pac Kinnich assured himself as he happily sank his few teeth into a chewy tortilla, for I survived, and the two lovers, Ixchel and Cheveyo, are to this day still trapped underground.

BOOK

FOUR

❧ 53 ❧

D o not worry about Chief Turquoise Smoke," Balám said. "My spear is thirsty to drink his blood. Go back to Mayapan, brother. My men and I will see that your people are well protected." Balám was eager to embark upon his new path: eradicating the despised Chichimecs from the face of the earth. And he would start with the local tribe, whose chief had made it clear the intruders were not welcome. "You must decide," Balám added impatiently, eyeing the object of their attention: a mysterious grass hut that had been erected on the beach.

Kaan agreed that they should move on, but Ixchel had ordered this risky halt in hostile territory. And because she had ordered it on religious grounds, there was nothing he could do.

"Chief Turquoise Smoke only grudgingly allowed us to pass through his territory," Balám reminded him. "But now he sees how we sit here, as if here to stay, and he deems it a challenge. He is amassing his warriors, brother, and they outnumber us. We cannot win. But if we strike at night when they are asleep, we can be assured a victory."

Kaan's people were camped on the shore of the Bay of Campeche, a sparkling green sea on one side, rolling green hills on the other. In between stretched a beach with sand of a dismal gray due to the volcanic peaks that bordered the area. A hundred campfires crowded the beach, with people going about their daily business of weaving baskets, spinning cotton, carving wood, talking, laughing, and arguing; children were running and playing, small dogs barking, turkeys gobbling in wicker baskets. Observing all this made Kaan think once again of a moveable city. Few Mayans made up the throng now as more Nahua people had joined—wives escaping abusive husbands, girls seeking marriage, men abandoning farms where the soil was poor and the rain merciless. They brought their lame and their sick, those without hope, those *with* hope—for a better life in the paradise of Aztlan.

The crowd had grown because of the magic and the mythos of Ixchel, who had been brought out of the ground after twenty years. To the people, she was the Earthbound Goddess, no matter how much she denied it. Just as Quetzalcoatl had died and gone to Hell, dwelling among the dead for three days, so had Ixchel died, to sojourn in the nether realms and return reborn.

They also believed her daughter was special. Myths had grown around Tonina so that people spoke of her life on the sea, living among dolphins, not a human girl at all but existing as an exotic ocean creature until the gods brought her forth and made a human female of her. The people loved Tonina and thought she had magic powers like her mother. Kaan recalled what she had told him of her upbringing on Pearl Island, what an outsider she had been, how her peers had mocked her and even suggested there was something wrong with her for her family to abandon her to the sea. But now she not only belonged, but was the heart of this great traveling crowd as the people followed them—the Earthbound Goddess and her daughter raised by dolphins—to the mythical paradise of Aztlan.

Farther along the beach, on the other side of a grass-covered jetty, Balám's men and camp followers were going about their business, which entailed the constant training of warriors. "To protect your people," Balám said, although there were those close to Kaan who whispered suspicions that Balám had other motives for building an army. But Kaan trusted his friend and welcomed the protection.

They were now deep into enemy territory and each tribe they encountered was led by a chief who wanted to slay the intruders first and ask questions later.

This was the Isthmus of Tehuantepec—Nahuatl for "jaguar hill"—a region filled with ancient mystery. In the jungle nearby, gigantic heads carved from basalt rested on the ground, as if the statues were buried up to their necks. Their features were foreign, with thick fleshy lips, flat noses, and heavy brow ridges over rounded eyes. The rock was black, as if

that were the giants' skin color. No one knew who had carved them or
what became of those ancient sculptors. They had lived here long ago,
the locals said, and then vanished.

It had taken Kaan and his people thirty-two days to reach this place,
longer than he had anticipated because they had been impeded by summer storms and unfriendly tribes. Every region they passed through required exhausting negotiations for safe passage. Local chiefs would say,
"You are not a caravan, therefore you must be an army." They especially
did not trust Balám and his Mayan warriors.

Chief Turquoise Smoke was no exception. Kaan's people had been
forced to pay a tribute of cacao beans and jade, and even then the chief
would not allow them to camp in his own lush green valley filled with
lakes and streams, where beautiful women rolled tobacco leaves all day—
cigars being their main export—insisting instead that they set up camp on
this gritty, gray-sand beach. And here they had sat for the last four days.

Because of the hut.

Ixchel and H'meen had bent their heads over the herbalist's books,
studying her charts and the stars, until Ixchel had announced that she
and Tonina must erect a special hut for a three-day ritual that involved
no men.

No men indeed, Kaan thought now as he scowled at the shelter that
had been built by women only, and had been attended to by women as
they went in and out all day, carrying bowls and gourds, musical instruments, food, incense, and clothing. On the dawn of the first day, Ixchel
and Tonina had entered the hut. It was now the morning of the third day
and they had yet to come out. But the ritual must be ending soon, for the
people's attention was now on the hut, especially the women and girls, as
they drew close, watchful, with an air of anticipation.

The mystery baffled him. Kaan knew of Ixchel's urgency to find her
husband, inquiring at every opportunity if a shaman named Cheveyo
had passed through. Kaan knew she was worried about Tonina's vision in
the Time Temple—a valley strewn with the dead, a smoke-blackened sky,
and Cheveyo calling for help. Yet, despite her anxiousness to find him,
Ixchel had called a halt and insisted upon conducting this mysterious
three-day ritual on the beach of Tehuantepec.

"If you leave now," Balám said close to his ear, "you could reach Maya-pan by the autumn equinox." Kaan did not need Balám to persuade him to return to Mayapan. The need to track down the men of the consor-tium consumed him night and day. But he now had another, more com-pelling motivation for leaving this area: his growing ill-ease in Nahuatl-speaking country where Mayan was not known except as a for-eign tongue. The customs were strange here, the gods unfamiliar. Even the ball game was not the same but played with different rules. Each day he found it a struggle to maintain his Mayan-ness. Kaan feared if he let down his guard, if he weakened for one moment, he might lose his iden-tity. If he did, who would he be then? *If I am no longer Mayan, will I sim-ply disappear and fly away on the wind?*

But he could not leave Ixchel and Tonina. They had a long way to go before they reached their destination through the Valley of Anahuac and beyond, over mountainous terrain and through hostile territory. He could not desert them now for his own selfish purpose.

"By the gods," Balám said in a growl, "if it were *my* son those devils had murdered, I would have seen them strung up by their testicles long ago."

"Enough," Kaan said in a low voice. Squinting at the hut, wondering about the smoke spiraling up through the hole in the roof and the sound of chanting coming from within, he thought: What are they doing in there?

He trembled. He was losing Tonina, even though she had never really been his. Ixchel was teaching her basket weaving, to speak Nahuatl, call-ing her Malinal, preparing her for the day she embraced her true self.

"Do we just stand here," Balám said in disgust, "and let Turquoise Smoke annihilate us because of that woman?"

Realizing he could not arrive at a decision, to stay, to move on, or to return to Mayapan, until Tonina and Ixchel had come out of the hut, and aware that Chief Turquoise Smoke was growing displeased with the presence of the invaders on his beach—he had granted them one night's stay only—Kaan stepped away from Balám and strode toward the hut, the morning sun in his eyes.

Women and girls crowded around the grass shelter, chanting and clapping their hands, making it difficult for Kaan to push his way through. H'meen was there, wearing a tunic and skirt that he recognized as clothing she wore for special occasions. "Blessings of the gods, noble Kaan," she said. "You have come at the right moment. We are about to celebrate."

"Celebrate?"

H'meen finally explained what the men could not be told before: that the three-day initiation marked Tonina's official acceptance into her tribe as a woman. "What we Mayans call the Descent of the Gods ceremony."

Kaan nodded. He himself had celebrated the Descent of the Gods when he had turned thirteen, the traditional age for the ritual.

In Tonina's case, however, a new date had had to be selected since she had missed her ceremony while on Pearl Island, and Ixchel had decided that it should be Tonina's twenty-second birthday, a date comprised of two lucky numbers: nine and thirteen.

H'meen fell silent when Ixchel emerged from the hut, smiling graciously and holding up a hand for attention.

Kaan marveled at the gradual change in Tonina's mother after they left Palenque—how, with the restoration of health and vigor, her body fleshed out and grew youthful; her spine straightened and she walked taller. In this morning's sunlight, she carried herself with regal bearing, making him think of queens. And even though her hair remained white, it was glossy and thick, and he knew that men in his group found Ixchel sexually appealing.

She said something in Nahuatl, in a strong, ringing voice that drifted out over the campfires, drawing attention from the hundreds camped on the beach. As one by one the small groups fell silent, Ixchel called out her announcement again until, eerily, the entire length of the beach was silent, with only the sound of seagulls in the air.

Kaan did not understand what she had said, but saw how everyone paid attention, watching the hut, and he was filled with a sense of drama. He looked out over the water where local fishermen sat patiently in dugout canoes, watching tall white herons wade through the shallows. Each long-legged bird was anchored by a tether that allowed it to roam a distance but not to fly away, and each had a collar tied around its neck, leaving only enough room to breathe. The fishermen waited for a bird to plunge its head suddenly into the water and come back up with a wriggling fish in its bill. The collared herons could not swallow and so the men plucked the fish from the bills with ease.

A prosaic scene, Kaan thought, and yet he sensed that the world was about to change forever.

Finally another figure emerged from the darkness of the hut, to stand tall in the bright sunlight for all to see.

The first thing he noticed was her hair, swept up now in two rolls, one on either side of her head, and bound with colorful ribbons, a sign that she had left girlhood behind. The enchanting seashells, he noted sadly, were gone. But the swept-up style exposed a long graceful neck that had been hidden before, and Kaan thought it added to the illusion of Tonina's tallness. The plain white tunic and skirt had been replaced by ones of vibrant colors and patterns—shimmering greens, blues, and reds that complemented her honey-hued skin. Necklaces and bracelets accented the outfit, giving Tonina the look of a noblewoman.

But more stunning was her face. It had been scrubbed clean of paint and decoration so that her features were clearly seen in the morning sunlight—the wide expressive eyes, the fine nose, the strong jaw and high cheekbones. Kaan felt he was looking at Tonina for the first time—a new woman he had never met before.

And she was beautiful.

His heart was suddenly heavy. As Ixchel announced first in Nahuatl and then in Mayan, "Today we shall have a great feast in honor of my daughter, Malinal," Kaan looked at Tonina, now Malinal, and thought: *I have lost her.*

When Tonina emerged from the hut, she blinked in the blinding sunlight. After three days of prayer, fasting, and learning from Ixchel the secrets and mysteries of womanhood, her first thought was to search the crowd for Kaan.

What was his reaction going to be? He had told her he had been raised to despise his own race. Would he now despise her as well? She found him standing next to H'meen. Their eyes met. She smiled tentatively and watched for his reaction, her heart racing.

Kaan tried to return Tonina's smile when her eyes met his. But her transformation was more than just hair and clothing and a face free of paint. Tonina was a stranger. She was Nahua.

And then suddenly—

His breath caught. He stifled a cry. In an instant, Tonina was more than beautiful, more than a transformed young woman, she was his blood and breath and bone. His sudden physical desire for her was a palpable ache. Never had he desired a woman so deeply and sharply as he did Tonina in that startling moment.

And then his eyes played tricks, replacing Tonina with the image of another woman from long ago. His mother, young and beautiful, new to Mayapan and not yet adapted to Mayan ways, her hair worn up in two rolls, a colorful tunic over a colorful skirt, Nahuatl words tumbling from her lips as she told her small son the myths and history of their people, and—

Chapultepec.

That was it! The word, the name, the place that he had been trying to remember since leaving Mayapan, that his mother had told him to memorize but which he had purposely forgotten. Chapultepec! It came back to him. It *all* came back. . . .

He stood for one frozen moment beneath the summer sky while all the world around him underwent so drastic a change that he thought the sun was going to fall from the sky. Then he turned and bolted from the beach, pushing through the crowd, away from the hut and the new woman who stood before it, throwing himself into the jungle that fringed the gray-sand beach. Kaan plunged blindly through palm trees, ferns, and vines, his throat tight with an unescaped sob as he held his breath, pushing giant green leaves and lianas from his path until he found himself alone amid thick greenery—a man alone in the world, without a name, newly born from the loam and the moss and lichen of the rain forest.

Falling to his knees, he let the sob escape. It was followed by another as his chest heaved with pent-up emotions, and the invisible walls within him came crashing down, barriers that had for years protected him from unwanted memories. Words rushed back from his past—*auakatl* . . . *chichiltik* . . . *kali* . . . *kuakuake.* Random, unconnected words, but he knew their meanings: "avocado" . . . "red" . . . "house" . . . "beetle."

Nahuatl. The language of his boyhood.

He collapsed to the jungle floor as the past washed over him like a tropical rain: hot days in the royal kitchen where his mother was the lowest worker, scrubbing pots and grinding corn, before she rose to tortilla-maker, and then to supervisor of the tortillas, and then to chief cook of the entire kitchen. Chatting with her boy in her native tongue, filling his head with the myths of his people before he was befriended by Balám and he became Mayan and he worked to build walls in his mind to keep the memories from escaping.

Chapultepec.

"Never forget, my son," she had said, making him repeat the word, asking him each day if he remembered it until he was old enough to leave the kitchen and live in the barracks where ballplayers trained, living with Balám and other Mayan boys, and then youths, and then young men. Kaan the chameleon had taken on their ways and language and customs, adopting their gods and myths and beliefs, pushing the world of the kitchen and the little Chichimec boy and his Nahuatl-speaking mother so far from his mind that the day came when he had forgotten the word she wanted him to remember always.

But now it was back, wakened from its slumber by the sight of Tonina transformed.

"Chapultepec," he whispered, sweat-drenched and weak. Kaan sobbed into the grass and earth of the Tehuantepec rain forest, a man caught between two worlds like a rabbit caught between two dogs, each pulling until the helpless animal was ripped in half.

He lay for a long time, letting the past swim over him, capture him, carry him back, until he was spent and exhausted and he had no idea where the sun was in the sky. As he sat up, wondering which way was east and which was west, he brushed twigs and leaves from his drenched skin and knew that he had reached a turning point in his life.

Struggling to his feet, Kaan swayed for a moment, then caught his equilibrium. Through his pain he saw clearly that there was only one choice. There had only ever been one choice. And perhaps, he told himself as he began to walk out of the jungle, perhaps—the gods willing—it was not going to be as difficult to say good-bye as he had once thought.

A seat of honor was crafted out of driftwood and soft ferns, and Tonina was ceremoniously seated upon it, to oversee the feast like a reigning queen while fire pits were dug, musical instruments were produced, and *pulque* flowed. After days of traipsing through hostile territory, the people happily seized upon this day of festivities and careless abandon.

Tonina knew she should be happy. She was no longer the outcast she had been on Pearl Island, unwanted and considered homely because she was so different from the others. Now she resembled other Nahua women and was recognizable as a member of one of the seven tribes of Aztlan. Belonging at last. But worry dampened her joy. Where was Kaan? No one had seen him since morning, when he had taken one look at her and had fled into the jungle. Now the sun was setting and he was nowhere to be seen.

The late afternoon air was filled with the aromas of steamed mussels and clams. To the merriment of flutes and drums, people feasted on tortillas and beans, tomatoes and avocados. Cigars and pipes laced the ocean breeze with pungent smoke. For this one day they forgot their worries, their infirmities, their reasons for leaving farms and families to join in a quest that, if they were to give it serious thought, held no more promise than the smoke in the air. It did not matter. The girl on the throne had become one of them, reminding them that though they hailed from different tribes and clans, they were in fact one people, speaking one tongue, worshiping the same gods, and walking the same path: toward Aztlan and home.

But there were those who were not so pleased. At the periphery of the boisterous crowd, Balám and his warriors stood alert and watchful, knowing that Chief Turquoise Smoke was mustering his men for attack. As Balám kept a keen eye on the pathetic rabble celebrating what was in his mind a worthless ritual, he, too, wondered: Where is Kaan?

Balám was hoping Chief Turquoise Smoke *would* attack, so that Balám's men could show the Zapotec dogs what superior warriors Mayans were. He and his soldiers would fight valiantly—not to protect this miserable crowd, but for the glory of their own race. And after a victory on this beach, Balám would lead his men to greater victories, all against the day the Chichimec menace was eradicated and the gods rewarded Balám with the return of his precious daughter.

Although he had still received no word as to Ziyal's whereabouts, despite broadcasting a handsome price for information about the Mayan child bought on the Mayapan slave block, Balám was not worried. When he had sacrificed blood to Buluc Chabtan back in Palenque, and had been visited by a series of visions, one of them had been a message from the war god himself, assuring Balám that the gods were watching over Ziyal and protecting her against the day their servant, Balám, was reunited with her.

"Cousin!" hissed the young man at his side, jabbing Balám's arm. "Look!"

Balám peered over the heads of the celebrants and realized that, farther up the beach, the edge of the crowd had fallen silent. The silence spread like ripples on a pond, until the red-gold afternoon was silent except for the breaking of waves on the shore.

Balám gripped his spear and pressed his lips together. He could not believe his eyes.

Tonina also stared in disbelief as the crowd parted to admit a newcomer to the festivities. She almost did not recognize him.

The long jaguar-tail was gone. Kaan's hair hung straight and loose, trimmed at the shoulders, with bangs now covering his forehead, cut evenly over the eyebrows. The square haircut framed Kaan's face in a striking way, Tonina thought, making him more handsome than ever. The barber who had done the work had also given Kaan a warrior's top-knot: a handful of hair gathered into a ribbon at the crown, and cut very short so that it stood up. Kaan's plain white loincloth had been replaced by one dyed in bright blues, yellows, and reds, drawing attention to his hips, loins, and thighs. His plain mantle had likewise been replaced by one of such a deep and vibrant scarlet that it looked hot to the touch.

Kaan came to a standstill before Tonina, bowed respectfully, and then, lifting his chin, said in a proud, ringing voice, "Honorable ladies, I have come to pay my respects. I am Tenoch of Chapultepec."

~ 55 ~

Not a sound was heard, save for the whispering surf, as everyone stared in shock. And then the murmurs began, spreading through the crowd until everyone was talking and marveling at once. Smiling, Ixchel said, "Come forward, Tenoch of Chapultepec." Her voice shook with emotion, for here was the answer to her prayers: that Kaan should find his true self. Now there could be a marriage, her daughter safely joined to a man of honor and courage. In her long, lonely years in the cavern, with no companionship other than a bird that could not speak, Ixchel had dreamed of one thing: someday holding a grandchild in her arms.

Cheveyo's grandchild.

As Kaan stepped up to Tonina's "throne," and saw the look of awe and joy on her face, he wondered why he had fought so hard and for so long against this inevitable metamorphosis, for this new man was who he really was—not a "new" man really, but the one he had been born to be. Had his mother known this? Was that why, even though she was dying, she had insisted he make the pilgrimage to Teotihuacan?

All his life he had pretended to be Mayan. But now that he knew who he was, he suddenly felt empowered as new strength entered his bone and gristle. When I return to Mayapan it shall be as Tenoch of Chapultepec. I will show the men of the consortium that my people are not without pride and honor. And they will curse the day they were born.

"Chapultepec," Ixchel said again, frowning suddenly. "Grasshopper Hill?"

Kaan drew aside his mantle to expose the fresh tattoo on his chest.

After he had staggered from the jungle, weak from his revelation, but energized also, he had sought out one of the many barbers who traveled with the great migrating crowd, and the man had worked his skill beneath the privacy of a giant mahogany tree. Kaan had then quietly sought out a family who specialized in expensive textiles, spinning and dying fine cottons for sale to rich men and nobles. Lastly, he had found a tattooist who was an expert in Nahua tribal symbols.

The wound was still scabbed with blood, but Ixchel saw the symbol clear and recognizable, designating him as a member of the Grasshopper Hill People—*chapultepec* in Nahuatl.

"The day I received this mark of my tribe, when I was a boy, I tried not to cry," he said with a smile, "although I did. And then I had forgotten what the mark meant, and it had grown distorted over the years. But now it is back, the name of my tribe."

"Do you know the name of your *clan*?"

"I have forgotten it, noble Ixchel."

As he shifted his attention to Tonina, who was staring at him with her lips parted, neither saw the frightened look that swept across Ixchel's face.

"Forgive me for interrupting your special celebration, honorable Malinal," Kaan said, "but I arrive in some urgency. It has come to my attention that Chief Turquoise Smoke is planning to attack us this coming night. I intend to intervene on your behalf."

"Intervene?" Ixchel said in alarm, her eyes going to the dense jungle behind them, imagining the warriors amassing there.

Kaan turned to One Eye, who was gawking with his jaw hanging down, and said, "My friend, I want you and H'meen to pay a visit to Chief Turquoise Smoke. Tell him that Tenoch of Chapultepec begs the chief's presence at an important feast, that we wish his blessings upon our celebration, that we wish to do him honor."

One Eye did not question the order. He and the royal herbalist were the logical choices as the only members of this great crowd who would have any worth in the eyes of the Zapotec leader. What One Eye did question was the drastic transformation in Kaan. And then he looked at Tonina on her throne and the question was answered.

Balám pushed his way through and strode up to Kaan, his eyes narrow with suspicion. "What are you up to, brother?" he growled, looking Kaan up and down in disgust. "Have you lost your mind?"

"Never has my mind been more clear, brother," Kaan replied. "You said there was no other choice, we had either to leave this place at once or fight Turquoise Smoke. But you were wrong. There is a third choice."

"And what is that?"

"To *befriend* Turquoise Smoke. I vanquish my enemy, brother, when I make him my friend."

"And how do you propose to achieve such an impossible feat?"

"By using two weapons Turquoise Smoke will not anticipate— humility and respect." Kaan smiled. "No worthy leader can resist the opportunity to appear magnanimous."

"You invite disaster," Balám warned. "But do not worry. My warriors will be ready when your attempts at friendship fail." He turned and strode away, his cousins falling into step behind.

While they awaited word from Turquoise Smoke, Kaan invited everyone to resume the festivities, which they happily did, all chatting now about the change in their leader, agreeing that he cut a splendid figure, that they all had known he would eventually come to his senses and realize where his true blood lay, complimenting themselves on having the wisdom to follow such a hero.

Kaan turned to Tonina and said quietly, "Now I know why I could not stop looking at you in the Mayapan marketplace when I first saw you. I must have sensed the connection between us even then. I know now it is not by chance that we were thrown together, but the working of our mutual destinies."

He leaned forward so that only she could hear, and said with passion, "Tonina, you once asked me why I was reluctant to be a leader, and I said it was because of something my mother told me as a boy. Do not ever be a failure, she said. It was her biggest fear for me, and soon it became *my* biggest fear. But Tonina, when I saw you come out of the hut this morning, the sight of you triggered forgotten memories. And out of those memories came the realization that I had misunderstood my mother's words! When she said do not ever be a failure, I took it to mean, 'Do not ever fail.' But they are not the same, and in fact mean the opposite. All these years, those words held me back. But they will hold me back no longer."

There was more, but he could not speak of it here, or even put into words the new feelings, new revelations that filled his mind like a brilliant sun. He would explore it later, and come to terms with the startling realization that his mother had *not* been ashamed of their race after all—she had not fostered in him the disdain for their people that Balám and other Mayans felt. It was others who had imprinted that prejudice upon young Kaan's heart. He knew now that his mother had in fact been proud of their race.

And now he wished to do *her* proud.

The sun dipped behind the rain forest, casting long shadows on the beach. The scarlet of Kaan's mantle grew deep and lush. Tonina could not take her eyes off his face—he was still Kaan, and yet he was not. It was as if, she thought, the final acceptance of his true self had opened the doorway to a new inner power and self-confidence. She sensed that all his doubts and worries had dissolved, for before her stood a man strong and confident, sure in the knowledge of who he was and what he was born to do.

She wanted him to take her into his arms. She longed to feel the crush of his lips on hers. She wished these hundreds of people would vanish, leaving her alone with this man she so desperately and urgently desired.

And then she thought: Today marks the day of my birth, twenty-two years ago, in the Mayan city of Palenque, to Ixchel and Cheveyo. But the day also marked the birth of Tenoch of Chapultepec, and she knew that, for the rest of her life, she would look upon this as the most important day in her life.

Kaan fought the impulse to gather Tonina into his arms and carry her off to a private place, where they could be alone together, to touch and feel and make love away from prying eyes, for now they could truly be together at last. But the immediate protection of his people came first.

He drew back from Tonina just as a commotion erupted at the edge of the forest. Chief Turquoise Smoke had arrived.

The pompous Zapotec chief paraded slowly toward the center of the beach crowd, accompanied by aides and wives, slaves and attendants, a short, big-bellied man heavily ornamented with shell, bone, and feathers, but whose eyes were keen, betraying a sharp intellect behind them.

Tension filled the air as the silent crowd nervously parted for the ferocious-looking Zapotec warriors, whose spears were topped with human skulls. As he came to a standstill before Kaan, Turquoise Smoke's eyes narrowed, and then widened as he saw before him a familiar face, yet a different man, one who had only four days prior called himself Kaan and who had dressed as a Mayan. But now he called himself Tenoch and dressed in Nahua fashion, so that Turquoise Smoke wondered if this man was possibly one of their own.

Tonina thought the chief a curious-looking man, his skin so dark as to be almost black. His eyes were extraordinarily round and slightly bulging, and his nose was fleshy and flat. And then she realized he resembled the strange Olmec heads in the jungle and, seeing that many of those who had come with him bore the same features, wondered if his tribe were descended from that distant race.

They took seats on woven mats while women brought *pulque* and platters of food. Turquoise Smoke's heavily armed soldiers stood behind their chief while people crowded around in a circle to watch the momentous meeting. Tonina remained in her driftwood chair at one point of the circle, while Ixchel sat opposite. H'meen was at Ixchel's side, blank paper on her knees, brushes and ink pots ready. One Eye was part of this inner circle, for his good luck.

In the Grand Hall back in Mayapan, Kaan had witnessed many audiences with His Exalted Goodness, when visiting dignitaries came with offers and requests, and so he knew that in negotiating an agreement, one never got down to business right away but began with endless compliments and flattery, calling upon the names of every god one could think of, blessing every member of each man's family. After spilling libations to the gods, and tossing morsels of food into the fire, he and Turquoise Smoke toasted each other's clans and tribes and gods with *pulque,* with everyone politely waiting for Turquoise Smoke to sample the steamed clams before they could descend upon the tempting delicacies themselves.

And when Turquoise Smoke was satisfied that he and his party were being treated with respect, he invited "honorable Tenoch" to state his business.

Kaan surprised the onlookers by not telling the chief what he and his people needed. Remembering what he had observed in the Grand Hall, Kaan instead told Turquoise Smoke what Kaan and his people were *offering*. The trick was to convince Turquoise Smoke that Kaan was doing him a favor, not the other way around; to make the Zapotec chief believe that he could not live without the goods and services provided by Kaan's people, to make it seem to the chief that the advantage was all his with no sacrifice on his part—that all Turquoise Smoke had to do in return, Kaan said, for cotton, baskets, expert hunters and fishermen, for girls for his unmarried men, for the good luck of a dwarf and a royal herbalist, for the prayers and praise and loyalty of hundreds of new citizens—for all this generous bounty all the noble Zapotec chief had to do was to provide the protection of his army.

"For how long do you require my protection?" the chief asked, knowing from four nights prior that this man and his strange crowd were journeying northward on a quest to find a mythical ancestral home.

Kaan produced a bark-paper map. He and his people were following an ancient trade route that extended from Teotihuacan north of the Valley of Anahuac to Chichén Itzá in the far east, and Copan deep in the south. "We are here," he said, pointing to the glyph indicating Turquoise Smoke's settlement. The highway through Tehuantepec was a continuation of the Mayan White Road and had been used by merchants and travelers for over a thousand years. "We go to the Valley of Anahuac."

Turquoise Smoke chewed his cigar as he frowned at the map. He had never learned to read. "Where is Zempoala?"

"Here," Kaan said, pointing to a glyph.

"Very well," Turquoise Smoke murmured. "That is the territory of the Totonacs, with whom I am allied. You and I are now allies as well, Tenoch of Chapultepec, and so my army will travel with you as far as the limit of my territory, at which time we will help you to negotiate further protection from Chief Acayucan, who is married to my sister."

But before he sealed the agreement with his thumbprint in his palm,

Turquoise Smoke held up a fat, nicotine-stained finger and said, "One thing. I do not trust that Mayan and his warriors."

"Do not worry about Balám. He will do as I say."

"So be it!"

The crowd broke out in cheers and words of admiration. Kaan himself was amazed at his innate skill as a negotiator and diplomat. But he knew the skill had come from knowing who he really was. Kaan the Mayan would not have succeeded so well.

"And now to seal our treaty," the chief said, rubbing his fat hands together, "we will arrange marriages."

Kaan blinked. "Marriages?"

Upon a signal from Turquoise Smoke, a shy young girl was brought into the circle. The chief said to Kaan, "To join our two tribes, you will marry my daughter."

Then the chief pointed to Tonina and said, "And I will marry *her*."

Balám gazed admiringly at the item that had been brought to him under the cloak of secrecy. By the flickering torchlight of his beach encampment, he beheld the beautiful crown of gold, jade, and amber. "Fit for a queen," said the man, who had not explained how he came by such a royal treasure.

"Indeed," Balám murmured as he handed the man five ocelot pelts, twenty pieces of jade, and a gourd of *pulque*. A high price, but the crown was going to go on Ziyal's head the day he became ruler of the world.

Balám watched his secret visitor disappear into the jungle, then he turned to look out at the Bay of Campeche, where starlight reflected on the sea. His hand went to the little pouch that hung about his neck, containing his daughter's baby tooth, and sweet memories flashed behind his eyes: Ziyal riding around the house on his shoulders, giggling as he tickled her on his knee, the nights sitting vigil at her bedside when she was ill. *The feel of her little arms around his neck. Her soft breath on his cheek. The way his heart soared with joy every time she called him* "Taati."

Soon, my precious one, his mind cried as he sent his thoughts out over the waves and up to the stars. Just a little longer, my sweet child, and *Taati* will be with you once again.

Carefully packing the crown into a basket stuffed with dry grass, Balám listened to the night for other sounds.

After watching the repugnant spectacle farther up the beach—Kaan working a peace treaty with the Zapotec dog—Balám had given orders to his men to wait until midnight and then sneak into the encampment where Turquoise Smoke's warriors were bivouacked. "Make sure they are all asleep," Balám had said, "and then take your knives and . . ." He smiled grimly. By reducing Chief Turquoise Smoke's army, Balám was achieving a two-fold goal: weakening the fat Zapotec leader, and thinning the ranks of the soldiers who had been engaged to protect Kaan's people.

Exchanging wives! Balám thought in contempt. Marrying an enemy's daughter or sister was how weak men kept the peace. For Balám, a true warrior, there was only one way to maintain peace: through military might. He was going to become the supreme chief in the land not by marrying other men's sisters and daughters, but by *slaying* them. Only in this way could an enemy be truly subjugated.

Balám thought about Kaan's change from Mayan to Chichimec and knew it was a sign from the gods that the time had come for him to part ways with his former friend and brother. But first he was going to find Kaan's new Chichimec tribe and slaughter it to the last man. But the problem was: what tribe? "I am Tenoch of . . ." What? Balám had not heard the rest.

Hearing sounds nearby, he turned to see his men stealing back into the camp, bringing captives tethered together. Balám nodded in satisfaction. He counted about a hundred. They were pushed to their knees before him, their heads hanging in shame. It was the worst dishonor for a soldier to be taken captive without a fight, without having even drawn a weapon. Balám knew that Turquoise Smoke would not want them back—men caught while they slept! He knew also that they expected to be executed now, and in such a state of dishonor that it would send them straight to the Ninth Level of Hell.

But the prince of Uxmal surprised them. "Join me and you will have the glory of fighting the lowly Huastecs in the north, you will have spoils and plunder and women, and if you die in battle, you go straight to the Thirteenth Heaven."

As they prostrated themselves before him, swearing loyalty, Balám saw a vision of the military force that was going to grow, the ranks swelling until a great army spread from his feet to the horizon, the army with which he was going to conquer the world, starting with the man who had betrayed him.

K aan paced impatiently in the moonlit glade.

Where was Tonina?

Hearing the rustle of leaves, he spun around, and there she was.

She carried the Book of a Thousand Secrets, protected now in a new feather wrap, but as she entered the glade and saw Kaan there, waiting for her, all her mother's warnings and alarms were forgotten as she dropped the book and ran to him.

Kaan's arms encircled her, his lips pressed hers. Tonina clung to him, tears stinging her eyes. She wanted to cleave her body to his and stay that way forever, alone in this moonlit glade, away from the hundreds sleeping in the beach camp, away from duties and responsibilities and ... taboos.

"Am I dreaming?" he murmured as his hands explored her slender body, feeling her heat through the fabric of her new clothes—Nahua clothes, like his own, as if the textiles themselves were of a new race, a new breed.

Taking her face in his hands, Kaan looked deep into her eyes and said, "When I saw you standing in the sunlight this morning—I was overcome with such intense desire that I could not move. I wanted you in that moment, I wanted to join with you, I wanted you and I to be *one*. And then I knew who I must first become. Beloved Tonina, out of my passion to possess you, my new identity was born."

Tears sparkled in her eyes. Mistaking them for tears of joy, he kissed each one as they rolled down her cheeks. "I feel as if I died in the cenote and when you breathed life into me, a fresh new man had been born, and in the days and months that followed, like a newborn I had to learn to live all over again, how to feel, how to listen to others, how to understand them and myself. It was as though I had received a second chance at life."

His mouth touched hers in a tender kiss. He tasted tears, felt her lips tremble beneath his.

"But you have given me more than life, Tonina. Where I once knew only shame for my race, I now feel pride. This is your gift to me." Kaan's face twisted briefly in pain as a memory came back, one that he had pushed from his mind long ago. "When I was twelve years old," he said in a tight voice, "I was in the marketplace with Balám and other boys. I encountered my mother and she spoke to me. I turned away, pretending not to know her. The other boys asked me who she was and I said I did not know. I am so sorry for that! To have treated my mother so cruelly. I wish now she could understand the pride that fills my heart, as it must have filled hers. Tonina, I had thought it would be so hard to shake off the mantle of Kaan the Mayan—and yet, when I came to my senses, alone in the jungle with nothing but memories and my conscience, I realized that perhaps it was not going to be as difficult as I had thought to say good-bye to the man I once was."

A night breeze swept through the trees, rustling branches and fronds, stirring Kaan's straight, shoulder-length hair. Tonina watched his lips as he spoke, wanting to kiss them, but knowing that he needed to speak what was in his heart. His voice was deep and rich; she could listen to it forever.

"When famine swept through the land, my father and mother left their ancestral home to go in search of a better life for me and my sister. My sister died young, and then my father died in a tree-felling accident. But *I* grew strong, I grew to be a hero. And my mother rose in the ranks to become the chief cook of a royal kitchen. Tonina, I want to find her family and let them know what a brave and successful woman she became."

Tonina buried her face in his neck, dug her fingers into his hard muscles. There was so much to say, so many words stood on her lips, but she was afraid to give voice to them. She wanted only to be a part of this man she loved so deeply and desired so sharply that she sent a mental prayer to the gods that they lift a new burden from her.

His mouth met hers again, in a stronger, deeper kiss. She felt his hand slide down her thigh, lifting her skirt, touching hot skin beneath. "Wait," she whispered.

He drew back and gave her a questioning look. His hand touched the cowry belt, badge of her purity, still around her waist, and he understood her hesitation. "Tonina, we will marry in the morning," he said, "and then we will be together for the rest of our lives."

"Marry—"

"I have already arranged it!" he said, having wanted it to be a surprise, but realizing now that he must assure her his intentions were honorable. "As we speak, Hairless is out with a hunting party. Our guests will feast on deer after we have tied our mantles together."

"Kaan," she whispered. "We cannot marry. Not yet."

"Why not?"

She drew back. The book. She had dropped it. Breaking away from his embrace, a painful, physical separation, she searched the forest floor. Finding the book in the grass, still protected in its feather wrap, she brought it into a pool of moonlight and hurriedly turned the folded pages. "Here," she said, handing the book to him.

Kaan scanned the page and came upon the familiar symbol: It was the same as the tattoo on his chest.

"Grasshopper Hill," Tonina said. "On the shore of Lake Texcoco."

"What of it?"

"Kaan, *my* tribe lived on Grasshopper Hill."

He waited. A lone night bird called out from a towering treetop. Frogs and cicadas clicked and buzzed and croaked in the night. The air was heavy with humidity and warmth. But when Kaan saw the look in Tonina's eyes, he felt a chill. "What does that matter?" he asked, a cold presentiment stealing through his body. "What does it matter where our families lived? Tonina, this is about you and me, no one else."

"Kaan, you and I might belong to the same clan, or to the same family. What if our mothers were close cousins? The laws of gods and ancestors would forbid us to join together."

He wanted to bellow his outrage at this twisted injustice. When he was Mayan and she an island girl, when the chasm between them was so wide it seemed uncrossable, they were freer to take physical pleasure together than they were now, with the chasm gone.

He wanted to throw the book and the taboos to the night wind and take Tonina right there. Once again, his impulse was to curse the gods, smash their idols, vent his fury on the unseen world. But, unlike another fateful night in his past, when he had not restrained himself and the gods had demanded his sacrifice in the cenote, Kaan struggled to control himself. A small voice of conscience warned him of the ill luck that could befall the innocent people slumbering on the beach should one of the most sacred laws of the gods and ancestors be broken.

"It is unfair!" he cried, remembering when Balám fell in love with Six Dove, the agony they had gone through as the priests had spent days tracing their kinship lines, searching for the smallest taboo. The laws governing marital unions had been laid down long ago by the ancestors, and although many of the rules made no sense, they were still respected. No one knew why women of Tortoise Clan could not marry men of Red Hawk Clan while women of Red Hawk Clan were permitted to marry men of Tortoise Clan! Or why River Clan could never marry Locust Clan. The rules had been set down back in the mists of time and were not questioned.

Kaan himself had had to rule on such a union, when his people were camped at a village near Tikal and two young lovers had wanted to marry, but the elders of the two families had forbidden the union on kinship grounds. After hearing both sides, Kaan had been forced to rule against the star-crossed pair, for according to the Code of Mayan Law, two people with the same clan name on the father's side may not marry.

Could such a cruel irony happen now? That the very name that had caused his transformation and joyous emancipation turn out to be the instrument that kept him apart from the woman he loved?

"We must know your clan name," Tonina said, and the spark of worry in her eyes made his throat tighten in agony. Changing his name had not changed his conscience. More than ever, Kaan felt bound by a strict code of honor, for now he was Chapultepec and must show the world his people were not lawless savages.

He stepped back, afraid of his own physical weakness, afraid his body would act without listening to his conscience. "Tonina, when my memories came back this morning, another word came back, one which my mother spoke often. *Tonali.* What does it mean?"

"*Tonali,*" she murmured, marveling that so powerful a word sounded like her island name. "It means 'fate, destiny, what you were born to do or to be.'"

"Whenever my mother spoke of Chapultepec she spoke of *tonali.*

Does my destiny lie on Grasshopper Hill in the Valley of Anahuac?" He turned his face into the warm night wind, looking westward in the direction of a highland valley that lay months away from the jungle of Tehuantepec, yet he felt its pull as if it were just beyond the trees.

"Tonina," he said, taking her by the shoulders, "nothing happens by chance. Everything that occurs in our lives happens for a reason, for we are governed by the gods. And if I am being led to my destiny, then I must follow."

"I will go with you," she said. "We shall go to Chapultepec together."

He drew her tightly to him. *Yes.* "No. You must stay with your mother, Tonina. I can travel faster on my own."

Kaan was right. Tonina knew where her duty lay. Ever since Palenque, she had felt a new force within her, a new burning need: to make up for the terrible thing that had been done to her parents—her mother forced to put her child on the sea, and then buried alive, her father told that his wife and daughter were dead. Tonina felt driven to find Cheveyo, to reunite him with Ixchel, to make up for the pain and the lost years.

Reaching for the medallion she had worn since she was a baby, she lifted it over her head and placed it around Kaan's neck, saying, "Search for the red flower, my love. And if you find it, wait for me there."

"No," he said. "I will come back. You are on your way to the Valley of Anahuac. We follow the same highway. After I have learned who I am at Chapultepec, what I am being called to do, I will rush back to meet you. Be faithful to the map, Tonina, and I will find you. And stay close to Turquoise Smoke, for he will protect you."

After the Zapotec chief had said that Kaan must marry his daughter, he had been persuaded to let his daughter marry another man in Kaan's circle, and had been persuaded himself to take a woman other than Tonina. And now, because of the ancient custom of exchanging family members, with each group having an interest in keeping the other safe, the two were allies.

Kaan cupped Tonina's face between his hands and said, "I was once self-centered and gave no thought to the suffering of others. While I would not call myself callous or heartless, my view was narrow, and although it did not make me a bad man, I was no hero either. But you have opened my eyes. And for this, and so much more, I thank you. And I love you." He bent his head and kissed her again, softly and sweetly, shuddering with desire.

And then he quickly stepped back, to allow air and the night to come between them, for he teetered on a dangerous brink and knew that his own self-discipline was as tenuous as the moonlight that streamed between the branches. One more moment with Tonina, one more word from her, and he would capitulate.

As he gazed longingly at her in the moonlight, Kaan saw Tonina in her many surprising incarnations—the naïve girl commanded to perform as a fortune-teller in the Grand Hall of Mayapan; the rebellious girl who ran from him outside of Uxmal and demanded he take over leadership of the people; the alluring creature who drew him into the seductive waters of Lake Peten.

The woman she had been, in his arms, just moments ago, ready to surrender to his love.

"When I return, we will marry," he said. "And on our wedding night, my dearest Tonina, I will honor you with my love and with my body."

≈ 57 ≈

Dark storm clouds hugged the horizon, but Kaan's farewell was celebrated beneath a clear summer sky, an occasion that was both joyous and sad, as all knew he was embarking upon an errand of discovery and reunion, but a journey that also required he go alone.

Hairless threw himself at Kaan's feet and cried, "Master, what have I done to displease you?"

Kaan lifted the big man to his feet, amazed at the tears streaming down the broad Mayan face. "You have not displeased me, dear friend. Do not be afraid. I am still Kaan the ballplayer. The man you have followed all these months is still here. But I am another man as well. And when I return, I will make it all clear to you."

Ixchel said, "My tribe are nomads; we have no permanent home, for we are searching for Aztlan. They might be at Chapultepec, I do not know. This is what you must find out. Here are four names you will need." She had asked H'meen to write them on paper in both Mayan and Nahuatl glyphs. "They are my mother's parents and my father's parents. Seek out their descendants. It is imperative, noble Tenoch, that we make sure you and my daughter are not closely related."

"Do not worry, honorable Ixchel," Kaan said, adding, "and I will inquire about Cheveyo along the way."

One Eye stepped forward to offer Kaan some advice. "If you encounter the Mud People in the Reed Flats, do not compliment their women, for the men will stone you to death." He gave Kaan a few pieces of jade and useful words in Nahuatl, such as "peace" and "friend," then called upon Lokono, the Spirit of All, to watch over him.

H'meen gave Kaan a gift of medicinal herbs and a strengthening tea, as well as a protective amulet that was once worn, she averred, by the first *h'meen* of Mayapan.

Finally, Kaan elicited a promise from Balám to stay with the group and protect them until he returned. "They are making their way to the Valley of Anahuac, brother, and just beyond is Teotihuacan, where you are heading."

Balám replied, "You have my promise, brother, that your people will be protected, for I do not trust that toad Turquoise Smoke." Then he narrowed his eyes and said, "Will you no longer take revenge upon the men who murdered your wife?"

"I have not forgotten my duty to avenge her death. And I *will* return to Mayapan and see that justice is served. But I know now that I must first find my people, find out who I am, for only then can I stand before Jade Sky's assassins in strength and honor."

"Where exactly do you go now, brother?" Balám asked, having tried to learn the name of Kaan's Chichimec tribe without success. After the feast, Ixchel had asked her people not to speak of Kaan's true identity. To Kaan himself she had said, "There is power in names. Your enemies can use your name against you. This is why our creator god Huitzilopochtli forbade us to call ourselves Aztec until we find our home. Do not tell anyone who you are until you have found your family."

"I will tell you when I return, brother," Kaan said solemnly.

His final good-bye was with Tonina, as he gave her a copy of his map and showed her the points along the way where they might once again meet—Matacapan, Tlacotalpan, Reed Flats, Heron Bay—reminding her once again to stay on the ancient trade route. And then he kissed her on the lips in front of the gathered crowd and murmured a promise to meet her again on the highway to the Valley of Anahuac.

58

Hairless opened another gourd of *pulque* and drank freely, forgetting in his inebriation to first pour a libation to the gods.

He sat alone on a driftwood log, away from the main camp, alone beneath the moon and stars with only the crashing surf for company. He was feeling profoundly sorry for himself. Kaan was no longer a hero ballplayer, and that was all Hairless had lived for. Since leaving Mayapan, Kaan had played the game very little. And then came the tragedy of Hairless's beloved wife dying the horrible way she had. And now his new wife was cheating on him with a flute maker.

As he took another long drink of the liquor, Hairless dragged his large hand across his mouth and began to sob. He longed for the old days when the ball game was his life, when he lived for the thrill of victory, the wagering, carrying his hero on his shoulders. Hairless had been willing to follow Kaan to the ends of the earth, as long as they eventually returned to Mayapan and the tournaments.

But then there was Kaan—*appearing in the crowd as a despised Chichimec!*

Tossing aside the empty gourd, Hairless rose and stumbled blindly into the forest, heedless of vines that tripped him and sharp fronds that sliced his flesh. The world had been pulled from beneath his feet.

When he staggered into a night camp where men sat around small fires, and women filled the air with the familiar pat-pat of tortilla-making, Hairless came to a swaying standstill and blinked.

His bleary eyes settled on Balám, who gave him a startled look. As Balám slowly rose, Hairless remembered that *here* was a prince of the Maya and a true hero of the ball game.

Balám approached the sobbing man, knowing who he was and understanding his pain—a few of Kaan's other supporters had also felt betrayed by his transformation from Mayan to barbarian. Balám laid a hand on Hairless's broad shoulder and said, "Have you come to tell me something, friend?"

Hairless saw two Baláms before him, and then he felt sick to his stomach. "Tell you?" he mumbled. And then he thought, Yes! I need to tell you! I need to set the world straight again. I am a simple man who lives for only one thing! Go and fetch Kaan, set him right, and bring him back so that we can return to Mayapan and the games.

"My master is going to the highlands, your exalted lordship," he said with slurred speech, "to Lake Texcoco in search of a tribe named Chapultepec. My master says he is Chapultepec, but you have to tell him that he is not."

Hairless fell to his knees, sobbing, and then he slumped to the earth and, in the moments before he passed out, remembered too late how Kaan had risked his own life to pull him from a deadly quagmire outside the city of Palenque.

Balám and his men were ready to leave just before dawn. As he surveyed their broken camp to make sure nothing was left behind, and that there remained no clue as to their destination—the great mass of people still asleep on the beach would believe he and his Mayans had continued on to Teotihuacan—and satisfying himself that he had left a clean camp (with the exception of the bloody head separated from the giant hairy body of Kaan's traitor), Balám told his cousin to quietly move the men out so that they were not detected.

"There is one thing I must do first. I will join you up ahead."

Balám knew it was Tonina's habit to bathe each morning in whatever water was nearby, and so he knew where she would be at that moment—alone, chanting her prayers, removing her clothes, and preparing to swim in the surf like a fish.

Spying through the dense trees, he saw her on the shore as the sky was beginning to pale, naked, except for protective necklaces and a rope belt around her waist. Because she was praying, Tonina did not hear him sneak over the cold sand, and was taken by surprise when two strong arms seized her from behind, clamping around her waist, one arm holding her pinned to a powerful body, the other hand tight over her mouth. She struggled, tried to scream and bite and dig her heels into the sand, but her attacker was stronger and dragged her back into the cover of trees.

The assault was brutal and painful as Tonina struggled against a power she could not fight. He pinned her arms over her head and forced her legs apart. Her screams were muffled; she could not push him off. All his fury and rage, bitterness and despair went into the attack—Six Dove lying dead on the slave block, Ziyal crying, *"Taati!"* as she was being carried away. You should have chosen my wife! his mind silently cried as he lay siege to the fortune-teller who had chosen Jade Sky in the Grand Hall, destroying Balám's life forever.

When he was done, he knelt over her and, withdrawing his obsidian knife, severed the cowry shell belt. His eyes met hers—there was no fear on her face, no weeping or shame, just defiance and anger. He liked it. He wished he could stay and use her a few more times, or take her with them and let his men enjoy her. But her people would look for her, pursue, and get in the way of Balám's destiny.

As he started to walk away, Tonina flew to her feet and raked her nails down his face before one blow to her head sent her flying, to land unconscious on the ground.

Before catching up with his army, Balám tucked the cowry belt into a small deerskin bag and, sneaking into the sleeping camp on the beach, found the dwarf asleep next to the white-haired *h'meen*. Balám kicked One Eye, and when he had his attention, threw the deerskin pouch at him, growling, "Give this to your master when he returns."

59

When Tonina's monthly time came and went and no flow appeared, she consulted with H'meen, who gave her a blood-strengthening tonic. But when her second monthly time did not show, she confessed her suspicion to H'meen, who, without asking questions, planted five little mounds of beans, which she then watered with Tonina's urine. If the seeds sprouted, H'meen said, it was because she was with child. If not, the missed menstrual cycle was due to other causes.

When H'meen showed her the tiny green sprouts five days later, Tonina knew that her worst fear had been realized. She was carrying Balám's child.

The prostitute watched the stranger at the campfire, gauging his wealth and station in life. He was young and strong, traveling alone, and he sat by himself instead of joining the other travelers who had stopped here for the night for a meal and a safe place to sleep.

This place of rest, nestled in woodland foothills inland from the sea, had no name and resembled the many other rest stops along the trade routes—makeshift settlements that had sprung up long ago at intervals of one day's march, when travelers and traders found natural places to stop for the night and band together for protection and commerce—and it consisted of pole-and-thatch shelters, grass huts, stone shrines to a variety of gods and goddesses, wicker pens for animals, and merchants' stalls, dark and empty now but ready to be opened in the morning for business. A few enterprising men had erected sturdier hostels of wood and stucco, with private rooms and adjoining steam baths, for the wealthier travelers.

But this man whom the woman of pleasure studied had not rented a hut for the night, even though he appeared to be able to afford it, but rather had staked out a small space among the many squatters in which to spread his sleeping mat. He had eaten a simple supper of tortillas, declined *pulque* and tobacco, and now sat staring into the flames in the manner of a man with something on his mind.

A woman, she thought, sensing a profitable evening. A man who sorely missed a woman could be most generous.

But when she approached, softly saying, "Blessings of the gods," and smiling sweetly, he looked up, frowned at her with a vague expression, and then, understanding her intent, shook his head and said, "No, thank you," but politely, not gruffly as some men did.

She sighed and moved on. There were still plenty of lonely men in the camp.

Kaan returned to his brooding contemplation of the fire and heard again Ixchel's words the day he left: "Time and space cannot separate two hearts joined by love. Whether you and Tonina stand in close proximity or a continent apart, it makes no difference, for love spans all time, all space, and connects you. My beloved Cheveyo's people believe in a faith called Oneness, in which all things in the universe are connected."

Kaan realized this was how Ixchel had sustained herself in the underground cavern, by reminding herself of her connection to Cheveyo, no matter where he was, knowing that their love bound them together. Ixchel's hope and optimism gave Kaan hope as well. Nonetheless, the separation from Tonina was worse than he had imagined, and he yearned to turn around and go back. But Chapultepec beckoned, and was still many days away.

The peace of the camp was disrupted by the late arrival of a group of men who had apparently continued to travel after sunset. As it was rare for guests to arrive so late after dark, they drew everyone's attention, and they were eager to tell their tale as they called for *pulque* and tortillas and invited themselves to sit near the largest campfire, where the remnants of a deer still turned on a spit.

Kaan paid little attention until he heard the word "Mayan," and then he snapped his head up. His Nahuatl was still flawed and so he caught only scraps of the men's urgent report, but it was enough. A small army led by a Mayan prince was pushing its way through the countryside, laying waste to all in its path. What was unusual about this invader, said the frantic newcomers (who turned out to be refugees from a ravaged town), was that instead of slaying the men of the village or taking them prisoners, the Mayan chief offered them the choice of joining his army as soldiers under his command. The small army, the refugees said, was headed for Teotihuacan.

Kaan stiffened. Balám!

Y ou must tell your mother," H'meen said gently, believing the baby to be Kaan's and mistaking Tonina's fear to be because of the kinship taboo.

They were camped in green hills near the ancient town of Matacapan on the gulf, with Turquoise Smoke and his army nearby, guarded and watchful. This was Olmec country, where a civilization had once flourished. Now, only mysterious mounds dotted the maize fields, along with a weed-grown pyramid that the locals said had been founded centuries ago by the same gods who had built Teotihuacan. No grandeur remained, just ruins and rubble, as families struggled to grow tobacco and earn a living from its export.

In the two months since departing the Isthmus of Tehuantepec, the great traveling crowd had made little progress due to storms and floods. Having stopped frequently to seek shelter and high ground, Tonina and Ixchel were not as far along the trade route as they had hoped. And Ixchel's anxiety was growing. She had witnessed an omen several sunsets ago, a coyote devouring a young rabbit, and took it to mean that Cheveyo was in trouble, for he was Rabbit Clan.

And so she spent her free time studying the Book of a Thousand Secrets, searching for answers. It was for this reason that Ixchel had secured lodging in a small stone house belonging to maize farmers.

When the light from her doorway was suddenly blocked, she looked up and saw her daughter standing there. Although Tonina was in silhouette and Ixchel could not see her face, she knew all the same—she had known from the moment it happened, the day after Kaan left and Tonina had grown quiet, stopped eating, had withdrawn into herself. Ixchel had both feared and known that they had taken the forbidden step, that the Book of a Thousand Secrets had not been sufficient warning to stop Kaan and her daughter from crossing a taboo threshold.

When Tonina rushed to her and, falling to her knees sobbing, confessed that she was with child, Ixchel's heart broke in two. She held her daughter and they rocked together for a while, and then Ixchel's practical side took over. After living twenty years underground, she understood the preciousness of time, that not a moment should be wasted, least of all in recrimination and self-pity.

"When Kaan returns," Ixchel said, holding her daughter at arm's length, "you and he will marry. It is the only solution."

"No!"

"Daughter, whatever kinship taboo he might find, we can work around it. The legitimacy of your child is more important. And after all, it is not as though you and Kaan are brother and sister, or paternal cousins even."

"He must not know about the child."

"But he is the father, it is his right—" Ixchel froze. Seeing the fear in her daughter's eyes, and something else—a deep shame that should not stem from an act of love—she looked back over the past two months, viewing Tonina's attitude again, and, remembering Kaan's strict code of honor, realizing that he would never have crossed a taboo threshold, now she saw something different. "What happened, Daughter?"

Hanging her head, Tonina haltingly confessed about Balám's attack, and when she was done Ixchel sat in stony shock. She had not trusted Balám from the moment she first met him at Palenque. At the time she had thought her mistrust stemmed from his likeness to Pac Kinnich. But now she realized that her instincts had detected something about his true nature.

"The gods will punish him," Ixchel said, embracing her daughter again, wishing she could take away her pain.

"Mother, we cannot let anyone know the truth. I will not have my child born with so terrible a stigma." On Pearl Island, children conceived in violence were treated as pariahs, for it was believed the violence was bred in their blood. On some islands, a child of rape was buried at birth.

Ixchel agreed, but for other reasons. After Mayan and Nahua custom, there was shame in an unwed girl getting pregnant. Mother and child were ostracized, and became outcasts in society. "You must be married at once," she said decisively.

"What man would marry a girl who is already pregnant?"

"I will find someone."

"Mother—," Tonina began. And Ixchel saw the plea in her daughter's eyes.

"I will find a man," she said firmly, "who will marry you and who will not demand his rights as a husband. A marriage in name, for the child's sake, and for your honor's sake."

"Who will believe it? The child will be born two months early."

"It does not matter. Those who are not fooled into believing the child is your husband's will believe it is Kaan's. Either way, you have preserved your honor and their respect. And your child will know no shame."

"Mother," Tonina said, taking Ixchel's hands firmly in her own, "Kaan must never know of this. He must never know it was Balám."

Ixchel looked into her daughter's eyes and understood. "Do not worry. Kaan will never know. And now I will find you a husband."

After further questioning of the men who had escaped the slaughter in their village, Kaan confirmed that the man responsible could only be Balám. But why had he left Ixchel's people after promising to protect them? Had something happened? A fight with Turquoise Smoke?

Are Tonina and the others now completely without protection?

Kaan wasted no time. He would not wait until morning. Because of late summer storms and flooding, it had taken him two months to travel this far, but with Tonina's group on the move northward, it should take less time for him to meet up with them.

As he shouldered his packs, his spear, bows and arrows, and left the camp, hurrying through darkness toward the main trail, he chastised himself. I should have married her that night. I should not have been persuaded to leave. If Tonina has come to harm, it is my fault!

Ixchel discovered that it was not easy to find a man willing to marry a pregnant girl, especially as she had to be circumspect in her search. When she brought One Eye into her confidence, he eagerly volunteered, declaring that he believed the child to be Kaan's and therefore wished to do this favor for his friend. In truth, One Eye knew who had fathered the child. When Balám had kicked him and thrown a deerskin pouch at him, telling him to give it to Kaan, One Eye had naturally opened it to see what was inside. He had recognized the cowry belt at once, and guessed what had happened. But he kept this knowledge to himself, for Tonina's sake.

Ixchel thanked One Eye for volunteering. However, for the subterfuge to be successful, the man would have to be someone whom people would believe Tonina would bed with. And she knew that Kaan would never believe it of his friend One Eye, or any other man in their crowd. Kaan would become suspicious, and perhaps learn the truth.

Above all, the fact that the baby was Balám's must remain known only to Tonina and herself.

And then Ixchel realized that there *was* one man whom Kaan would believe Tonina would marry, and who could have fathered the child, for he was a man who had already expressed interest in making Tonina his bride.

Chief Turquoise Smoke was housed in a splendid tent where he was protected from the elements and could enjoy pleasures away from prying eyes. It was here that he granted audience to Lady Ixchel, a beautiful woman who intrigued him.

Taking a seat on the richly woven mat where food and drink had been set out, Ixchel first observed social amenities, then she said, "Two months ago you expressed interest in my daughter. Are you still interested?"

The chief shrugged. "She is spoken for, is she not? I do not steal other men's women. I do not need to."

Ixchel pressed her lips together and braced herself. The success of her mission called for blunt truth. "My daughter was attacked and raped."

He shrugged again. "She should have been more careful," he said as he surveyed a bowl of avocados, selecting one and peeling it.

"And now she is pregnant."

Popping the stone out of the avocado, he stuffed the creamy green fruit into his mouth and munched juicily, washing it down with *pulque*, waiting for the woman to get to the point.

"She needs to be married."

"What about Tenoch of Chapultepec?" he asked, picking his teeth as he selected another avocado.

"Tenoch has traveled far from here. We would not be able to get word to him and have him return for a timely wedding. She needs a husband *now*."

Turquoise Smoke narrowed his eyes, finding the snow white hair curiously alluring in one so young. He would guess Ixchel was not yet forty. "You want me to ask among my men?"

"I want *you* to consider the arrangement, honorable Turquoise Smoke. But there are conditions," she added quickly when his eyes sparked with sudden interest. "You will publicly declare that the child is yours and you will not demand marital rights. The marriage will be in name only; my daughter is not to be touched. I am willing to pay any price you ask. But you must keep our agreement a secret."

He thought about it, weighing the advantages. In the eyes of his men, he would have added a nubile and attractive wife to his harem, and would, in seven months, produce a child that proved his virility. And even though the agreement stipulated no marital relations, was the mother going to be with them every moment? The luscious Tonina would be his.

"What will you pay?" he asked.

She presented the gifts she had brought—jade, amber, blank books, a handsome Nahua mantle—but he dismissed them all. Then the chief gave her a look that left no room for misinterpretation and said in a husky voice, "You are a very handsome woman, honorable Ixchel."

Her heart stopped in her breast. Once again she was trapped, except this time it was no underground cavern. But it might as well be. She thought of her daughter, the shame, the stigma. And the decision was made. "Just tonight," she said in a tremulous voice. "Just this once, and you will marry my daughter and honor our agreement?"

He smacked his lips as his eyes roved her body. "Tonight will be enough," he said, and he stepped out of the tent to bark orders that he was not to be disturbed until morning.

Ixchel closed her eyes, and as she began to undo the ribbons in her hair, she silently cried: Forgive me, my beloved Cheveyo.

∼ 60 ∼

At a place on the eastern coast that would one day be called Ve-racruz, Tonina and her people turned inland to follow a westward road that would take them into the mountains where high passes led to the highland valley of Anahuac. Once again, Tonina was moving away from the sea, away from her dolphin spirits, and she felt a fresh ache in her heart.

It was also four months since Kaan had said good-bye, and their parting was still painful and sharp. She wondered if he had reached Chapultepec. He had said he would be there by the winter solstice, which was now just days away. How long he would remain among his tribe he had not been able to say, nor when he expected to start the journey back. But he had told Tonina that the distance between them would gradually shrink as she and her people continued their northwestward trek.

However, the large, cumbersome crowd had made little progress in the four months since they had left Tehuantepec, hampered by late summer storms, one ferocious end-of-season *huracán,* and finally, on the flat and humid coastal plain, by fever that had broken out, with many lying ill while those few unaffected nursed them under H'meen's supervision.

Now they were resting at the base of foothills that gradually became steep mountains covered in pine forests. Behind them lay the sea, ahead lay dormant volcanoes and snow.

And Kaan.

Tonina looked back through the trees, down the narrow path in the direction of the sprawling camp. She could have collected water from a closer source, but Tonina needed to be alone, to think.

Her mother never told her what Turquoise Smoke had accepted in payment for marrying her. But he had staged a splendid ceremony with much feasting and entertainment and, true to his word, had not touched her on their wedding night. After two months, Tonina had been able to respectably announce her pregnancy. She sensed that there were those who suspected she was already with child when she married the chief, but she knew they believed it was Kaan's. As he was everyone's hero, Tonina was forgiven, especially as she had taken the honorable steps and seen to it that the child had a legal father.

But what was going to happen, the gossips whispered, when Kaan came back?

Tonina also worried about Kaan's return, but for other reasons. Under no circumstances must he be allowed to see the baby. The child would bear none of Turquoise Smoke's features—the near-black skin, round eyes, flat nose—but rather Balám's red coloring, prominent nose, and slanting eyes, and Kaan would know the truth.

Tonina could not let that happen. She was too familiar with Kaan's deeply entrenched sense of justice. If he knew what Balám had done to her, he would track his former friend to the ends of the earth and then call him out in a fight that he could not possibly win.

As she bent to fill her gourd in the cool stream, she tried to think of what she could do to ensure that she would never see Kaan again.

M any people, large caravan, and soldiers," the maize farmer said, and pointed to an eastward trail into the foothills.

Kaan thanked the man and hurried on. He had found Tonina at last.

As he struck off down the path that led through an emerald valley misty with waterfalls and clear blue ponds, Kaan told himself that he was glad Balám had broken his word and abandoned the people, leaving them at the mercy of Turquoise Smoke's questionable honor. It had forced him into a decision he should have made four months ago, when he had been persuaded against his better judgment to leave Tonina and go to Chapultepec to investigate their kinship lines.

It had felt wrong when he left, wrong during the trek along the highway, and wrong when, two months later, camping in the protective company of a resting place, he had learned about Balám's broken promise. But now he was going to make things right. Kinship lines be damned, he was going to marry Tonina.

A s Tonina bent to fill the gourd from the stream, she felt the child move in her womb and experienced, once again, the conflicting emotions of love and hate—love for the child, hatred for its father. Pressing her hand to her lower back, she straightened and was startled to see a stranger approaching on the narrow trail. She watched him, her eyes widening, her mouth dropping open as she thought her mind was playing tricks on her. The stranger resembled Kaan—

"*Guay!*" she whispered.

K aan stopped on the path, staring at a vision he could not believe. She was not the island girl who had traveled with him these past months, in his memory and in his heart, but the new Nahua woman she had changed into, with her hair swept up into two coils attractively framing her face, exposing a long, graceful neck. Bright colors suited her, he thought, as the scarlets and yellows of her tunic and skirt brought out the honey glow of her skin. She also looked different yet again somehow, but he could not pinpoint in what way. She seemed not as slim as before, her face seemed fuller. It made him think she must be eating well, which was a good sign.

Dropping his travel packs and weapons, Kaan broke into a run. Tonina stood immobilized. When he neared, she dropped the water gourd and flew into his arms. He groaned with joy. She wept on his shoulder, holding tightly to him as if she were falling.

"I cannot believe—"

"I thought you—"

"I prayed—"

"I dreamed—"

His mouth sought hers in a desperate kiss. She tasted him. He inhaled her scent. Tonina in his arms. Kaan holding her.

Finally he drew back to drink in the sight of her, the unpainted face with its leaf-shaped eyes, strong nose and chin, the wide mouth that had dominated his thoughts. "Tonina, I have been on the road back to you for two months, ever since I heard of a small army being led by a Mayan prince marauding the land. I suspected it was Balám. What happened? Why did he leave?"

Tonina's throat tightened as the terror and shame of that moment rushed back—Balám dragging her into the trees, pinning her down, forcing himself on her. "We do not," she began, struggling to breathe, "we do not know why he left. We woke up the morning after your departure and he and his men were gone."

Kaan pressed his lips together. "He betrayed me. He promised to stay. He broke his promise because I changed, because I was no longer Mayan. And he left you here unprotected."

"Hairless left, too. We do not know where he went."

He thought about this, then nodded. Hairless was a kind and simple man, whose thoughts followed but one track—the ball game and its heroes. "He will have gone back to Mayapan."

Kaan took her by the shoulders and when he bent his head to kiss her again, Tonina stopped him, saying, "Kaan, a lot has changed in your absence."

He gave her a questioning look.

"I am married."

He stared at her.

"It was out of necessity," she quickly added. "There is no love."

His hands fell away from her shoulders. "What do you mean, 'married'?"

"Kaan," she said as gently as she could, wishing she were far away. She could not bear the pain she was about to inflict upon him. "I had to get married."

"*Had* to? Who did you marry?"

"Turquoise Smoke," she said, adding again, quickly, "out of necessity."

He stared at her a moment longer, and then he realized: Balám's departure. Recalling that marrying Tonina had been one of Turquoise Smoke's original points of the treaty, Kaan realized that the dishonorable chief had seized upon Balám's departure to get his wish. "Turquoise Smoke threatened to leave all of you," Kaan said angrily, "unless you married him."

Tonina remained silent. She was not exactly lying. She *had* married the Zapotec chief out of necessity—merely a different necessity.

"But, Tonina, you can divorce him and marry me. It is a simple thing. He cannot contest it. And I will fight him if I must."

"Kaan, I am pregnant."

He stood rooted to the spot, his eyes on hers as if he had turned to stone. The breeze played through his hair, lifting a strand of his bangs, causing his handsome scarlet mantle to flutter. Tonina heard bees nearby, the whine of a dragonfly. The shadow of a red-tailed hawk swept over the ground.

Kaan released the breath he had been holding. Now he understood the change in her appearance. Even beneath the loose tunic and skirt, he could see that her figure had filled out. And he noticed now that she no longer wore the cowry shell belt. That prize had gone to Chief Turquoise Smoke.

"I should never have left. I thought Balám would stay and protect all of you." Kaan was hurt and angry, and knew he would never recover— Tonina pregnant by another man!—but he blamed himself and vowed to make it up to her. "I am so sorry," he said, touching her cheek, "to have left you in a position of having to defend yourself and our people. What a terrible decision it must have been for you. And that man—" He could not bear the thought. Turquoise Smoke with Tonina. . . .

"I will never leave you again. I will stay by you no matter what. I know you must think now of the child. And Turquoise Smoke will not want you to divorce him. Certainly not to have another man raise his child."

"Kaan," she said softly, "you must go. There is . . ." Her throat tightened. "There is nothing for you here. You belong at Chapultepec, where you will find your mother's family and tell them what a courageous and wonderful woman she was."

"I will not leave you!" he cried.

She trembled on the brink of capitulation. To divorce Turquoise Smoke would be so easy. And then she and Kaan could be lovers, could be husband and wife; but it would be at the expense of Kaan's happiness after the child was born and he saw the truth. For his sake, to prevent further heartache and poisonous thoughts of revenge, she must not let him stay.

"We walk two paths," she said with tears in her eyes. "You must find your people and I must find Aztlan. Go to Chapultepec," she said. "Find your people, Kaan. And then return to Mayapan. Forget me."

His body shook as his face twisted in pain. How could he go? And yet how could he stay, and watch Tonina go to another man's bed each night? To watch her belly grow with the offspring of another man? To know that he had lost her after all, as he had thought four months ago when she emerged from the hut on the beach?

The urge to once again curse the gods rose to his throat. He lifted his face to the sky and wanted to damn them all, those cruel, fickle beings who played games with men and women.

And then his shoulders slumped. Kaan's eyes welled with tears as he looked at Tonina one last time. "He will let you continue your search?" he asked, meaning Turquoise Smoke.

"Yes," she whispered. "He will not impede a holy quest. He is rather proud of it, I think."

Kaan lifted a pendant from around his neck and dropped it into Tonina's hands—the medallion of the red flower. "This was what you were born to do," he said in a voice filled with pain. "This has been your *tonali* all along. How foolish of me to think the gods had brought us together for a reason. We are pawns in their complex games. And they are laughing at us."

One Eye knew of Tonina's penchant for going off alone, and so he had appointed himself her solitary guardian, although she did not know it. Following at a distance, and always hidden, One Eye saw to it that Tonina was protected. This morning was no exception, and the dwarf had witnessed the remarkable encounter by the stream from behind tall boulders, and he had heard every word.

Tonina had not told Kaan the truth. But he *must* know, One Eye told himself. Otherwise, the dog Balám would go unpunished for his crime. One Eye had not told anyone that the child was Balám's, not even H'meen. If such information were to leak out, the people's ire would be great. To learn that their beloved Tonina had been raped would enrage them to such a degree that they might turn into an unruly mob bent on revenge.

The great traveling throng had grown, with new followers of the goddess Ixchel. And now her daughter had been given elevated status. After Tonina had emerged from a symbolic "underground"—the grass hut on the Tehuantepec beach—transformed as her mother had been, the magic and mystique of the two women had intensified. Cheveyo, the husband and father, had joined the pantheon, as those who had lived at Palenque twenty years ago remembered him and spoke of the kind and wise shaman, liking the idea of following his trail to Aztlan (although One Eye had heard a strange rumor that no one believed, that Cheveyo had also been entombed in one of the many subterranean caverns around the city and was still there to this day). Finally, there had been Kaan's transformation when he had arrived at Tonina's Descent of the Gods feast a different man. The people believed that the gods were at work—that the beach and everything upon it had been touched by the supernatural.

And perhaps they had, One Eye decided as he thought of the gentle love that had grown between himself and H'meen during their journey with Tonina. Not a sexual passion, but a deep bond of caring such as One Eye had never experienced. For once in his life, he thought of another's welfare before his own. Was that not a miracle?

And so he could not let any in the massive encampment know the truth about Tonina's child. But Balám needed to be punished. He could not be allowed to get away with what he had done. One Eye decided that Kaan would make sure justice was served.

When he was certain Tonina was out of visual range, he left his hiding place and ran after Kaan. "Noble Kaan! Or is it Tenoch?"

Kaan turned and, seeing the dwarf, smiled. But it was a sad smile, One Eye noticed as he came breathlessly up the path. "By my great-grandfather's bones, it is good to see you again, noble Kaan! You won't be staying with us?"

"I came only to . . ." Kaan's voice drifted away as his eyes searched the green landscape for a vision. But she was gone.

Holding out his hand, One Eye said, "This is for you," and handed Balám's deerskin pouch to Kaan.

"What is it?" Kaan asked, barely looking at it as he tucked it into his travel pack.

And in that moment, all the regrets of One Eye's life coalesced into one as he suddenly wished with all his might that he could call back his rash act, wishing he could snatch back the deerskin pouch. For he saw, in that instant, the depths of Kaan's sorrow, the searing loss and pain. And One Eye realized that it would be monstrous to add the truth of Balám's attack on Tonina to Kaan's burdens. But how could he ask for the pouch back without arousing Kaan's curiosity, without explanation?

"I wanted only to say that I wish you well on your journey," One Eye said miserably, cursing himself for a coward, cursing the day of his birth, and cursing the day he had chanced to steal a purse of pearls from a fellow islander in the marketplace of Mayapan.

61

M other, I cannot go to the Valley of Anahuac."

Ixchel understood her daughter's fear, but she said, "Many people live there. It is unlikely that, as we pass through, we shall encounter Kaan."

But Tonina was too frightened to risk it. And if Kaan heard of a great crowd of people entering the valley, following a goddess who was leading them to Aztlan, would he be able to stay away? "I cannot take that chance. We must find a different route."

Finally, Ixchel agreed.

Neither One Eye nor any other experienced traveler in the crowd could advise them—the eastern trade route was the one most commonly taken—and so Tonina decided to seek Turquoise Smoke's counsel. He needed to know of their change of plans anyway, in case he had no allies in other territory.

"No allies at all," he said after she laid her proposal before him, "but I believe I can arrange for safe passage for you to the central trade route. It is a mountain trail, very difficult, but it will take you far west of the Valley of Anahuac, which you say you no longer wish to visit. Let me confer with the leader of a caravan camped nearby."

As soon as Tonina had come to him with her dilemma, the chief had seized upon it. Turquoise Smoke was not a happy man. He did not like the turn of events when Tonina announced she was pregnant. It was obvious nobody believed the child was his, and he suspected his men laughed behind his back.

The whole thing had been a mistake from the start, and unprofitable in the end. His night with Ixchel had been disappointing. She had lain cold and distant beneath him and had given him no pleasure. And he had not been able to bed the girl, despite his being her husband. As soon as they had knotted their mantles, the mother had whisked her daughter away to live among women. He saw Tonina only on religious days, when she sat with him during festivals and feasts, enacting a charade no one believed.

He had been trying to think of a way to get out of the marriage while saving face, and now she had brought the solution herself. The merchant train camped nearby was heading to the coastal town of Acapulco, which was Nahuatl for "place that is thick with reeds." Their band included three hundred porters bearing panther pelts, cotton from the lowlands, Chiapán amber, and, known only to the caravan leader himself, illegal quetzal feathers. "But we travel to the west coast," he said to the Zapotec chief. "We do not go north."

"I don't care where you take them, I want only to get rid of them," Turquoise Smoke said truthfully. "I will pay you handsomely to tell them you will take them north past the Valley of Anahuac. When and where you abandon them is up to you."

They sealed the deal with five bushels of Zapotec cigars.

Before leaving for the westward route across spines of towering mountains, Tonina thanked Turquoise Smoke for marrying her, and promised that once the child was born, and she had spoken its names before the gods and the people, she would publicly divorce him. This suited him fine, for then she could no longer lay claim to his lands and goods (not that she had so far, but he knew how women changed once they gave birth).

As the great crowd, now larger than ever, picked up stakes and resumed its journey, this time in the company of a protective caravan, with Ixchel and One Eye and H'meen in the lead, and Tonina saying a silent farewell to Kaan, whom she would never see again, the caravan leader studied his map and decided he would leave this ragtag mob at a place called Olinalá, a desolate spot where the snowcapped mountains touched the sky.

BOOK FIVE

62

The midwife was grimly silent as she laid her hands on Tonina's abdomen. Although the Tlahuica woman had said nothing, Ixchel knew the situation was serious.

They were camped near the mountain town of Cuauhnáhuac, Nahuatl for "place at the edge of the forest" (and which a future race of men would alter to Cuernavaca, deeming it more easily pronounceable). The Valley of Anahuac was north, a mere three-day journey, so that as Tonina lay beneath the hands of the Tlahuica midwife, she thought about Kaan, knowing that he would be there by now, in that valley, because she had said good-bye to him five months prior. Had he found his people? She prayed that he had, and that he had found happiness at last.

She brought her thoughts back to the local midwife who had been invited in for a consultation. Tonina knew her situation was worsening. And Ixchel blamed it on the strenuous journey they had just completed.

The Acapulco-bound merchant who was to have brought them to the western edge of the Valley of Anahuac had abandoned them near the village of Olinalá in the south, high in the mountains of a region called Oaxaca. Without the guidance and protection of the caravan, the frightened crowd of pilgrims had turned north at Olinalá to follow Ixchel along a strenuous trail through mountains and high valleys where they had seen snow on higher peaks, and experienced bone-chilling frost at night.

Ixchel had tried to thin the crowd, urging families to settle in the towns and villages they passed, advising girls to find local husbands and men to find local wives. But the call of Aztlan was strong, and had grown in the months since they left the eastern trade route to traverse the mountains.

They were not totally without protection, however. To Turquoise Smoke's surprise, when he had arranged for the seekers of Aztlan to journey under the protection of an Acapulcoan trader, a number of his warriors had elected to go with them. Some had fallen in love with women in Ixchel's group, others thirsted for adventure and exploration. And not a few had become enamored with the prospect of living in the paradise of Aztlan. So he had released them from their oath of loyalty to him, easing his own prickled conscience, for he knew the people were going to be abandoned.

When Tonina's labor started, they had made camp outside of Cuauh-náhuac. But after a few contractions, labor had stopped. Her water broke and now there was a steady trickle of blood. The baby was alive but could not—or would not—come out.

The midwife finally rested back on her heels, clicked her tongue, and said, "Baby will die. Mother will die." Then she gathered up her medicine bundle, traced a protective sign in the air, and left.

"Mother," Tonina gasped. "Leave me. Go without me. . . . Find my father."

One Eye was hovering nervously outside the grass hut Ixchel had been able to obtain for shelter and privacy. He was not alone. A crowd had gathered to pray and burn incense. When they saw the midwife leave, a communal wail rose up among the pine trees. And then Ixchel appeared, telling One Eye to fetch H'meen at once.

The royal botanist was not well herself. Although it was mid-spring, the nights were cold. And because of the alpine elevation, the air was thin—taxing enough for a robust person. While Ixchel had grown younger, H'meen had grown older. She suffered from altitude sickness, which brought on nausea, headache, fatigue, and difficulty breathing, and which she treated with gingko and sarsaparilla. The mountain chill had exacerbated her arthritis and rheumatism, and she had also lost another tooth. H'meen now bound her head in a cotton scarf, for her hair was so thin her scalp was exposed to the sun and cold. She was constantly terrified of falling, for a broken leg or hip would spell her doom, and there were many foods she could no longer tolerate.

H'meen's wants were simple: to live to see her seventeenth birthday.

When One Eye came for her, she did not want to leave the warm hearth and her sleeping mat. But Tonina was in trouble, and One Eye pleaded with his brave, good eyes.

Bringing her medicine kit, H'meen knelt beside Tonina and felt the swollen abdomen, as the midwife had. The baby did not move, although she heard a faint, rapid heartbeat. And then she knew: The baby did not want to be born. "A tea of pennyroyal will stimulate contractions," she said to Ixchel. "But it is only an assist—the baby must be persuaded to enter the world. If he refuses, then the contractions will kill both him and Tonina."

"How can a baby be persuaded to be born?"

H'meen closed her medicine kit and rose to her feet. "Someone must take a spirit-walk with Tonina and explain things to the child, assure him that he will be received in love and has nothing to fear."

"How is this spirit-walk achieved?"

"There is a cactus which the Nahua called *peyotl*. It contains tremendous powers to transport one who drinks it into the spiritual realm."

"Do you have this cactus?"

"I obtained some in Oaxaca."

"Do you know how to do the spirit-walk?"

"Yes, but I dare not. It is taxing enough for a healthy person. Extremely dangerous for me. I am sorry."

Ixchel gave her a shocked look. "You will not do it?"

Wearily, the elderly girl shook her head and left the hut.

H'meen was conserving her strength. She wanted to live long enough to see Aztlan. Though she was not Nahua, and though the seven caves were not the place of her own people's origins, it was said that the waters of the paradise cured all ills. She prayed she would live long enough to drink of those waters and have life and youth restored to her.

One Eye ran after her. "H'meen, you are the only one who can save Tonina."

"If I do, I will die!" she cried.

"*Please.* Save Tonina."

"If I attempt it, I will die," she repeated. Then she said more gently, "One Eye, it is fate. You are going to lose one of us."

He wept until his deformed body shook with bitter sobs. He loved them both and could not bear to lose either. Cynical One Eye, who had once regarded women as idle entertainments. "Please do not let her die!"

H'meen looked at him with a hurt expression. "Then you choose Tonina over me."

"No!"

She turned away, to return to her small camp among the pine trees.

One Eye dried his eyes and went back into the hut and, kneeling next to Tonina, removed from around his neck the pouch that carried his great-grandfather's bones, and placed it on her abdomen. He began praying to Lokono as he had never prayed before, wondering if the Spirit of All would even listen to an old miscreant such as he.

"One Eye," Ixchel said, seizing him by the shoulder. "You must go back out. Find someone to help! We cannot just let my daughter die!"

And then H'meen was in the doorway with her medicine kit.

As she came to kneel at Tonina's side, she said to One Eye, "I am sorry for my words. I know you do not choose Tonina over me."

Opening her medicine kit, she brought out a small gourd, stoppered with gum. Slipping her arm under Tonina's head, she coaxed her to drink.

"What is that?" Ixchel asked.

"Pennyroyal. It will stimulate contractions."

She next opened a deerskin pouch. "I will need your prayers, One Eye. And yours, too," she said to Ixchel. "While Tonina and I walk in the spirit world, we will need help from your gods. Now please bring me a gourd of water."

One Eye flew out of the hut and was back in a moment, handing her the gourd. As H'meen began to drop a powdered herb into the water, Ixchel said, "Wait," and went through Tonina's things. "Use this," she said, handing H'meen the transparent goblet. "This will increase the potency of your medicine."

H'meen chanted an ancient Mayan magic formula as she stirred the ground-up *peyotl* into the water, calling upon the spirits of the Otherworld to open doorways and allow visitors to enter. As Ixchel lit incense, and she and One Eye murmured prayers in their own dialects, H'meen

lifted Tonina's head again and put the goblet to her lips. Tonina took a sip
of the bitter brew. Then H'meen took a sip. Back and forth in the smoky
incense, to the steady rhythm of murmured chants, H'meen and Tonina
drank the *peyotl* until the cup was drained.

H'meen looked at One Eye and saw in his eyes that he knew one of
them would not be returning from this journey.

The hut began to change; the grass walls swam like water until they
dissolved. One Eye and Ixchel vanished, and then the forest and the
mountains, leaving H'meen to stand alone on a barren plain where
stunted plants struggled on sandy soil, and bleak dry lava beds lay to the
left and right. Beyond the plain, she could not see. If there were mountains or sea, she could not tell. The sky, however, was dark with black
clouds.

She looked down and saw a little boy sitting on the sand, crying. "Why
are you crying?" she asked, and when he looked up, H'meen realized she
was looking down at him from a greater height than she was used to, as
if she stood upon a stool. And when she held out her hand to him, she did
not see her own hand, spotted with age and deformed with arthritis, but
a young unblemished honey gold hand, and she realized she was also
Tonina. In their shared vision they had joined to become one. H'meen
felt Tonina's youthful strength and vigor, and she relished it.

"Why are you crying?" Tonina-H'meen asked again.

"I am afraid," the little boy said, slipping his tiny hand into hers.

"Do not be afraid," Tonina-H'meen said as he rose to his feet. "You
will be loved and cherished in our world. Come and join us. We will keep
you from harm."

He looked at her with big, soulful eyes that slowly turned yellow. The
boy grew taller, his limbs lengthened and stretched, and his hair swam
down to his shoulders until Tonina-H'meen realized he had changed
into Brave Eagle.

"You have come back," Tonina-H'meen said, joy filling their hearts.

Brave Eagle held out his cupped hands and they saw that he held the
red flower. "You have found it?" they asked.

"Hurry," he said. "Find the caves. They are in danger of destruction."

"Where *are* the caves?"

Brave Eagle did not respond as he underwent another metamorphosis until a third person stood before them. H'meen had never before seen a man dressed so: a deerskin tunic and leggings decorated with fringe and beads. She had also never seen a man wear his hair in two long braids. To H'meen he was a stranger, but Tonina recognized him as Cheveyo, her father.

"Are you three separate people?" Tonina-H'meen asked. "Or are you one person?"

"We are the Oneness in which all souls are joined," Cheveyo said.

"Are you a god?"

"We are all gods. But you must hurry now. You must find the caves so that Pahana can return to us."

Tonina-H'meen wanted to embrace him, but the sky darkened and Tonina remembered her prophetic vision. Reaching out with hands spotted with age and twisted with arthritis, H'meen realized she was no longer joined to Tonina. When the handsome Cheveyo took her hands, she said, "You must leave this place. It is dangerous for you. Go away at once!"

Severe pain suddenly ripped through her and Tonina realized H'meen was no longer a part of her. "Tonina, go back without me," she heard H'meen whisper. "Find Aztlan."

"I will not leave you!"

"Go. . . ."

Tonina looked down at her hands still clasped in Cheveyo's, young hands, old hands, unblemished, deformed, changing as he held them. Tonina's father said, "You cannot stay here, noble botanist. It is not yet time. You still have more service to the gods. Return with Tonina."

Another violent pain and Tonina's eyes snapped open. She was having contractions. As she cried out, H'meen slumped to the floor of the hut and One Eye rushed to her side.

Ixchel went to Tonina and saw that the child was coming.

"How . . . ," Tonina said breathlessly. "How is H'meen?"

Tenderly brushing white hair from H'meen's face, One Eye looked into her eyes and smiled. "You came back," he murmured. "My dear lady, my sweet lady, you came back to me."

"Push," Ixchel said. "Before your child changes his mind."

H'meen looked up at One Eye and whispered, "I am all right. One Eye, I felt what it was like to be young and strong. I saw Cheveyo, I saw the caves, I saw the red flower."

"Push!"

One more contraction and the baby was coaxed into the world.

Overcome with relief and joy, her eyes filled with tears, Ixchel tied the cord and severed it with an obsidian knife, and then examined the small mewling infant. Ten fingers, ten toes. Placing him in Tonina's arms, she whispered a prayer to Quetzalcoatl to watch over and protect this new life.

Tonina gently pressed her lips to the soft skull. A little boy. Her son. Not the offspring of an enemy, not the fruit of an assault, but her child, nurtured by her blood and her love. There was nothing of Balám in this tender little creature, no evil, no stigma. She would not flatten his forehead or cross his eyes, nor insert clay beneath the bridge of his nose. He would grow to be as he was, a proud and handsome Mexica. Bringing him close to her lips, Tonina whispered his name into his tiny ear: "Tenoch."

63

Springtime, Kaan thought as he waited impatiently for the guards to confer among themselves. Tonina had said her child would be born in the spring. Had she given birth by now?

As his impatience grew—he had been in the Valley of Anahuac for three months and still had not been reunited with his people—a thought flitted across his mind, something to do with springtime and Tonina's child. But as he tried to seize the thought, the two guards came back and Kaan knew by the looks on their faces he had a problem on his hands. He prayed he could negotiate with them. He had grown desperate.

Twice, he had nearly found his tribe, only to have missed them by mere days. The Mexica, as he had discovered they were called, kept on the move because they had so many enemies. And now there was talk that they might leave the Valley of Anahuac altogether to go in search of land untouched by man. But finally he had found them, and nothing was going to keep him from meeting Chief Martok and pledging his loyalty to his tribe.

The secret camp in the hills west of Chapultepec was jealously guarded, and the Mexica were wary of enemy spies. Kaan had been warned that his chances of being allowed to bribe his way in, or of getting killed, were equal. He hoped for the bribe, although he had nothing of value to offer. The five-month journey from where he had said good-bye to Tonina had taken every possession he owned, down to his colorful mantle and loincloth, so that once again he wore the plain white garb of a peasant.

After leaving Tonina by the stream, Kaan had retraced his steps northward along the east coast trade route, and when he had entered country known for brigands and thieves, he had purchased a place in a large caravan that was bringing seaweed and shells to the eastern town of Tlaxcala. From there he had joined a group of pilgrims going up to Mount Tlaloc for a festival in honor of the rain god.

That was where, three months ago, he had reached the mountain pass that crested between the peaks of Popocatepetl and Iztaccíhuatl, and there he had paused to take in the vast, smoke-filled valley spread before him. With settlements and towns hugging the lake's shoreline, the valley was green with acacia and oak, laurel and cypress, and patterned with farms that raised beans, corn, and cotton.

Kaan had paused also to catch his breath, as the road from the coastal plain had brought him to a plateau so close to the sky that he thought he could reach up and touch it. When the wind shifted, he had caught the acrid smell of sulfur drifting from the thin column of smoke spiraling out of the snowcapped crater of nearby Popocatepetl.

Descending the path down the mountain, he had gone straight to Chapultepec Hill, only to find that the tribe who had once lived on the forested mount on the western shore of Lake Texcoco had been forced out by the chief of Culhuacán, who jealously guarded the hill's freshwater springs. The evicted tribe were called Mexica, and as they were nomads, no one could say for certain where they were at any one time.

And so Kaan had become part of the busy traffic on the many trails and dusty roads that covered the valley like a spider web, finding places to sleep, exchanging cacao beans for tortillas, never staying in one place for long, inquiring everywhere about the people who had once lived on Chapultepec.

He discovered that Lake Texcoco was lobed like a three-petalled flower, with the three large but shallow bodies of water connected by narrow straits. The smallest and southernmost, Xochimilco, was fed by clear streams bringing snowmelt from the mountains and so it was a freshwater lake. The northern lake abutted land rich in minerals that leached into the water, making it reddish and briny. The central and largest lake, Texcoco, was not so much a lake as a soggy swamp of mud and puddles and sawgrass, not deep enough to swim in, and with water so brackish the people who lived on its shore relied on water from the freshwater springs of Chapultepec.

Around this lake a loose federation of warrior kingdoms coexisted under a shaky alliance that did nothing to promote peace, for Kaan had found crime rife wherever he went. Each village had its own laws and judges and punishments. Bribery was a way of life. As there was no central authority, raids upon neighbors were frequent, with the inevitable retaliations in an endless cycle. And a stranger such as himself, traveling alone and without a declared allegiance to this tribe or that, was suspect everywhere he went.

Nonetheless Kaan soon discovered that he liked the atmosphere of the Valley of Anahuac. Was it because of the rarefied air, the plateau being so close to the sky? Because, even though people had lived in this valley for centuries, there was a feeling of newness here. This was a flourishing and growing center, not like the decaying Mayan cities to the east and south. There was a vibrancy in the air and Kaan wanted to be part of it.

And Tonina, too. He had not given up on making her his wife, and had devised a plan to that end.

Kaan suspected that Turquoise Smoke would not want to range this far from his tribal land, and so he felt confident he could work an arrangement with the Zapotec chief, involving divorcing Tonina and allowing her to remarry. As for the child, Kaan suspected that, like most tribal chiefs, Turquoise Smoke regarded the offspring of a secondary wife primarily as a bargaining chip. Kaan believed he could take Tonina *and* the child, if he offered Turquoise Smoke a tempting enough arrangement.

But he was worried. It had been five months since he had said goodbye to her beside the stream. The group should have reached the valley by now, and yet wherever he went, asking about a large group of pilgrims on their way to Aztlan, inquiring particularly of caravans and traders who came up from the south, he heard no news.

Had something happened to them? Had Turquoise Smoke abandoned them, or worse, forced the great crowd to turn back to the isthmus? Kaan had been starting to wonder if he should retrace his steps and search for them when a salt harvester had told him he could find the Mexica camped in the mountains west of Chapultepec.

Now he was torn between duty and desire. He felt a responsibility to his mother to find their people, to reunite with them for her sake. He also wanted to find Balám. Because Balám had abandoned Tonina and her people, she had been forced into an unthinkable marriage. Kaan knew his erstwhile teammate was in the vicinity, for he had heard more reports of brutal pillaging by a bloodthirsty Mayan army, the chief of which did something unheard of: Instead of sacrificing the defeated soldiers to the gods, he offered them places in his growing army.

Finally, Kaan's own curiosity made him want to stay and get to know these Mexica, for had not Ixchel said that was the name of her tribe? If so, then these were also Tonina's people.

The two burly guards came back and said, "If you wish to gain entry, you must pay a price."

Kaan stifled his frustration. He had already shown them the Chapultepec tattoo, which they themselves sported on their chests, and so they knew he had a right to an audience with the chief of the Mexica. Yet they demanded a bribe, and he knew there was nothing he could do.

Perhaps there was a time when Kaan the Mayan would have given up and left. But he was Tenoch of the Mexica; he had a right to be here.

But Kaan had nothing with which to bribe the guards. When his resources grew thin, Kaan had found places to sleep in the nearby forest, and when game was elusive, he had learned to eat cheaply on cakes made of green algae harvested from the lake. But now his purchasing power was at an end. Stripped of jewelry, fine clothing, and anything worth trading, he had nothing left with which to bribe the men who guarded Martok's secret mountain camp.

But he was determined to get inside. If he lost this chance, and the tribe moved out of the valley, Kaan might never find them again.

They told him to open his travel pack and let them see what he had. One of the guards pointed to a small deerskin pouch at the bottom, neglected by Kaan for it was but a good-luck token from One Eye. "What's in there?"

Kaan shrugged. "Old bones, I think. Of no worth to any man but the original owner."

"Let me see."

Kaan loosened the drawstring and looked in. He pulled out the cowry shell belt and, recognizing it, frowned. "This is for you," One Eye had said. He hadn't specified that the pouch was from himself, but Kaan had not realized that at the time. Why had Turquoise Smoke asked One Eye to give him Tonina's purity belt? As an insult? A challenge?

"The bag is nice," the guard said, reaching for it.

But Kaan held on to it, noticing the stitchery for the first time. Mayan. Willow Tree Clan.

Balám's clan.

And then it came to him, the elusive thought that had flitted around in his mind. Tonina had said, "After the child is born in the spring, my mother and I will continue to Aztlan." But the reckoning was wrong. Rapidly calculating backward, Kaan realized in shock that, from the day of Tonina's wedding to Turquoise Smoke, nine months would place the baby's birth in the *summer*. Kaan had assumed she was two months pregnant at the time. But counting back from spring made her four months pregnant.

And Balám had left the isthmus four months prior.

"Holy Mother Moon," Kaan whispered. Throwing the belt and pouch back into his travel pack, he turned on his heel and sprinted away from the two guards.

"Never mind!" they called after him. "We will let you in to see Chief Martok without payment."

But their words fell on deaf ears as Kaan's heart thundered in his head with a rage he could taste in his throat. Balám had attacked Tonina, for surely it could not have been consensual. But why? And then he knew: Kaan had become Tenoch. He had shaken off his Mayan disguise, and Balám could not abide that.

How could I have been so blind?

"What are you afraid of?" the Mexica guards called after him, and then he heard words of insult and laughter.

They thought he was a coward. It did not matter. Nor did it matter that he might be losing his only chance of being reunited with his people. He was driven by one thought: to find Tonina.

64

Balám knew Kaan was in the valley, calling himself Tenoch of Chapultepec as he searched for the great crowd of pilgrims traveling northward in search of Aztlan.

Balám's latest spies reported that Kaan had yet to pick up Tonina's scent. But Balám knew where she was. While Kaan was but one man, Balám had agents in many camps, reporting daily on the movements and activities of the tribal chiefs around Lake Texcoco, and so it was an easy matter to pick up rumors of strangers and other visitors to the valley. Therefore he knew what Kaan did not know, that the island girl and her ragtag pilgrims were following a northward track to the west of the Valley of Anahuac, and that they would soon bypass the valley altogether.

Balám was brought out of his thoughts by the arrival of an anticipated visitor, Cocoxtli of Culhuacán, a local chief who wore so many impressive feathers he looked like a turkey. With the intention of forming an alliance, the two factions met with great ceremony in a thicket of willow trees near the southern shore of the lake, each chief accompanied by impressively dressed lieutenants and heavily armed soldiers. They spoke words honoring each other's gods and ancestors, spoke wishes for good luck and long life, and even commented on the fine summer weather, hoping that the rain held off for a little while. Spies from both sides reported that Cocoxtli's army was discreetly bivouacked in their own home camp outside of Culhuacán, while Balám's four thousand warriors were camped on the barren plain to the south, so that each leader was satisfied that the other could not order a sudden, surprise attack.

Finally they settled down at the campfire, two powerful men bedecked in tall feathers, heavy jade necklaces, facial paint, and mantles as brilliant as butterflies. They poured libations to the gods and then mutually tasted *pulque* decanted from the same gourd, to discourage poisoning. Cocoxtli then surprised Balám by informing him he had been at Mayapan to watch the Thirteenth Game. "Your team was losing until Kaan threw the hoop ball. You did not play well that day, my friend. Why have you come to the Valley of Anahuac?"

Balám spun a tale so intricate and detailed that he had come to believe it himself: a tale of treacherous defeat on the ball field, enemies causing his downfall, a cousin in Uxmal turning the king against him—the whole world, it seemed, conspiring to drive the noble Prince Balám from his homeland to seek a place of his own elsewhere.

"But as you can see, there is no available land here in the valley," Cocoxtli said, eyeing the stranger suspiciously. All local chiefs had heard of the Mayan and were wary of him.

"I will not try to deceive so clever a man as yourself, lofty Cocoxtli. I come to *take* land. I believe in the strong governing the weak. I have heard that you govern in a similar manner, for did your father not drive the despised Mexica from Chapultepec and claim it for his own? And now *you* control the freshwater springs on Chapultepec? I see a kindred spirit in you, my friend, though our tribes come from lands far apart. A soldier is a soldier, no matter the color of his skin or the names of his gods. And I see a lucrative future for us both if we were to band together."

"Why should I trust you?"

"And why should *I* trust *you*?"

Cocoxtli relaxed, seeming to like Balám's answer and what appeared to be forthright honesty.

The negotiations went on through noon and into the afternoon, with a feast of roasted opossum, then *pulque* and cigars, as they structured the pact, adding to it, subtracting from it, each chief gaining a point, relinquishing a point, while scribes recorded the event, until the agreement was reached and both chiefs concurred that the treaty would be sealed in the traditional manner of exchanging household members to ensure the peace.

To Cocoxtli, Balám presented one of his cousins, the youngest of them who had joined him in Uxmal, after which, with great ceremony, Cocoxtli produced a princess from his own house.

The girl was so elaborately adorned with a flowered headdress that the blossoms cascaded over her like a tent.

"And now see the might of the Mayan!" Balám shouted as, shooting to his feet, he suddenly seized the girl by an arm and lifted her up. She let out a squeal as her feet left the ground, and Cocoxtli's men started forward.

But the chief stayed them with a gesture as he narrowed his eyes at Balám. "What treachery is this?" he growled.

"Buluc Chabtan demands blood, not marriage! Alliances should be sealed with sacrifice. Exchanges of family members should be for the appeasement of gods, not men!"

As Balám shouted about how marriage alliances were the way weak men kept the peace, that *he* was going to become the supreme chief in the land not by marrying other men's sisters and daughters, but by *slaying* them, both sides tensed and readied for a fight. The girl dangled listlessly from his grasp. She had been drugged, as was often necessary, for a screaming or protesting child was thought to bring bad luck upon a treaty.

"Lower your weapon, Mayan," Cocoxtli cautioned, eyeing the flower-decked child. "There will be no blood sacrifice today."

When the child moaned, threatening to ruin the good luck of the day's negotiations, Cocoxtli's two top advisers—men in splendid robes and impressive feathers—exchanged a wary glance. Soldiers shifted nervously, and the day became charged with sudden tension.

"You think we are weak?" Balám boomed, drawing his arm back for what would be a forceful thrust of the knife.

"Put the child down," Cocoxtli said in a low voice.

Balám thrust his knife into the girl's stomach, declaring in a booming voice that he sacrificed her in the name of Buluc Chabtan, Mayan god of war.

Dropping the child, he braced himself for Cocoxtli's attack, ready to give his warriors the signal. The sacrifice had been a planned strategic show of strength, to demonstrate Balám's lack of fear of Cocoxtli's gods and army. Now he would show how well his soldiers fought.

To Balám's surprise, however, the Culhua chief merely looked at him in disgust and said, "I expected as much. Treachery and deceit! There were rumors that you had planned to lose the Thirteenth Game on purpose. I would have suffered heavy losses had you done that." He pointed to the child writhing on the ground. "Did you think I would trust one of my own daughters with a devil such as you? As it is, I gave you a Mayan princess, which I thought would please you."

Balám blinked. Mayan princess? He looked down, then used the bloody tip of his knife to sweep blossoms from the girl's face. Frightened eyes looked up at him. "*Taati?*" she said, blood gurgling in her throat.

"I paid a high price for her at the Mayapan slave auction," Cocoxtli said, "declaring the kingly right of *tu'ux-a-kah*—'pleasure of the gods'— so that no man could bid higher."

Balám froze as every vein, tendon, and fiber in his body turned to stone. "Ziyal?" he whispered.

"I was assured she is a daughter of the royal house of Uxmal. I thought I could use her to my advantage here in the Valley of Anahuac, as no other chiefs can claim possession of royal blood. But I see my effort was wasted." He spat on the ground. "Our alliance is over."

He paused and looked back at Balám, now kneeling over the dead child. "Your sacrifice to your god was worthless. The girl was not even a virgin."

Suddenly bellowing in a rage that shocked his cousins, Balám sprang to his feet and ran after Cocoxtli, unearthly howls tearing from his throat, spittle flying from his mouth. The cousins caught him and struggled to restrain their outraged leader. "Do not start a war," they warned as Balám shrieked like a man possessed, his face scarlet with fury and pain. "We must get away from here," Balám's companions said, knowing that the Culhua chief would return with his army.

Oblivious of the men who restrained him, Balám pulled away and ran back to Ziyal, gathering her lifeless body in his arms. He wept and howled as he rocked with her, his cries filling the valley so that even the most hard-hearted among his men felt tears spring to their eyes.

"Come back to me, my precious one!" Balám yelled. "Do not leave me!" He placed his hand upon her abdomen, where his dagger had gone in.

He felt moisture there. Bringing his bloody fingers close to his face, he sniffed. And then he touched his tongue to them and tasted the salty, metallic properties of his daughter's life force. His cousins watched as Balám bent his head to press his mouth to the wound, where the blood was pooling on cotton, growing dark and cool. Closing his eyes, he lapped up the blood and felt Ziyal's power enter him, and he knew that this was how the gods fed, what it was like when human sacrifice was offered to them.

As he lapped up the blood that had seeped through her cotton tunic, Balám felt shock and outrage and grief dissolve like sand in water, and he shuddered with another blinding vision. Just as the gods had opened his mind in a marketplace near Tikal, and again at Palenque, revealing their divine purpose to him, so now was Balám enveloped in a blinding white light and he was struck by so astonishing a truth that he cried out.

Ziyal was not dead.

She was living again. In him. And having drunk her blood, he thirsted for more, as he realized this was how he was to achieve godhood, by drinking the life force of his enemies.

And then the vision changed, grew dark, as fresh anger and realizations crept into his mind. Kaan was the cause of this. He was responsible for an innocent man slaying his own precious daughter. But simple killing would not be good enough, not any longer. For Kaan, something special.

And then it came to him. Kaan's punishment and torture would be to see his own people siding up with his enemy—Kaan, to be slain by his own tribe!

Balám lay for a long moment, his body covering Ziyal's, until finally he stirred to life. Rising to his feet, shaken and drenched in sweat, but with a look of awe on his face, he turned to his companions with a blood-smeared mouth and said calmly, "We will give my daughter a sacred burial, for she is now a goddess. Then we will retreat to the mountains in the north, and there we will plan our final attack upon this valley."

"But Cousin," one of the nervous young men said, thinking of Chief Cocoxtli and his large army, "we are not yet strong enough."

Balám nodded. "I know this. And that is why we are going to forge an alliance with a tribe that is strong but also is as despised as we are."

"Who?"

Who indeed? "The Mexica."

Kaan's tribe.

65

W hat is *that*?" One Eye said suddenly, looking up from the embers he was stirring. They were camped in a forest in the highlands of Michoacán, many days west of the Valley of Anahuac, in
Purépecha territory. Nearby was the village of Pátzcuaro, which in the
Purépecha tongue meant "place of stones."

Everyone turned in the direction of the trees. A strange sound came
from up the trail. Tonina's few soldiers were immediately alert, spears
and bows and arrows ready. They listened as the peculiar sound drew
closer—it was the sound of hail on a stone roof, or large bones rattling.
"Ghosts!" someone cried, for the sun had set and night now blanketed
the mountain forest.

But the beings who emerged from the trees and into the camp's torchlight were men—porters with tumplines across their foreheads and
heavy loads on their bent backs. They were preceded by a stocky man in
a plain loincloth and mantle of woven maguey fiber—poor man's
clothing—and walking with the assistance of a plain wooden staff.

"Blessings of the gods!" he called out in Nahua.

One Eye instantly relaxed, and gestured to his campfire companions
that this man was no threat. He was a trader, one who traveled great distances importing and exporting goods the length of the land from the
barbarians in the north to the Mayans east and south. One Eye knew this
because of the stranger's humble attire. Traders were known to be im-
mensely wealthy, and went to exaggerated lengths not to show it.

"I am Oxmyx of Amecameca," the visitor boomed expansively, eyeing
the skinned hares roasting on a spit over flames. "A purveyor of drums!"
he added, and gestured to one of the porters to open his woven sack and

produce its noisy goods. When everyone saw the brown and pink bony armadillo plates, they laughed. It explained the peculiar noise the small caravan had made as it moved along the trail.

Oxmyx was bald—rare among the Nahua peoples—and his nose had only one nostril, so that he made a peculiar whistling sound when he breathed. He smiled at those gathered around the campfire, then he looked past them, at the myriad campfires and clusters of people occupying this forest high in the mountains between the Valley of Anahuac and the west coast. Neither a caravan nor an army, he noted, and not really a tribe, as he saw various forms of dress, hairstyles, and skin color. His keen eye also noted that there seemed to be a lot of sick and lame among them. Pilgrims to a holy site? He had never seen so large a group of worshipers traveling to pay homage to a god. Hundreds were camped among these fir trees. Perhaps a thousand.

With just a handful of warriors protecting them.

"You are welcome to share our fire, noble Oxmyx," Ixchel said, and his porters immediately unburdened themselves and got busy making a small camp of their own.

"Praise the gods," he said, rubbing his hands together against the mountain chill. "Those hares look good, but I am full of meat. Have you tortillas?"

Ixchel apologized, for they had eaten their last corn cakes days ago. Oxmyx satisfied himself with sweet potatoes that Tonina fished out of the embers.

"Where are you bound?" Ixchel asked, noting that the trader didn't bother to drop some crumbs for the gods before devouring one hot potato in an instant.

"I carry cotton to tribes in the north, noble lady, and in exchange they give me armadillos. My porters and I have subsisted on meat for too long. We crave tortillas and corn. But this is my last trip." He helped himself to another sweet potato. "Textiles for drums was once a lucrative venture, but nowadays the bribes are too steep. Violence is everywhere, dear ladies. There is no law and order. At each border I am required to pay tribute to the local chieftain for safe passage. By the time I reach home, I shall be impoverished."

"And where is home?" Ixchel asked politely. One of the hazards of travel was the necessity to offer hospitality to other wayfarers, who sometimes ate more than their fair share. Supplies for her people were dwindling, and hunting had not been good in these forests, as the late summer had brought punishing rains.

"Amecameca, at the southern end of the Valley of Anahuac," he said, his mouth full of orange pulp.

At the mention of Anahuac, Tonina felt a sharp pain in her chest. When they had passed by the Valley of Anahuac, her heart had yearned to go there. She had felt an irresistible compulsion to leave the group and take her baby to the land of Lake Texcoco.

Kaan was there.

She ached to be with him. He filled her thoughts night and day. But for his sake, and the baby's, she could never be with him. As long as he never saw the child, Kaan would believe he was Turquoise Smoke's. But should Kaan learn the truth, that the baby was Balám's, she knew that Kaan's life would be destroyed by a hunger for revenge. And so, as they had made their way past the valley and beyond, she had pored over the Book of a Thousand Secrets to remind herself of her quest and her destiny.

Her baby, Tenoch, was three months old and slumbered on her back, safely swaddled in a baby board.

"And where are you and all these people bound?" Oxmyx asked, retrieving yet another sweet potato. To Ixchel's alarm, he was now consuming *their* share.

"We are pilgrims searching for Aztlan," she said.

He grunted. Men had been searching for the mythical Aztlan for generations. What made this woman think she could find it? He shrugged. He himself did not think the place existed outside of men's imaginations—like the Fountain of Youth or the Seven Cities of Gold that had called to men's hearts since the beginning of time. He supposed there was a need in some people to go questing, while others were content to stay home.

"You have come from the direction in which we are headed," Ixchel said hopefully. "What can you tell us?"

He ate more slowly this time and chewed thoughtfully, wondering if they could offer chilies with beans. "You are searching for caves, honorable lady. The world is full of caves."

"Perhaps this will help," Tonina said, showing him her medallion.

He studied it, then shrugged. "It looks like a lot of flowers I have seen."

"This one has magic healing properties."

"So do a lot of flowers," he said, wondering when they were going to offer him *pulque*. He scanned the vast camp that seemed to go on forever, with small fires and clusters of people and makeshift shelters disappearing among the trees. He didn't see anyone smoking cigars or pipes. Were these pilgrims *that* poor?

He brought himself back to his hostess and her peculiar companions—a dwarf, a very old woman who wore her hair in maidenly fashion, and a young woman with a baby on her back. Hope and yearning shone in all their eyes.

"Why do you search for this flower?" he asked.

"It is said that it grows near the sacred caves of Aztlan."

He sniffed, causing his nostril to whistle, and wondered if he could take another potato. His hosts were not eating. "The only red flower that I know of that cures ailments does grow near some caves. But I do not know if the caves are necessarily sacred."

Ixchel tried not to get her hopes up as she asked, "What do you know of this flower?"

He scratched his bald head where mosquitoes had feasted earlier that day. "The petals possess healing qualities. Not the roots, though. Those are bitter and can be poisonous. The leaves produce a nice balm for rashes and burns. And it is said, though I cannot vouch for it, that the pollen makes a man virile."

"Where does it grow?" Tonina asked excitedly, unable to restrain herself.

"Near my home at Amecameca."

Ixchel stared at him. "In the Valley of Anahuac?"

"The same."

She exchanged a look with Tonina. Was it possible Aztlan could be *there*?

"Where exactly is Amecameca?"

"At the foot of a snow-covered mountain called Iztaccíhuatl," he said, speaking a Nahuatl word that meant "white woman."

Ixchel gasped. She looked again at Tonina as they both recalled the glyph on the first page of the Book of a Thousand Secrets. Next to the pictograph of a red flower was the symbol for *iztaccíhuatl*: "white woman."

Cautiously, Ixchel said, "I have never heard of a mountain called White Woman."

"Perhaps you know her as Sleeping Lady."

"Yes!"

"Then possibly you do not know that when Sleeping Lady walked this earth as a human female, when she was the lover of hero Popocatepetl, her name was White Woman. When she and Popocatepetl were turned into mountains, her name became Sleeping Lady because she sleeps next to her lover, our hero Popo who guards the southeastern entry to the Valley of Anahuac."

Ixchel stared at Tonina, who in turn sat frozen in the light of the campfire. One Eye and H'meen shared their shock. They were to turn *back* to the Valley of Anahuac? And then they knew that, yes, tomorrow they would turn around and retrace their steps, for the Book of a Thousand Secrets placed the red flower and Aztlan near a "white woman." And Oxmyx had said that Iztaccíhuatl was snow-covered: *Aztlan* was Nahuatl for "place of whiteness."

As Tonina was thinking of what she was going to do when they encountered Kaan, for surely he was there now, at Lake Texcoco, Oxmyx belched and then yawned. "Honorable hosts, my weary porters and I thank you. We will retire now and be gone at daybreak. If you decide to go to Amecameca, ask for my house and I shall repay your splendid hospitality."

As he rose and wrapped his mantle about himself, Oxmyx offered a final warning: "If you do go to the Valley of Anahuac, do not get too close to the mountains, for even though his lady slumbers, Popo is very active. Of late, his black smoke has filled the sky."

～ 66 ～

Kaan had searched the valley and surrounding mountains. He had asked at every farm and village, had stopped every traveler and trader, he had supported himself on manual labor—tilling fields, chopping wood, hauling fishing nets—with but one thought: to find Tonina.

Now, after devoting the entire summer to his search and finding no trace of her or clues as to her whereabouts, he had decided he must go back to the eastern trade route, back to the placid stream where he last saw her, or to the ends of the earth if necessary. If he had to uproot every tree, tear down every mountain, Kaan would not stop until he had found Tonina.

Though the route through the high mountain pass was only a footpath that cut through steep rocky walls, it was heavily trafficked. Priests, pilgrims, and penitents came here because shrines to the gods sat at this cold, windy summit that stood, by the measure of future men, two miles above sea level. Traders and travelers also passed this way, and so enterprising merchants had erected wooden stalls in the inhospitable environment where no trees or bushes grew, selling hot food, blankets, and fur capes at exorbitant prices.

It was late summer, the day gray and drizzly. Kaan trudged with others along the trail between the two volcanic peaks, Popocatepetl and White Woman. During his trek to the eastern coast, he would first visit the hilly town of Cholula, and then on and on, searching every village and farm, every hill and valley for Tonina, going as far as the Isthmus of Tehuantepec if he had to, since it was possible Turquoise Smoke had taken Tonina back to his home.

Or would the chief have abandoned her, once the child was born and everyone could see that it was not his?

Balám. Kaan had never tasted such hatred, never known such fury and rage. He wanted to tear his former friend limb from limb for what he had done to Tonina.

Kaan had heard of the incident with Chief Cocoxtli in which Balám had insulted the Culhua chief by slaying a princess that had been given to him as a gesture of alliance. The whole valley spoke of it. No one knew exactly where Balám and his army had retreated to. In the north, it was said, to the region of Tlaxcala, where he was given sanctuary by a violent tribe.

But Kaan would not go after Balám now. He had to find Tonina first.

As he steadily gained altitude, and the morning sun blessed the eastern slope of the mountain while to the west a huge cone-shaped shadow spread like a blanket over the valley, Kaan turned his back upon the Valley of Anahuac and his people, the Mexica, with only one goal blazing in his heart.

67

H ow large *is* this invading army?" Balám's guest asked.

"My spies tell me it is a thousand strong."

Martok wrinkled his nose. "And you say it is led by a woman?"

"A *holy* woman. She has convinced them that the Valley of Anahuac belongs to them."

The Mexica general nodded. Religious fanatics. They could be ferocious fighters. "I will confer with my lieutenants," he said, and rose from his place at the campfire.

As Martok strode away, Balám spat on the ground. He hated dealing with barbarians, but an alliance with the Mexica tribe was necessary to his purpose.

Balám's vast military camp, hidden in the mountains north of Lake Texcoco, was alive with industry—warriors trained in mock fights, the clashing of clubs filling the air; craftsmen manufactured javelins and spears, bows and arrows, and fashioned shields of glittery pyrite that the soldiers would wear on their backs, to blind their enemies when they turned around; and women stitched padded cotton vests by the hundreds, to be stuffed with rock salt for protective armor. Even the children of the camp followers were put to work, hauling water and waste, foraging for nuts and berries.

All to one end: destroy Kaan and take over the world.

Ziyal was now a goddess. Balám had artisans working on a portable shrine that would be carried into battle. Upon the gilded wooden throne he would place a stone effigy of the goddess, which three stonemasons were at that moment carving. Ten thousand warriors were going to bow to her and pay homage. They were going to spill blood for her, and speak her name with reverence and honor.

As Oxmyx, the importer of armadillo drums, approached Balám with a look of displeasure on his face, the Mayan wondered if he should sacrifice him as well. Oxmyx knew too much.

After Ziyal's sacrifice, when Balám had outlined his new plan to his men, a cousin had asked, "How will you bring Kaan to the battlefield? Will you send for him? Challenge him? We do not even know where he is!"

But Balám had looked out over the shallow lake and, seeing fishermen in their flat-bottomed canoes, had seen the solution. The way to get Kaan to come to the battlefield was to lay bait.

The island girl and her ragtag pilgrims.

"It was a long way around," Oxmyx now complained, the annoying whistle sounding in his nose, "to give the illusion of arriving from the north. A strenuous journey for me and my men. And it kept me from my home longer than I liked."

Balám paid no attention. All he cared was that his plan had worked. When his spies had told him that the group of many hundreds was moving northward away from the valley, he had needed to find a way to turn them back and bring them *into* the valley, knowing that when Kaan got wind of them, he would follow like a bee to nectar.

To do the job, Balám had chosen a man without a conscience. Oxmyx was not bothered by the fact that his charade with the woman named Ixchel and her curious companions was leading them into a fatal trap. In this world, he thought, it was every man for himself. Oxmyx would lose no sleep over it.

And whatever conflict was coming, he was going to be well away from it, because he lived here in Tlaxcala. Despite what he had said to the lady named Ixchel, he had never even visited Amecameca. Nor did he ever plan to. It was rumored that the people in the Valley of Anahuac were bracing for trouble; even the peaceful farmers and villagers were laying in food and water stores, bandages and medicines, praying night and day. Tension was building as local soldiers were seen parading and training, and the ateliers of the weapons makers were blazing day and night.

War was coming. No one was safe.

Balám slowly rose and, reaching for the obsidian dagger at his waist, said, "One more word of complaint, my friend, and you will have *no* nostrils through which to breathe."

Oxmyx fell back a step, then turned and made a hasty exit.

Martok returned, a large man in military attire, with the green feathers of high rank. "Our two tribes," he said, "are alike, noble Balám, for nowhere in the Valley of Anahuac are we welcome. My tribe has not been allowed to settle there in generations. We lived awhile on Chapultepec and were driven off like dogs. And now you, too, have been forced into exile."

Balám had told Martok the same story he had told Cocoxtli.

Martok said, "My officers agree that our two armies combined would be a formidable force, and the chiefs of Lake Texcoco would see the wisdom in granting us places to settle."

Martok did not like having to forge an alliance with the outsider. The prince of Uxmal had raised his army under dubious conditions— offering condemned men places in his ranks. And he maintained their loyalty by impaling deserters on upright posts, to die slow painful deaths as a deterrent to others who did not feel loyal to Balám.

However, united with this new army, Martok would finally have the manpower to seize land that was rightfully theirs and establish a home that would put an end to the wanderings of the Mexica.

"But we have stipulations," Martok continued. "Whomever we engage in battle, there must be minimal loss of life. We want prisoners for negotiating peace. We cannot achieve our victory through dishonorable slaughter. We fight for land, for a home. We Mexica pride ourselves on our code of honor, and we expect you to follow it as well."

"Agreed," Balám said, spitting into his palm and pressing his thumb to it in the ancient tradition of sealing pacts. He would agree to anything Martok said, because once victory over the other tribes was theirs, he planned to turn his army against Martok's—Kaan's people—and slaughter them utterly to wipe them once and for all from the face of the earth.

68

Another death. Another day of hopelessness.

"We cannot stay here, Mother," Tonina said as she watched women cover the body of their loved one and prepare him for burial. "There is no food. We will die of starvation."

When they had arrived at this sylvan wilderness six days prior, a timber region between two dormant volcanoes and a gorge so steep that there were no towns or villages nearby, they had found piles of animal bones picked clean, mounds of fruit rinds and nut shells, scattered seeds, and human waste—signs that a large group had camped here until the food was gone.

"Like locusts," Ixchel had said when she had brought her people here one late afternoon, intending to spend the night and rest. Seeing the plucked trees, naked berry bushes, and cold craters where campfires had burned, she had recalled witnessing a locust invasion when she was a girl; clouds of flying insects descending upon the farms outside of Palenque, stripping crops down to dry stalks. Whoever had passed through here in recent months, whether it had been a large caravan or a small army, had not respected the gods or spirits of this place. Nor had they honored the ancient customs for wayfarers, an unwritten tradition that stipulated a traveler was never to deplete an area of its resources.

The previous occupants of these woods had been selfish.

The problem was, which way had those selfish men gone? If they were on their way to the west coast, they posed no threat. But what if the gluttons were on their way to the Valley of Anahuac, traveling just days ahead of Ixchel and her people?

While she and H'meen and others had tried to determine which direction to take next, a new problem had presented itself. The people rested here but had eaten at bare subsistence level, so that many had grown weak and could not continue the trek. Now Ixchel faced a curious conundrum: The longer they stayed here, the weaker her people became, and the weaker they became, the more they were forced to stay here.

She was baffled. Ixchel had prayed to the gods and spirits of this forest, to no avail. Under other circumstances, she would have concluded that this place was cursed. And yet, how to explain the butterflies?

When she and the people had first arrived here, there had been a few of the black and gold beauties fluttering about. Each morning since, there seemed to be more. And as everyone knew that butterflies were the spirits of dead warriors returning to earth in radiant war robes, this place could not be cursed.

As Ixchel heard the wails of mourning for the poor man who had just died of starvation, she felt the cold grip of panic. *Was* there a way out?

She had attempted different methods of divination, including Tonina's transparent prophecy cup, but the gods were not speaking. She and her people could not go west, because Cheveyo and the sacred caves lay eastward. But where was the gluttonous horde? She had tried to send scouts to determine the level of danger in either direction, but the few men among them who were warriors had grown lazy and indolent, and refused to take orders from a woman.

Ixchel knew that if she did not find a solution soon, they would all perish. Their diet now consisted of grasshoppers and caterpillars, beetle larvae and termites. Although nearby streams had fish, there was not enough for so many mouths, and so Ixchel's people fed on frogs and freshwater snails and crabs. Men who were able scoured the area for game, while women hunted for birds' nests and children sat watch with snares at rabbit and squirrel holes. But it had been many days since the men had been able to bring in anything larger than a hare. And although bows and arrows could bring down owls, ravens, and hawks, these birds were sacred and it was taboo to kill or eat them.

There were other perils as well. Because they were starving, the people tended to recklessly eat anything they found, with disastrous consequences. When they had come upon a patch of milkweed, a mob had descended upon the wild plants to devour the milky sap and fruity pods stuffed with seeds. An entire clan of men, women, and children was dead by nightfall. H'meen had examined the remaining plants and informed Ixchel that this was not the species of milkweed that could be boiled and consumed by humans. It was a strain known as "butterfly weed," as only butterflies could ingest the plant and survive.

Ixchel established a new rule: If an unfamiliar plant could not be found in H'meen's botanical books, they were to search for its seeds or berries in the scat of a wild animal. If found, the plant could be eaten since the flower or shrub had not killed the animal, and therefore it would not kill them.

But hunger drove reason from people's minds, and Ixchel feared there might be further poisonings. Especially as it appeared they had entered a region thick with the poisonous milkweed, and its sap and fruit were appealing to the eye.

But at least the people were warm, and that led to another cruel irony: With wood plentiful, the people had enough fires to keep the cold away. But the smoke also kept the larger game away. Their choice, it seemed to Ixchel, was to die of cold or hunger.

Kaan was sorely missed. Without their hero to lead and govern them, the people had lapsed into lawlessness. Stealing was rampant, as were squabbles over food and fights over women. Ixchel noticed that famine triggered a curious promiscuity, as men and women sought quick, desperate couplings—perhaps, she thought, to sate their hunger in other ways.

And so with each day in this inhospitable forest, Ixchel's anxiety grew. She feared that Popocatepetl was going to erupt and destroy the caves, and kill Cheveyo. Oxmyx, the armadillo merchant from Amecameca, had said the volcano was filling the sky with black smoke. Just like in Tonina's prophetic visions. Gripped with urgency, Ixchel had volunteered to go alone, to leave the crowd here and make her way to Amecameca on her own, but Tonina and the others would not let her, for her own safety's sake.

"Mother," Tonina said again now, as the wails of mourning subsided and a period of silent prayer began. The deceased had been a well-loved storyteller. "Something must be done."

Ixchel met her daughter's eyes and nodded in silent consent. She knew what Tonina had in mind, and it terrified her. Ixchel was certain she would never see her daughter again.

Tonina stepped into the crude grass-and-stick shelter she shared with Ixchel and looked down at her five-month-old baby, sleeping soundly and warmly upon a bed of fur. Tenoch was healthy and fine, with two bottom front teeth, able now to lift his head, to roll from his stomach onto his back, to babble cheerfully, and smile all the time. A happy, sweet little soul.

Tonina's heart moved in her breast. She had not known such love existed. Not the kind of devotion-love she had felt for Huracan and Guama, or girlish love for Brave Eagle, or even her woman's love and desire for Kaan—her love for Tenoch was so deep and vast and consuming that it was as if the love were part of her flesh and blood and had been sleeping in her muscle and sinew, to be born when the child was born.

It was going to be the worst torture to be parted from him. But the people were starving, they were dying, they needed to be rescued from this nightmare. Tonina would go alone, without her baby, for she could not put him in jeopardy. And she would move swiftly, back to the Valley of Anahuac, across the plain to the settlement of Amecameca where the armadillo trader had said sacred caves were tucked into the base of the White Woman. The magic of the caves and the red flower would tell her what to do, perhaps empower her, or even lead her to her father.

If I can bring Cheveyo back . . .

And what if she encountered Kaan? It was a prospect she both yearned for and dreaded. It did not matter. Her people had to be saved.

Tonina decided that she would leave at first dawn, and creep out of the camp while everyone slept. She knew that Ixchel and H'meen would take good care of her baby and see that he was fed by one of the other nursing mothers.

When she heard a sudden commotion outside, people shouting, feet stamping the earth as men and women ran past, Tonina stepped out of the hut and, when she saw what was causing the stir, froze in shock.

Kaan!

He emerged from the forest behind three men whom he marched at spearpoint. A bloody mountain lion was draped over his shoulders.

Everyone recognized the three as two brothers and an uncle traveling together, corn huskers by trade who had joined the group at Cuauhnáhuac. Two were carrying Kaan's travel packs, and one carried his mantle. They stumbled along as he prodded them with the tip of his spear. Their mouths were strangely bloody.

Entering the circle of the main camp, Kaan threw the carcass to the ground at Ixchel's feet and, without a word, crossed in front of the startled company, went straight to Tonina, and gathered her into his arms. "I thought I would never find you," he murmured into her hair.

"Kaan," she whispered.

Releasing her, he turned to Ixchel and said, "Blessings of the gods, honorable lady."

"It is good to see you again, noble Tenoch," she said with emotion.

"These men killed this animal and I came upon them as they had started to gorge themselves on it." The cat's belly was split open, innards spilling out. One Eye rushed forward and, with the help of two other men, dragged it away to be dressed and cooked.

"They were eating it raw to avoid building a campfire lest you should detect the smoke or the aroma of roasting meat."

He looked at the three men in disgust. "They were going to stay hidden until they had consumed the beast entirely."

Ixchel turned horrified eyes to the three men, who knelt on the ground, heads bowed as the people crowded around, their rage palpable in the air. "They took food from children's mouths," Ixchel whispered.

"What would you have me do with them, honorable lady?"

She scanned the faces—gaunt, pale, with haunted eyes—and said, "Turn these men over to mothers. They will determine the punishment."

Kaan nodded. As soon as he said, "So be it," women pushed through the crowd—mothers who had seen their children weaken and sicken and die from starvation—and laid hands upon the three. The men begged and pleaded for mercy as they were dragged away, and while many in the crowd followed to witness the execution, most stayed, to look upon Kaan in awe.

He wore no mantle, so that his broad shoulders were smeared with mountain lion blood. He was a vision of health and strength. He looked like a god. And when he spoke it was with a powerful commanding voice. "There is deer in those woods, noble Ixchel," he said, pointing in the direction from which he had come. "I will organize hunting parties. Soon your people will be feasting."

As the onlookers cheered and praised him, and women broke down into tears of relief and gratitude, Kaan strode to Tonina and looked into her eyes. "I was so worried," he murmured, as if they were the only two in the forest. "When I heard of a great throng of pilgrims wandering in these mountains, starving—" He took her by the shoulders. "Are you all right?"

"Yes," she said, lost in his eyes, mesmerized by his nearness. Was it truly Kaan, or was she dreaming?

"And your baby?"

Taking Kaan by the hand, she led him to the crude shelter and lifted the deerskin flap to allow him a look inside.

"A boy," she said, the breath caught in her chest. From the dense trees, screams could be heard, but they could have come from the moon, so little did they reach Kaan and Tonina.

"He is beautiful," Kaan murmured. "Like his mother." He smiled, and then he grew somber. "This is not Turquoise Smoke's child."

The screams reached the sky and drifted over the tops of pine trees to echo off nearby summits—three men who would not share food, being skinned alive by the mothers of starved children.

Tonina tipped her chin and said, "He was fathered by another. But bastard children are despised universally, whether in the islands, or in Mayapan, or in the Valley of Anahuac, and I would not have that happen to my child. I wanted him to grow up with honor."

"And so you married the odious Turquoise Smoke."

"He did not touch me, Kaan. It was a marriage in name alone. And when Tenoch was born and Ixchel severed his cord, I spoke his name out loud, and then I divorced Turquoise Smoke by publicly repudiating him after Mayan and Nahua fashion. I am free, Kaan."

"You named him Tenoch?"

She smiled. "After a hero of the Mexica."

"You could have told me the truth," he said, speaking quietly. "If I had known, I would have married you."

She blinked. "The truth?"

"I know the boy is Balám's."

She sucked in her breath. "How did you find out?"

He told her about the cowry shell belt and she closed her eyes against the memory of that terrible dawn. "I am so sorry," she whispered.

"There is nothing to be sorry about."

"Balám stole so much from us."

"He stole nothing. We are here, aren't we? Together?"

As the screams died down, Kaan turned in the direction of the trees. He would order the corpses to be hung from nearby branches as a reminder that the stealing and hoarding of food would not be tolerated.

"But still," he said, "I wish you had told me the truth. I cannot bear the thought that you went through this ordeal on your own. And we wasted precious time apart."

"If I had told you, would you have let Balám go free? For even now I suspect there is revenge in your heart."

"I am going to kill Balám. If I have to, I will spend the rest of my life hunting him down."

"That is why I did not tell you! I knew it would consume you. Now all you can think of is revenge. Forget Balám. Help me find the caves of Aztlan."

He nodded and said, "I will help you. Lake Texcoco is only three days away for a healthy adult moving at a jog. Your people, however, are weak. It will take twice that long to reach the valley. And they will need protection. The valley is not safe. Clans fight clans, tribes raid tribes. There is no central law." He scanned the smoke-filled camp, the people who stood at a polite distance, staring at him, hope glowing on their starved faces. "But we can do it. I will choose men to be guards. I will train them, and then," he looked down at her with a smile, "I will take your people to Aztlan."

"Kaan, did you find your tribe?"

"I followed them everywhere, Tonina. I am Mexica, like you," he said with pride, "but they are without a home, and they are despised because they are proud and arrogant and believe they are the chosen of the gods. No one wants them to settle nearby and so they are forced to keep moving. But there is no available land left in the valley, it has all been claimed, with the exception of a barren rock in the middle of the swampy lake which no one wants. I came close to meeting the Mexica leader, but then I realized what Balám had done to you. I turned away and went in search of you. And then, oh, Tonina, the most wondrous thing happened!"

He paused, suddenly overcome by the sight of her, her nearness, the brightness of her eyes—the moist lips, parted in awe. Although onlookers still stared, standing in the smoke-filled clearing to gaze upon Kaan as if they were witnessing a miracle, he bent his head and pressed his mouth to Tonina's. She hooked her arms around his neck and leaned in to him, tears sparkling at the corners of her closed eyes.

When he drew back, he said, "I was traveling through the mountain pass on the trail to the eastern coast when I heard the crack and thunder of an avalanche. I and my fellow travelers were in no danger, but I stopped to listen. And I thought I heard a woman's voice whispering on the wind. I could not make out the words, but I sensed that she was speaking to me. I turned toward the peaks of White Woman and suddenly remembered the glyph for *iztaccíhuatl,* meaning 'white woman,' in the Book of a Thousand Secrets. I turned back, Tonina, for I knew beyond a doubt that you would come to the Valley of Anahuac. I believe now that is what White Woman was telling me in her wind-voice. To turn me back from my eastern trek, to set me on the path westward . . . toward you."

He took her by the shoulders and said with passion, "Twice have I tried to find my tribe, and twice was I called back. I know now why. *This* is my destiny, here with you, Tonina, not on some faraway hill that means nothing to me. You are my universe. You are the breath in my lungs. Here is where I belong. I care nothing for kinship taboos, Tonina. Whatever was forbidden generations ago means nothing to us now, in this moment. Say you will marry me."

The mountain lion was consumed utterly, including its brains, eyeballs, and tongue. As Kaan saw to the portioning out of food, reminding the people of his law of sharing, he decided that tomorrow he would remind them of the other laws he had laid down, and to which all must adhere. Then he would gather up the able-bodied men and turn them into an efficient fighting force once more.

He had washed the blood from his shoulders and changed into fresh clothes and now sat cordially with his friends because, although his thoughts were on Tonina, formalities must be observed. Even so, he and Tonina both declined to eat of the mountain lion, having appetite only for each other, as they anticipated the coming night together.

Kaan said to those sitting in a circle around the campfire: "Balám is secretly negotiating pacts with other tribes, knowing the deeply rooted rivalry among the various groups inhabiting the Valley of Anahuac, each striving to be the dominant tribe. For generations, there has been a shaky peace there, just as there was in the realm of the Maya. Balám is striving to turn allies against each other. As a consequence, the other chiefs are meeting in secret, to form pacts against the interloper. But bad blood runs deep. Old grudges and ancient feuds are being dredged up as Tepanec turns against Mexica, and Culhua against Mixtec."

He told them this to alert them that the way to Amecameca was not going to be easy.

And then the feast was done and it was time for Kaan and Tonina to speak vows before their friends. Since it was a second marriage for both, there was no formal ceremony. After Mayan and Nahua tradition, each simply declared to be married to the other and that was it. H'meen recorded the union in the chronicle that she had started the day she left Mayapan, which was now many pages long.

It was time to retire. H'meen tactfully invited Ixchel to share her humble hut for the night, and Ixchel thoughtfully took the baby with her so that Tonina and Kaan could be alone.

While Ixchel's hundreds of pilgrims slept, for the first time in many days under the blanket of peace and security—their leader was back, everything was going to be all right—Kaan slowly untied the ribbons that bound Tonina's long hair in two rolls on either side of her head. She loosened the knot that secured the mantle at his neck, letting the plain white cotton slide from his shoulders, exposing a muscular chest that she had seen so many times, but which she was now *seeing* for the first time.

She bent to kiss the Chapultepec tattoo. He kissed the places on her face where white symbols had once been painted.

Their mouths came together in passion and hunger. Hands eagerly explored. Tonina felt like a virgin, as if no man had ever touched her. And indeed no man had, for Balám had been a beast and his coupling with her had been an assault. *This* was lovemaking, this was yearning and caressing, delicious and erotic. Kaan's penis felt strange in her hand, but good also, as she guided him into herself, feeling herself rise up as if on a warm ocean current.

The steady rhythm was pure ecstasy as she closed her eyes and delivered herself completely to Kaan. She felt his kisses on her face and neck, felt his hands on her breasts, teasing a nipple, sucking, and when she came to orgasm it startled her. She gasped. Her eyes flew open.

Kaan watched her, delighting in the glow on her face as he felt her body shiver and shudder with wave after wave of pleasure. And then he allowed himself his own release, kissing her as he did so.

They heard the call of an owl and inhaled the pine scent of fir trees. But those things no longer existed. Kaan and Tonina were back in the marketplace of Mayapan, their eyes meeting across the crowded quarter, seeing each other for the first time through the haze of campfires, and knowing, somehow, that they belonged together.

I t was still night when Tonina awoke to find Kaan looking down at her, a smile on his face.

She reached for him and brought his head down to meet her mouth in a deep kiss. Then she sat up, her long hair falling over her breasts. They ached. She must feed Tenoch. And then she remembered Ixchel's assurance that he would be taken care of by one of the other nursing mothers.

A full moon sailed across the night sky, shedding light into the crude shelter that was little more than branches leaning against a thick tree. In the silver light Tonina filled her eyes with the sight of Kaan's magnificent body. She saw the scar on his thigh and remembered when he had received the wound, saving her life during the hurricane at Copan. It seemed so long ago.

Then she looked deep into his eyes, aching for him to make love to her again. But first she had to speak what was in her heart. "Kaan, I am dedicated to finding the caves of Aztlan."

"I know," he said, brushing a strand of hair from her cheek.

"In the Book of a Thousand Secrets, my mother recorded my father's history, joining it to her own. She recorded what he had told her of his people, how they had once been enslaved in a kingdom called Center Place, far to the north in a land of canyons and mesas, and that they had broken their bonds of slavery and had been led to freedom by a mythical tribal mother called Hoshi'tiwa, chosen by the gods to find a home for her people so they could prepare for the return of Pahana, the bearded white brother whom they called 'lost.' And now it is my mother's destiny, and mine as well, to find Aztlan, our home, so that we can prepare for the return of Pahana-Quetzalcoatl."

"I know this, too," he said gently. "And I will keep my promise to take you and your people to Amecameca. I know the valley well. In the months that I lived there I made many friends. I will see that your people have safe passage to the caves."

"And after that?" she asked, terrified of his answer.

"And then I have to go in search of Balám."

"Please do not do this," she whispered, her throat tight. As she had feared, she was losing him to revenge.

"I *must* find Balám, Tonina. And when I kill him, it will be no swift death. He will linger painfully until he begs for death."

"Kaan, it does not matter. I do not even think of Balám. If I have forgotten what he did, why can't you?"

He took her by the shoulders and said, "My love, you must find the caves of Aztlan, for that is your *tonali*. And I must find Balám, for that is my *tonali*. It is the will of the gods."

"But I do not wish for you to take revenge on my behalf. I do not wish you to follow this path."

He kissed her and stroked her hair. "My dear one, it is not so simple.

This was destined long ago, from the day in an alley in Mayapan when a gang of boys tormented me."

"You told me Balám saved you from them."

"They had cornered me behind the Kukulcan temple and were throwing rocks at me. Balám stood up for me, drove them off, and befriended me, introducing me to the warden of the ballplayers' barracks. But what I did not tell you, Tonina," he said, his forehead knotting at the painful memory, "what I have never told a soul, not even Jade Sky, is that Balám was the leader of that gang. In fact, it was he who led the assault on me that day."

He paused, remembering the frightened and hurt little Chichimec boy huddling against the wall, trying to protect himself from the stones that stung and cut. "And then, suddenly, Balám told them to stop. He drove off the other boys and offered me his mantle to dry my tears. And then he became my friend."

"Why did he do that?"

"It had been a wager. Even as a boy, gambling was in Balám's blood. He had bet the boys that I would not run, that I would let them pelt me with stones. His friends thought they could make me run, and I did not. So Balám won the wager, and I thought at the time that that had made him feel amenable toward me. But as I look back, Tonina, I see things differently. After I left the Isthmus of Tehuantepec and was no longer in proximity to Balám, I experienced a strange clarity of thought. In my desperation to be Mayan, I always believed nothing but good of Balám. I aspired to be just like him. And so when I looked at him, I saw only what I wanted to see, not what my eyes really saw. But in these past months of journeying alone I have come to an understanding about the relationship between those two boys long ago."

He paused and, in a high branch, the owl called softly again. In the distance, another owl called back in response.

"Something in Balám needed me," Kaan said. "He needed my inferiority, as it was perceived in the eyes of others. In order to feel worth within himself, to raise himself up, he needed someone near him whom he saw as inferior, whom his friends saw as inferior. I was the son of barbarians. I was not Mayan. With me at his side, his sense of worth was lifted. I see now that he has always hated me, even though he called me brother."

Tonina caressed his cheek, kissed it, and whispered, "I am so sorry."

There was great pain in his eyes as he said, "A clever cook disguises the taste of spoiled meat by glazing it with something sweet. That is how I have always looked at Balám, glazing him with a goodness that hid the rottenness underneath."

"I understand," Tonina said, "but are you so sure this is your *tonali*? I always thought the gods had greater things in mind for you."

He smiled sadly and said, "To you, Tonina, the gods have given lofty aims. To me, they have assigned a more earthbound and prosaic path, if indeed the gods guide me at all."

"And after you find Balám? After you kill him?"

But Kaan could not see beyond that, and it filled Tonina with sadness. It seemed a purposeless life, one without a *tonali* at all. She knew he had been born for greatness, but she did not know exactly what. And unless she could tell him what that greatness was, she knew she could never change his mind.

"How long will it take you?" she asked tearfully.

"That, too, is in the hands of the gods."

She drew him into her arms and closed her eyes once more against the world outside, to live only for this moment, and for Kaan's love.

69

Tonina awoke troubled.

She had slept poorly, visited by strange dreams and haunting images. The prophetic vision had appeared again—dead people strewn on a plain, black smoke in the sky, and her father calling for help. This time there had been more—people running every which way, blind and terrified amid chaos and bedlam. It looked like the end of the world.

Dawn had not yet broken, but the sky was beginning to pale. She looked down at Kaan, slumbering peacefully at her side.

Here, now, was yet another love—one she could never have imagined. She had thought, before now, that she was in love with Kaan. But the completeness that had come with their physical joining had expanded her love for him to such a degree that she wondered how the human heart was capable of containing it.

She never wanted to be parted from him again.

And yet, once more, as the gods seemed to wish it, their paths would be diverging. But Tonina had no argument, no way to persuade Kaan from his obsession to find Balám, no words to convince him that he was meant for greater things.

She closed her eyes and, shivering, prayed: *Please, Lord Quetzalcoatl, send me a sign. . . .*

Tonina listened to the dawn silence, saw pale light slice through the sticks of her crude shelter and then—

A strange sound.

Wrapping Kaan's mantle around herself, she looked out. The forest lay in deep shadow, with dawn breaking through the overhead trees. She smelled the smoldering scent of cold campfires and warm embers, and heard sounds common to the morning—someone urinating in a nearby bush, Poki's familiar yap as he no doubt chased a lizard that had escaped the cooking pot, sounds of lovemaking, and an infant wailing.

But amid these forest sensations Tonina detected something that had not been there the night before.

Emerging all the way from the hut and straightening, she looked around, waiting for her eyes to adjust and for day to break. She attuned her ear to the strange sound—like a hum, the vibration of a plucked string, or someone moaning. It seemed to come from near and from far at the same time, as if she were enveloped in the sound.

As pale light crept into the forest and turned dark silhouettes into familiar objects, Tonina's eyes widened. And as she began to realize what she was seeing, her shock turned to awe, and then to joy.

The world was covered in butterflies—millions of them, black and orange, fluttering, quivering, their wings creating a hum as they covered every branch, every pine needle, weighing the limbs down with butterfly weight, there were so many.

She heard a snap and saw a branch fall to the ground, covered in butterflies.

As the pearl light of a new day bathed the bleak camp, the gold of the butterflies filled Tonina's vision—they blanketed every tree and bush, every stalk of grass, every hut and tent and shelter, as if they were a snowfall of golden flakes. She held her breath, trembling beneath Kaan's mantle, and suddenly, all in an instant, a new knowledge filled her mind, as if the top of her skull had been opened and the gods were pouring their ancient wisdom into her head.

She fell against the tree that supported her crude shelter, causing butterflies to flutter up and away. She was unable to breathe as god-wisdom cascaded like liquid sunlight into her brain, a luminous waterfall of blinding ecstasy as she saw the butterflies, clustered peacefully together on the laden branches, transform into something new; different beings, growing before her eyes, changing, filling out until Tonina gasped and felt sweat sprout over her body.

The butterflies had become the people of the Valley of Anahuac.

She saw them as clearly as if she stood at the summit of Popocatepetl, looking down upon the villages and towns, the farms and settlements hugging the shores of Lake Texcoco. The butterflies had become all the scattered tribes and clans of Aztlan—*and they were joined together living under one rule.*

So vibrant and grand was the vision that Tonina began to weep, but they were tears of joy as she saw the people tilling the land, exchanging goods, visiting neighbors, honoring the gods, and giving praise to their leader—Kaan. She saw no more crime, no more raids and wars, people living together like the butterflies, in the glorious Oneness promised long ago by Quetzalcoatl-Pahana, as prophesied in the Book of a Thousand Secrets, foretold by a mythical ancestress named Hoshi'tiwa who had lived in a land of mesas and canyons.

The revelation faded, the camp returned, the butterflies quivered on tree branches, and Tonina found herself leaning against rough bark, her cotton mantle covered in the fluttering, golden creatures.

"Kaan," she whispered when she finally collected herself, reaching into the shelter to shake his leg. "Kaan! You must come and see!"

He sat up, rubbed his eyes, and, when he saw her, smiled. "Come here," he said playfully.

"No, you come here. There is something you must see. A miracle happened during the night."

Wrapping a fur pelt around his waist, he stepped out of the shelter, yawned, and blinked. When his vision focused, he frowned, and then his eyebrows arched. "Mother Moon!" he whispered. "Where did they come from?"

"They were sent by Quetzalcoatl," Tonina said in excitement, not knowing that she was witnessing the annual migration of a butterfly that would one day be called "monarch," and that these millions of butterflies had just ended a flight of three thousand miles, begun far in the north at a place someday to be called the Great Lakes. "I prayed to Quetzalcoatl, I asked him to send me a sign, and this was what he sent."

Kaan looked at her. "A sign of what?"

"I prayed to him to reveal to me your *tonali*. And this is the answer!"

Amusement played at the corners of his mouth. "My destiny is to be a butterfly collector?"

Taking him by the arm, she turned him to face her, so that he could see the seriousness in her eyes, so she could make him understand the momentousness of what she had experienced. "You have been chosen to unite the fractured tribes and clans of the Valley of Anahuac and unite them under one rule."

The amusement played a moment longer, and then vanished. "Tonina," he said with a sigh, "for reasons I cannot fathom, you see a leader in me. You have seen this since we left Mayapan. But I assure you, that leader does not exist. And to unite all those squabbling factions? It would be an impossible task for the most determined of men."

But she would not be dissuaded. Lord Quetzalcoatl had shown her the way. "It is your *tonali*," she said with conviction. "The whole highland region is hostile and at constant war. It will never end unless the various factions unite. Think of Mayapan. That is what our people need. A solid center, with rules and laws. You are the leader they have been waiting for."

"It cannot be done," he said, "even with a strong leader."

"Tell me this; how can a butterfly, the lightest creature in nature, weigh down the branch of a pine tree to the point of breaking it? Look there! That branch broke as I was looking at it. A butterfly *can* do it, with the help of its companions! Enough butterflies could move a mountain. Kaan, this is the Oneness of my father's people. Look at the butterflies. How did they come here, to this place, at the same time? They do not speak, they have no books, there is no communication among them, and yet they know where they belong and where they all must go. Connected, Kaan, by the invisible threads of the cosmic Oneness."

She looked at the glorious orange and gold creatures quivering and humming, weighing down tree branches so that they could be heard snapping. "Kaan, I know now that the gods brought you here to unite the seven tribes of Aztlan. It is no coincidence that my mother and I are being led to the sacred caves where the red flower grows. You are part of that divine plan. It is the will of the gods that you should bring order and leadership to Lake Texcoco."

She pressed on: "When you told me about Balám last night, it wasn't just about you and your past with him, was it? And it isn't just about what he did to me. You are going after Balám because you suspect he has secret plans to subjugate the tribes in the Valley of Anahuac and set himself up as supreme ruler, enslaving them under Mayan rule. And now that you are a proud Mexica, you cannot abide this."

Kaan looked at her, stunned by her perception and wisdom, for she had guessed right. "I will stop him," he said grimly.

"And what good is stopping Balám when nothing good comes of it? When nothing changes for our people? They will continue to roam, being forced off every piece of land by other tribes. Or perhaps another Balám might come along. You must take a stand, Kaan."

"I *will* take a stand," he said grimly. "You can be sure of that. But, Tonina, I am no ruler."

"You have been since you set foot out of Mayapan. You have been the leader of all these people ever since."

"They chose to follow me, I did not force them to."

"And that is the mark of a good leader! Not the man who forces others to follow him, but a man whom people choose to follow. Kaan," she said with passion, her fingers digging into his arm, "if it is our destiny to live in the Valley of Anahuac, if the red flower is there, and the sacred caves, as prophesied by Huitzilopochtli, then I want it to be a place where my son can grow strong and tall and with honor, and where respect for law and tradition is upheld."

Kaan did not reply, as sunlight filled the clearing and men and women came out to remark in wonder at the miracle of the butterflies. He kissed Tonina and then strode away, to organize hunting parties, to find food for the people, and to prepare them for the trek to the Valley of Anahuac.

As the day warmed up, the gold and orange butterflies fluttered to the humid forest floor, so that by mid-afternoon they covered the ground like a brilliant living carpet. The people went about their business, being careful not to step on them. Kaan and Tonina saw to their duties, both wanting to turn away from the burden that had been thrust upon them. They wanted to run away together and find a place to live safe, peaceful lives. But they had responsibilities—Tonina to find the red flower and the caves of Aztlan, Kaan to stop Balám from slaughtering their people.

Our people, Tonina thought as she watched him drill his warriors in readiness for battle. She had once been an island girl, diving for pearls. He had once been a Mayan hero of a ball game. But now she was a Mexica woman, guardian of the Book of a Thousand Secrets, and he was Tenoch of Chapultepec, destined to be hero of the Mexica. Never had they been closer; never had they been further apart.

They departed the forest camp three days later—a stronger group now, having eaten and nourished themselves, filled once again with hope, and protected now by strong young men eager to please their hero Kaan. All were imagining the paradise they were going to find at a place called Amecameca.

When they reached the head of the western trail, a scout came running to inform Kaan that Balám's army of eight thousand was on the move.

"Where is he headed?"

"Straight for Amecameca."

70

When the strangely quiet and somber procession of pilgrims, numbering over one thousand, entered the western end of the Valley of Anahuac, they paused to look at the snowcapped mountains on the other side.

Everyone was full of hope—the sick and the lame, the elderly, the childless women and loveless men, H'meen riding in her basket with Poki in her lap, and One Eye, reaching up to hold her hand. Did Aztlan and its wondrous cures and miracles lie just ahead? Was it possible the gods had kept it a secret so that these people would find it again on this day? H'meen thought, I will grow young and One Eye will love me as a woman. One Eye thought, I will grow tall and H'meen will love me as a man.

As they came down from the hills and entered the valley where corn and cotton grew, scouts reported back that Balám's army was still advancing toward Amecameca.

The pilgrims skirted the shallow lake, while farmers paused in fields to watch the enormous mob walk past, merchants came out of their homes, and fishermen straightened from their nets, to comment and wonder. Farm wives came out with gourds and skins of freshwater—showing generosity to holy pilgrims brought good luck upon one's house—and when a small earthquake rumbled beneath the valley floor, causing huts and houses and trees to sway, the women told the pilgrims that the ground had been shaking for days, that it was a warning that Popo, as the volcano was affectionately called, was going to erupt. Proof lay in the great cloud rising from the volcano's peak, dispersed by the prevailing winds, turning it into a gigantic mushroom.

Ixchel's excitement turned to fear and anxiety. Was this where Tonina's prophetic vision would come to pass? She thought of the dead strewn about in the vision. Was she leading these innocent people to their deaths? And where was Cheveyo?

At sundown they camped at Xochimilco, a settlement at the southern tip of the lake. Here they marveled at the floating, artificial islands of flowers and crops—a clever use of mud and water in an area of limited land. They purchased food and supplies from nearby villages and farms, and then Kaan led the people in prayers as, once again, the ground rumbled.

The next morning they set out after prayers and sacrifice of incense and food to the gods, and as they left the lake far behind and neared the mountains, they saw wooden posts in the ground, bearing glyphs that warned of danger. For people who could not read, some posts bore the drawing of a man standing next to a cone-shaped mountain, with rocks flying from the top of the cone, hitting him on the head. This was the hazardous "outfall" area of the volcano, where debris dropped to earth whenever Popo was angry.

When Ixchel saw these, she knew that this was indeed the plain in Tonina's vision, for Popo was now spewing black smoke into the blue sky. She looked about at the hilly countryside dotted with stunted trees. Ancient lava beds, black and barren, lay nearby, proof of prior eruptions. Surely her beloved Cheveyo was here! But where was the red flower the armadillo merchant had promised?

Amecameca was still half a day's march away, but the sun was setting, so Kaan brought the weary, frightened, and anxious pilgrims to a halt at Tlamanalco, a cluster of huts hugging a stream near a small forest that provided protection.

Scouts reported that Balám's army was camped at the edge of an ancient lava bed where nothing grew. He blocked the way to Amecameca.

Kaan's "moveable town" was used to setting up camp efficiently, and soon there were lean-tos among the laurels and oaks, grass shelters, *hamacs* strung in trees, mantles draped from branches, anything that would provide privacy and mark territory. Fires were soon glowing and cooking aromas quickly followed, while children got down to the business of exploring and playing, turkeys and dogs were set free from their crates, and the usual music, laughter, and arguments began.

For Kaan and his handful of warriors, however, it was a different matter. Tonight was not just another night, because tomorrow was not just another day.

As Kaan held Tonina in his arms within the shelter of their makeshift tent of woven mats and cotton mantles, he silently asked Mother Moon to lift this burden from him. Grant me one more day with my beloved Tonina. Give me one more sunrise, one more sunset with her. Send Balám and his army away. Grant us peace and passage to the sacred caves of Aztlan.

He tightened his hold on Tonina while she slumbered in his embrace—their lovemaking had been with such desperate urgency that she now slept deeply—and wished them both away from the valley, up into the stars, back to the innocent days of their first nights outside of Mayapan.

He had not known how to start a fire. He laughed softly at the memory, and then grew somber.

Kissing her on the forehead, he eased Tonina down and left the shelter. He must see to his warriors. But first he stopped at Ixchel's camp, where she was poring over the Book of a Thousand Secrets, and told her she could take the baby back to his mother, for he would soon need feeding. Then Kaan sought a private place among the dense trees that were bordered on one side by farms stretching back to Lake Texcoco, and by a barren plain on the other, where Balám's army waited.

Here, unseen, Kaan knelt at a small boulder and, pressing his forehead to the cold, hard surface, prayed again to Mother Moon.

"Luminous lady, hear my confession. I am guilty of the sins of pride and anger. Twice, I cursed the gods and committed sacrilege. . . ."

In a shelter that had been constructed by H'meen's attendants, loyal men who were with her still, all the way from Mayapan, solid, simple men who knew their purpose in life—to serve the royal botanist—One Eye held H'meen in his arms as she cried softly. "Please do not go," she whispered. But he was not going to let Kaan face Balám alone—Balám who had lied and cheated, threatened to hurt Tonina back in Copan, and then had almost killed One Eye himself, raking him with painful, bloody "jaguar claws." There came a time in a man's life, One Eye realized, when even the craftiest and most cynical of fellows had to stand up for what was right.

Besides, he told himself, being a dwarf had its advantages. *I shall slip beneath the edge of Balám's vision, using his own shield as a blind, and thrust my knife upward into his gut, twisting, turning. . . .*

Ixchel looked up at the stars, and then at the dense trees, wondering if Cheveyo was nearby. She was consumed with the compulsion to leave this camp, leave these people and the path to the caves, and go in search of him. As they had trekked through the valley, she had inquired along the way about a shaman named Cheveyo, asking if anyone had heard of him, or knew his whereabouts. Perhaps he was on the other side of the lake. Or was he at the caves by now?

Cheveyo, my beloved. I am here. Wait for me. . . .

Having finished his prayer of confession, Kaan rose and turned in the direction of his warriors' camp. He knew they would not be asleep. They would be waiting for words of encouragement from their commander.

What was he going to say? *We are four hundred twenty-six against eight thousand.*

Kaan shuddered with fury and anguish. Those good men were surely going to die tomorrow. And yet he could not turn back. The showdown must be faced. And it was going to end in slaughter.

It was an injustice, he thought, that innocent people should die tomorrow, because the fight was really only his. This had nothing to do with tribal honor or territorial rights. It was two men who had old scores to settle.

"Oh, Mother Moon," he whispered, lifting his face to the sky. "Tell me what to do. Guide me."

Suddenly remembering another god, as if Mother Moon had whispered the reminder in his ear, Kaan removed one of his necklaces and opened the small pouch that contained the lock of Jade Sky's hair, a small blue feather, and the statuette of Kukulcan. This last he brought out and clasped tightly in his hand. He closed his eyes and prayed mightily to his wife's god, the One Who Would Return. And as he prayed, he remembered that Kukulcan was the Mayan name for Quetzalcoatl, and since Kaan was in the Valley of Anahuac, among Nahuatl-speaking people, he realized that it was more respectful to the god to call him Lord Quetzalcoatl and to address him in his native tongue.

And so Kaan prayed to a god he barely knew, Kaan who had never considered himself a religious man, pouring out his soul and heart and fears and yearnings, sending them up to the impersonal stars where Mother Moon sailed in radiant effulgence.

He waited for an answer.

And Quetzalcoatl spoke.

71

Dawn arrived, the morning air thick with the stench of sulfur.

Although Kaan had slept little, he felt keenly alert and energized because he knew he had been born for this moment, that all his days had been in preparation for this one day. Only the gods knew what the outcome would be, but Kaan was untroubled, knowing that he faced the coming trial with a pure heart, and with honor.

Tonina was silent as she watched him prepare for combat in the pale light filtering through the trees. He drew a thick black stripe of paint across his face from ear to ear, over his nose and cheeks, whispering a prayer as he did so. He tied the warrior's topknot on the crown of his head with a ribbon from Tonina's hair, again whispering a prayer. And as he knotted his mantle over one shoulder, he invoked the protection of Mother Moon and Lord Quetzalcoatl.

When he was ready, with spear in one hand, club in the other, he faced Tonina, who had said not a word since waking. "Do you trust me?" he asked quietly.

"Yes."

"Then believe me when I say that I have no intention of dying this day. I cannot, for to die would be failure, and you know how I feel about *that.*" He smiled playfully. "Know this," he said, growing serious again, "no harm will come to you or our people today."

"How can you say that? Balám's army outnumbers you, they are trained fighters, they have many weapons."

"But Balám has one vital weakness which will be *my* weapon. Do not worry. We shall be the victors here today."

"How do you know?"

"I know, dearest Tonina, because last night I prayed to Lord Quetzal-coatl for guidance, and he spoke to me, as he once spoke to you. It was knowledge I already possessed but had forgotten. Lord Quetzalcoatl made me remember it."

Kaan kissed her one last time and left the protective woods with his men who numbered four hundred twenty-six, to face Balám's eight thousand.

Tonina watched him go, her heart swelling with love and pride, then she turned to her mother and said, "I cannot let him go out there alone. We face this enemy together, Kaan and I."

"I understand," Ixchel said softly. She, too, felt strangely unafraid, for she had spent the night studying the Book of a Thousand Secrets, and had greeted the dawn with the sure knowledge that the gods were with her people today, and that a miracle was going to save them. Nonetheless, she said, "Give me the baby," holding her hands out.

But Tonina would keep Tenoch with her, strapped to her back in his baby board, where he belonged.

Before she went to join her husband, Tonina moved through the camp, among the hundreds of people, asking them to join her, to stand up with Kaan, reminding them of how he had taken care of them. When she saw their reluctance, when able-bodied men shook their heads and looked away, she said, "Noble Kaan made all the decisions for you, fought for you, kept you safe. You benefited from his protection and he asked nothing in return. It is time for *you* to give something back." But they drew away, shaking their heads.

Tonina stared at them in disbelief. To a farmer who had been with them since Tikal, she said, "You had lost your crops to a forest fire and then the rains washed all the soil away. You were impoverished and starving when noble Kaan invited you to come with us and to enjoy our bounty and his protection."

The farmer hung his head and did not stand up.

To a family crouched around the neighboring campfire, she said, "You have been with us since we left Mayapan. Noble Kaan has taken care of you, provided for you." ·

They averted their eyes and remained silent.

From campfire to campfire she went, growing desperate, angry, Tenoch riding on her back as she reminded this woman or that youth, this married couple or that divorced man of everything noble Kaan had done for them. "When your child lay ill, Kaan brought the crowd to a halt and made camp until your son was well again. And you, when someone accused you of stealing, did Kaan not prove your innocence and restore your honor? How can you all abandon him now?"

But they drew back, casting their eyes down, afraid.

Tonina looked at them and thought: So be it. Retrieving a spear, and with her baby strapped to her back, she left the people she had come to love and think of as her family, and walked in the direction of the battlefield. At her side were Ixchel, One Eye, and H'meen, with Poki close at their heels. They sent silent prayers to Heaven as they walked, Tonina calling down the protection of Lokono and her dolphin spirits; Ixchel entreating Lord Quetzalcoatl and Cheveyo's Pahana; One Eye invoking the power of his great-grandfather's bones; and H'meen sending a respectful supplication to the local gods of this valley.

When she reached Kaan, to take her place at his side as he faced Balám's formidable army in the early morning sun, Tonina looked around at the barren, hilly expanse with stunted greenery and dry lava beds, and recognized it as the bleak landscape from her *peyotl* vision.

She looked across the barren strip of neutral ground between the two opposing forces, an expanse of perhaps a thousand paces, with warriors on the other side, lined up and silent. Seeing Balám for the first time since his assault upon her, Tonina marveled at the difference now between him and Kaan, recalling when they had dressed so similarly back in the marketplace of Mayapan, worn their hair the same, sported the same body paint and tattoos. But now only Balám wore the Mayan jaguar-tail beneath his showy headdress while Kaan had hair falling to his shoulders, straight and square, bareheaded except for the warrior's topknot. And while Balám had covered his body in fearsome red paint, Kaan's own copper skin glowed beneath the early sun.

As Tonina came to stand at his side, with Ixchel and H'meen and One Eye behind her, Kaan smiled at her, his heart expanding with love and admiration.

The plain was silent as thousands of men stood in tense anticipation; the only sound to be heard was the snapping of pennants and flags, the distant cry of a red-tailed hawk, a stifled grumble from Popo's belly. Balám's warriors were arrayed in costumes that ranged from simple loincloths to padded armor; many had painted bright stripes on their bodies, many were adorned with animal pelts, bright feathers, and shields painted in bold colors.

Balám was magnificently arrayed in deep blue and magenta robes with a plumed headdress that almost doubled his height, his chest displaying heavy necklaces of teeth and claws. Kaan was less splendidly dressed in just a white loincloth and mantle, but no less impressive for the simplicity.

As the rising sun broke over the plain, Balám shouted, "Hear me, Kaan! You are at this place today because I summoned you here!" Balám could not resist gloating over the way he had engineered this glorious moment of conquest. *He* had chosen the battlefield, *he* had decided who was to fight. "I sent the armadillo merchant to lure you here," he shouted across the great space between them, so that those hiding in the nearby woods could hear. "I knew the girl would come, and you would follow. There are no sacred caves in this place. And now I have you where I want you."

Enlivened by their chief's shouts, the warriors in the front lines executed feints and fake attacks, in the ancient tradition of Mayan and Nahua warfare—soldiers dashing forward and back, pounding spears on shields, releasing unearthly howls that filled the valley. The shouts were picked up as, line after line, all the way to the rear of the army where Balám's cousins had been deployed to prevent desertions, the warriors added their own screams until the roar of so many eager fighters drowned out the grumbling coming from the hot throat of Popocatepetl.

Standing behind Balám were the heralds and standard-bearers, waiting for the order to attack. When Balám gave the signal, the heralds would lift massive conch trumpet shells to their mouths and blare the signal, and then the standard-bearers would break formation, to dash in predetermined directions for the warriors to follow.

Before the commencement of any battle, however, it was traditional for the opposing leaders to meet on the neutral ground between their two forces. As Balám waited for Kaan's response, he kept an eye on Tonina. He had given his men special orders: The girl was for him alone.

As Kaan stood at the head of his few hundred men and surveyed the massive army that opposed them, listening to the collective roar as it filled the valley and then died down, he noted the various tribes represented among Balám's ranks, surprised by how diversified they were— Zapotec, Otomi, Mayan. While many stood in proud, fierce poses, some looked guilty or hung their heads in shame. Kaan knew why. They were taking orders from a foreigner and being forced to fight their brothers. Even though the Valley of Anahuac was splintered with myriad squabbling tribes, they were all Nahua, and many traced their roots back to Aztlan. This army was being led by a Mayan. He was not one of them, he did not speak their tongue, and he worshiped strange gods. Most of Balám's warriors had been given the choice of death or joining him, and so they had been subjugated and enslaved, stripped of honor, and forced into service.

It was not right. Warriors should be proud. They should be fighting for a cause in which they believed, and following a leader whom they respected and honored.

His gaze went back to Balám, setting eyes on his erstwhile brother for the first time since leaving the isthmus, fifteen lunar months prior, and his body shuddered with a rage he could taste.

This man had raped Tonina.

And suddenly Kaan was remembering the day, when he was twelve years old, when he had encountered his mother in the Mayapan marketplace. She was delighted to see him because he had moved into the ballplayers' barracks by then. And *he* was pleased to see *her*. But when she spoke to him, and he was about to reply, he had caught the disapproving look on Balám's face, and Kaan had turned away, pretending he didn't know her, hurting her. The new look on Balám's face, which at the time Kaan had taken to be one of admiration, he now realized had been one of triumph. Kaan also realized now that he had been under this man's thumb for most of his life, manipulated by his own need for Balám's approval. But now he was Tenoch of the Mexica, and he saw before him a man who did not belong here in the Valley of Anahuac.

This is our land.

Kaan thought these thoughts all in an instant, and in the next, he felt new purpose flood his being. It was as if his soul had been enshrouded in dark cloth all his life, and now the cloth was falling away, and he was seeing and understanding for the first time. All the months and days of reluctant leadership, he had felt as if the duty of authority were being thrust upon him—taking charge, laying down laws, passing judgment— all done without wanting to, but because he had no choice.

But now he *wanted* to.

Tonina was right. There *was* more to his destiny than just revenge against Balám. He *had* been born to lead, and to unite the tribes of this valley.

By mutual signal, Balám and Kaan broke ranks and strode out to meet on the neutral ground between the two armies, where the names of the gods were invoked, where last-minute truces were sometimes made, or final vituperative words were spoken.

Kaan gave Balám no chance to speak. "The hour has come for you to pay for your crimes, Balám. For what you did to Tonina."

Balám responded with a sneering grin. "I see you did not waste any time in getting her with child."

Kaan blinked. "I have a proposition for you," he said.

"Propositions are for cowards!"

"A wager," Kaan said, and the sneer vanished from Balám's face.

The idea had come to Kaan while he was praying to Quetzalcoatl. His heart had been pure and his desire earnest, and so from the distant stars the answer had come—*Prince Balám has one weakness. Through this weakness you can defeat him.*

"I propose this," Kaan said as he saw keen interest light up in the

Mayan's eyes. "You and I alone will fight. No weapons, just our hands. The winner will be the victor of this battlefield."

Balám sniffed. He glanced right and left. He narrowed his eyes at Kaan. The temptation was great. It was the supreme gamble—the wager of a lifetime. "Do you mean to say that if I win," he said, "your people become my prisoners?"

"And if *I* win, your army disbands and my people are allowed to continue to the caves."

Balám pursed his lips, rubbed his thigh, looked over his shoulder, and bit his lip. He had never known such temptation. He had never wagered for such high stakes. He nearly shivered with ecstasy.

And then he thought: A battle without casualties would mean winning many new worshipers for the goddess Ziyal.

"Very well," Balám said, and gestured to his first lieutenant to join them, while Kaan summoned One Eye. After Mayan and Nahua tradition, these friends would hold the combatants' possessions, see that the fight was fair, and make sure the winner was awarded his prize.

But instead of holding Balám's massive feathered headdress when it was handed to him, the lieutenant—clad from ankle to neck and wrists in tight ocelot skins—shouted, "We came to fight! Cousin, you cannot rob us of this glory! You mock the gods with this wager!"

Balám was outraged. "How dare you defy my wish! You must honor my decision."

The cousin spat. "We will not!"

"By the blood of Buluc Chabtan, I will have your testicles for this!"

The cousin—younger, taller, and stronger than Balám—straightened his back and shoulders and said, "Cousin, we have followed you through the Nine Levels of Hell to reach this glorious moment. Our spears have lain idle, our daggers have slept. We kept our mouths shut. But now I must speak. It was your obsession with gambling that brought you to this place. It was nearly your ruin. We will not allow it to ruin *us*."

Balám's face grew redder than the paint that covered it; his neck bulged and veins stood out. But the cousin would not back down. Silence fell over the valley so that the only sounds came from snapping pennants and flags. Kaan held his breath, praying Balám would not back down.

But he did. To Kaan's surprise, he growled, "You are right, Cousin." Then he turned to Kaan and said, "Your warriors against mine. We fight to the death." Retrieving his great feathered headdress, Balám strode back to the front line of his army.

When Kaan returned to Tonina and told her that his plan had failed, he insisted she go back to the safety of the forest. "Take Tenoch away from here. One Eye, take H'meen and Ixchel back."

But they would not go. If they were all to die, then so be it, they would die together.

Kaan turned to address his men. "The hour of honor is upon us. Fight well and the gods will receive you into their radiant kingdom."

He looked at each of their proud faces. The evening before, he had walked among them as they had sharpened their spears and recited the prayer of confession. He had given them words of encouragement and had shown no fear. Now he said, "Think of this as a game! We are simply two teams facing off on a playing field. I will go for Balám." The men understood. It was a common strategy on the ball court. Eliminate the captain, and the team loses cohesion. "You men cut a path for me," he said, pointing to the four Nine Brothers, "and strike at Balám's lieutenants. Each of you choose a man and focus on that one man, as you would an opponent on the playing field. Stick to that opponent until he is eliminated and then move on to the next. Concentrate on getting to the other side of the battlefield. Do not think of this as a fight but as a run to a goal."

Then he turned to face Balám's army, watching for the signal when the conch trumpets would sound for the fight to begin.

To Kaan's surprise, Ixchel suddenly stepped forward, proud and tall, the Book of a Thousand Secrets embraced in her arms. She called out to Balám, "Noble prince, the gods summon us to a place in the foothills behind you. It is our destiny to go there. Will you part and allow us to pass?"

Balám made a rude gesture that left no room for interpretation, and at that same moment, the ground rumbled so that the soldiers thought it was another earthquake. But it was the stamping of thousands of feet as another army appeared from the foothills, lining up with Balám's soldiers while an impressive chief strode forward to stand next to him.

Kaan turned to Tonina and said, "Go! This is no place for you or our child. Take Ixchel and One Eye and H'meen and go. I beg of you."

Before she could respond, they noticed Balám's ranks begin to shift and murmur, and then to laugh. Puzzled, Kaan and Tonina turned around to find their own people coming out from the safety of the woods—women, children, and old men, carrying sticks and rocks and knives. No match for the Mayan warriors and their newly arrived ally, but a proud and honorable militia nonetheless.

They were led by H'meen's attendants, who said, "Forgive us for our cowardice, noble Kaan. We were afraid. But when we saw this second army arrive, we knew we could not leave you to the slaughter."

Balám and his men roared at the ridiculous sight, but then slowly their laughter died as the people kept coming and the sheer numbers impressed them; the determination on their faces, young and old, male and female. It wasn't that the people could win, for Balám knew they did not stand a chance. What angered him now was that they were there for Kaan voluntarily, unlike his own soldiers, whom he must threaten or *pay* to keep loyal.

As Balám raised his arm to give the signal to attack, the chief of the second army frowned and growled at him, "What *is* this? You said we were to fight a fierce enemy, an invading tribe that would certainly guarantee no room for land or settlement. But, Balám, *old women*?"

Without waiting for an explanation, the chief stepped forward and bellowed, "Who are you?"

"I am called Chak Kaan of Mayapan! But by birth I am Tenoch of Chapultepec!" Kaan shouted back. "Who are you?"

"I am Martok, chief of the Mexica." He gestured for Kaan to meet him in the barren neutral space. "Show me proof of who you are!"

Martok was a surprisingly ugly man, even for a soldier who had seen much combat. His forehead was scarred back to the crown of his head, where no hair grew, the result of a burning torch that had been flung at him, so that the skin from his eyebrows to the top of his head was puckered with unsightly scars, and bald. Martok's remaining hair was wild and untamed, growing long and snarled from a shiny crown. Kaan had never thought a bald man could sport so much hair. Nor did Martok braid the unruly gray-black tresses as other soldiers did, but let the whole cloud settle over his shoulders and down his back. The nose had been smashed, too, but what soldier's hadn't?

When the Mexica chief came close, Kaan drew aside his mantle and exposed the Chapultepec tattoo.

Martok scrutinized it, then, satisfied with its authenticity, said, "When we lived on Grasshopper Hill and we thought it was our permanent home, we adopted the tattoo as our tribal emblem. But then we were forced out and now we roam once again in search of a home."

He looked past Kaan and narrowed his eyes at Ixchel, wondering about the feather-wrapped bundle in her arms, thinking of what he had just heard her say about caves, gods, and destiny. Who *were* these people?

The ground shook and warriors looked at each other nervously. And when the wind shifted, sending acrid sulfur and gas fumes over the plain, their nervousness grew. But Chief Martok ignored the tremor and the smells as he looked keenly at Kaan. "How do you come to have a Mayan name?" he asked. "And how is it you speak our tongue with a Mayan accent?"

"I have been searching for my people since I left Mayapan, where my mother and father took me many years ago."

The chief's face suddenly cleared and he said, "Those who left! I remember! There was much strife in this land, and famine. We were so unsettled, roaming the four cardinal points, that some of our people picked up their families and their possessions and went in search of a better life. We heard that many did not make it."

"My parents and I made it to Mayapan," Kaan said, appreciating for the first time the suffering and sacrifice they had endured for the sake of a better life for their son. "Honorable Martok, why are you fighting alongside this Mayan?"

"We need land, son, it is that simple. But wherever we go, we are despised and told to move on."

"What about Aztlan?"

Martok blinked. "What about it?"

"Did not your god Huitzilopochtli say you must roam until you find Aztlan?"

"We do not all believe that the home Huitzilopochtli promised to us is Aztlan itself. It is a matter of interpretation of the ancient myths and prophecies. *My* people believe that Huitzilopochtli did not speak of the ancestral home but a new land, such as is found on the shore of Lake Texcoco. And that he will lead us to it by showing us a sign."

"What sign?"

"Enough talk!" Balám shouted.

Martok shouted back that he would not do battle with a kinsman.

"Then I fight alone!" Balám cried, and, raising his sword with a chilling scream, raced toward Kaan, his thousands of soldiers bolting to follow close on his heels, their throats also emitting blood-chilling howls.

They drew near. Kaan's few hundred raised their weapons. And then—

The sound of thunder that filled the valley was deafening; the ground shook and the sky exploded in such a massive black cloud that the morning sun was instantly obliterated. Everyone on the plain, and in the valley and beyond, turned to see majestic Popocatepetl erupt in a ferocious display of anger and indignation. The soldiers and chiefs and lieutenants and women and old men and children stood rooted to the spot, staring spellbound at the billowing cloud that grew and expanded and flowed outward in whites and grays and blacks until instinct took over and feet and legs found life and everyone began to run in all directions.

In living memory, no one had ever seen such an explosion from Popo. The great noxious cloud was vast and angry, and quickly rolling down the slopes toward the valley. The volcano spewed gas and ash as the cloud threatened to surge over the valley like a giant tidal wave, engulfing everything in its path in a choking darkness.

Objects began to fall from the sky—fragments of stone and crystal, chunks of pumice and glass shards. "Help me get this off!" Tonina cried, and Kaan hurriedly untied the straps of the baby board. Once the infant was in Tonina's arms, they ran.

But where to run to? Where was shelter from a sky raining rocks and stones?

As Kaan hurriedly led Tonina and the baby to the protection of the woods, they did not see Balám coming at them from behind, his spear aloft. Balám drew back, took aim, and, as he was about to let fly the spear, froze, a look of shock on his face.

One Eye stood before him, his dagger thrust hilt-deep into Balám's belly.

When they heard the strangled cry, Kaan spun about to see Balám sway and fall. One Eye ran to stand over him, his bloody dagger raised high. "Stop!" Kaan shouted.

It was getting hard to see. The dense cloud of ash and gas was rolling closer, the mountain no longer visible, nor the settlement of Amecameca and the ancient lava beds. The world had been thrown into chaos as thousands ran blindly in panic, calling out to loved ones, dropping unconscious as debris continued to rain down.

Telling Tonina to run deeper into the trees, Kaan dashed back to the fallen Balám, seizing One Eye's wrist.

"Master!" the dwarf cried, while the ground rumbled and volcanic ash fell all around. "Let me do it! He sent you far away from Teotihuacan! The message-carrier lied about the red flower in Copan! And I was never attacked by a jaguar! It was this dog! Let me kill him! It is my right!"

But the ground shook, throwing One Eye off balance so that he toppled and fell.

"Take care of Tonina!" Kaan shouted, pointing to the woods. Taking Balám by the arms, he dragged the Mayan to the shelter of a massive oak tree where others huddled in terror. Kaan knelt next to Balám as the rumbling subsided and the ground grew strangely still.

While smoke and ash and gases continued to spew forth from the crater, darkening the day, turning the sun into an eerie orange ball, Balám gasped for breath. Blood gurgled in his throat. "We were good together, you and I . . . ," he rasped. "We were brothers. Heroes."

Kaan slipped an arm under Balám's shoulders, this man who was his enemy yet for whom he now felt only pity.

"Your child . . . is it a boy or a girl?"

Kaan said grimly, "I have a son."

"Brother!" Balám said suddenly, his eyes rolling from side to side as blood bubbled in his mouth, and the wound in his belly ran scarlet. "Hear my confession. . . ."

He spoke in Mayan, beginning his prayer with *k'inn kiichpan,* "beautiful sun," which Tonina had once mistaken for "agony." But Balám *was* in agony, Kaan knew, as he struggled for breath, strained to get the prayer out and then list his sins so that he would be taken up to Heaven.

"Kaan, my brother, I killed Jade Sky."

With the mountain rumbling and people screaming, Kaan was not sure he had heard correctly. "What did you say?" he asked, bending closer.

"I killed her. I was going to . . . stab her . . . knife . . . but she fought . . . struggled . . . I punched her . . ."

Kaan stared at Balám, at the face he had once wanted to emulate but now despised, and as the horrible truth sank in, as he watched the fleshy, bloody lips speak a confession so terrible it could not be believed, Kaan did in the next instant believe it.

Releasing an anguished cry, he shot to his feet and glared down at the fallen Mayan. The heat and anger of Popocatepetl now boiled and expanded in Kaan, as his rage turned volcanic.

Jade Sky . . . attacked by a *friend*—

He felt something slimy grab his ankle. Kaan looked down and saw Balám's bloody hand holding him.

"It was for Six Dove and Ziyal . . . ," Balám gasped. "And I have followed you since, planning my revenge."

Kaan could barely speak as tears of rage streamed down his cheeks. "If you hated me so much," he said through clenched teeth, "why did you not kill me back in Mayapan?"

"I needed you," Balám said, blood sputtering out of his mouth. "After Six Dove and Ziyal were taken from me, you became my reason to exist. I lived only as long as you lived, brother. Thoughts of revenge kept me alive.

"There is more . . . ," he whispered. "So much more. . . ."

Kaan looked down, his hands curled into fists, and watched dispassionately as Balám died.

And then darkness fell.

Complete and total darkness, like a night without moon or stars, as the great volcanic cloud reached the ground and enveloped the world in an embrace of black smoke and acrid fumes. Birds started to drop from the sky, landing dead in sickening thuds on the ground. Dangerous glass shards and pumice fell all around. There was no light. It was impossible to breathe. Ash settled on heads and shoulders. To Kaan's horror, trees were starting to ignite and burst into flame.

His eyes and lungs burning, he cried, "Tonina!"

He found her with others. She was breathing into the baby's mouth, as she had done for Kaan in the cenote at Chichén Itzá. "We must get out of this!" she gasped.

Kaan turned in a slow circle but could see nothing but black smoke. Which way to run?

Suddenly, Chief Martok emerged from the smoke, a large knot of warriors with him. "Come with me!" he boomed. "I will show you the way!"

The ground rumbled again, people shrieked, and more rocks and birds fell from the sky.

As those huddled with Tonina began to follow Martok, Kaan once again squinted into the burning smoke. They were completely enveloped in it, inhaling deadly gases, their eyes and throats on fire. Which way was which? The mountain continued to rumble and cough out smoke and ash and gas. Would there be a lava flow this time, as in the days of the ancestors? If so, they had to move *away* from Popocatepetl.

Kaan put an arm around Tonina, who held little Tenoch close, protected beneath Kaan's cotton mantle. But as they started to follow Martok, Kaan sensed that they were going the wrong way.

As he paused and looked over his shoulder again, to see a man run by with blood streaming down his face, suddenly, through the smoke, a large bird swooped low, nearly hitting Tonina.

It was an eagle.

They stared at it. How could it be alive when other birds were dropping dead from the sky? Suddenly, Tonina knew.

The dream back in Mayapan, Brave Eagle saying: "When you are most in need, I will come."

"Wait!" she called to Martok. "Not that way! This way! Follow the eagle!"

The bird flew low, circling back when the people fell behind, making sure they followed—in the opposite direction from where Martok had wanted to take them.

After they had gone a short distance, Kaan told Tonina to keep going, that he had to turn back and help others. And then he disappeared back into the volcanic cloud.

72

When they finally staggered out of the dense cloud, the injured and bleeding survivors looked back and saw the plain strewn with bodies, some dead, but most merely unconscious from the smoke and gases. Tonina realized that her prophetic vision had come to pass.

Then where was her father?

Martok brought the group to a halt to allow them to rest, and for stragglers to catch up, many of whom were holding on to each other, coughing as they emerged from the smoke. Overhead, the eagle lazily drew circles in the sky.

Ixchel first helped Tonina, to make sure the baby was all right, then she checked on H'meen, to see that she had come through the inferno safely, a wheezing Poki in her arms. One Eye had seen to it that the royal botanist was unharmed. As others sat dazed, or tried to gain their breath, Martok stood with arms akimbo, surveying the perplexing crowd that had squared off against Balám's army.

Striding up to Ixchel, who was examining a bump on the forehead of one of H'meen's attendants, he said, "Who are you people? Where did you come from?"

Assuring the attendant that he was not bleeding, she said to Martok, "We came to the Valley of Anahuac to find the caves of Aztlan."

"Aztlan! But everyone knows Aztlan is in the far north."

Ixchel nodded. She knew that now, after hearing Balám's boast about luring them into his trap. "We are also searching for a man named Cheveyo, whom we expected to find here. A shaman. Do you know anything of him?"

Martok rubbed the puckered scars on the top of his bald head. Like everyone else, his hair and shoulders were dusted with volcanic ash. "Yes, Cheveyo, the holy man with an interesting tale!"

Ixchel gasped. "You have heard of him?"

"I met him! Shared *pulque* with the man. He said his wife was Mexica and that was why he sought us out. He told us of having been buried in a cave underground near Palenque. He had managed to escape, but his wife had not. That was long ago, he said, and he had been roaming since, searching for Aztlan. He rested with us a while and then he left. It is interesting. Cheveyo had planned to stay with us longer, and he would have been here today, except that he had a dream warning him to leave."

Ixchel wiped tears from her eyes. "A dream?"

"Strangest thing. He experienced a vision in which an old woman told him to leave this place, that it was not safe for him. Cheveyo said that although the woman in his vision appeared old, he knew that she was a girl not yet seventeen."

Tonina and H'meen exchanged a glance, recalling their shared *peyotl* vision.

"Where did he go?" Ixchel asked, filled with new hope.

"He mentioned a monastery he wished to visit, just beyond Tlaxcala. I would imagine he is there still."

"Is the monastery far?"

Martok shook his head. "Two days."

"Thank you," Ixchel said. When she found Cheveyo, they would resume their search for Aztlan together; a journey of months or years, it did not matter.

As Tonina crooned to her crying baby, she kept an anxious eye on the wall of smoke that so filled the eastern end of the valley the mountains could not be seen. Where was Kaan?

The sun rose in the sky, and more people emerged from the smoke, stumbling, coughing, holding on to each other, soldiers and warriors, women and children. Tonina began to panic until finally Kaan appeared, a child in his arms as he led a group of people out of the darkness.

She ran to him and they embraced. Then he squinted around at the enormous crowd that had gathered on the plain—Balám's soldiers, Martok's men, and Ixchel's pilgrims, joined together in catastrophe. Smoke continued to rise in the sky, the ground trembled on and off, but they were safely away from the falling debris and poisonous gases.

"Where do we go now?" Martok asked, and Kaan looked up at the eagle circling overhead. It had led them out of the smoke. Would it continue to lead them?

Tonina also looked up and had the same thought. Remembering the prophecy of Huitzilopochtli in the Book of a Thousand Secrets, that an eagle would lead the Mexica to their home, she cupped her mouth and called up to the sky, "Honorable Brave Eagle, for that is who you are! It is me, Tonina! We thank you for leading us from peril. But are we to continue to follow you?"

In answer, the giant bird swooped low, causing people to duck, and then up again, to shoot away in a straight line toward Lake Texcoco. The people followed, with Kaan, Tonina, Ixchel, and Martok in the lead.

They trudged all morning, through the day, and into late afternoon, far enough away at last from the great smoking volcano to be able to breathe again, and to look about with eyes that did not burn, steadily following the eagle until, with the sun hanging low in the western sky, they saw the bird fly out over Lake Texcoco and finally come to rest on the barren rock in the middle of the vast marsh.

As the thousands gathered along the shore—warriors and pilgrims, farmers from nearby whose crops were covered in ash, villagers whose homes had collapsed—they stared at the eagle, and saw now two startling details: that it held a serpent in its beak, and that it was perched on top of a prickly pear cactus growing out of the rock.

And blooming on the cactus, brilliant scarlet in the late afternoon sun, was a red flower, its petals curving upward to form a cup.

"This is the sign!" Martok declared in amazement. He turned to Kaan. "Son, this is the sign I spoke of. The sign Huitzilopochtli promised us."

"Yes, it is so," Ixchel said reverently, her voice trembling. "For ten generations we have roamed this land as outcasts, unwanted, without a home of our own. But long ago, the god Huitzilopochtli told us that an eagle would lead us to our home, and we would find the eagle perched on a cactus with a snake in its beak."

"How shall we reach it?" One Eye asked, thinking that although the lake was shallow—not deep enough to swim in—for a man of his stature it would be a difficult trek across the soggy swamp of mud and puddles and sawgrass.

Kaan studied the wide, mosquito-infested marsh, already envisioning the firm, dry paths they would create for easier access to the shore, ridges of packed earth rising above the bog. Eventually stone and cement would replace the earthen paths, and the island would be a center of commerce and travel.

"Divide into groups," he said, "with strong men and women carrying the weak and the old across. We shall establish a camp at once to claim that rock, and bring water in skins and gourds. We will welcome any who wish to join us, but we will not allow anyone to push us off."

He felt comfortable as a leader, and he now shared Tonina's vision of a central rulership in the Valley of Anahuac, with laws, unification, and safety in travel and trade benefiting everyone. H'meen's Book of Laws, begun in a forest outside the city of Uxmal, would be the foundation.

They began the crossing, with strong men carrying the weak and the children, others determined to make it through the marshy expanse on their own; a thousand people from a thousand walks of life, bearing a thousand dreams and faiths, united in one hope.

Kaan and Tonina reached the enormous boulder first, to look up at the eagle perched majestically on the cactus. It did not fly away at the arrival of so many humans. There was enough dry land around the boulder to support many of the arrivals, and when Ixchel arrived with One Eye and H'meen—both having been carried by stalwart men—she found a smaller section of the great boulder that jutted out like a shelf.

Or an altar.

Here, Ixchel prepared a place for the first prayers in their new home. H'meen found a dry spot to sit and address her chronicle, opening paints and brushes, wanting to record the symbol of the eagle while the details were fresh, with Poki happily exploring his new home. One Eye, the practical one, scouted for what dried wood and brush he could find, for the sun was setting and they would need fire on this small island.

Kaan surveyed the boulder and its limited dry base, the swamp extending from it, and the distant shore from which people were still coming.

Beyond, Popocatepetl had stopped erupting, but smoke continued to fill the sky and would do so for months to come. Kaan's ties to Mayapan were now severed. The members of the consortium were innocent of his wife's murder. Jade Sky and their son were enjoying the bliss of the Thirteenth Heaven. His mother was dead by now, too, and as she had led an exemplary life, she would have recited the prayer of confession, so that she, too, existed in bliss with the gods. He also knew that, in his long absence, the king would have seized his wealth and property.

Kaan did not care. His life in Mayapan had been but preparation for this day. He would never think of that city again, or of Balám and his former life. Already Kaan was thinking of ways they would expand the barren rock into a larger island, bring land to it, create floating gardens like those at Xochimilco, and then bring timber and stone, and built a great city there, with writing and arts, science and religion.

Standing at Kaan's side, Tonina surveyed the swamp that surrounded them. She was near water again. It was not the sea, nor a lake of any depth, but it *was* water. And perhaps in time, as they built up the land with floating gardens, and created causeways to the shore, the water that streamed to this place from the mountains could be contained and the lake made to grow. And she could swim again.

Looking back over the events that had brought her here, Tonina finally understood why Brave Eagle had been so insistent, that day on the terrace of the royal garden, that they return to Jade Sky's villa instead of leaving the city. His every act had been to prevent her from going south to Quatemalan, guiding her instead to Kaan. To join their destinies together.

She had not yet told Kaan that she suspected new life had begun within her—a child in whose veins would flow the blood of Cheveyo's people far to the north, a race called People of the Sun, as well as the blood of the Mexica, and the blood, too, of an ancestress three hundred years ago who had lived for a while with the shipwrecked Northern Sea Men, strangers who had reassured them that Quetzalcoatl would return.

Tonina saw that Martok's warriors were now being joined by another great crowd of old men, women, and children—the Mexica mothers, wives, and sisters of his soldiers, who had stayed in their camp awaiting the outcome of the battle, but who now hurried to the shore of the lake to join their men in the sloppy trek to the cactus rock. As Tonina watched, she was stunned to see how they resembled Kaan, and she knew they must resemble herself as well for they were her tribe, too, the Mexica, so that she wondered if she was now looking into the faces of cousins, aunts, and uncles.

To Tonina's surprise, the great crowd did not, as she had feared, descend upon the red flower and ravage it in a fight for its healing power. Instead the many hundreds approached respectfully and in awe, realizing that they were part of a religious miracle, part of a momentous day, knowing that the gods were there, invisible among them, working their magic and good luck. The people sensed that they were special, that the gods blessed them for the great sacrifices they had endured in order to find this new home.

Tonina turned her eyes to Brave Eagle, who finally spread his magnificent wings, lifted himself off the cactus, and flew up into the sky to circle for a moment. As he did, Tonina sent him a silent prayer: Dear Brave Eagle, one last favor, please. Tell my brother dolphins what happened to me. If Pearl Island still exists, if Guama and Huracan escaped the big storm, please ask the dolphins to let them know I am well and happy.

The eagle gave a cry and flew away.

Tonina lifted a string from around her neck, at the end of which hung a small pouch she had worn since leaving Pearl Island. Before stepping into the canoe to be taken to Mainland, she had bent and scooped up sand and put it in her little medicine pouch that also contained a small blue periwinkle and a dolphin's tooth, powerful talismans that would forever connect her to the islands. Now she opened the pouch and poured the marine contents into the waters of Lake Texcoco—pieces of Pearl Island and its surrounding sea—so that Tonina would always be in her two homes: the old and the new.

Watching Tonina's touching ritual, One Eye fanned the flames of a new fire and looked at H'meen, thinking that, considering the disaster she had just survived, she looked remarkably healthy and robust. It was hope that did it, he knew, like a rejuvenating elixir.

One Eye knew the one secret of H'meen's heart. She had never voiced it, but he had seen the look in her eye whenever she cradled little Tenoch in her arms. People had died this morning; there were sure to be orphans. If not, One Eye would seek a poor farmer with too many mouths to feed and, after ancient tradition, purchase the youngest. One Eye would give H'meen the child she secretly yearned for. They would tie the knot so that she would know marriage and, the gods willing, and H'meen willing, One Eye hoped to gently and tenderly help her to experience the physical bond between men and women.

As H'meen moistened her paints and proceeded to outline the eagle glyph on a new page of her chronicle, she decided she was going to choose a bright, healthy child from among Ixchel's followers and train the child to be the next *h'meen,* passing along her vast accumulated knowledge, handing down her books and the chronicle of their journey from Mayapan.

H'meen wanted to live for many more years, but knew she would not. But then, she asked herself philosophically, do any of us know how long we will live? Thinking of those killed that morning by the eruption, she thought: The secret to life is to live each moment as richly and thankfully as possible.

Arriving at the island with two children in his arms, Martok immediately sought the handsome Mexica woman with the glorious white hair, Ixchel, who had come through the volcanic catastrophe with a book clasped to her bosom. A fine woman. He wondered if she was married. It had been a long time since the grizzled war veteran, himself a widower for years, had looked upon a female with anything other than a lascivious eye. But now he, too, as if a kind of magic were working spells in the late afternoon air, was thinking it would be nice to tie the knot and settle down.

But Ixchel was thinking of Cheveyo. Although she planned to go in search of him, it occurred to her as she cleared ash and twigs from the rocky ledge that surely the residents of the monastery at Tlaxcala would hear of the eruption and the eagle that had saved so many lives—the miracle of the cactus and the serpent and the rock. Cheveyo would come at once to witness it for himself.

Upon the rock altar, Ixchel placed the Book of a Thousand Secrets, and next to it the gray-metal crossbeamed Tree of Life from the Northern Sea Men. Tonina set the glass goblet next to the cross, and Kaan added the statuette of Kukulcan. Joining the solemn ceremony, One Eye removed the pouch containing his great-grandfather's bones and added them to the sacred objects.

Martok wondered out loud: "What shall we call this place?"

They had seen the stone stelae of the Mayans who had tried so hard to keep their names alive. But not even stone lasted forever. And then Tonina came up with an idea. "We shall give this place a name that will live through the generations. Each time someone speaks it, they will be speaking the name of the man who brought us here." She smiled at Kaan and spoke his Mexica name: "Tenoch." Adding the Nahuatl suffix *titlan*, meaning "place of," she said, "From this day forward, our new home will be known as Tenochtitlan."

"And though we are still Mexica," Ixchel added, "our origins lie in Aztlan. Lord Huitzilopochtli said we could not call ourselves by our real name until the eagle had led us to our new home. But we are here now, and so we can call ourselves the People of Aztlan—*aztecatl*. We are Aztec."

Finally Ixchel added, "It is prophesied in the Book of a Thousand Secrets that in the year One Reed, Lord Quetzalcoatl will return to us, arriving from the east on his raft of serpents. We will be ready to welcome him when he comes."